No. 2 GIVEN WITH No. 1.

THE OUTSIDERS OF SOCIETY

OR

THE WILD BEAUTIES OF LONDON

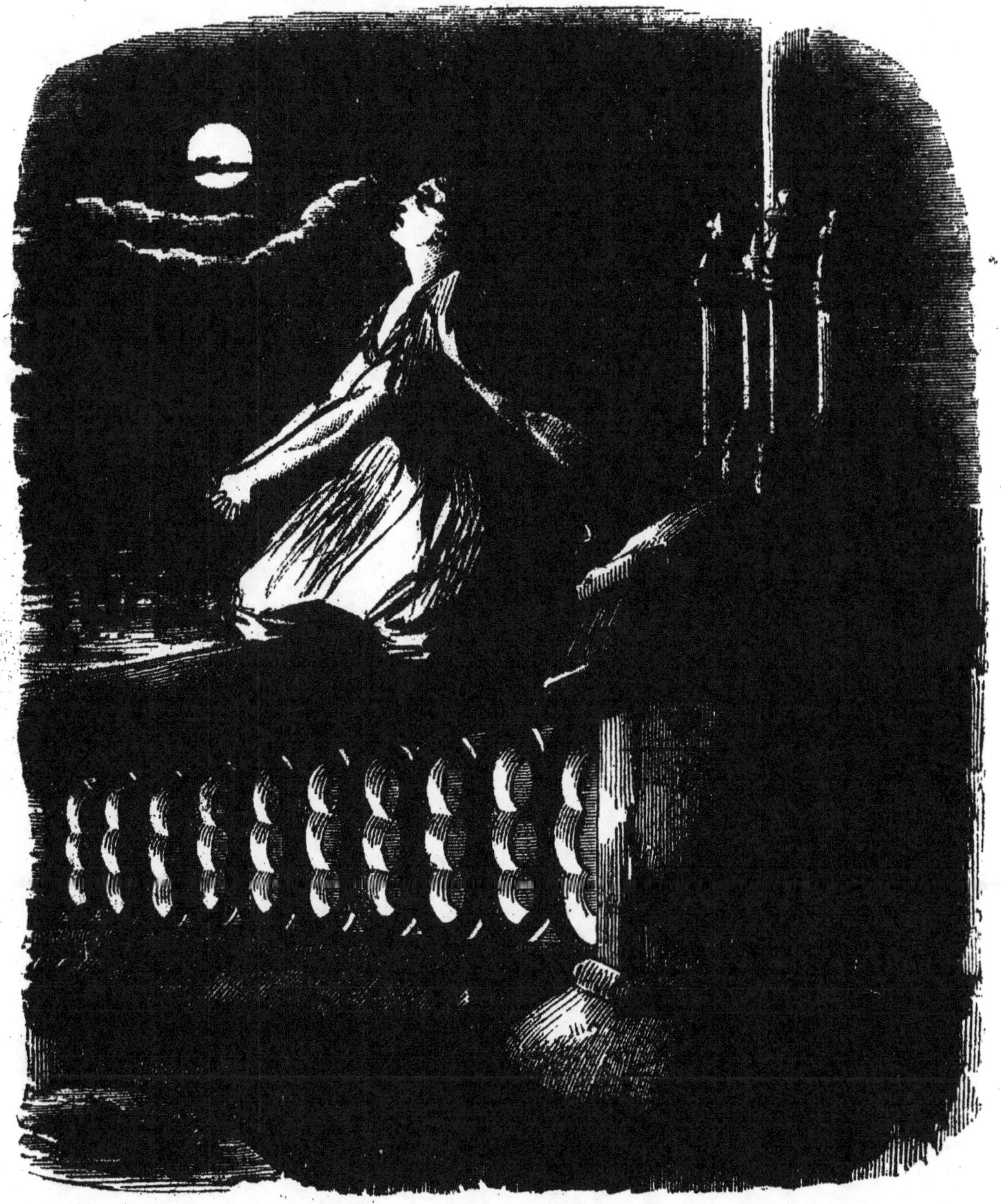

LONDON: PUBLISHED BY HENRY LEA, 112, FLEET STREET, E.C.;

THE

OUTSIDERS OF SOCIETY;

OR,

THE WILD BEAUTIES OF LONDON.

WITH ILLUSTRATIONS.

LONDON :

HENRY LEA, 112, FLEET STREET, E.C.

AND ALL BOOKSELLERS.

THE OUTSIDERS OF SOCIETY;

OR, THE

WILD BEAUTIES OF LONDON.

[HIS LORDSHIP CONTEMPLATES HIS VICTIM.]

INTRODUCTION.

ALTHOUGH I do not hold mankind in so high opinion as perhaps many others do, still, for the sake of humanity, I will assume that limited is the number amongst us who are totally lost to all sense of philanthropy, and for whom the sight of a fellow-creature apparently in distress kindles no sympathy, no momentous feeling of charity.

We must all in the course of our existence, be it brief or long, have been thrown more or less among persons for whom we felt an unaccountable antipathy, amidst scenes which we would willingly have not witnessed had a choice been left to us in the matter.

And have we not some of us, at least once in our life, been induced from various circumstances to ask ourselves this simple question, "How do some people manage to live?"

Some have sought a clue to the mystery and

found it—others, less persevering, have allowed the passing thought to be dismissed from their mind without bestowing any further interest upon those friendless, lonely beings who abound in every large town.

For be not mistaken, reader, their name is legion.

That nomade tribe, without any settled home, any honest occupation, wandering in and about London, doing nothing whatever to look forward to a remuneration upon which they can fairly reckon, living " *au jour le jour*," changing daily the scene of their exploits, moving from suburb to suburb, now imposing upon the charity of their fellow-brethren, then resorting to every imaginable scheme to earn sufficient to satisfy the cravings of the most brutal passions, is heartrendingly immense.

Look at their pale features, their sunken eye, their emaciated bodies, shivering during the cold winter's night beneath their shattered and dirty garments, and as Christians answer me—Does not the whole outward appearance of these doubtful wanderers convey to a thinking mind many an unknown tale?

Of misfortune, of honest but unsuccessful industry sometimes it speaks, but ever the wretched condition of those unfortunate beings betrays the natural consequences of years of debauch, of sin, and of uncontrolled licentiousness.

Doubtless many of those were born under a lucky star ; at a given time they, too, were justified in indulging in dreams of future happiness, had they not dashed them to the ground.

Had they not themselves been the instruments of their own ruin—irretrievably blasted their once bright and hopeful career—step by step dragged themselves through the ignominious ordeal of a felon's cell—levelled their respectability to the crouching height of the gutter, finally to be cast, after years of social degradation, upon a world that denies them, upon a society that will no longer acknowledge them as any of its members?

But let us not give too hasty a judgment. Some from choice—yes, let not my meaning be misunderstood—yes, from a choice—brought on by the education which they received (if such a name can be given to their rearing up)—by the sad and pernicious examples of immorality ever set before their youthful nature, causing them to embrace, at a glance, the gratifying enjoyments of ill-gotten wealth, without bearing in mind the consequences which cannot but follow—have willingly, and with their eyes only partly opened, walked towards the path of infamy. Others, too confiding, too trustful, too honest, and too good, have looked upon the world with noble and upright ideas—their endeavours have been crushed, their honourable intentions suspected and condemned, their behaviour unjustly punished ; and from their fall they have arisen again, and they have struggled and prospered, and, after being culprits, they have become judges, while others have still failed.

Are you aware also, my readers, that at the present moment at which I am writing, there are in this huge metropolis a large number of human beings plunged in the most abject ignorance, and that, notwithstanding our charity schools, our city missionaries, our enlightened constitutions, there are thousands to whom Providence is but a name—who look upon their father and mother as " good people," but who have no further respect for them, and who, at a moment's notice, if it suited their purposes better, would part from them, never to see them more, without the slightest regret—who have spent their youth without their action being controlled, their mind educated—who, at the age of fourteen or fifteen, look upon concubinage as a pleasant and innocent state of socialism—who consider that to be dishonest is no crime so long as you are not found out—and to whom the very suggestion tending to induce them to control their nature, to prevent them indulging in all kinds of licentiousness and dissipation, and to mend their ways, would sound as preposterous !

Such as they above described form the nucleus of a large family, which I will divide into three classes :—

Firstly—The pickpockets, professional beggars, costermongers, night-cabmen, prostitutes, skittle-sharpers, shoeblacks, that " try their own hook" and belong to no society ; men on the look-out, in all night places of public resort, for gentlemen returning home " groggy ;" and billiard captains, that are ever ready to back the red or the white when their " pal" is playing and visitors in the room.

Secondly—Keepers of night-houses ; assistants, that stand without to induce people to go in ; prizefighters ; bill-discounters ; " go-between" commission agents, lately whitewashed, and insolvent years ago ; book-makers, not " good for any amount ;" men that will set girls on town ; publicans that never intend to pay for their stock, however flourishing the business may turn out ; and tipsters of " dead certainties" for all race-meetings throughout the kingdom on receipt of twelve postage stamps, and such like.

Thirdly—The lucky tout ; " the man that has married a beauty ;" the fortunate horsebreaker ; the well-off spendthrift ; the reckless *roué* ; the broken-down swell, that still manages to keep up appearances ; the promoter of public companies ; the unprincipled gentleman ; the astute " black-leg," that has had wit enough to keep clear of Newgate ; the hypocritical " respectable woman ;" the pettifogging lawyer ; and all the bright followers of such worthy individuals.

These last ones—forming the last and third class—are the best off ; they manage to exist. They are " hard up" sometimes, but there is too great a scope for the display of their talents, and they never starve, literally speaking. What would you call them ? Outcasts ? No, for some of them do move in society. Swindlers ? No, that is too harsh a term. No, that will not do either. What name shall we give them ? As we shall make acquaintance with them as the tale proceeds, the reader may wish to know. Why, I am at a loss myself—oh ! no, I am not— I will denominate them, appropriately, I hope, " THE OUTSIDERS OF SOCIETY !"

CHAPTER I.

A BIRD'S-EYE VIEW OF A LONDON LOCALITY—WE ARE INTRODUCED TO THE ABODE OF OUR HEROINE —A DEATH-BED—THE ARRIVAL OF LORD VINE-YARD.

WHO does not know Long Acre, and who has not passed through it ? Only few of those who belong to that class which include the upper ten thousand, and very few of these who may be reckoned among the members of the less fortunate community, are unacquainted with the spot. But if, alike a country road which is familiar to the surrounding peasantry, Long Acre is a part of the town known to many Londoners, similar to the road, also, it has its sinuosities. By the sinuosities of the road, I mean the ascents and descents which a coach has to undergo in its tract; whereas, by the sinuosities of Long Acre, I allude to the ups and downs of life which are plainly perceptible in the numerous alleys and lanes which swarm around it. One takes but little heed of the jerks he sustains during a summer tour, indeed he forgets them nearly as soon as the journey ends; and thus it is with the lounger walking through our huge metropolis. Although in every large town there is always an everlasting panorama unfolding itself before the gaze of the person whose mind is bent on close observation, he stoops not to inquire into the misery around him. He witnesses sad and dreary scenes, but these are soon obliterated from his mind by occurrences of a more pleasant and livelier nature; and whether it is a drama or a vaudeville which is being performed as he strolls along, neither makes nor leaves any very deep impression upon him.

Long Acre, however, I will venture to say, if known by nearly everyone, is still more familiar to that class of west-end lawyers who tread daily their way to their chambers in Lincoln's Inn, to the inheritor of a large fortune who has sometimes occasion to visit the many carriage factories which abound in the locality. Towards nine o'clock in the forenoon how deeply engaged seems this gray-haired individual walking in a sharp and brisk step towards his dusky office; while towards four in the afternoon how careless and *sans souci* appears his young man, who dashes out of a hansom. One is ending life—the other is beginning it. One knows well the ropes of a ship in which he has weathered many a storm; the other is merely stepping on board. But who are those two imaginary persons? one may ask, for the sake of argument. Is the first individual poor? is the second rich? and what is the meaning of that formal crape round the young man's Lincoln and Bennett? Passer-by, inquire not, but walk on. Inquire no further, for you know not what volumes are contained in a crape. At times, it tells a sad and melancholy tale; at others, it proclaims the realization of dreams of opulence, and a mark of mourning which apparently bespeaks to the world that natural grief attending the death of a parent, is often longed for by the wearer as the conclusion of hopes fostered in some crying emergency! If for some it implies the possession of a rent-roll of so many hundreds or thousands a year, for others it is a sad blow—distress—poverty; it is the beginning of a wretched and endless litigation, which must ultimately break a gallant heart, unfit to bear the many reactions and deceptions inherent to the stern and cruel intricacies of the law. And yet, notwithstanding the wretchedness which exists, notwithstanding the proud misfortune which would rather weep than beg, the world will go on as it did of yore, and the sun will rise and pour forth its rays over smiles, and will set amidst an ocean of tears! And how can you reconcile the silvery laugh with the hollow sob—joy with grief —light with darkness? As long as human nature will be human nature; as long as mankind will be allowed to indulge freely in its evil and wicked propensities; as long as wealth and power will sway society; as long as the pangs of

hunger will be felt; as long as misery will be crushed, and real virtue unrewarded; life for some will be hard and bitter to bear. Oh! *si jeunesse savait, si vieillem pouvait!* What a new era for mankind! Oh! but for a few years of gaiety in youth, how many bitter tears in old age!

Now that we have digressed, it is right that we should go on with our tale; and, as the French say, *retournons a nos moutons,* if we wish not to encroach upon the patience of our readers.

In the immediate vicinity of Long Acre there are many lanes—many a poverty-stricken spot— which in themselves form a neighbourhood known by the name of the "Seven Dials."

When you leave Leicester-square—that infamous locality of London, that plague of the metropolis, where vice, infamy, incest, prostitution, congregated from every part of the continent, seem to walk hand-in-hand; with brazen foreheads, drunken, besotted faces, rejoicing over their infamous career, and gloating over their ephemeral and short-lived triumphs—you come to Coventry-street.

You may either go to the right or the left— towards Piccadilly or towards Long Acre; and if you wind your steps towards the latter, you must come to the spot where our story began.

Not more than a few years ago did the events which we are about to relate occur.

On the right-hand side of Long Acre there stood a short narrow lane, that has entirely disappeared to-day.

There were not many houses in it—seven or eight; and these were broken-down, old-fashioned, wooden dwellings.

Had anyone passed through this row of small cottages on a winter's night of the year 18—, he would not have been stopped in his course by an unforeseen occurrence.

No carriage-sound rattled in the distance— there were no shrieks, no screams to be heard— not even a drunken man's voice reeling home.

Everything around was silent and still.

No light was to be seen in the lane, and yet there was a light in the last house.

But where was it?

In the front or the back? in the attics or in the underground part?

Well, it was in the rear of a most melancholy-looking abode in the whole row; in a small room, in which a cupboard, two straw chairs, and a wretched bedstead, upon which a woman was lying, composed the whole furniture.

She was a woman, indeed; ere long she would be a corpse, for her pale features and sunken eyes plainly showed that life was rapidly ebbing from her frail and emaciated form.

She was leaving the world, and yet she was young.

She was dying, and yet she seemed to cling to a life which must have been burthensome to her, if we can form an opinion from the outward appearances now before our gaze.

Poverty, misery, the utmost wretchedness, were peeping—if we may so far carry out the way of speaking—peeping through the key-hole, and yet she wished to exist.

Perhaps she trembled to appear before One to whom she would have shortly to give an account of her stewardship.

No, her fears did not come from that course.

She had a daughter—a sweet, lovely creature of sixteen—whom she was about to leave behind her, and she felt more frightened at the prospect of her child remaining in a world she knew, than she was herself at exploring a world she knew not.

The daughter was there; she stood leaning by her mother's bedside, with a cast-down and gloomy countenance.

Near her a tallow candle was casting its fitful glare over her beautiful features.

As it shed forth but a very doubtful and uncertain light upon the miserable contents of the low abode, it appeared, to all intents and purposes, to be destined to have the same fate as the dying inmate upon whom it was shedding its flickering beam.

It was nearly burnt down to the socket, and would shortly die out, and leave two lonely beings to part from each other on this earth amidst the darkness of night.

Sad and terrible farewell, indeed!

It was bitterly cold.

There was no fire, and shortly there would be no light.

Surely this would have rendered the scene more heartrending.

The poor girl shivered and trembled, and her eye wandered vacantly around her.

The fact was plain, and need not be disguised.

The dying woman had sent for help to the parish, but owing to some informality in her request, that help had been denied to her.

Thus Mrs. Wilson was doomed to breathe her last.

Suddenly she rose up from her pillow, and she, in a faint voice, murmured, "Oh! Lydia, I can scarcely respire; bring me the basin quickly—quick!"

She had scarcely spoken when a gush of blood rushed like an overflowing stream from her nostrils and her parched and pale lips, and stained her soiled and ragged bed-clothes with a crimson hue.

"Child! child! I feel I am worse. Where is the doctor? He might, perhaps, do me good."

And the poor woman mournfully shook her head, as if she thought that to hope was a sin.

"Dearest mamma," the daughter replied, "he called about twenty minutes ago. You were then so overcome and exhausted by what you had undergone, that you did not notice him. He, however, said that he would call again shortly."

"Shortly! shortly! But I shall be dead then," exclaimed the patient, in a subdued and exhausted tone of voice. "Shortly. Ah! Indeed!"

And she spoke no more.

There was an earnestness in these words which made Lydia's blood run cold.

For awhile she looked truly like one of those unfortunate inmates who abound in the asylums devoted to the care of lunacy cases.

Her soft blue eyes kindled with a strange and indescribable expression of awe, and she placed her hands against her forehead as if she wished to hide from her gaze that which she thought was too much for her to bear.

"Do not cry, Lydia," the mother pursued, in a painful tone. "I may live yet, although"——

She did not complete her sentence.

She trembled to speak.

What could she say to bring relief to the anxious mind of her child?

Dying people, in many instances, are excessively selfish, and this can easily be explained. A succession of acute suffering drowns, in the

being who is about to be launched into eternity, all thoughts of the world. Hence it has been noticed that the voice of nature is stifled sometimes.

And frequently, in the agonies of death, a mother will not remember her own child, and, even if she does, by a wayward and unexplainable turn of her feelings, she will refuse her farewell blessing.

Mrs. Wilson was not one of those.

She was fully conscious of her state.

She knew it was of no avail to nurse her child with hopes which could not be realized, and she wished to make the most of the few instants that Providence had allotted her.

She loved her Lydia fondly, tenderly, and such was her affection that, although the minutes were reckoned, she could still perceive, in the misty and cloudy territory which unravelled itself before her dying and now nearly unconscious sight, a lonely star, which she thought would ever keep her in mind of her child.

Poor Lydia remained watching Mrs. Wilson's movements with silent distress. What on earth had she done to be so sadly tried by misfortune? She was young, innocent, guiltless of any bad deed, and yet she suffered deeply.

The silence which reigned was suddenly interrupted by Mrs. Wilson, who said—

"Lydia, why am I taken from you? I wish I could live for your sake only, for I am tired of life. Oh! Lord," she exclaimed, after a moment of respite, "I can't, I won't die; I must take care of my child!"

Was the prayer heard? No one has as yet been able to fathom this mystery. But, whether it was or not, the request was not granted by the Omnipotent Dispenser of all things. The words which Mrs. Wilson spoke could not be uttered without a great exertion on her part; so she was taken worse. She lay down, then she rose restlessly on her pillow, and then she looked towards the entrance of the abode as if some noise had attracted her attention. The patient was not more than thirty-nine years of age. Her countenance, although harassed by much fatigue and sickness, was still noble and handsome, notwithstanding the ravages of distress, which were powerless in depriving it of a certain commanding majesty.

"Child," said Mrs. Wilson, after a few moments, "I must pray now; why have I not done so before? Oh! God," she said, "forgive me for my sins, and take care of my poor child whom I am leaving behind me unprotected, without friends to take care of her, or wealth to smoothe down the sorrow which my loss will inflict upon her!"

Lydia, who had fallen upon her knees as soon as her mother had began her appeal to Providence, murmured "Amen!" in a low and nearly inaudible voice.

Now Mrs. Wilson felt in earnest the pangs and the agonies of that cruel disease which was dragging her from those she loved. She was thirsty, and she called for some potion, which she drank with avidity; but this afforded no relief to her pains, for her weak stomach was unable to support the cold weight which was administered to it.

Thus a few drops of a soothing draught was the last blow to the moribond.

"Oh! God, oh! God," she ejaculated, "spare me; I am dying! Oh! Lydia."

She had scarcely spoken when an individual entered the room. He was old and gray-haired, and he remained for a while contemplating the sad scene before him. From the white tie which surrounded his broad neck, he might have been taken for one of those numerous and worthy men who form the influential body of the Church of England.

"Console yourself, my poor woman," he said; "God is good, and to Him we never apply in vain. Fret not; I will take care of your child."

"Oh! thank you," Mrs. Wilson slowly replied, looking earnestly at the stranger; but her gaze had scarcely met that of the new comer than her lips quivered, her eyes began to sink deeper and deeper, and, as if she feared the contact of the new friend and protector of her child, she sank back on her couch.

Mrs. Wilson was no more.

The hand of death, which makes such terrible ravages among the rich as well as among the poor, which spares neither the lord nor the peasant, had at length seized hold of one more of its victims.

The stranger now approached and felt the pulse of the deceased.

He shook mournfully his head, and in a slow and subdued tone he thus addressed Lydia—pretty Lydia, whose lovely blue eyes, damped by many a tear, sparkled like two diamonds of the purest water—

"Come, child; come along with me; your poor mother will never again in this world speak to you. In heaven only will you meet her now."

These words were uttered in an affectionate tone of voice, and yet Lydia did not like the sound of that voice, and she feared the speaker.

Why? She knew not.

Who could the stranger be? She had no remembrance of ever having seen him before.

"I will not go with you, sir," the girl replied, after a pause; "I will remain here. Mamma is only asleep; she will awake, I know."

No answer was made; but the stranger took Lydia by the arm, and he clasped his hands round her smooth, rosy neck, and he kissed her affectionately.

And Lydia wept, and she trembled when the lips of the stranger touched her forehead.

"Come with me, my beauty, I beseech thee," the stranger pursued. "I will take care of thee."

"Oh! mother! dearest mother!" sobbed the maiden.

The tallow candle was gradually ebbing away, and darkness was spreading by degrees in the room, and Lydia would stand by her mother's corpse.

Something white laying upon the floor now seemed to attract the stranger's attention. He stooped and he picked up a letter, which was addressed, "To the Right Hon. the Earl of Vineyard, House of Lords."

"What can Mrs. Wilson want with me now that she is dead?" his lordship thought. "She never applied to me while she was alive."

And he was about to depart, when he fancied he heard a sarcastic laugh.

He turned round, and his features assumed a snowy white.

He listened, and he fancied he saw Mrs. Wilson rising upon her bed, and holding out her fist towards him in a threatening attitude, and he fancied still that she was endeavouring to speak, that she was trying to hurl anathemas against

him, and to rush against him like a wild tigress from whom her little ones would be stolen; and that he would have been strangled by her, had not Lydia been in her way—Lydia, who was calling her mother by the most endearing terms, but who received no answer, and yet thought that she heard a strange voice softly whispering into her ears—

"Beware of the new comer, for he will be your ruin—your evil genius!"

My Lord Vineyard was a strong-minded man. He had been amused, it is true, nay, frightened, in his youthful days by ghost stories—otherwise he really would have believed he had seen what was but the freak of his imagination—of a brain muddled by copious libations after dinner.

However, at one time he had been greatly terrified. He now again recovered his usual composure. He listened attentively.

He heard no sound—he saw no ghost. He looked outside.

The night was now bright and clear. The heavens were covered with stars, and everything around was silent and still.

He endeavoured to persuade Lydia to leave the wretched abode where the corpse of her mother lay cold and motionless.

But the maiden was dumb to his entreaties.

He whistled sharply and swiftly, and a man who was standing at the end of the alley responded to his lordship's call.

Lord Vineyard spoke a few words to him, who appeared to be his valet—his confidant—one of those individuals who always "hang about" noblemen, gentlemen of property, who require similar persons to carry out those matters where they do not wish to take a prominent part themselves.

We should think that his lordship had given instructions to his attendant to take care of Lydia, for he still remained outside the abode when he had departed.

A few minutes afterwards the roll of a brougham was discernible a few yards away, and at the very time that the vehicle was hurrying on, the last gleam of the candle lighted on a sweet angel kneeling.

It was Lydia — unfortunate Lydia — whose features buried in her two tiny hands, and silently kneeling by the bed-side, was deeply engaged in prayer.

Poor maiden! Poor girl! Thou knewest not what thy lot was to be. Otherwise thou wouldst have fled away, instead of remaining in that lonely alley, watched by the agents of vice and dissipation, whilst thou prayed for the spiritual welfare of thy departed mother!

CHAPTER II.

A FEW WORDS OF EXPLANATION.

WHEN Lord Vineyard reached his home, he read Mrs. Wilson's letter. The contents of it were short, but peremptory. She bid him attend to the expenses of her funeral, and to place her daughter in a way of supporting herself. The first part of the note he strictly carried out; whether he fulfilled her other wish remains to be proved. Mrs. Wilson was, therefore, buried in a becoming manner, shortly after the scene which we have related in the previous chapter. Her child at first cried and wept bitterly, but a new life now opened to her. Before she was poor and friendless, now she was rich and encumbered with visitors. Notwithstanding her mother's wish, Lydia had obeyed Lord Vineyard. He promised her happiness, and she believed him; he furnished a house for her, and she inhabited it; he bought her a brougham, and she rode in it; he gave her money, and she managed to spend it; and, in exchange for all these gifts, he wanted her affection, and Lydia endeavoured to like him. But, reader, be not mistaken; Lydia loved Lord Vineyard only as a daughter.

Besides, the time since her mother's death was so short, that she could not yet appreciate him in his full value.

Now, I will say a few words *en passant* which will, I think, be found to be true by many. If, by the death of a dear relative, we are suddenly cast upon the world, and called upon to seek a livelihood, while before we have led a happy life, an existence deprived of all cares, we will feel the loss with no small share of despondency; whereas, if the scales are turned, and if one person less in the world rids us of incumbrances, and places us in a better position than we had hitherto enjoyed, we will grieve, no doubt, for some time, but our grievances will soon be forgotten in the whirl of pleasure, and amidst the numberless gaieties of the world.

And thus it was with Lydia. Had she found herself destitute and forlorn, and no one to help her, she would have fretted and grieved sadly. She would have solicited Providence, and, if in vain, she would have fought her destiny, and, may be, have emerged successfully from a weary and difficult struggle. How profitable, however, it would have been for her had such an alternative taken place! Lydia was now rich, and apparently happy for the time being. Her house, which was situated in one of the numerous streets which branch off from Piccadilly, was the most coquetish residence that could have been chosen. It was gorgeous inside, and neat and tasteful outside.

Lord Vineyard, who had many a time thought of Lydia Wilson, had spared no expense to ornament the cage in which the little nightingale was to be kept a prisoner. Surely the evil genius did the things well!

But how happened it that Lord Vineyard came in so *apropos* to witness Mrs. Wilson's bed scene? I must explain that. My lord had hired a person to be constantly in attendance in the neighbourhood, to let him know the progress of Mrs. Wilson's disease; and, when the crisis had arrived, he lost no time in hurrying to the spot where he could seize upon his prey.

I will not, like some novel writers, begin my story by telling my readers that everything I relate is strictly true. On that head I will remain silent, and let them judge for themselves; and I think that it will require very little discernment on their part to find out whether my work is based upon real life occurrences, or whether it is only a few ideas emanating from a wayward brain.

When Lord Vineyard had left the poor abode where Mrs. Wilson had breathed her last, he stopped for awhile in the street, and reflected deeply ere he entered his carriage. The scene which he had witnessed had made a lasting impression upon him, and he knew not how he could dispose of Lydia—whether he would enable her to occupy an honourable place in society, or whether he would make her his mistress. As we have perceived by the few lines above, he had

come to the last resolution. Lord Vineyard was a cool, calculating individual. A proud name in "Burke's Peerage" sounded well in the eyes of the world; but if people only knew the infamy attached to it! If they did, what matter! Lord Vineyard was thought wealthy; he had a town residence and two country mansions. He was a clever statesman, a good politician, and his public life was worthy of the utmost praise. Not so, indeed, with his private life; Lord Vineyard knew how to be infamous. Who cared about a humble little girl? Surely very few. Now that I have gone so far, the reader may naturally be curious to know why Mrs. Wilson appeared to have such a decided antipathy for Lord Vineyard. I will enlighten him on the subject. When Lord Vineyard was a few winters younger, like most young men he was careless, extravagant, and fond of pleasure. Years ago, then, he was staying at his uncle's, the late Lord Vineyard, to whom he was the heir-at-law. We will all be foolish; well, he was so. A pretty *soubrette* was always in Dashmore's way. She flirted, joked, laughed, smiled with him; and he returned the compliment. He said he loved her, and I believe she admitted the same feeling. Out of such intercourses results will occur. A fine healthy boy was brought in this world one fine October morning. The mother died; the child lived. This was unpleasant, and it would certainly have been much more in accordance with the present earl's wishes had the contrary taken place. But we cannot always manage things as we like, or, if we did, what a queer world this would be! Mrs. Wilson, at that time, was housekeeper to the late Lord Vineyard. For a good consideration, Dashmore made it worth his while to acquaint her with the secret. The child was made away with (sent to some neighbouring farmer, who gave the little urchin more than he had appetite for, and he was smothered). "Would—could those things be accomplished in a civilized country?" will exclaim some Baptist clergyman. Whether they will take place again or not, I am not in a position to say; but I know that similar deeds have been perpetrated. Since the day, then, that Mrs. Wilson was an instrument to the proceedings above related, she never had one moment's peace of mind. Lord Vineyard, on that account, thought her an ignorant woman, and himself an intellectual man. He persuaded himself that, after all, there was no murder, and that it was all an accident. In the course of time, and with due regard to appearances—namely, according to circumstance, the maid and the child were buried with due honours. The county magistrates never suspected anything, and even if they did, the uncle of the present lord was a popular landlord, a generous nobleman, and out of philanthropy they would not, under any considerations, have broken the poor old man's heart by laying to his nephew's door a charge which, if well proved, would have inflicted upon his proud coat of arms a stigma which it would have required centuries to wipe off. Mrs. Wilson knew the kind of man Lord Vineyard was. She knew with whom her child would have to deal, and she naturally looked upon so worthy a guardian with indescribable bitter disgust. This was the reason for which Mrs. Wilson disliked—nay, hated—Lord Vineyard. The feeling, I believe, was fully reciprocated, and when she died his lordship felt much relieved. No one knew his little peccadilloes, and he was sure never to be detected. In this respect he was sensible enough, for he and Mrs. Wilson were the two only persons that knew of the transaction. The infirmary surgeon who attended the abigail (my lord's physician not being thought necessary in so vulgar a case) was persuaded by Mr. Dashmore that she died of dropsy. The medical man had his doubts —in fact, he was nearly certain of the contrary— but he was a careless sort of fellow, and a ten-pound note soon cleared away whatever will he had of diving deeper in the matter. I do not wish my readers to believe for one single instant that I intend to describe my characters opened to corruption for the sake of pecuniary motives; indeed, nothing is further from my mind. Even provided that I were inclined to do so, I would certainly not attack the medical profession. During my eventful career, I have met many of its members, and a finer class of men, in my opinion, does not exist. On the whole, they are a generous, kind-hearted set of fellows—ever willing to support the orphan and the widow, and never shrinking from the discharge of their arduous duties they are called upon to perform. But now *revenons à nos moutons.* Two heads are better than one, and when the young infirmary surgeon was persuaded by Mr. Dashmore and Mrs. Wilson that everything was "all right," he believed them. The poor woman was dead, and what matter was it to him how she died? Thus he thought, and there was an end to the affair.

But Lydia, what was Lydia doing now? Very little, and a great deal. She was thinking. Oh! how pretty she looks, as she sits in her boudoir. Now she rises, and she walks about. She treads the velvet pile, and she does not dislike the softness under her feet. Why, I never noticed her little brodequins before. What charming extremities she has! How nicely made you are, Lydia! What a pity it would have been had you been allowed "to waste your sweetness on the desert air!" How kind of Lord Vineyard to take care of you, and to drag you away from that horrid dirty lane! And the mother? she is gone. Do you ever think of her, now that all your wishes and whims are granted? Of course you do, often? Oh! yes, very often. You will forget her, though, and that before long? Oh! never. Lydia is bewitching. Her lips are like two cherries; her teeth, so white; and her hair, so luxuriant and so glossy. Lydia is just the kind of being that a painter would have longed for to complete the heavenly picture of his romantic imagination—and no wonder! Nature, who is so parsimonious with some, has been extraordinarily generous with her gifts to her. Her eyes, dark blue, have something which betrays more than I could say—the capricious desires of woman when her heaving breast does swell; and yet Lydia is not much more than seventeen, and I might perhaps venture to assert that the innocence and joyousness of childhood has scarcely given place to the more sober charms of womanhood.

Now Lydia looks round the apartment, and she seems satisfied with the tasty manner in which it is decorated. The ceilings of the rooms are ornamented with costly designs; the walls are covered with a paper of a rich and lively pattern, considerably enlivened by masterpieces of the Italian school, and by modern pictures owed to the genius of the living celebrities. Oh! if Lady Vineyard could only step into your boudoir, and reckon at a glance the profuse expenditure displayed by all the little "nic-nacs" carelessly lying about, how you would smile, Lydia! but she would look daggers. If her ladyship was aware of you having such a "Rembrandt," and those two pictures of Poussin—and there, also, is the bed-scene, so well painted by Fragonard—the question would be, Where did my lord find the money? for, although his lordship is thought a wealthy man, he is comparatively poor. His wife is extravagant; his estates are not entailed; and one day there will be a crash! Oh! if my lady knew my lord's doings, she would make him remember he has a wife, and she would threaten him with Sir Cresswell Cresswell's court. Keep good hours, my lord, and do not tell my lady that a heavy discussion at the club is the cause of your remaining out so early in the morning. But what did my lord say he saw in you, Lydia?—a deep likeness to a departed child? Oh! do not believe him. To carry out his end he will play with the most sacred feelings. Shun him—remember your poor mother, Lydia—it is time yet. She seems to hear these words. She sits down. She hides her lovely features in her pretty hands. Weep, Lydia, weep. Shed tears of innocence. Thy youthful, innocent garment is still as pure, as white as the snow which falls from the canopy of heaven.

But Lydia is not weeping for any very sad consideration. Lord Vineyard promised her a pet dog—a small Italian greyhound—and she needs somebody's love. She is restless. She looks outside the window. Oh! what weather! it is raining. The sun was shining but a minute ago. Now Lydia must work.

She takes up a little embroidered collar, which is lying on an ebony *table à ouvrage* by her side. She is about to begin her task when the sounds of footsteps ascending the staircase are distinctly heard, and a decent-looking maid makes her appearance, conveying to her mistress a letter on a metal salver.

Lord Vineyard had chosen the servants, and he had taken good care that his *protegée* should be well attended to.

Lydia reads the letter.

"No greyhound to-day. However, I must console myself for a while. Kate, do you know what the French say when you are longing for a thing?"

"No, miss."

"*Tout vient à point pour qui soit attendre.*"

"Oh! what is the meaning of that, miss?"

"That you will get everything in good time."

Kate, who was a fine specimen of the Emerald Isle, and whom Lord Vineyard had engaged, notwithstanding that ridiculous "no Irish need apply," which portrays so well the English antipathies towards their Irish neighbours, looked at her mistress and smiled. I am not very certain whether a full sergeant in Her Majesty's Royal Horse Guards did not at that moment appear before the bewildered eyes of the *femme de chambre,* who left the room immensely astonished at the rapid progress Miss was making in the *parlez-vous* language.

Lydia was a clever, quick-minded girl. She had heard my lord say that French phrase, and she remembered it well; and the poor mother's request had been, perhaps, very easily forgotten.

Lydia was about to read Byron's "Don Juan," that my lord had brought her as a little keepsake, when Kate again appeared, to announce that my lady's brougham was waiting. She flew to her dressing-room, and, a few instants afterwards, she was driving towards Kensington alone—alone with her thoughts.

CHAPTER III.

MY LORD AND HIS PUPIL—LORD VINEYARD COMES OUT STRONG.

THE brougham rolled rapidly over the pavement, conveying in its swift course the object of Lord Vineyard's affection. As the fiery steed dashed along with uncommon rapidity, many a passer-by halted to admire the stylish appearance of the whole concern, which in club parlance would have been termed "a first-rate turn out." Even the coachman was irreproachable in his "tenue." His livery coat and his doeskin gloves fitted him to a nicety, his cravat set without a crease, and it was easy to perceive that he was careful in the brushing of his hat, which had evidently been manufactured by some west-end tradesman. As he sat coaxing with his whip the horses which required no punishment, he felt a great man—at least, in his own estimation—and I should venture to say that he would by no means have been flattered at being placed on a par with the insignificant footman who stood by his side. Lydia, in the meantime, lying luxuriously in the brougham, was puzzling her brain in the hope of fathoming the reason of Lord Vineyard's sudden kindness. She knew him to be a married man—to have a family—a large and gorgeous town establishment to keep; and, in the innocence of her youthful imagination, she could not come to any conclusion satisfactory to herself concerning his lordship's profuse generosity. Lydia until now was virtuous, candid, and handsome. She belonged besides to that golden period of life during which the mind, ever confiding, ever trusting in sunshines, forgetful of the storm which often succeeds bright days, spreads before itself the future in warm, glowing colours. She saw a dazzling picture of happiness unfolding itself in lively shades before her inexperienced gaze; it foreshadowed, she thought, new and lovely scenes, and, satisfied with a cursory glance, she dreaded to dim her sight by too long a contemplation. She was indulging in a dream which pleased and flattered her taste, and—why I know not—she feared to awake to sad reality. Had she tried to account very hard for every little incident in my lord's behaviour which came under her notice, she might, perhaps, have guessed part of the truth. Alike the sailor on the ocean, who sees breakers looming in the distance, she might have detected danger in the dark clouds gradually appearing in the sky, and have endeavoured while it was time yet to prevent her frail bark from coming into contact with the rocky and dangerous cliffs yonder—treacherously hidden at intervals by the foaming waves. Alas! a day would come when bitter thoughts would crowd themselves in Lydia's mind, and fill her heart with despair and sorrow, but how could the poor girl prevent the accomplishment of that destiny which was rapidly hurling her to a sad and dreary fate? My Lord Vineyard, in the meantime, was sitting before his writing-desk, penning a few lines of that work which was to astonish the literary world. The book, I believe, has never been published, but, if I remember aright, it was a treatise on the "Immortality of the Soul." It would be inconsistent with my purpose were I to attempt to conceal from my readers the various feelings which from time to time actuate the behaviour of those who are to play a part in the course of this story. Very few will be disposed to excuse Lord Vineyard's conduct; I for one shall not endeavour to palliate it. I will merely restrain myself to saying that his way of acting was excusable, if any deviation from the path of religion and morality can be excused when brought about by the promptings of love. Truth, above all things, is in many instances more difficult to believe than fiction. Byron, I believe, has said before me something to the same effect. Trusting, therefore, that my reader will rely on so good an authority, I beg of them to credit the following. Lord Vineyard had reached the age of sixty without ever having loved. Many individuals have been and will be found to be very similar to his lordship in this respect; the cases, however, I am happy to say, on behalf of the ladies, are solitary ones, and do not by any means form the generality. To infer, then, from the above statement that Lord Vineyard's heart was closed to every feeling of tender affection, would be dismissing the subject at issue in rather too summary a manner. To say that his mind was so taken up with political matters that it could not be made the slave of some genial warmth, would also be enclosing the bounds of my lord's imagination without too limited a sphere. Further, to sum up by concluding that his nature partook too much of that selfishness—inherent to certain unprivileged men—to leave him any scope for the enjoyment of reciprocated love, would indeed be doing a great injustice to my lord's *tout ensemble*.

No, Lord Vineyard had walked for many years in that wide demesne over which Venus sways with uncontrolled power, and he had always until now been allowed by this sometimes indulgent goddess to proceed unmolested. Once he saw Lydia—then he was another man. His heart began to throb—he fancied himself wandering under some hallucination, he looked upwards, and he beheld Cupid smiling in the distance. It was a long time ere he could extricate the arrow from its bleeding position, for Lord Vineyard was enamoured of Lydia. The contrast between the two beings was great; an attempt to blind youth and old age was not an every-day occurrence. So deep, so great was Lord Vineyard's sudden passion, that it could easily have been suggested that he was worthier of a seat in a lunatic asylum than in Her Majesty's House of Commons. Constituents, however, do not always think the same. In one word, Lord Vineyard's passion was the only tie that bound him to this earth. It was the tenure by which he held his life; it was the spark of his existence, which, once extinguished, would render him wretched and miserable. Lord Vineyard loved Lydia, and, when a man at his time of life takes to love-making, it is a step which generally entails results of a most original nature. Lord Vineyard was a man of the world, and, although many of his countrymen had in his presence turned into ridicule the system of matrimony adopted by our gallant allies and neighbours across the channel, he had, nevertheless, suited himself regardless of *qu'en dira le monde*, and his union was more a *marriage de convenance* than an exchange of love sanctioned by the parson. Lady Vineyard, before her marriage, had a few thousands a year in her own right. Lord Vineyard, at that time the Hon. Mr. Dashmore, was heir presumptive to his uncle, an Irish peer, and was thought a

[THE BEAUTY AND HER MAID.]

good *parti*. Lord and Lady Vineyard met in society, and they agreed to spend their income together, until something should turn up. It was a kind of bargain highly in accordance with the requirements of both parties. The future lord wanted money, the future my lady wanted a title. Unfortunately for the would-be " my lady," no settlements were made at the time — the marriage having been carried out expeditiously, so as to suit the purposes of the future lord's counsel, who impressed upon their client's mind the necessity of his having the uncontrolled management of his wife's goods and chattels. Whether there were a few little claims which the lawyers wished to have settled, is an item best known to the parties concerned, and upon which I look as being excessively probable, although nothing was said about this very interesting topic at the time. There are, indeed, matters which it is wiser to leave in the background The marriage was duly performed, and its announcement published in all the fashionable newspapers of the day. Lord Vineyard, therefore, had led but an indifferent matrimonial life. He never found in the conjugal embrace the emotions he sought, and when he saw Lydia he felt as happy as the weary digger who, after a few weeks' toil, hits upon a longed-for gold-nugget. " Women are roses," said Shakspeare. This is an opinion which no one would venture to contradict ; but I may add, if they are roses, alike roses they require a deal of attention, which could not be too constant. If they are well looked after they will bloom at a given time ; whereas, if they are neglected, they will shortly fade away, and their beautiful colour soon forsake them. Lord Vineyard knew these things; furthermore, he was aware that nothing subdues a woman's heart quicker than everlasting kindness, and he resolved to love Lydia. Love in the abstract is certainly in my opinion the most extraordinary feeling to which human nature is amenable, and although it is a subject which has been commented and dwelt upon by our greatest poets, our most enlightened writers, our moralists, and by almost every intellectual and deep-thinking man, so inexhaustible is the topic, that there is still scope for further writing. It is a warm affection which has always existed, which has been kindled in a multitude of breasts in a variety of shapes and forms, and which will, until the end of time, be always new to those who first experience it. He would be a bold being who, in the erroneous and misplaced valuation of his own strength of mind, should endeavour to persuade others of his being fully competent to withstand whatever temptations might fall in his way. If we must believe the French, love may be compared to a fountain, from which, some day or another, we shall be compelled to draw a few drops to quench an unexpected thirst. To love, and to be loved, is the ideal dream for the realization of which many long in vain. Longfellow tells us "that there is nothing holier in this life of ours than the first consciousness of love—the first fluttering of its silken wings—the first rising sound and breath of that wind which is soon to sweep through the soul, to purify or to destroy." What truth there is in these few words! for, however cold, however ungrateful one's heart may be, man will still remember in old age a feeling kindled in the days of youth, when everything smiled before him. Sensations awakened in the human breast —whether they made the heart palpitate with joy, or caused the pulse to quicken under terrible apprehensions—whether they were torments or pleasures, pains or delights—whether inspired by objects worthy or unworthy of admiration, can never be forgotten. So great, indeed, is love's magic control, that it exercises an indescribable influence over the bearings of everyday life. It induces him whom passion has chosen for his slave, to commit either the noblest deeds or the worst actions. It plays with human nature like a child with a toy—now raising the soul to a higher life, and then levelling it to the lowest ebb. No one has as yet successfully accounted for the waywardness of a feeling, the depth of which it does not belong to humanity to fathom; it has its secrets, its mysteries, which have and always will exist, and which can be summed up thus: that love can be written upon, but never definitively explained.

Lydia was perhaps indulging in similar thoughts, having just returned from her daily drive, when ten silvery sounds emanated from a splendid piece of workmanship which rested on the chimney-piece.

"My dear girl," said Lord Vineyard, on entering the little *salon*, "your clock, I am happy to perceive, is perfectly right. How are you to-day, my charming little angel?" he continued, after a while.

"Delighted to see you," replied Lydia, as her lips opened in a smile, which displayed a faultless row of teeth. "The rain was beating the window so hard and so ceaselessly, and the sighs of the wind were so monotonous to hear, that I was getting quite frightened here by myself, all alone in my glory."

"Lydia, you must not give way to foolish fears," my lord replied. "But there is no necessity for musing always by yourself, if you dislike the idea of it. Why do you not ask Mrs. Haltering on a visit to you? She is a good-hearted woman, and she might turn out a very useful companion to you for the time being."

"How strange, my lord, that you should say so," the girl replied. "When I was driving out to-day, I called at her place in Kensington. She was out of town for a day or two, but I left a few lines trying to induce her to do the very thing you suggest as soon as she returned."

"When I hit upon a good idea, or happen to say something funny, which would almost at the same time have occurred to the mind of my friend the Marquis de Limayrac, the French *attaché*," the lord replied, "he generally answers me— '*Mon cher lord, les beaux esprits se rencontrent.*'

"I will say the same to you, Lydia; your charming mind has met mine;" and as he spoke my lord took Lydia's tiny hand into his, and there he kept it.

Lydia allowed her rosy nails, her white and soft fingers, to come in contact with those of Lord Vineyard; and she looked at him with timid astonishment.

She felt no delightful sensations in the pressure of a strange hand.

"I'll tell you why, Lydia," his lordship said. "I should like Mrs. Haltering to spend a few weeks with you; she is a woman who knows what is necessary to get on, and she might make somebody of you."

"Oh! yes," replied Lydia, "I would like so much to be 'somebody,'" and a silvery laugh followed her exclamations; "but what must I do?"

"Become a fashionable star in the London season," Lord Vineyard replied.

"But for that," Lydia said, "I must learn to play and sing on the pianoforte. I think that I could stand on a horse's back and hold a pair of reins; but I must excel in riding, and I must become a capital whip."

"And if I knew these things thoroughly, my lord," Lydia inquired, after a moment's reflection, "should I be somebody?"

"Of course you would," my lord replied, and the idea that his pupil could ever attain such superiority made Lord Vineyard's heart palpitate with a natural glow of pleasure and pride.

He continued, after a while—

"Lydia, listen to me. If you could combine cleverness in the field with a certain amount of accomplishments in the drawing-room, you would attain an *apogee* of excellence which I think no woman ever possessed. I have had some experience in society, and I feel confident that I never yet met a lady who was perfect in every respect. I will tell you, Lydia, what my *beau ideal* is. Every man to his taste—I say that before I speak for fear that you should laugh at me."

"Well, what is your *beau ideal?*" Lydia coaxingly inquired.

"It would be a woman who could clear a five-barred gate in the morning, as well as a *morceau* of Meyerbeer's in the evening. Unfortunately, women are incomplete. She who dazzles a musical party would never win the sympathies of an old fellow like me, who has always considered fox-hunting to be the first and last thing one should learn to do properly. But perhaps I am behind or before my time."

Lydia listened attentively to the words my lord spoke. She said nothing, but, from the steady manner in which she kept her eyes fixed upon the speaker, it was no difficult matter to guess that she was drawing her own conclusions. I am not wrong in my assertion, for Lydia was indeed forming a plot, of which the inoffensive and laudable nature was to endeavour to turn out "somebody."

"My lord," she slowly began, "to-morrow I must begin to learn how to sing, to play on the piano, to drive, and to do everything first-rate."

"You are settling matters rather too quickly, my dearest pet," my lord replied. "If you wish to learn all the things you mention, you shall learn them. Nothing, I assure you, will give me greater pleasure than to put you in the way of retrieving a neglected education; but you talk like a child—how can you learn singing unless your voice is suited for it."

"Oh! with regard to that, I am in no fear," Lydia replied. "Did you not, my lord, tell me yourself that the sounds of my voice were the sweetest you ever heard?"

This answer, which flowed from the lips of a girl of seventeen, caused the wrinkles on my lord's forehead to extend, his eyes to brighten. In fact, he was rather pleased at his having been caught in his own net.

"To become thoroughly acquainted with all the accomplishments you speak of," Lord Vineyard continued, "it will require time—and some time, too."

"What matters that?" Lydia replied. "I will be such a good pupil—so zealous, so docile, so attentive, and so laborious, that I will learn a great deal in a short period."

As the girl spoke, a beam of happiness flashed across her lovely features.

"There is nothing like being one's own trumpeter," continued Lord Vineyard, who wished to tease Lydia, and who did not by any means dislike the sudden craving for education entertained by Lydia.

Now my lord drew his chair closer and closer to that of Lydia, and he kissed her tiny little hand, which he still held in his manly grasp.

"Oh! I love you so much, Lydia!" he said.

I do not think that this avowal was necessary to convince the young girl of the truth of my lord's love. She kept her eyes bent upon his features, and she saw his flushed countenance and the brilliancy of his eyes, which at one time almost frightened her.

And she was about to rise, when my lord kissed Lydia again and again; and as his lips fell upon her silky and warm eyelashes, his frame quivered as if it were shaken by some delightful sensation until then unknown to him.

And Lydia was at a loss to understand the extraordinary behaviour of her new protector and friend, and then she thought of her mother, and then the death scene appeared before her, and her cheek turned as white as snow.

There is a Providence in everything, so my lord noticed her altered looks.

"What is the matter with you, Lydia?" he said; "are you unwell?"

"Say good-night to me, and leave me now. I would feel so happy if I were left alone."

Lord Vineyard obeyed Lydia.

"To-morrow I will see about your masters, and next time I see you, you will tell me whether you approve of them."

Lydia answered not; she stood silent, and looked at his lordship with her big blue eyes.

Lord Vineyard approached her, and he wished her adieu; and as he descended the staircase the picture of an angel came before him, with a crown of laurels and a sweet smile, and then he thought of the syrens, who were said to live in forests, to dwell in rivers and valleys, who were so heavenly and yet so earthly, who appeared so trustworthy and yet were so deceitful, and whose whole time and occupation were spent in sowing their numberless attractions in the path of those they wished to lead to perdition.

Was Lydia an angel or a syren? As the story proceeds, the reader will be able to answer that question for himself. I will not, therefore, dwell any longer upon this point, but begin another chapter to attend to matters of perhaps more importance.

CHAPTER IV.

LYDIA AND HER NEW FRIENDS—A SKETCH OF TWO OUTSIDERS.

LORD VINEYARD kept his promise to Lydia. Next day, early in the morning, he went in search of the best masters he could procure, entered into final arrangements with them, and, after having recommended them to pay particular attention to their new pupil, he left their respective abodes, perfectly satisfied with the manner with which he had discharged his difficult task. I say difficult, because it was no easy job to choose masters who were not known to those who were wont to give lessons to his daughters during the London season; for Lord Vineyard had a family, about which we shall have occasion to speak as the story proceeds. On the following Monday, Lydia's boudoir was filled with educational books, musical albums, drawing cahiers, pencil-cases, colour-boxes, grammars, dictionaries, and a variety of objects of a similar description. She had now the tools to work with—it remained for her to employ them to advantage. It would, however, have been preposterous on my lord's part had he expected Lydia to become, in a few weeks, a maestro on the pianoforte, or a thorough French scholar, or had he thought that a few lessons in drawing would enable her to take fair copies from original Italian pictures, and that a little training in singing would just suit her for the faultless performance of any of the different selections from the operas en vogue. Lord Vineyard knew better, and he felt satisfied to wait, provided the pupil would do justice to the masters, and in the end prove worthy of the attention which would have been bestowed upon her. The mental accomplishments would require time ere they would be perfectly mastered; but as to the riding and driving, my lord fretted little about. He felt confident that Lydia had rather a horsy taste, and that ere long she would excel in taming the most vicious mare, or in cleverly managing the freshest pair that ever dashed out of Tattersall's. In thinking thus, Lord Vineyard was perfectly justified, as time will show. Lydia, on her part, would exert herself—she would, I doubt not, make the most of her time. She had never had an opportunity of a refined education, and she would not allow the present one to escape. She had, in all probability, many years of existence before her, and what will not a few years accomplish? Progress in learning does not depend on the time actually spent in study, but entirely on the taste that a person may have for a particular thing. I have known an instance where a student in six months became so familiar with music, that his tutors were astonished with his wonderful perception, and with the extraordinary rapidity with which he would carry out the slightest hint given, whether during the hours of tuition or not. Lord Vineyard used to assist at the lessons, and as he stood leaning over Lydia's well-shaped shoulders, he presented more the appearance of a father watching his daughter, than an old *roué* watching his victim. Had Lydia been born in another class of life; instead of being poor, had she been rich, how different would have been her lot! One forenoon that Lydia's fingers were running over the wiry notes of the piano, a tap was heard outside the drawing-room door, and two ladies entered the apartment. Ere a word could have been said, Lydia was in the arms of the elder person, who was no other than Mrs. Haltering, about whom we have previously spoken.

"Allow me," Lydia said, "Mrs. Haltering, to welcome you and your friend. I was expecting you for the last few days, and was at a loss to account for the reason which kept you away so long."

"My dearest girl," Mrs. Haltering replied, "I was down at Brighton until yesterday evening; and, as you can see," she continued, "I lose no time in visiting my old acquaintances. Permit me, Lydia, to introduce you to Mrs. Leicester. Although our acquaintance is not of very long standing, I have taken a decided fancy to her, and I hope sincerely that you will feel like myself towards her."

Lydia looked towards Mrs. Leicester, and she could not help being struck with her beauty, with the neatness of her toilet, and with a kind of *je ne sais quoi* which she possessed to an eminent degree, and which at once enlists friends on behalf of those who realize the portrait given below.

Mrs. Leicester was quite young; she could not have seen more than twenty-three summers, even had she seen so many. Her eyes were of a dark brown, and, when they rested upon any particular object, they shone with a peculiar and extraordinary lustre. Her lofty and high forehead was crowned with a profusion of silky glowing hair, falling in two wavy ringlets round her lovely countenance. Her aquiline nose might, perhaps, have been considered by some to be too prominent, but the disproportion was not striking enough to contrast disagreeably with the loving expression of her features. Her lips, which nature had carefully coloured with a brilliant rosy hue, were, perhaps, too pouting to be strictly in accordance with the exquisite delineaments of her well-shaped mouth, but this is a point against which I will say nothing, as I consider pouting lips to be in themselves a great beauty. They betray more than I would or could tell; a something which would undoubtedly be spoiled by explanation, but which adds considerable charm to the many attractions Providence has so profusely bestowed upon the prettier and gentler portion of humanity. Mrs. Leicester had besides a most charming figure. Although she did not look precisely *passée*, yet it was easy to perceive that she had led rather "a fast life," and that, ere long, she would reap the benefit of an exis-

tence spent in draining to the dregs the cup of pleasure and volupty. Mrs. Leicester was consumptive, and, like all the women thus afflicted, she had, strange to say, an unaccountable craving for experiencing strong emotions. Now that I have given my readers Mrs. Leicester's portrait, I think it only but fair to divert our attention to her friend. Mrs. Haltering was as different from Mrs. Leicester as night is from day. She was, nevertheless, an extremely lady-like person, who, in her day, must have been remarkably handsome. She was not above forty, and, had she lived at our British court when George IV. passed so favourable an opinion concerning women who had reached her time of life, doubtless she would have had but very little trouble in encircling within her wily nest the royal favours. Not a wrinkle could be detected on her forehead, not a silvery spark in her dark and abundant hair; her skin was soft and white, and her hands well-shaped and slightly *potelees*; her bust was still good and well preserved; and the darkness and brilliancy of her eyes well worthy of a Spanish woman. This is only but a sketch of Mrs. Haltering's *physique*, but now let me picture her *au moral*.

Mrs. Haltering had only made but one *faux pas*: she had unfortunately been rather too gay to suit our extremely liberal and sometimes indulgent code of society. She had, it is true, been duly and formally married to a worthy gentleman, who for years had worn with distinction her majesty's scarlet uniform, and who had acquired in the end his spurs on the field in the East Indies. He had, however, been obliged to enter at length into a *séparation amicale* with his *soi-disant* better half, leaving her an annuity of £300, which was a great deal more than she was entitled to by marriage settlements. This would have been a sufficient allowance to a person of moderate habits, but it was only a trifle for one who had been all her life accustomed to reckon and to spend other people's money by thousands. Mrs. Haltering, therefore, not wishing to live like a pauper, resolved to make most of her respectability. She was not very particular in making acquaintances, and remarkably easy and free in effecting introductions. She was always busily occupied in forwarding some scheme or another of which no one with a fair amount of *bienséance* would have approved of. She would be the means of bringing about clandestine engagements; would let lodgings, or part of her house, in the season, in the hope of becoming acquainted with some wealthy or respectable family, out of which she might make something. She never would be at a loss for a reply, and always make her exit with flying colours out of any scrape she would fall into. When in conversation with one person she would astonish the walls with the filth of her conversation, and the extraordinary nature of her philosophical, orthodox, and religious ideas. When surrounded by a few people, she would be taken for an angel, so chaste and so innocent would she appear! Mrs. Haltering was constantly abusing her husband (women in a similar situation always do); would condemn the doctrines of the Church of Rome when talking to Protestants, and *vice versa*; would be constantly speaking about her distinguished relations, always omitting to say whether she claimed relationship on her side or on that of her husband; would be acquainted with lots of noblemen to whom those kind of persons are of an immense use; speak of "my lady so-and-so," to whom she never was introduced; would be under obligations to women under gentlemen's protection, but would never know "unfortunates;"—indeed,the word itself would make her blood run cold, and cause her to shrink with disgust; would know "Burke's Peerage" by heart, and occasionally take part at whist when money was to be won; was as bland as an angel in some cases—as deceitful as a demon in others; would be constantly borrowing five pounds, and never lending a farthing; living at the rate of £500 a year, and always pleading poverty; would get immensely in debt, and always be clever enough to keep out of trouble; would never in her opinion forget her dignity as a lady, and yet do everything to suit her purposes; she would wear costly jewellery, and always be dressed with unassuming elegance; would *chaperon* young girls, and make them pay dearly for her services; would gratify every whim; would go to church on Sundays, and shroud all her peccadilloes with her "respectability" and Mrs. Major Wilkinson on her pasteboard. In fact, she was a selfish and bad woman, but not worse than hundreds of others who live and move in the world, and who belong to a class which, if it was well looked into, would be found to be composed of an immensity of numbers—male and female—which I have already denominated by the name of "The Outsiders of Society."

When the introduction took place between Lydia and Mrs. Leicester, the former lost no time in entering into a little chit-chat conversation with her newly-made acquaintance. She felt a certain affection for her—and why so she knew not. Was it because Mrs. Leicester was young and dazzling like herself, or was it because she looked upon Mrs. Haltering as a woman too advanced in life to countenance the wayward exuberance of her imagination? She would have been at a loss, no doubt, to analyze the nature of the sudden friendship springing up in her whole being. There are things for which we cannot account, and the tendency which she experienced towards Mrs. Leicester was one of them. How pretty, how charming, how bewitching the two women looked, as they sat side by side, whispering to each other, while Mrs. Haltering was glancing over the woodcuts of some fashionable magazine.

"I shall be quite jealous of you, Lydia," said Mrs. H., after she had opened and closed nearly every book on the table, "if you go on like you do. Why, you and Mrs. Leicester are talking so, that one would fancy you had a world of new things to say to each other."

"Now, do not be too severe," Lydia replied, smiling. "Mrs. Leicester was asking me what I did with myself in the evenings. You see," she continued, "that our chat does not relate to matters of very great importance."

"I never said it did, but I do not like to be left alone. The fact of the matter is this; I am of a very jealous disposition, and if I hate anything, it is whispering."

"Some people say it is very bad taste besides," returned Lydia, who wished to show Mrs. Haltering that she was up to a joke as well as anybody else.

"When did you see Vineyard last?" Mrs. Haltering remarked. "I want to speak to him."

"I am expecting him here in the evening," Lydia replied, "when he is going to make me the present of a nice Italian greyhound."

These words had scarcely been spoken when the rattle of a carriage was heard, and my lord jumped, rather than walked, into the drawing-room with the most charming little dog that ever was seen, bundled in his arms. He threw it upon the ground, and the animal, without asking any-one's permission, went quietly to the sofa, where it made itself quite comfortable for the time being; but it was not allowed to remain there long ere Lydia took it and placed it in her glossy silken dress.

"How are you, my dear girls?" my lord said, in recognising the two strange ladies, and in advancing towards Lydia, by the side of whom he sat for awhile. "I have just left the club, madam," he began, after a few moments, addressing Mrs. Leicester, placing a certain emphasis on the words, "and I saw your friend Williamson, who begged of me to tell you that he would not see you for a few days, as he intends. running down to Lincolnshire to-night."

"I think he might have taken the trouble to wish me good-bye ere he went," Mrs. Leicester thought, but she was accustomed to the *sans façon* manner with which women of her class are sometimes treated; so she said nothing, but took very good care to make Williamson repent, at the first opportunity, for his want of courtesy.

"And how has my darling been spending her time since I saw her?" my lord inquired, addressing Lydia, who was too much occupied in admiring the soft hazel eyes of her tiny dog to answer the question just placed in unbecoming hurry.

"I have been studying very hard," Lydia replied, "and my masters are very satisfied with my progress."

Mrs. Haltering now looked towards Lydia. She did not know what the word study implied, emanating from a person whom she thought was meant for anything but study.

"Oh! I am happy to hear that," my lord replied. "If you keep on, some day you will astonish us all."

Mrs. Haltering was too knowing to attempt to find out the meaning of the words she heard. It is true she saw in Lydia's possession a great many books that had, in her opinion, no business to be there; but through carelessness she had not made inquiries concerning that particular thing. She resolved, therefore, to find out for herself how matters stood. The idea that Lydia, in the position she occupied, could ever dream of improving her education was a thing which never flashed across her. Now she pulled out her watch and looked at it.

"Mrs. Leicester, it is now two o'clock," she said. "We must go to Swan and Edgar's at three, to see about that dress and to meet our friend Patrick Langdon."

"Ere you go," Lydia said, "you had better have a bit of lunch. It is about my time, and I am certain that my worthy friend will not object to the proposal."

As she spoke, the young girl cast her fine features on those of Lord Vineyard, who, of course, assented to the suggestion.

The wine, which was already decantered, stood upon the sideboard, from which it was removed to the dinner-table; and to summon the servant, who soon appeared with a tray upon which flourished a heavy capon and a Yorkshire ham, was a feat accomplished in less time than we have taken to describe it. The knives and forks were soon at work, Mrs. Haltering doing ample justice to the hospitality of her new friend, whom she over and over again congratulated upon the selection of her golden sherry—a beverage which she evidently relished, if a hasty opinion can be drawn from the frequent and various times she refilled her glass.

Mrs. Haltering, when at table, was what one would call a "jolly woman." She knew that it would be ridiculous on her part to assume the *role* of a maiden, ready to faint after a couple of glasses of sherry, and consequently she made the most of the occasion, and lost no opportunity of drinking my lord's health, coupling it with that of Lydia.

Lord Vineyard made no answer, merely acknowledging the compliment by a parliamentary bow. His lordship was sometimes witty after dinner; but all the Amontillado in the world could not have made a young man of Lord Vineyard before ten o'clock in the evening.

The repast was soon terminated, and shortly afterwards the two ladies left, leaving Lydia and his lordship together.

CHAPTER V.

LYDIA AWAKENS—INSIGHT INTO DETAILS WHICH OCCUR EVERY DAY—HEARTRENDING REVELATIONS—FRIGHTFUL DISCOVERY—HER SORROW—SHE TAKES A DETERMINATION.

HOURS of bliss, like the hours of sorrow, only last for a while; and, however anxious we may be to remain beneath the voluptuous and enervating influence of Venus—to drink from her golden cup the sweet nectar of love—a moment must come when, willingly or not, we are compelled to stray from a Mahometan heaven to things of a less pleasant nature, when even the remembrance of the most gratifying enjoyments are often marred by the stern and more sober realities of every-day life.

I give expression to the above sentiments, as they were exactly similar to those which crowded themselves on Lord Vineyard's mind upon the morning which followed the day during which we introduced the reader to two female acquaintances of Lydia.

It was about nine o'clock in the forenoon, and Lydia, carelessly lying upon her couch, was awakened by the warm rays of the sun, which, peeping through the window, set upon her beautiful eyelashes and induced her to rise.

She looked around the apartment, and no one was nigh; and yet she fancied that, but a few instants previously, she had heard the sounds of Lord Vineyard's voice.

Where was he, then?

Surely he could not have remained with her since twelve o'clock last night?

She remembered, it is true, that Lord Vineyard had called in the evening, after a short absence from her; that together they had partaken of a sumptuous supper; that at least three bottles of Moselle had been opened, and that she, for her part, had drunk the best part of number one. She remembered, too, that she had drunk the sparkling wine out of a clear, limpid, crystal glass, which she had allowed to slip from her rosy fingers and to get smashed to pieces. She remembered all that, and, while she puzzled her brain, the thought dawned upon her, that it

struck her at the time that the Moselle had rather a strange taste; that shortly afterwards she was taken unwell; that she felt sleepy; and that, anyhow, she struggled towards her boudoir; and that she had reached it just in time to give way entirely to a slumber—to a repose which she needed to soften the unaccountable torpitude which had suddenly seized hold of her frame, and for which she could assign no reasons.

This was about the extent of Lydia's recollections—more she knew not. She stretched forth her arms, opened her eyes wider and wider; and she walked towards the splendid looking-glass to gaze upon her features; and—must it be confessed?—she was indeed ashamed of herself! A dark, blueish circle surrounded the lower part of her eyes, which were quite red, and which presented all the outward appearances of one who had been indulging rather too freely in bacchanalian excesses; her lips were whitish and parched; and, strange as it appeared to her, the bloom of her youth had, for the time being, entirely forsaken her.

Gradually she became uneasy; and at length she thought that there must have been something literally wrong somewhere.

And, despite all, her fanciful imagination reverted to worldly matters, and she could not help admiring the beautiful furniture around her; and to realize to herself the idea that it was all her own, caused her to smile placidly.

What had she already paid for these things?

This she wished to know.

She was not yet positive of it, but she suspected as much. To satisfy the anxiety of her mind she took a resolve, which she immediately carried out by laying hold of the bell-pull and shaking it strongly and repeatedly, while, in her uneasy suspense, her pretty little foot was beating the carpet beneath it.

Not many seconds had elapsed ere a servant answered the call.

It was Kate, whom we have previously seen.

Upon the girl's cheek there rose a blush as soon as she confronted her mistress. She had not been long in London, and she was beginning to think that, if she had any respect for the future welfare of her Roman Catholic soul, the sooner she returned to her priest, to her potatoes, and to the yelling and picturesque cottages of the Emerald Isle the better. She had seen quite enough, and sure, in her opinion, the big town was no place to send innocent colleens, if noblemen were all as bad as she heard they were, and to corroborate which statement she had Lord Vineyard before her. If they were all as unscrupulous, licentious, and unprincipled as Lord Vineyard, and if his lordship could be looked upon as a fair representative of an English aristocrat, the morals of Mayfair must have been relaxed indeed, as he never lost an opportunity, when he saw her, of slapping her well-shaped and round shoulders, or of taking hold of her pretty chin, a handling which Kate by no means approved of.

"At what time did I go to bed last night, Kate?" Lydia curiously inquired, and meanwhile she stood before the looking-glass, placing some order to her toilet, which no word could have better described than the French *deshabille*.

Kate looked at her mistress's dissipated appearance, and she remained dumb.

After a while, however, she began—"Why, ma'am, you ought to know better than myself. My lord told me, once I had laid the supper things, to go away, and as he particularly informed me that he would not require my attendance any more, and you seemed to coincide with him, it was not likely that I should trust myself in the way again, when I was not wanted."

There was seemingly a good deal of bold impertinence in the girl's speech, but Kate was far from bad-hearted, and she meant no harm. It was more her manner, and the total ignorance in which she was of the right appreciation and the true meaning of every sentence which she uttered, which caused her to speak as she did; and although, emanating from her lips, such language as hers was inoffensive enough, coming from any one else it would have been insulting in the extreme.

"Repeat what you said, girl," Lydia pursued; "I caught not the first part of your sentence."

And these last words were pronounced in a genuine tone of voice that no guilty person could have ever assumed, and which strikingly betrayed the partial ignorance in which Lydia must have been of all that had taken place.

Kate mused for awhile, as if to collect her thoughts, and after she had complied with her mistress's request, she continued, in answer to Lydia's repeated queries—

"Yes, as far as I can remember, 'tis all he said. Oh! no; I forgot," she went on; "what a stupid girl I am, to be sure. I had scarcely closed the door, ma'am, when his lordship called me back again."

"Go on; pursue," Lydia ejaculated, who every instant was getting more and more interested, and anxiously so, too! "Pray do hurry on—you can have no idea of my anxiety."

Kate smiled.

She thought her mistress was acting, and she was doing her part remarkably well; so she continued perfectly unconcerned, and as if she were relating a story of the most casual occurrence, knowing not to what extent every syllable she pronounced tore and lacerated Lydia's feelings.

"Oh! it was only for a trifling detail he wished me back; but as you wish me, ma'am, to tell you all, I will not deny anything."

"Yes, yes," Lydia pursued; "he called you back—what for?"

And the girl's eyes brightened up with a strange expression.

"True, ma'am," the abigail pursued, "and his lordship said—'Look here, Kate; your mistress is not very well to-night; she has been taken unwell; and I really do not know what's the matter with her.'

"I asked his lordship whether I should go to fetch Dr. Saunemany, who lives in the square, and he replied—

"'No, no; never mind. I daresay she will be all right shortly. Just pour me out this bottle of eau de Cologne in the basin, and give me that bottle of salts standing on the chimney-piece.' These are his very words, Miss Lydia, and, troth! I do not omit a word. 'Now, like a good girl,' his lordship continued, 'leave the corkscrew and one or two bottles of wine close at hand, in the event of my being thirsty.' I acted as he bid me, and when I had done all that he required of me, he enjoined me not to come in the room again, unless he called me. You, Miss Lydia, looked at me during the whole time which he spoke, but you never said a syllable. Your eyes had a strange expression, which I never saw with you before; but as you did not appear to object to any of my

lord's actions or words, I went to my room, where I remained until this morning, when my lord's voice woke me up."

Kate had stringed together the above sentences without taking breath at any of the words; and thus Lydia's curiosity was soon satisfied, but there were one or two things besides which she wished to know.

"And has his lordship slept here, then?" she inquired, nervously.

And her features became as white as snow; her heart began to palpitate with quick pulsations within her agitated breast; her pulse became feverish; and her dark eyes shone with extraordinary lustre.

"Slept here? of course he has, Miss Lydia! What a strange question! And you do not know it! Why, that's odd enough! Twenty minutes gone eight I called a Hansom for him, and it is but a few instants the roll of the cab was heard outside."

And Kate was about to indulge in a long rigmarole of her own, and in her ignorance she was about to give a sly look to her mistress, while she was inwardly muttering to herself—"Why, she has a front, too, to deny it after it is done! What an oily one she is, to be sure! Did you ever see such a little Touch-me-not before! Oh! the English girls! What degradation!"—and so forth; and thus she was indulging in these freaks of her imagination, when her gaze reverted to that of Lydia, and, as if by magic, she stopped short.

Terrible in her bitter rage—superb in her despair, stood poor Lydia!

Noble and queenly was her whole demeanour as she paced to and fro—her expressive blue eyes brightened up by those tears which she would not shed—her lovely breast heaving heavily from those outraged feelings which lacerated her inwardly. At times she presented truly the handsome and melancholy picture of an innocent woman cruelly injured—while at others her countenance assumed so revengeful and so haughty a look, that one might have been tempted to assign her a place among that disobedient group of doomed angels, who feared not even a god's wrath, and who are said to have gloated and rejoiced over their downfall, when hurled by an omnipotent hand from a seat of glory!

Thus, with a mind a prey to the most excruciating reflections, Lydia remained alone with her shame.

She was no longer the innocent, spotless creature whom we have pictured in the beginning of this story. Now she understood her real position.

Now she began to fathom the reasons of Lord Vineyard's generosity. The truth with its sad smiles dawned upon her, and too late she became acquainted with her protector and friend in his true light. The systematic and slow steps which he had taken to effect her ruin could no longer be a mystery to her.

No doubts could remain to her as to who and what she was.

For his unaccountable kindness Lord Vineyard expected a reward; he had obtained it. What did the poor girl care for wealth? for all the luxuries she enjoyed? for the many amusements which he threw in her way? Of what avail was that education which her seducer wished to thrust upon her, if she was to become an outcast? —an outcast of that society whose entrance a cold world would deny to her. If friendless and lonely, she was doomed to end her days among a golden youth—a libertine old age which reflects not ; to die in the hospital, with the remembrance only of those gay, short-lived days when she received those homages bestowed to the queen of the hour—when she sold her smiles to the highest bidder.

Lydia thought over all those things. Acutely did she feel the loss of that gem which woman ought to hold so dear; bitterly could she have exclaimed with the poet Waller—

> "Oh ! that I had my innocence again,
> My untouched honour ! But I wish in vain,
> The fleece that has been by the dyer stained,
> Never again its nature's whiteness gain'd."

And she would have given the world, if she possessed it, could she have recalled what had taken place.

Men cannot understand the feeling which women will experience when situated in the same predicament as the poor girl.

She sometimes had dreamt of Lord Vineyard marrying her. Examples which had occurred in high life—related to her—were present to her mind, and warranted her in persuading herself that such a conclusion might take place. Stranger things than those had been wrought ere now ; and the fulfilment of the hypothesis which she would have delighted to see carried out was by no means an impossibility, although there was a life which stood awkwardly in her way— although a sacred consideration for the name he bore ought to bind Lord Vineyard to the mother of his children, and make it incumbent upon him not to violate the respectability of his home by the intrusion within it of his fallen victim.

And while her mind was thus wafted upon the wings of fancy, a voice would keep whispering— "And what right has Lydia to complain ?"

Had she not willingly, and with her eyes opened, acted as she had ?—entered into a bargain with Lord Vineyard—for what else could you call it ?

There was love on one side, interest on the other.

True, if she wished to look upon her misfortune in another way, she could.

Her career, if thus it can be termed, was not that of her own choice.

But albeit it at first she had shown some reluctance to live under Lord Vineyard's protection, had she ever made any step since her mother's death to free herself from his contact ?

He had offered her wealth, and she had accepted it. She had lived under his tuition unmolested for a while, and the bloom of her youth had not hitherto been faded by any corrupt stigma, but how could she expect such disinterestedness to last for ever ?

Little did she know the ways of man, if she fancied that it could be so.

Lord Vineyard had played with her like the tiger plays with the timid doe, ere he grasps it within his merciless claws and tear it to pieces.

Better a thousand times Lydia had been snatched away from this earth, sooner than be allowed to live to see her disgrace !

CHAPTER VI.

LYDIA'S OVER-HEATED IMAGINATION DRIVES HER TO SIN—A SCENE OVER WESTMINSTER-BRIDGE.

"OH ! Lord Vineyard, you monster !" Lydia muttered, and, unable to suppress her sorrow, she at length fell upon the sofa behind her, and gave vent to her tears, to those tears of which she could no longer hinder the rapid overflow.

She wept freely and bitterly, and she felt momentarily relieved.

And, as if she became ashamed of her weakness, she rubbed her eyes—damped by a brilliant moisture—and she thought it childish, unworthy of a woman, to keep on crying.

Under the impression of these reflections, she rose, and pondered over what she should do.

The worst had come. How should she mend matters ?

She wondered still, and mused silently, and seemingly she asked herself one or two questions, for she soon soliloquized, as if in answering some unknown questioner, "What can I do to escape him ?" she suddenly exclaimed.

She had pronounced these last words quite aloud.

Should she run away, leave that home which she owed to her guilt, thanking his lordship by a few lines for his kindness, cursing him for the dastardly advantage he had taken of her youth ?

She was uncertain how to act.

If she went away, some other one would soon fill the vacant place.

Then, again, she pondered over the few years of her childhood, and fancied that then she was happy.

Could she now have returned to misery and poverty, willingly would she have done so.

It was, however, impossible. To alter what had taken place was beyond her control.

That power belonged to no one—not even to the Divinity above.

How could she redeem her past conduct ?

She was without sterling friends, without relations.

How, we ask, can a poor girl retrieve the loss of her reputation ?

London is a huge city, a vast metropolis with an immense population, swarming with a myriad of charitable societies, abounding with generous and wealthy hearts, willing to help distress ; but what difficulties are strewn before the path of those poor girls (who are anxious to reform) to bring their cases before those beings— those charitable beings, ever ready to listen to the voice of real misfortune.

To whom was Lydia to go to seek redress ?

Would Lord Vineyard suffer by her revelations ?

Were there not thousands and thousands situated as she was ?

And why should she act thus ?—would that palliate her guilt ?

His lordship had not been cruel and rough to her ; his treatment was kind in the extreme.

If she left the home where she was, poverty— utter want—stared into her face with its hideous glare.

She would apply to a milliner's shop—then she would obtain employment.

But she would not try—she was not up to the task. She could easily ascertain that by the beating of her pulse—the quick pulsations of her heart.

Even had she endeavoured to obtain a honest living, she could not have done so.

It will, perhaps, be hardly credited that any occupation, any duty, however hard and irksome to discharge—with a trifling remuneration attached to it—is eagerly sought for by a multitude of maidens, respectable, well-conducted, and

[LYDIA TAKES A RASH STEP.]

strongly recommended, some of them even possessing an amount of education known only to those who are in the way of becoming acquainted with the working girls, with the price given for their labour.

All the thoughts which we have jotted down were precisely those which occurred to Lydia's mind in rapid succession.

She hid her features within her hands, and mused silently.

The day had elapsed; the night had come, and she had not even rang for her servant to bring her any food, so engrossed was she in her reflections.

She looked at the clock; it was long past midnight.

She walked towards the window, and she gazed outside.

The pavement beneath shone in the moonlight, and both sides of the street were literally deserted.

Far away she saw Piccadilly.

She lived at the West End, as we have already said, and Lord Vineyard had taken lodgings for her in one of those streets which, branching off Piccadilly, lead into that fashionable part of London where some of the highest aristocrats of the land do dwell.

Lydia closed the window which she had opened with a nervous shake of her hand.

Her bonnet was close at hand; she seized it eagerly.

She took a warm cashmere shawl lying carelessly upon the sofa, and she went to the glass; and, after having placed it upon her shoulders, she gazed upon herself to see whether it nicely fitted.

Not a word did she speak; not a sigh did she give way to.

Only her demeanour was strange. Her eyes possessed a queer expression.

She sat down again.

"The people will think me mad, I dare say, when they hear of it," she muttered. "What matters? there are no cares, they say, where I go."

The roll of a carriage attracted her attention.

"Would Lord Vineyard dare to face me to-night?" she whispered.

And she rushed towards the window again and looked outside.

The vehicle had stopped its course a few yards yonder.

A gentleman and lady stepped out of it.

"That's the happy couple that got married two days ago," Lydia muttered: "How delighted the girl seems in jumping into her young husband's arms! She is fortunate, that woman. She is not an outcast like me. O God! will you forgive me?"

Lydia pronounced these last words with a subdued bitterness that no human pen could adequately describe.

Pen, ink, and all the materials for writing now attracted her gaze. They were strewn here and there upon a table covered with a beautiful cloth.

She wrote a few lines. She began the letter, "Lord Vineyard;" she concluded, "unfortunate Lydia." She folded up the paper, placed it in an envelope, and left it upon the mantelpiece, so as to attract the notice of the first person that might step into the room.

"Have I got anything more to say, anything else to do?" Lydia mused, and she looked around her.

Her little dog—Tiny she called it—which Lord Vineyard had given her, now came up from the inner room, where the unconscious animal had been dozing all day long.

"Good-bye, Tiny," she said, taking the Italian greyhound within her hands. "Good-bye; you will soon have another mistress, for you are a pretty creature. Good-bye, good-bye, Tiny;" and with these words she shed a tear.

The only friend Lydia had in the world was her dog.

Such was Lydia's farewell of her first home.

With a quick step she walked on.

A minute or two found her in Piccadilly.

She looked interesting and pretty, Lydia did, and one or two gentlemen endeavoured to speak to her—to make her acquaintance.

The first one was an old man. His legs would not carry him long. The second was younger; and, although once rebuked, he persisted in following her.

He addressed Lydia once, twice, thrice. She answered him not.

"There is something mysterious about that girl," he thought. "She ain't dressed like a dashing horsebreaker going to Mott's or to the Argyll. I have nothing particular to do, so I'll watch her."

"Sir," said Lydia, vexed at being followed and repeatedly spoken to, "will you desist watching me? I have my reasons for wishing to remain undisturbed."

This sentence was pronounced in a preremptory tone that admitted of no reply.

The young individual felt it; he made some kind of apology and bowed.

He was, however, taken quite aback. Receptions of such kinds are not often met with, moreover, when a stranger, whose attire and manners proclaim him to be a gentleman, addresses one of those birds of night, generally speaking, seeking fresh scenes and pastures new.

The manner of Lydia had struck the stranger as exceedingly extraordinary.

In no ways deterred in his determination of watching her, he relinquished not his pursuit.

Lydia, meanwhile, hastened her steps, and she never turned her head once to see whether her wish had been complied with or not.

Had she done so, she would have perceived the young stranger in the distance.

Who was he?

Lydia never stopped to inquire.

Who was she?

This the young stranger resolved to find out.

Lydia could not see him, and he could not see her.

And the poor girl ran rather than stepped, and it was as much as the mysterious individual could do to keep up with the girl's swift pace.

She had now reached the top of the Haymarket.

Never in her life had Lydia seen so much bustle, such crowds, before. In the day her brougham, doubtless, had driven through that infamous spot of the metropolis; but, unaware of the character of the place, she had not bestowed any particular attention upon it.

She had great difficulty in forcing her way through the numberless loungers.

She met with an insult at every step she took.

"Move on, move on!" she would hear the policemen ever saying to those around her; and her arms would be pinched, and her waist would be encircled by the profligate frequenters of that night resort.

"Who are you pushing, there? Can't you look out?"

"Oh! ain't she proud to-night, Maggy."

"Pretty girl, that."

"Will you come and have a drink, my pet?"

Such were the exclamations that Lydia gave rise to, and that struck her ears as she stepped onward.

And she saw the reigning queens of the day—the wild beauties of London—swarming like so many bees; the Turkish Divan, blazing forth with the rays of a thousand lights; the public-houses radiant with jets of gas; the coster-boy, singing out, "All hot, all hot! who will buy?" the melancholy-moving coffee-shops; the flower-girls with their faded bouquets; the cabmen on their seats, looking for a fare; the destitute vagrants begging for alms; and yet she noticed all these things—they heeded her not in her course.

These numerous tokens of the pleasures and gaieties of life; these unmistakable signs of grovelling poverty, of silent distress, shook not the determination she had taken.

Across Waterloo-place, along Whitehall did she wend her steps; and now she was standing upon Westminster-bridge.

To throw off her bonnet and shawl was the work of an instant; to fling away far from her a valuable bracelet that Lord Vineyard had given her, was a feat accomplished quicker than we could describe it.

And then, with dishevelled hair, with imploring features, with a heart heaving as if it threatened to burst, she clung upon the parapet.

Thus she stood upon her knees.

She gazed upwards and then downwards, and the dark and deep waters of the Thames running in their channel frightened her not.

Their gloomy appearance beneath shook not her resolution.

And she stood still—with her hands closely crossed together.

Evidently she was muttering a prayer.

God knows how long she would have remained in that critical position.

Suddenly she heard the sounds of footsteps. She turned round, and saw a man closely approaching the spot where she was.

It was he who had followed her.

She would be frustrated in her design were she to await his arrival.

Hence she made up her mind at once.

Now he was close upon her.

" Stay ! stay ! whoever you are," he exclaimed.

" Oh ! God, forgive me !" was the only answer.

A second elapsed, and the form of a woman was seen falling from the bridge immediately afterwards, and a loud splash was heard in the stream yonder.

The Thames had received another of its victims, and once again everything around reassumed for a while its former stillness.

*   *   *   *   *

The man who had witnessed the scene will, ere long, be introduced to our readers.

He stooped and he picked up the bracelet; that at once struck his gaze. At least he had got something belonging to her ; and, like a maniac, he ran towards the right end of the bridge, singing out as loud as he could bawl—

" A woman drowned ! A woman drowned ! For God's sake, help ! help ! help !"

Thus speaking, he disappeared amidst the shades of night, which were rapidly darkening the surrounding neighbourhood.

CHAPTER VII.

WHEREIN NEW SCENES ARE DESCRIBED—WE MAKE THE ACQUAINTANCE OF " POLL."

STORMY has become the night—the few passengers about, sheltered beneath umbrellas and capes, hasten as rapidly as possible each in his own direction. The gas-jets in the shop-fronts make a brilliant stand against the exterior dreariness, with but little success to the purses of their owners, for no one stays to look within—the streets, in fact, being almost deserted.

The wind, too, is in high spirits to-night ; anon a sudden gust sweeps round the corner of one street, and howls its passage through another, driving the rain and sleet into the faces of the passers-by, and causing terrible discomfiture to the possessors of umbrellas, who are compelled to fight many a tough battle with their refractory protectors, and, in some instances, shut them in valiant despair, and trudge onward unprotected.

Occasionally the blasts vary their amusement by hurling a tile, slate, or chimney-pot with thundering crash into the fortunately nearly vacant streets.

The rattle of cabs, also, is unceasing, for a storm is a most agreeable windfall to cab and omnibus drivers.

The old clock from the belfry of the magnificent church of St. Mary Overies—better known, perhaps, as St. Saviour's—had pealed the last stroke of nine, when a sudden uproar, a shouting and screaming, aroused the attention of the hastening few. A coster-woman, without either bonnet or shawl, dressed in the habiliments of her class, and driving before her an empty barrow, has been well-nigh caught under the wheels of a rushing cab. The shrill tones of the woman, loudly vociferating her opinion of the driver, in no very measured nor graceful language, are plainly discernible above the ready explanation of the latter, and the queries and answers of the bystanders.

It seldom takes long to raise a crowd in London. It is wonderful with what celerity an uproar immediately becomes the centre of a large, gaping assembly ; but now the rain, damping the ardour of curiosity and anger, for want of encouragement the disturbance is quickly over. Those who paused for a moment, hastily retrace their way ; the cab drives off, followed by a derisive sarcasm from the woman, who, seizing the handles of her barrow, proceeds after it along the fine High-street, now completely disfigured by the ugly leaden coffin thrown across it for the convenience of the Charing-cross railway.

Going along at a tolerably quick rate (not on account of the rain, it seemed, from the apparent indifference with which she regarded it), in a short time she reached St. George's Church, and, turning to the right, pursued her way down the narrow and dirty lane which here transects the Borough—running from the Old Kent-road to Southwark-bridge, and called respectively, Kent-street, and the Mint. Down the latter, then, went the barrow, and after it the woman.

Have my readers ever been to the Mint?—not the Mint of pecuniary celebrity, but the Mint of unenviable notoriety, in Southwark. If not, if they desire to behold pictures of the lowest degradation and filthiness, of the deepest villainy and most abject poverty, here they lie open to the inspection of all.

Here live, perhaps, one-third of the thieves of London when not absent on government commissions. To these must be added numerous keepers of the commonest lodging-houses, at most of which beds, or substitutes, can be obtained at 2d. or 3d. a head per night.

Most of the bird-fanciers of the metropolis seem to have taken their quarters, too, in this respectable locality.

Brush-makers and publicans, from the numerous houses devoted to these, would appear also to thrive and luxuriate ; certain it is that there is no demand for brooms within the Mint— cleanliness being one of the virtues most strongly objected to.

Thus, lodging-houses, public-houses, aviaries, brush repositories, old-clothes shops, and eating-houses, with a moderate assortment of private dwellings—that is, those having *no acknowledged* profession—all scattered together in the most picturesque confusion, form the majority of the Mint buildings, which itself consists of the main street to Southwark-bridge, crossed by numerous lanes and alleys—again divided into courts—and, in a few instances, shadows of squares.

The houses present a most dilapidated condition, inducing one to believe them built at some very remote period, and left partly finished ;

here a window threatens to come out upon the heads of the passers ; there the roof has given way, and a rafter projects some three feet over the parapet ; here, again, the parapet, in part, has fallen, and more seems about to follow ; there the whole house itself threatens to come down entire, and huge beams and shores prop up its bulging sides and front against its neighbours. But the inhabitants are in no wise troubled ; and as for repairs, to the memory of the oldest inhabitant, no workman (save to embellish with gaudy colours some public-house or haunt of vice) has ever been known in the more secluded spots of this almost unknown region.

One caution must be given to any adventurous explorer—"take care of your head." The good people here are remarkably shy of strangers, and often give them a welcome from an upper chamber by the contents of a wash-basin, or other domestic utensil, which may happen at the time to need emptying ; or a salute with a brickbat is not unusual when the seeker for information intrudes his attention too forcibly upon the habits or customs of the residents.

Into the Mint, then, turned this woman ; and, as she is one of the principal characters of this work, this time in perfect security let us follow her.

After progressing some distance down the main street, bidding occasionally good-night to an acquaintance within the half-opened doors of the gin-palaces, blazing with light, reeking with smoke and steam, the breaths of the numerous occupants resting like webs upon the window-panes, whilst peals of boisterous laughter, oaths, coarse jokes, imprecations, mingling with the rattle and clash of glasses and mugs, issued into the streets ; when midway down, turning to the right, through a dismal half-lighted passage, she presently entered an apology for a square, surrounded by ruinous though once rather superior houses, and halted before one of them, from one of the windows of which streamed a flood of light and shouts of merriment.

There is just light enough to perceive the house to be in a terribly ruinous condition. The doorway in the centre has lost many of its bricks, which lie heaped beneath one of the front windows ; formerly it boasted a fanlight, but this has long since disappeared, and the aperture is closed with a board, upon which a roughly-painted figure of a mangle may be seen.

The stone steps of the doorway are removed ; one lies by the heap of bricks, another, broken in two, is lying a little distance off, whilst a third does duty still a foot or two from its proper position.

The windows especially are worthy of attention. Evil deeds, we are told, love darkness ; probably this is the reason why so many panes are broken and their place supplied with old hats or remains of linen stuffed into the chasms. Not more than four or five whole panes are to be met with in any given window, of which, perhaps, a dozen are scattered over the front of the building.

Each was formerly provided with outside shutters ; two now hang, one by a single hinge, threatening with every blast to fall ; the others have disappeared.

At one end of the ruin an open shed afforded a resting-place for some half-dozen barrows. Placing her own amongst them, without fear for its loss— as the old saying, "Honour amongst thieves,"

does hold good amongst the class most addicted to pilfering—she raised the latch, the sole fastening of the door, and entered the house.

A candle stuck in a bottle on a ledge over the door of a room to the right, from whence came deadened sounds of merriment and jollity, merely made darkness visible, casting, as it did, but a glimmering and uncertain light upon the scene.

She stood in the hall. In front appeared the base of a staircase, whose enormous balustrades and heavy oaken banisters had hitherto resisted both the attacks of time and the ill-usage of the occupants.

To the right and left were doors leading to the rooms on either side, and a narrow passage led behind the staircase to the back of the building.

The inner view amply corresponded with the exterior, the same ruin and havoc plainly written on the face of all.

The panelling is eaten and decayed, the doors warped and ill-fitting, and the once white wainscotting has become a most unpleasant yellowish brown, and it needs no practised eye to tell water and paint have not made its acquaintance for years. On a portion of it is sketched with charcoal a rude representation of a couple of women fighting, the fist of one making intimate acquaintance with the nose of the other, and beneath is scrawled "Judy Callaghan her mark."

Drawings in the rough of gallows and their swinging fruit are numerous, for men mostly treat with levity the thing most to be dreaded : thus, the class most likely to take a "dance upon nothing," as one of themselves has facetiously termed it, are the most inclined to be humorous upon the subject.

Several huge heads, with pipes of still more astonishing dimensions are scattered over the surface ; and the flickering of the candle, nearly extinguished by the gust which entered on the opening of the door by the woman, rendered them all the more ludicrous and repulsive.

Without casting a glance around, the woman commenced ascending the steps ; but the creaking boards arousing the attention of the party, one of them opened the door sufficiently to put his head and shoulders outside, and shouted after the retreating woman—

"Hillo! is that you, Poll?"

Receiving no answer, he repeated his question, with the addition of an oath, and "Confound yer! can't yer answer a feller when he asks a civil question? I suppose it's her in her tantrums," he added, after a pause, turning to his companions.

"All right, Bill ; I heerd her put up the wehicle," replied a voice. "Shet the door ; it's jolly cold, blest if it ain't."

Regardless of the voices below, the woman groped her way along the dark and narrow staircase ; and finally, drawing from her pocket a key, after a minute's fumbling, she opened a door on the first landing, entered, and banged it to after her. In the obscurity, her form might be faintly traced as she bent over the empty grate ; then a scratching succeeded, followed by the pale blue of the phosphorus, and then a bright flame lit up the chamber. Taking a candle from the hob, she lit it and placed it upon the plain deal table in the middle of the room.

—————

CHAPTER VIII.

AN INCIDENT IN THE BOROUGH—CHARLEY AND "HIS GIRL"—HOW HE TREATS HER—RESULT.

WE can now do what we have not been able to do before—namely, to examine the person whom we have just followed.

Now that she stands upright we perceive her to be of average height, her body finely formed, and her arms, naked to the elbows, roundly and beautifully moulded; her hair, of raven hue, disarranged by the storm, and escaping from its fastenings, falls in luxuriant masses upon her shoulders, protected by the light cotton dress and customary handkerchief. Her face would be noble and beautiful in the extreme, were it not marred by dissipation and wretchedness, and if there were not at times something absolutely repelling in the sardonic expression of the features and the deep sensual glare of the liquid black eyes.

Fetching some wood from a cupboard, she heaped it in the grate and covered it with coal taken from the same closet, and then lighted it by placing the candle to the bars; and soon a cheerful blaze illuminated and cheered with its rising and falling radiance the surrounding objects.

It was a large although miserable room, looking into the square, a couple of the broken and patched windows lighting it, its flooring sloping towards the front from the sinking of some of the lower beams.

Its wainscot, darkened with the fogs and smoke of years, and constant carelessness, is in places eaten away, disclosing the thick crossing-rafters of the walls, and affording openings for the exit of the damp, unwholesome aroma from the depths below. Over head the ceiling, broken through in one spot, reveals the secret of its construction by the hanging laths and plaster, whilst a huge beam runs the whole length of the apartment, and a hook in the middle, with a piece of cord still dangling to it, is terribly suggestive of what has been or yet may be.

A low bedstead with dingy drapery fills one corner, a chest of deal drawers the opposite; and these, with half-a-dozen chairs formerly caned, one alone now in a state of preservation, the others supplied with pieces of board for bottoms, treacherous indeed, from a habit they had of slipping away from the sitter, and the table in the centre, with a box by one window, form the principal articles of furniture.

Whilst the fire burned up she busied herself changing her wet dress for another hanging over the back of one of the chairs, and brushing her dishevelled hair before a remnant of a looking-glass stuck in an interstice of the panelling. This done she turned to the fire, and, drawing a low stool in front of it, sat down, resting her head upon her hands, and remained thus gazing at the flickering flames.

How many of us have conjured up visions of the past or future in the burning coals, have traced resemblance to long gone friends, or created realms of fancy for ourselves in the dying embers of our cheerful fireside.

Thus she sat pondering. She compared her present life, with its prospects of the future, with what it might have been had her lot been cast in another sphere of action. The past rose before her; it was but a chequered course of vice and misery. From a child, without parents, guardians, or friends, a foundling picked up in the streets and in false pity cherished by the vilest and most abandoned, she had passed through every scene of dissipation and sensuality that presented itself; she had drunk the cup of misery empty, and now, although still young and beautiful, yet disgusted and wearied with her being; she who, for aught she knew to the contrary, might be high-born and gentle, the companion, not *wife*, of a common costermonger, a prey to fits of withering anguish and remorse, willingly drowning her feelings in intoxication. Is it strange that she hated the world in its pomp and state, since she was not amongst its votaries, and ardently longed for the time or opportunity when she might be drawn from her present low guiltiness to higher and glittering scenes of infamy and pleasure? Never once occurred to her the idea of repentance or change.

Then awoke feelings of revenge. She knew the world cared not for her, she would not care for the world. What mattered the contempt of some, if from a lofty eminence of sin she could look down upon and despise many who she knew wanted but the power to excel, and therefore the more upbraided her? If the mistress of a churl, why not that of a noble? if the toy of the vulgar, why not of the patrican?

Then gloomier feelings prevailed. Let death come when it may; can it be more dreadful than a life of torment, than a hated, despised existence?

Still she mused, fleeting from thought to thought, indulging every feeling. Christianity teaches us to subdue, occasionally muttering to herself as some fresh or more exciting thought came. "Yes," half-rising in her emotion, she ejaculated with emphasis, "yes, Jack White hung himself in this very room; so much the more fool he. I've had my trials and hardships before this, but I was never mad enough for that. It might come to it still," she repeated, more slowly and gently, "if he"—and now the liquid eyes, glowing with sudden passion, rivalled even the flame of the coal itself, her bosom heaved, her whole frame dilated with suppressed excitement.

This again soon subsided, and softer feelings seemed to take possession of her breast. "If I could but lie down as I have heard some can, in far-off places and quietly rest; the green fields, they tell me, are very beautiful, and people are happy and live and die in peace amongst them." Silently tears rolled down the cheeks, pallid enough now, and the fiery eyes lost for a space their strained attention.

Meanwhile without the storm increases, lightning begins to thread the pitchy gloom, and distant thunder mutters its nearer coming.

A wild night indeed it is! The wind, more vigorous than ever, dashes the rain like showers of hail against the windows, and a gust more furious than the rest forces in several of the papers covering the vacant woodwork. With a shriek it follows up its assault, sweeping through, extinguishng the candle, and sending a cloud of smoke and dust from the hearth into the room.

Roused from her reverie, the girl walked to the window to close afresh the apertures. This effected, after some little trouble, she was about turning to her seat, when a fearful flash lit up the apartment, the square, the whole heavens, with lurid glare. Startled and alarmed, blinded with the intensity of the flash, she shrunk back, exclaiming, "Good heavens! what a frightful night." Crash! right over head, burst the thunder, as if responding to the words, so loud and tremendous, that the ruin shook and rattled, and many an echo awoke in the crazy building.

Hastily regaining her stool, the girl resumed her watching of the leaping flames.

Below, the merriment, hushed for a moment by the crash of the thunder, breaks out again still more exuberantly, as if to compensate for its sudden cessation.

Leaving the figure by the fireside, we must now join the party beneath.

A thick cloud of tobacco-smoke, overhanging and veiling everything within the room, prevents any very close inspection. However, we can discern a long table, with a mixture of both sexes sitting along each side of it, all smoking and drinking; forms along the wall are equally favoured by sitters, chatting, laughing, and joking, each provided with a clay pipe.

Four or five of the company, at the end near the door, are playing cards; several more are leaning over them, attentively watching the game; at the further end, a burly fellow, with cloth cap and fustian jacket, is loudly addressing the friends in his immediate vicinity, his speech being indistinguishable to those a few feet off.

Stationed beneath the window, behind the card players, is a group in rather exciting conversation; to these we must pay attention.

The place is lighted with four gas burners, one right at the further end, illuminating the rude bar, covered with mugs and glasses, behind which in rows are bottles; beside these, the handles of a small tap; over all, a tall, bony female keeps watch and ward.

"I say, Bill," remarked one of the group by the window, "is it true Harry Gatter's got to be scragged next week? what's it all about?"

"Well, you are a bloke, not to know all about it yourself by this 'ere," returned the party addressed. "I thought, blowed if I didn't, every kinchin knowed he was lagged for cracking a crib, and for"—here the speaker drew his finger significantly across his throat.

"More's the pity," replied the questioner. "Harry was a rare plucky one—as good a pal to work with as any I know. Well, here's luck to him."

Here, in response to a shout from the other end, a general chorus of "Order, gentlemen, order!" "Be still, there, will yer?" "Stow yer gab, Tom Rowney; don't yer hear the call?" "Order, there, for the chair," arose from a dozen throats. After no little persuasion and bustle, the required attention being obtained, the burly speaker, with the pipe in hand, commenced—

"Gentlemen, I ain't nothink of a speaker—stow yer larks, Bill Stiggins, will yer?" (This was addressed *en parenthese* to a friend emptying, by mistake, the orator's mug.) "But this 'ere's an occasion when a feller must use his jaw a bit. To cut it short, then, our old chum Harry Gatter's been nailed by the slops, and is to be turned off the hooks on Monday. He's been rayther misfortunate, and collored for walking into another bloke's crib with his own key, and as the kid wot owned the shop cut his jugler afore Harry got in, why, they said he done it, which every honest feller knows he didn't." (Here a chorus of assent to the last remark interrupted.) "In course he didn't. Well, then, as he vants a bit of something to keep up his pecker, let's give him three arty cheers, and drink his wery good 'ealth."

After the applause consequent to this pointed and rather able speech had subsided, the speaker went on to propose a toast.

"Here's a quick end to him, boys, and I can't say as how I knows much about the other place the parsons pratter about; but, if there's a crib to be cracked, why he's the boy to do it; so here's, as I said afore, a wery good 'ealth to him."

This being appropriately drank, and the three cheers duly given, three hisses for the peelers was next demanded by a gentleman in cords and furry cap, whose ferocious appearance and furtive glances led one to imagine the peelers would be rather careless of the hisses provided they could lay hold of the proposer. With considerable fervour, indeed, all joined in complying with the request, and the uproar again proceeded. The players at cards resumed their dealings—hardly true and just, perhaps—and a general desultory conversation ensued.

"Well, Charley, my boy, how's Poll?" inquired another of the window party of an individual far gone on the high road to intoxication, leaning carelessly against the wainscot, smoking, with his eyes half-closed.

Dressed in the coster's rough garb, his muscular frame gives evidence of great bodily power, his face strikingly sensual and bloated.

"I hear she's getting jolly independent, wants a good licking," continued the fellow.

"She's more likely to lick him," jeeringly began a second. "Ain't she, Ned?" A general titter followed the remark.

At the taunt, taking his pipe from his mouth with drunken gravity, Charley blurted out, "Poll's nothing to do with any of yer, so I hope yer won't interfere with what ain't none of yer business. As for licking, ugh, if I liked"——

"In course yer could, Charley, in course; we all knowed that. But Dick must have his chaff; musn't yer, Dick?"

Hereupon Dick broke into the deepest regret at saying anything annoying, and, with a wink at the rest, concluded, "It was only chaff, Charley, my kinchin. No offence, I hope."

Completely mollified by the ample apology, though not at all disposed to drop the subject, on account of the drunkard's mania to continue an argument long after the ground is cut from under him, Charley continued, "It's deuced improper to talk like that, Dick, when yer knows I can make her do what I like. I tell yer what, I'll fetch her down, I will, blowed if I don't! Ain't I good company enough for her? I'll see to that."

"Brayvo, Charley, that's the way to do it! There ain't a feller I more likes to see than Charley Wood when he makes up his mind to do a thing," said one.

"Can't Poll sing, too!" added another. "Talk about Jinny Linn, why she ain't a patch upon her! Fetch her down, Charley; let's have a song out of her."

"If she don't" —— he replied, with an execration; and staggering to the door, he opened it, and responding to encouraging smiles and nods by a drunken laugh, he groped his way up the staircase, followed by the laughter and cheers of his companions, who left the door ajar, to hear, as they termed it, "the jolly row."

Too absorbed in herself to heed or even to perceive his approach, the girl was rudely roused from her musing by the rough hand of the coster upon her shoulder. "Get up, will yer? What the deuce do you want burning coals for and moping by yerself, when yer can get fire and good company downstairs?"

"Because I prefer being by myself, and the fine company downstairs don't suit me," was the reply.

Scarcely had she finished the words, before the house rang again with a chorus chaunted in every key and pitch by the jovial party.

"There, do yer hear that?" Charley returned. "Come, now, like a good gal, and have some fun; besides, Jack Grady swears he'd sooner hear yer sing than Jinny Ling. Come, and cheer 'em up a bit; they're all down in the mouth acause poor young Harry's to take a dance upon nothing next week. Come along."

"I tell you I will not come for all the Jack Gradys in the world, and serves Harry Gatter right. Burglary's bad enough, without murder. If you like the good company so much, go and join them again; I seen enough of them before to-night."

"P'raps you think they're not good enough for yer," with a grin he retorted; "p'raps you'll think I'm not, too."

Receiving no reply, he repeated his question, adding, by way of emphasis, a few oaths, and shaking her roughly.

"Yes," she jerked out, passionately, "I do say so. I must have been a fool indeed when I took you, Charley Wood, for my fancy man."

Her words were not from the heart; although at times she did despise him, still there was yet some lingering affection for her companion; but, irritated now, and excited, the words came almost involuntarily but with biting force.

"What?" shouted the infuriated drunkard, "what? not good enough for yer, eh? I'll talk to yer about that. Just yer come now, when I tell yer, or it'll be the worse for yer, my gal."

She made him no return, and he continued—

"If yer can't win by fair means, yer must by foul; coaxing won't do, so I'll try force."

Still she replied not, save by a sarcastic and derisive laugh, and never moved from her position.

"Are yer coming?" he asked, in thundering tones, loath to put his threat into practice—perhaps half-afraid.

"Ain't I told you twice before I ain't? You ought to know by this time I mean what I say," she sneered.

"Will yer come now, before I make yer? I ask yer once agin," he said.

"You make me?" and she started to her feet, her splendid eyes again liquid with fiery passion, whilst her hands clenched the table with vehemence. "You make me? Ah! you know better than that."

"None of that, Poll, with me; yer not going to frighten me with that, yer ain't. By God, yer really looks handsome now! Give us a kiss, and come along," and he seized her by the waist, and commenced dragging her to the door.

"Keep off, Charley, if you value your life," she screamed; and, extricating herself from his grasp, she seized a knife, and vowed with a frightful oath to murder him if he repeated his attempt.

Half-sobered, and completely cowed by the appearance and resolution of the infuriated girl, who now presented a startling yet noble picture—her long black hair, swept from her forehead, falling in massy folds and glossy ringlets adown her neck and shoulders; standing upright; the blue veins upon her noble and expressive brow startlingly apparent; her feet firmly planted; her eyes wildly glaring—no wonder, then, the drunken wretch fell back, cowed and conquered by a spirit superior to his own, in so noble and yet how debased a frame.

"If yer won't come, then, yer won't," he muttered, after a pause. "It's unproper to force a gal against her will—kissing goes by favour. But I say, Poll,"—and he addressed her in a softer and more suppliant tone—"I swore downstairs I'd bring yer, and I can't go back alone. Why, yer knows, they'd chaff me like blazes. If yer won't come, why, there's an end to the matter; but it's damned hard a bloke should lose his pleasure, because his gal's in her tantrums. Come, hear reason, Poll; yer can be sensible when yer likes," and, with a last hope of persuasion, he turned to watch the effect.

"If you swore a thousand times, I would not go," she hissed between her teeth, "and you had better not try again to force me."

"Then, damn yer, if I don't remember yer, my gal, some time or other," he replied, throwing himself into a chair by the window, which groaned and creaked alarmingly beneath his weight.

With all her passion and fury, she yet felt some slight degree of disquietude at thus depriving her companion of his night's enjoyment; so, replacing the knife, she spoke, more quietly and kindly—

"Come, I'll fetch you a pint, and you can sit here and smoke your pipe with me; you used to do it once, why not now? I'm sure that'll be better than spending your money, and getting dragged 'into society,' as they term it."

Nothing softened by this appeal, he sat savagely smoking with short, jerking puffs. Taking his silence for consent, the girl took from the cupboard a jug, and descended the staircase.

"Here she is!" shouted a voice as she passed the door and turned past the staircase to the back of the house.

"Here's Poll, boys! I'm hanged if he ain't managed her, for all her temper."

A sneer passed over her features, but, making no reply, she stopped and tapped at the door of a room immediately behind that of the convivial meeting.

"Come in," uttered a voice, and, pushing open the door, Poll entered.

"Let's have a pint of half-and-half, Mrs. Callaghan," she addressed to the tall, bony virago superintending the drawing and distribution of numerous orders.

"Ain't you going to join 'em, Poll," asked the latter; "they're regular larky to-night."

"Not to-night," she replied, "I'm too tired; Charley and me rowed about it; but I would'nt give in, so he's going to make himself comfortable where he is."

"Here you are, then, my darling," and the woman handed her the overflowing jug. "Good night, Poll."

Softly she went through the passage, regained the staircase, and mounted to her own room.

Charley was still savagely smoking.

"Oh! you're come at last, have yer?" he yelled, as she entered. "Yer have been a hell of a time fitching a miserable pint; yer didn't think to bring any bacca, I suppose? Oh! in course not."

Setting the jug before him, she returned to her stool, the old expression again crossing her face.

Evidently seeking excuses and reasons for a quarrel, "Yer needn't keep all the fire to yerself," the drunkard shouted. "Does yer think no one likes to be warm but yer blessed self?"

For sole reply she moved the stool from its former position, and commenced rocking herself to and fro.

It was easy to perceive Charley was gradually working himself up to a fit of desperate drunkenness. Soon the pint disappeared, and the empty pot lay by his side.

For a time he savagely smoked, casting occasional brutal glances at the noiseless figure at the fire.

"I say, you Poll," at last he raved, "get me another pint. Do yer hear?" he shouted yet louder as she made no approach, but continued her rocking.

Thus aroused, "I'm sure you've had enough, Charley," she returned, noticing for the first time his real condition.

The intense passion pent within him, waiting but a spark to explode it, with the quantity of liquor swallowed previous to his ascent to Poll, rendered him now entirely beyond control; semiconscious, yet possessing in his strength awful capability for ill, the thirst for more liquor was about the sole idea left him.

The girl herself was startled at his aspect. Never before had she beheld him in so extreme a state, though drunkenness occasionally was common to both; yet the spirit within her never quailed, as she resolutely refused to stir.

"If," he yelled, "if yer don't go, by the living jingo, I'll murder yer!"

She moved and gazed upon him threateningly, but her power was gone now, and he repeated his assertion.

"Will yer go? will yer go, I say?" raising the jug from the floor and prising it in his hand.

Quickly she rose from her seat and stood before him. "If you do," and rage choked her utterance, "I'll never forgive you; I'll be your bitterest foe, your worst enemy; I'll return each blow with a thousand, as sure as there is a God in heaven."

How long she would have stood threatening is impossible to say—the two wild, untamed natures thus confronting each other—when, with all his drunken strength, he hurled the jug at her.

A shriek of pain followed, and she fell heavily to the floor. True to its mark, the missile struck her cheek, and bruised and bleeding she lay before him.

It was but for a moment. Darting to her feet, the blow unheeded in the intense excitement of the time, she shrieked rather than spoke, "Charley Wood, to the longest day of my life I'll remember this; in me you shall find your deadliest enemy. I'll hunt you for it through the world till I bring you to the gallows. I call heaven to witness"——

A blinding flash, a horrible sulphurous smell pervaded the apartment; then thunder burst over them with such stupendous power and crash as absolutely to deafen them both; the glasses below rang and rattled upon the tables; the revellers themselves were involuntarily stilled, and sat looking at each other in astonishment and dread. Charley was sobered in a moment; the whole scene darted before him, but it had not the slightest effect upon her in her delirious passion.

"You hear," she screamed; "heaven hears and answers me, and I curse you from the bottom of my heart."

Passion, rage, and the turmoil of contending emotions hindered her from proceeding. Casting one withering glance of hate and contempt upon the now cowering and repentant wretch, she swept from the room, down the staircase, and out into the fearful storm of the night, unheeding the fierce contest of the elements in the awful strife within; the pouring of the rain, the flashing lightning, reverberating thunder, alike disregarded and unfelt in the awful consuming furnace of emotions, and surging and playing within this tortured soul.

On she rushed, the few yet abroad gazing in wonder after her as she strode hastily and fearlessly through the cheerless thoroughfares; the rain falling in torrents; the vivid flashes of heaven illuminating but to plunge into deeper gloom the black, swiftly-rolling, and foaming river, meanwhile the tall, innumerable masts of the ships at anchor, creaking, tossing, and straining beneath the hurricane blasts of the wind.

All the world, indeed, seemed to have sought shelter away from the raging storm, save she who unheedingly hurried on through all the turmoil, impelled by the madness of passion and despair.

For a moment she gazed upon the swollen river, but the mind followed not the eye. Naught of the imposing scene was grasped; and, passing on again, she swept into the deep gloom of the now deserted city, and soon became lost in the labyrinth of the flooded streets.

Fury is soon spent, and the duration of extremely high excitement but transitory; and so, as the storm began to abate, so did the girl's intense passion. The dark, overhanging clouds melted away, the storm rolled its course into the abyss of night, the rain ceased, the wind, still boisterous, yet lost much of its force, whilst the lightning shone at ever-increasing intervals.

With her excitement went also her endurance, and after wandering unheeded through the gloomy streets, the girl retraced her steps; and, faint and exhausted, she found herself on the shores of the river, near Westminster-bridge.

A shouting of voices mingled with a heavy splash roused her attention; then followed a rush to the place where, panting and in curious suspense, she stood.

Boats were hastily put off by the watermen, over at their post, whom she soon saw wending their course towards a certain spot. Repeatedly and swiftly were the oars plied by the stout hearts engaged in their praiseworthy and laborious task, and smoothly and swiftly did the cutter glide along the dark waters.

At a loss for anything to say, she inquired the cause of the scene she beheld of a bystander close by her side. He heeded her not, and, seemingly wrapt up entirely in his own thoughts, his eyes bent forward, kept on scanning the deep.

She looked again, and it did not take her long to guess that a fellow-unfortunate had hurled herself into the depths of the river.

Loud, joyful exclamations were now heard, and through the mist of night she saw a white form appear on the surface of the water. She saw men leaning over the sides of the boat, and

[THE COSTER-LAD SHOWS HIS BAD HUMOUR.]

she saw them grasping that which appeared to her to be a lifeless body.

And the watermen returned to the water's edge, and when they had reached the side she was told to help in unfastening the tight dress which encircled Lydia's beautiful breast.

Thus did Lydia and Polly meet for the first time.

Thus began the acquaintance of the lord's mistress with the coster-boy's concubine.

Thus were thrown together, by the unfathomable hand of Destiny, two beings who are to occupy rather a prominent place in the course of this thrilling narative.

CHAPTER IX.

WHEREIN A NEW CHARACTER IS INTRODUCED IN THE SHAPE OF A "MAN ABOUT TOWN"—MRS. HALTERING AND HER OLD FLAME—A LITTLE SCHEME IS HIT UPON HIGHLY IN ACCORDANCE WITH THE IDEAS OF ONE OF THE PARTIES CONCERNED.

WHO was Patrick Langdon, whom Mrs. Haltering had condescended to call her friend in the early part of this story?*

Was he one of those fashionable *roués*—one of those dazzling, dashing spendthrifts, of whose

* See No. 1 of "The Outsiders of Society; or, Wild Beauties of London."

acquaintance the fair sex in general like to boast ?

Was he one of those well-to-do individuals who need no wit to get on among certain women—who would be called "good fellows, regular trumps," provided they drew their imaginative powers from Coutts's bank, their gentlemanly appearance from Poole, and their standing in society from a first-class horse-dealer ?

Was he allied to the nobility, and did he obtain his *entrée* in the aristocratic salons during the gay Parliamentary season ?

In short, could he be of any use to such damsels as Mrs. Haltering and her pretty and young friend, Mrs. Leicester ?

I should say not, for poor Patrick Langdon was on his last legs—*ergo*, being unable to help himself, he consequently could not be of any use to anybody else.

He was, indeed, a pitiable object now—the broken-down remains of an old stock. What the world denominates a man that has seen better days, was poor Langdon !

Once a dashing dragoon, he had sold his troop over regulation price, risked the same upon the "Flying Dutchman" with remarkable success, clearing a few thousands by the transaction, and finally retired, and strikingly illustrated the words that money easily got is easily spent.

He had kept racers—had his stall at the opera, and for a few years had launched into a career of extravagance and dissipation which had brought him where he was—to the foot of the wall.

Patrick Langdon, I need not say, was highly connected at one time. Poverty came—with it the old,—old story : his connexions, his wealthy friends, dwindled off as his coin melted away. Langdon's father had been a lord-lieutenant of his county, a colonel of one of Her Majesty's militia regiments, and it was a well-known fact that one viceroy of Ireland in a tour through the south had been so struck with Langdon's sister that he had made her a formal proposal of marriage, which the foolish girl had declined, to marry some penniless sub-lieutenant—now rusticating in Jersey, spending his days from the tobacco-shop to the billiard-room, and from the billiard-room to the neighbouring public-house ; and yet of what avail were all those remembrances to the late dragoon ?

It would not soften the heart of the cool-headed tailor who would refuse credit to Langdon—by whom he had made sufficient money to clothe him for the remainder of his life without loss. If he was hungry, and he would stroll in one of those West-end resorts where he had lavished gold as if he was of the same opinion as Shakspeare—"who steals my purse steals trash"—could he get a morsel of food from the owner of the establishment once so bland and smiling ?

This last query requires no answer, for it was all over with poor Langdon for the present, or at least until the conclusion of some Chancery suit, which would place him in the possession of a few hundreds, which would enable him to weather the storm—"to exist" for a while.

In his days of opulence, Patrick Langdon had met Mrs. Haltering—quite casually, too. He had formed a *liaison* with her one fine summer morning that he was taking a solitary ramble on the Brighton chain pier. He had been generous and kind to her when he had it ; and, now that he was in want, Mrs. Haltering occasionally

would help him on with a sovereign or two—perhaps more.

There is no woman so selfish and so depraved but what she has a little nook in the corner of her heart, which beats at intervals for some person or another. If Mrs. Haltering ever had loved anyone, she had loved our worthy friend Langdon ; but in her own way, of course. She would serve him if she could, and if she thought she could manage some good turn for him she would do so, and hence the reason she had appointed to meet him at the corner of Swan and Edgar's shop. Mrs. Haltering and Mrs. Leicester were not long in walking from Lydia's residence to the Regent-circus. They went and saw about a dress ; and when Mrs. Haltering had duly given her opinion to her friend concerning the trimmings and all the etcœteras, she suggested that it was time to move. Four o'clock had just struck, and the two women were emerging from the silk department when they encountered Langdon, walking leisurely, and as carelessly as if he were still the owner of Langdon Castle.

"Halloa !" he exclaimed, shaking hands with Mrs. Haltering, "is that you ? Why, there must be something good looming in the distance, for I had entirely forgotten the appointment I had to keep with you."

"You story-teller," replied Mrs. Haltering, in an affectionate tone ; "surely you will never change—you are incorrigible."

Mrs. Leicester had noticed Langdon when he had spoken to her friend, and, to use a slang word that I once heard a pretty horsebreaker make use of, she immediately "took stock" of him. That he was wretchedly in want was a fact plainly told by his shabby garments. He had on a dark blue coat, which required sadly to be touched up ; an antiquated waistcoat to correspond ; and a pair of light trowsers, of which the pattern dated, I should think, from the 1851 Exhibition. His boots were considerably worn out, but they had just been cleaned by the little boy at the corner ; and, a considerable amount of blacking having been infused in the holey parts of the "Balmorals," the socks and the leather were amicably blended together. The hat would pass in a crowd, for a great many Englishmen are not very particular in that part of their toilet ; and the pin stuck in his woolly cravat was not a very good specimen of the brass articles which come under the name of Birmingham jewellery.

"I say, I am so tired," Mrs. Leicester observed, "that I should like to take a cab home."

She said this because she was really ashamed to be seen walking with Patrick Langdon.

A four-wheeler was called, and then the two ladies and the "gentleman" were comfortably seated together.

Now that she was certain not to be detected by anyone of her acquaintance, Mrs. Leicester spoke to Langdon. She had heard Mrs. Haltering mention his name before ; therefore he was not a complete stranger.

"Do you know, Agnes," he said to Mrs. Haltering, "that you have always got deuced good-looking girls with you ? But how is it that you have not introduced me to your fair companion ?"

"I thought," Mrs. Haltering replied, "you knew Mrs. Leicester ?"

"I never saw her before," Langdon continued,

"and if I did I would not forget her easily. I seldom forget nice girls, for they are rather scarce with me now."

Mrs. Leicester was far from being annoyed or vexed with the observations of her new acquaintance. Langdon had been excessively handsome, and a handsome person does not become ugly all in a day. His face was red, it is true, and he bit his nails to the quick; but these were only trifling details.

"What would you give me, Langdon," Mrs. Haltering said, after a moment of silence, "if I placed you in the way of getting £500 a year?"

Langdon looked at Mrs. Haltering and mused for a while.

"Five hundred a year," he said, "would be a very good income, but a bird in the hand is better than two in the bush, and I would rather have five hundred pence in ready cash than all the expectations in the world. Ah! there was a time," he continued, in a saddened tone, as if he began to feel his position, "when I could have married well, but I must think no more about those things, for when I do, I am ready to curse myself for my past foolishness."

There is no knowing how long Langdon would have indulged in these melancholy thoughts had he not been interrupted by Mrs. Haltering, who pursued the conversation by saying—

"My dear Langdon, I am not joking, I can introduce you to an heiress!"

"By Jove! can you?" responded Langdon, who thought there might be some truth in what he heard. "She is old and wrinkly I suppose?"

"No, she is young," replied Mrs. Haltering.

"Young! what might be her age?"

"Twenty."

"Is she dark or fair?"

"Fair."

"Lady-like?"

"Extremely so."

"Good family?"

"So-so."

"Any flaw upon her character?"

"Not one."

"Has she many relations?"

"Well," replied Mrs. Haltering, "she has an old father who thinks that his daughter should always remain single, for he could not, he says, part with her under any consideration. The old gentleman has a very high opinion of me, and he never would question the respectability of any of my acquaintances. The little girl likes me very much, and she longs for a flirtation."

"Is she partial to military men?" Langdon now inquired.

"Oh! yes," responded Mrs. Haltering; "she spent a few years in Ireland, and she has returned from the Emerald Isle with the scarlet fever."

"It could not be better," exclaimed Langdon, who wanted to be acquainted with all particulars so as to be able to prepare his batteries for the day of action.

"You seem to be discussing the subject rather rashly," now put in Mrs. Leicester; "the heiress might not fancy Mr. Langdon, and then it would be all up."

"Faint heart never won fair lady," Langdon said, who was very fond of quoting proverbs. "Beforehand I feel confident of success; but I wish to know all about her; and, if it is not indiscreet, how came you to make her acquaintance?"

"If you wait patiently I'll tell you about it, but you must not interrupt."

"Ere you proceed," Langdon now asked, "what is her name?"

"Laura Wylde."

"Well, it will not sound so badly. Fancy," Langdon exclaimed, with a laugh, "the following advertisement in the *Times* newspaper: ' On the 1st, at St. Paul's Church, Knightsbridge, by the Reverend Irvine, Miss Laura Wylde, to Captain Patrick Langdon, late of the 14th Light Dragoons, and eldest son of the late Colonel Langdon, M.P., Langdon Castle, County L——. Would not my Irish friends open their eyes and stare? Oh! oh! it would be a good joke," and Langdon burst into a fit of laughter, in which Mrs. Haltering and Mrs. Leicester heartily joined.

"Agnes," Langdon resumed, "I know all about my future intended—she is only twenty, and you say she is fair; by-the-bye, I dote upon fair women; I think there are none to be compared to them; but I am rather of a dark complexion, and this accounts for the taste, I believe. Laura Wylde, besides, has, or will have, five hundred a year when she comes of age, and is not incumbered with a lot of confounded relations to watch all her moves, so I have a fair field now before me. I feel perfectly happy, but what about the story?"

Mrs. Leicester now said a few words to Langdon—evidently relating to the subject; and Mrs. Haltering began—

"Last season the upper part of my house was empty, so I resolved to try to let it. I put an advertisement in the paper, and a few days after Laura Wylde and her father came to see about the terms. We were not long in coming to some arrangement, and shortly afterwards father and daughter were comfortably located under my roof. The father, I must tell you, holds a very good civil appointment, and he is always absent from ten to four. Thus Laura used to feel lonely by herself, so she generally came down and chatted with me. We became very intimate, and, as a matter of course, I made way with the old father, whose absurd notions on red tape I never ventured to contradict. I never lost an opportunity to flatter him right and left, and, as it should follow, he took a great liking for me. When he had company he always asked me to increase the number of his guests, when I was introduced as Mrs. Major Haltering. Things went on smoothly and well until he took it into his old head to have a house of his own. I then lost him, but since I have been friendly, and I am on visiting terms with him."

"And where do they live?" inquired Langdon, who had always an eye to business.

"Onslow-square."

"Good situation! It is not a tip-top square, it is true, but there are in it some very good residences, and I believe they are all rented by wealthy families. The whole thing looks well, and suits me admirably. But when shall I meet her?"

"As soon as I can well manage it."

Langdon now became so happy that he lost all control over his temper. He began to laugh, to giggle, to rub his hands, to tap Mrs. Leicester on the knees, and to encircle Mrs. Haltering's waist.

"And what is your price for the introduction?" he asked, half-joking, half-serious.

Mrs. Haltering turned round, and cast a severe look upon Langdon.

She had seen Rachel performing at the "Français," and at times she assumed tragical gestures. She knew not what answer to give. Should she turn him out of the four-wheeler, and have no more to do with him? This would have been, on her part, a way of acting as foolish as it would have been detrimental to her own interests. She felt and knew that, and so she very coolly replied—

"I will require ten per cent. on the ready money you get, and eighty yearly out of the five hundred pounds income. I will, on the other hand, do anything I can to bring you always together. Now tell me, does that suit your book?"

Human nature is very extraordinary at times. Langdon had not a farthing property at the time, and yet he thought those conditions rather hard. He was, however, too sharp a man to let any of his feelings transpire at that particular moment; for, had he been so unwise, he would doubtless have lost the opportunity which offered of retrieving his proud coat of arms, which was getting rather rusty.

"Agnes," he continued, "you must get what you think right; we are old friends, and we need not stand on ceremony with each other. I will give you a written agreement as soon as I see Laura Wylde, entering into any clause you think fit to suggest. Can I say more, or speak more business-like?"

"Certainly not," resumed Mrs. Haltering. "Langdon, you are a regular brick."

"Mrs. Leicester," Langdon said, "you are a witness to the whole transaction, and it is now incumbent upon you to see that matters be carried out as they ought to be."

"I will have nothing to do with it," replied Mrs. Leicester, smiling. She knew that her position in life was such as to preclude her from respectable society, and she, therefore, thought it wise to decline a thing she would never be called upon to perform. She gazed dreamily and earnestly on Langdon and Mrs. Haltering, and she seemed evidently astonished with both of them.

The four-wheeler had now reached Mrs. Leicester's house. She shook hands with Mrs. Haltering and with Patrick Langdon, and departed, while the old friends remained in the vehicle.

"What shall we do now?" Langdon inquired, as the cab was at a stand-still.

"What you like," replied Mrs. Haltering, who had just received her quarter's annuity.

"I think I will dine with you to-day, Agnes. Indeed, I had no breakfast this morning," Langdon continued. "My landlady, annoyed at my procrastination to pay her bill, would not, she said—the old Jezebel!—put her hand in her pocket any longer. But what do I care about breakfast if I have a good dinner? I am of opinion that one meal a day is quite enough."

"I will not discuss that point with you, Langdon," Mrs. Haltering replied, "for you and I could not agree. Let it be settled that you dine with me, and tell the coachman to drive on."

Langdon put his bushy features outside the window, and, in a dictatorial tone, bid the coachman to "fire away." It was happily getting dark, for had it been otherwise, it is very probable that the Society for the Prevention of Cruelty to Animals might have summoned "coachy" for being too zealous and diligent in carrying out the gentleman's request. The poor horse could scarcely trot, and yet the driver was beating him in a cruel manner.

Surely, some of those coachmen are heartless villains. With this kind estimation of a respectable body of men I will conclude this chapter.

CHAPTER X.

SHOULD OLD ACQUAINTANCE BE FORGOT?—MRS. HALTERING TELLS A TRUE STORY—THE LODGINGS OF A BROKEN-DOWN SWELL.

LANGDON and Mrs. Haltering soon arrived at their destination.

The house which Mrs. Haltering inhabited was a large-sized residence; and, as she sub-letted the best part of it, for herself as well as for the convenience of her lodgers she kept it in first-class order.

The four-wheeler was dismissed, and with a quick step the widow alighted, being handed upon the pavement by Langdon—who in his poverty had not forgotten his manners, and who was always a gentleman when a lady was in the case.

He knocked at the door, which was soon opened by a sober-looking housekeeper.

Mrs. Haltering never had good-looking servants. Women on the *retour*—that is to say, past forty—seem to have a great reluctance to having pretty girls about them. They are good for nothing, they say, except to flirt with the gentlemen when they come to visit, with the grocer's boy, or the butcher's assistant, as *pis aller*, provided they are smart—young, like themselves, and wickedly inclined.

In a minute Mrs. Haltering was in her boudoir, closely followed by our friend Patrick Langdon, who walked quietly behind her.

The dinner—a plain, homely meal—was very quickly despatched by the good lady and her male companion, who had always a good appetite when he was "asked out."

When the two beings had satisfied the cravings of their hunger (and Langdon was famished), the conversation reverted to the day's business, and Laura Wylde and her good income, as a matter of course, were brought upon the *tapis*.

"Are you not a lucky fellow," Mrs. Haltering inquired, "to have such a friend as I am to you?"

Langdon bowed like a man who did not understand the immensity of his luck. "I feel very grateful, I assure you, Agnes, for your kind offer, and it remains now for me to make the most of my introduction. That I will try to do, you may rest persuaded. But I again ask you when will I see her?"

"She will be going to the opening of the International Exhibition. I will meet her with a lady friend and her companion. So if you like to be in the German Court at about four o'clock I will introduce you. Let her not guess by your manner that it is a concocted thing between us, but come and speak to me as if it were *par hazard*."

"We are only the 18th of April," Langdon replied, "and there are at least a couple of weeks ere the 1st of May. What is to be done in the meantime?"

"What you did before," Mrs. Haltering replied. "You must not become too anxious all of a sudden."

Langdon had no answer to make, so he quietly revenged himself upon the decanter. Mrs. Haltering now rose from the table and went to the piano, upon which she began to play one of those charming melodies of Meyerbeer, which are so delightful to a musical ear.

"I say, Agnes," Langdon now said, interrupting Mrs. Haltering, "I am looking over your album, and I have an idea. Would you advise me to have my *carte-de-visite* taken?"

"What for—to send it to Laura Wylde?" jokingly inquired Mrs. Haltering.

"No, I am not so fast as you seem to think," replied Langdon; "but it strikes me that if you added my likeness to that of the others, when Laura comes to see you she might hit upon me and be struck with my appearance."

"I thought, Langdon," Mrs. Haltering said, "that you had given up all those foppish ideas, which, although, they are very ridiculous, are excusable in a man of large means, but which are inexcusable in one who has nothing to rely upon."

"Not only your remark is bad taste," Langdon now replied, getting up, "but still it is a cruel one. Who brought me to the state where I am? Oh! not you, of course."

And the remembrance that Langdon still owed a balance at some jeweller's for costly pearls he gave to Mrs. Haltering, flashed across his mind and considerably irritated his temper; he bit his nails over and over again, and stood in the room silent.

Mrs. Haltering knew that she had been in the wrong, and that she had unwillingly offended an old friend, who was very ticklish when his good looks were called into question. La Rochefort could tell us that "*l'amour propre offensé ne pardonne famais.*" No one could have illustrated this thought of the great thinker better than our friend Langdon.

Mrs. Haltering now continued—

"Langdon, you are very easily annoyed; what did I do to vex you? You must learn how to control yourself, for if you betray any of your *mauvaise humur* before Laura, I would give very little for your chance of success."

"Do not trouble yourself about Laura," Langdon replied. "I will marry the girl, if I get what our adjutant used to say—who, by-the-by, died in the Crimea—'A fair field and no favour.'"

"My dear Langdon, can I promise you more than I have done?" Mrs. Haltering inquired.

"Certainly not; but why tease a fellow?"

Langdon pronounced these words like a man who is at a loss for something to say; and doubtless, had he thought better to appear in a different mood, he would have suggested to Mrs. Haltering the propriety of refilling the decanter, which was, I am sorry to say, heartrendingly empty.

"Langdon," Mrs. Haltering said, "now that we are talking of matrimony, I will relate to you a story which is strictly true, which happened in an English county not many years ago, and which, although rather terrible, is extraordinary enough to induce me to ask you to bestow a little attention to it."

"A story! egad! I am awfully fond of a good story. Let us have it."

And, to give a gentle hint to his lady friend, Langdon took up his glass and drained it off.

Mrs. Haltering guessed the pantomime of Langdon.

She went out upon the landing, and told her maid to run out to the wine-merchant's at the corner, who kept open until a late hour, and get a couple of bottles of his best sherry at three-and-six-pence.

Mrs. Haltering waited ere she began, and when the abigail had returned she thus commenced—

"Do you remember, Langdon," she asked, "that little girl, Miss Blake, that we met together at Scarborough four years ago?"

"Certainly. She was rather pretty, I think. If my memory does not betray me, she had a brother who used to keep rather sharp look out after her."

"The very one."

"Well, what about her?"

"The poor thing is dead."

"I am sorry to hear it; why, she seemed one of the healthiest girls I ever saw."

"What matter that, Langdon?" Mrs. Haltering replied; "does not the Bible tell us somewhere, 'Amidst life we are in death'?"

"No allusion of that kind, if you please," Langdon ejaculated suddenly. "There is disease of the heart in my family, and if we are to give up the ghost at a certain time, it is no reason why such an unpleasant winding-up should ever be kept before our eyes. I am fully aware that, if we acted rightly, we should all prepare ourselves for what I call the final jump. But I never think about death, and this is my motto—'After me, the end of the world!'"

"Fine morals! fine religion! fine sentiments, these, Langdon!" Mrs. Haltering followed.

"Never mind about that. I know that you are a very religious woman yourself, Agnes, but 'tis not the question at issue now. You were about to relate me a story about that little Irish girl, Miss Blake. I remember her quite well. She was one of the belles of the season. Such style! such manners! Indeed, I seldom saw her like before or since. I used to dance with her more than with any girl there. Nothing but fast dances would do for her—the dizzy whirl of the waltz, and the rapid stepping of the galops she extremely enjoyed. Slow quadrilles, old-fashioned polkas, she seldom patronized. And do you tell me she is dead?"

"She is," Mrs. Haltering replied.

"How long ago did the event occur?" Langdon inquired, in a saddened tone. "Although in my present circumstances, and considering the state of my exchequer, it is not probable that I should fall in her way, were she still in the land of the living, yet I am grieved to hear what you tell me. Why, one night I got awfully spoony upon her; and she flirted so pleasantly and so coquettishly, that I have not forgotten it yet. I am getting quite curious to hear all about her."

"I thought you would: hence I spoke."

Langdon kept on gazing steadfastly at Mrs. Haltering. After a while, he resumed the thread of the discourse.

"I am not a wealthy man, Agnes," he began, "anything but, you know; and if I were not as poor as a church mouse, I would not mind betting you five sovereigns to one that she did not drop off quietly, like the rest of the vulgar mortals do. Something leads me to think there must have been something romantically tragic attached to the girl's end."

"And there was," Mrs. Haltering replied. "She died by the hand of her husband."

"He got hanged, I hope, for it ?"

"Not at all ; he is still alive. He was returned M.P. for a borough but the other day."

"Great God ! you astonish me !" Langdon pursued. "I am getting quite interested. They tell us, it is true, that there is a good deal of vice in the world—that virtue often remains unrewarded ; and I have seen it myself, that poor, honest people sometimes starve ; but that a husband could kill his wife and not get punished for it is a thing that I never knew."

"You are a simpleton, Langdon," Mrs. Haltering replied. "You know nothing of life ; because you have managed to run stupidly through £3,000 a year—to give one-half of your patrimony to the lawyers, the other to a lot of heartless, wild beauties, of designing, coquettish women, who would not recognise you were they to see you again, you fancy that you are a genius of your kind. Let your mind be set at rest. Meanwhile, listen to the following"——

"All right ; go on ; I am all attention."

"Well, little Louisa Blake went to Scarborough again the season after we saw her. She was deemed by all one of the loveliest girls for miles around. Lots of fellows were after her. She had money, you know."

"I am fully aware of that," interrupted Langdon, "but what has that to do with the story ?"

"A great deal ; does not money sway everything ?" and Mrs. Haltering uttered these last words in a manner which Langdon doubtless understood, for all of a sudden he became as mild as a lamb.

"Miss Blake, then," Mrs. Haltering resumed, "had lots of admirers ; noblemen she had none, but barristers, enjoying their holidays, officers on the "look out," solicitors in good practice, young stock-brokers—caring for the girl, not for her money ; city men, with their cheque-books in their pockets, and fearing not to hear that their accounts were overdrawn, mustered strong— stylish looks, refined manners, surrounded her, yet she knew not who to choose. She dismissed the buoyant and unreserved youths from her list of worshippers ; professional men were apparently not within her taste ; and individuals belonging to the service she abhorred."

"Strange girl !"

"Very !"

"You have taken quite a bird's-eye view of society, Agnes," Langdon pursued. "You have, it seems to me, in one bold sweep brought all classes together ; out of which sphere of life, then, did she take a husband ?"

"I leave you to guess in a hundred."

"I am bad at riddles."

"Are you ?"

"Your question seems one to me."

"Does it ?"

"I should think so, from your speech. Proceed—tell me who that little Blake married ?"

"I will."

"No one knew him at the time."

"I hope they do now."

"Not yet."

"For God's sake go on."

"No one ever knew him then, nor do they now, I should think, except myself."

"Yourself ?"

"Yes."

"Why, you are an astonishing woman, Mrs. Haltering."

"Do you think so ?"

"Of course I do."

"Why ?"

"I will explain : you tell me that you are acquainted with a strange story, which purports to relate how a husband killed his wife, and you coolly confess it."

"Certainly."

"And pray how did you become acquainted with details which would make a capital plot for a moving novel."

"Easily enough."

"Easily enough !" exclaimed Langdon, opening his eyes wider and wider, and repeating Mrs. Haltering's words. "You must be a female detective !"

"Perhaps I am."

"I am glad to hear it ; a detective game is a likely one to pay, I am told."

"Sometimes."

"Are you speaking from knowledge ?"

"No ; yet I answer, you see."

"And do you see a man that got rid of a wife in a manner which is punishable by the hands of justice ?"

"I do not see him often ; he visits here occasionally."

"Does he ?"

"Of course."

"What is his name ?"

"Why do you want to know ?"

"I am anxious to hear it ? Are you satisfied ?"

"Perfectly."

"Louisa Blake's late husband is called Martin Dashwood."

"I never met him."

"Indeed ?"

"It is not likely you would."

"How so ?"

"Because he is an individual whose character very few people seem to understand. When he was staying at Scarborough he was quite a stranger there, yet he appeared to be quite at home. He managed to go everywhere, to be seen everywhere ; he bowed to every one—every one returned his salutation. They had met him somewhere, and yet they remembered not how they first got acquainted with him."

"What kind of man was he ?" Langdon now inquired, getting interested.

"I could scarcely describe him."

"Try."

"He is tall ; his hair curls naturally."

"Good-looking fellow, then ?"

"Anything but that, in my opinion," Mrs. Haltering replied. "His eyes are dark, bright, and piercing ; his mouth is well-shaped ; and although he seldom laughs, there is a constant strange smile ever lurking upon his tightly-compressed lips. His manners are cold and gentlemanly."

"Is this a faithful description ?"

"As accurately as I can make it."

"And was that the man that married that pretty Miss Blake ?"

"It was."

"From what you tell me—from the sketch that you have given me—I should think that he was anything but calculated to make an impression upon a girl's mind, and such a girl, too, as Miss Blake."

"Yet he did."

"There is no accounting for taste. And how did the whole thing wind up?"

"Naturally enough. She took a decided fancy to him; and, notwithstanding the watchful brother, she eloped with him, and a few weeks afterwards the marriage appeared in the papers.

"The busy tongue of gossip must have been busy about them," Langdon pursued.

"Well, it was: the people said that a dashing young girl like Miss Blake, with a good income in her own right, might have made a better match than to go and bind her future life to a being who was twice her age, and who had already been married three times."

"The marriage gave a clue to the mystery," Langdon pursued. "The world found out who that Dashwood—what did did you call him?"

"Dashwood. So far as this they did. In the announcement he was described as Martin Dashwood, Esq., of Dashwood Hall, County L——."

"He was a man of some standing, then?"

"Yes and no. He was outwardly, not inwardly."

"What do you mean?"

"What I say. That he lived in the county in good style; had a good income; and that, his antecedents being unknown, his previous career surrounded with mystery, he was visited by none of the gentry who dwelt in the neighbourhood. Three months after her marriage Mrs. Dashwood died."

"What about it? Surely there is nothing so extraordinary in what you have told me. I expected some startling revelation, and the whole thing can be resumed in a nutshell. A wayward girl marries a mysterious individual, and dies like everybody else. What is there good in all that?"

"A good deal. Miss Blake went down in the country with Dashwood; when that little bashfulness which ever follows matrimony had subsided, he asked her one morning to undress herself, and to allow him to roll her up in some of the blankets, and of the sheets, which laid upon the bed."

"Mrs. Haltering, you are cracked!" Langdon now exclaimed. "What a whim—a husband asking his wife to roll her up in blankets; what are you talking about?"

"Yes, I repeat what I say; Dashwood asked his wife to comply with his request."

"Did she do so?"

"Not at first."

"Did she afterwards?"

"She did."

"And what became of it?"

"Why, he tickled her to death! While she was so closely surrounded with the blankets and the sheets as to be unable to move, Dashwood tickled her under the palm of the feet. At first she laughed—she liked it, afterwards she disliked it—she shrieked; but, bent upon his work, Dashwood kept on. Hysterics followed; the crisis came; and she died."

"The story may be good, Mrs. Haltering, but I do not believe a word of it."

"You do not?"

"No, not a word of it."

"Well, Dashwood told me that he killed four wives in this fashion; and the proof of the pudding is in the eating, as an old proverb says. Ask any medical man whether the thing can be done, and give me an answer when I see you again."

"And did you listen to Mr. Dashwood? Did you listen to a man relating to you a threefold career of murder?"

"I did; and I laughed over it."

"Your duty as a woman, as a Christian, would have been to rush to some police-station, and give your information."

"Indeed; and who is to prove the murder? The body of Miss Blake has been lying underground for months; naught remains of that wavy pair, of those lovely eyes, of that splendid form, so much admired by all; it is now eaten by the worms—and would you want me to go and put myself to an immensity of trouble to prove a thing which I could not corroborate? to bring forth a statement for which I have no witnesses? Now, my friend, live and learn. Last time Dashwood came to see me, he brought me a very pretty bracelet—it was a good one. Vincent, in the Brompton-road, lent me thirty guineas upon it; do you think that I would fall out with a friend like that?"

Langdon listened to all he heard; he stood like a marble statue by the chair from which he had arisen—such revelations were too much for him.

"Do you tell me, Agnes," he inquired, "that your story is true?"

"It is."

"And is there no one to bring such a man before his judges? why, I would if I could—so, after that, I'll go; good-bye, Agnes!"

Thus speaking, Langdon wound his steps towards the door.

It was getting rather late, and, as he had to walk from Kensington to Tottenham Court-road—where he lived—he thought that it was high time he should effect his departure.

He held his hand to Mrs. Haltering, and, as he did so, he found that he felt a crimping paper within it; and so extraordinary was the sensation which he experienced, that he became quite contented.

"You are a good soul, after all, Agnes. Never mind what other people do; let the world jog along as it will, and let us poor outsiders get on as well as we can. I ought never to fall out with you;" and his hand made its way to his breast-pocket.

As he uttered the last sentence he walked downstairs, and, when in the street, he turned round to see whether he was watched; but, having satisfied his mind upon the latter point, he boldly entered a gin-palace, close at hand, and called for six of brandy, a threepenny cigar, and flung a five-pound note on the bar.

The maid looked at the wealthy customer with an eye of suspicion. People do not, generally speaking, call for the change of five pounds at twelve o'clock at night.

She asked him to write his name behind; and, so deliberately did he accomplish that little piece of etiquette (which, in my opinion, is useless; for, if the note is bad, where can you trace the signature of the individual?) that she no longer entertained any doubts about his genuine respectability.

Langdon strolled along; and, after an hour's walk, found himself safely located in his bedroom.

It was rather a dingy closet, looking over a bye-lane. The furniture corresponded with the abode. An old clay pipe stood on the chimney-piece, and, although it was winter, the fire-place was destitute of the smallest particle of coals, and it was evident it was not used often by the present lodger.

Langdon now felt himself rich; nay, he would not have changed his position with a peer of the realm—for such was his character.

As long as he had enough to go on for the time being, he never looked forward to the morrow. There are a great many improvident people like him in the world, I am also to say.

Langdon was as satisfied as man can be, with four glittering sovereigns in his pocket, and about nineteen shillings' worth of silver.

Sleep—that comforting slumber—was not long ere it closed his weary eyelids; and, as he never thought of what would take place next day, he soon dozed away, and dreamt that he was driving a pair in Hyde-park, and that Laura Wylde—the observed of all observers—was proudly sitting by his side.

Let us not disturb him for the present, and let us now return to matters upon which we must bestow a little more attention, as they are required to be fully entered upon to enable our readers to understand thoroughly the character of this tale.

CHAPTER XI.

LYDIA COMES TO LIFE AGAIN—A STRANGE COM-
PANION BY HER BED-SIDE—TWO WOMEN TALK
TO EACH OTHER—A NEW PERSONAGE APPEARS.

WHEN Lydia's senseless body had been taken out of the boat, it was ascertained that the poor girl was nearly dead, and that, unless the quickest remedies were at once applied, she would never again here below open those bright eyes that had produced so great an impression upon Lord Vineyard.

She was carried by the watermen to the first tavern they encountered, and, as the Royal Humane Society never refuses to pay for whatever expense is incurred by those who endeavour to bring people to life, she received plenty of assistance at the hands of those under whom she was placed.

Polly, the coster-girl whom we have seen in the Borough—who, by an indescribable whirl of events, just reached Westminster just in time to see the last act of the sad drama which we have done our best to relate—watched carefully the unfortunate woman who had tried to seek a hasty termination to what she believed must be a heart-rending story.

Although Poll was not dressed in the gaudy clothes which would have at once proclaimed her to belong to that class so useful and yet so despised, yet she appeared pretty; and those who witnessed the events which we have related were at a loss to account for the sudden appearance of that vulgar girl, in a spot where anything but business could have brought her.

But watermen are a silent class of men when engaged in the task which they were fulfilling, namely, fully bent on endeavouring to restore a life to mankind. They never ventured to ask any questions, which, however out of place they might have been at any other time, would have been unjustifiable at the particular moment to which we allude.

In any spot situated in the neighbourhood of the river, the refreshment-houses—or, if you like it better, the public-houses—are supplied with cards, which teach them how to behave in such needy cases as that which now offered itself to the worthy landlord of the "Dragon."

It would be useless here to describe minutely the place where Lydia was first taken; it would not enhance the interest of the tale, and were we even to do so, the chances are that we should not offer any clue to our readers as to the place where Lydia was conveyed by the watermen. The landlord has died; a fresh man has taken up the business; he changed the ensign—he has changed everything, and the whole concern is in noways similar to that which it was at the period when our story occurred.

By a delicacy which deserved the highest praise, the landlady bid her daughters (for she had three) to attend to the poor girl, and to procure for her whatever help would be deemed necessary under the circumstances.

Lydia's head was kept up, although at times it threatened to fall downwards in its unconsciousness; over and over again it was propped by the girls—who were women, and who, after all felt for the sadness of the position of Lydia, and who pitied her whatever her faults might have been. They had been brought up religiously—they had read the Bible, and they remembered the sublime words of an ever-merciful God, which relates to the poor frail creature that has sinned.

Lydia remained perfectly unconscious.

Her face was as pale as death—as that death which, but for a providential succession of events, would have taken her as one more of its victims. Her lips were of a violet hue; her silky hair, wetted by her sojourn in the water, hung stiffly about her neck; and she looked, indeed, like those poor corpses that are exhibited at the police-stations to await identification.

The remedies were applied. A surgeon was called in; and, having brought to bear all the talents he possessed, the scientific man soon made her have a full knowledge of her own being.

Gradually she began to breathe easier, and she was placed into a warm bed, lined with hot blankets, and she felt a sudden comfort, which caused her to be herself once more.

It was, indeed, a happy incident for her that she had been followed; for, had the case been different, she must have found in a watery grave a termination to her insanity—for it was only a temporary state of madness that impelled Lydia to act as she had done.

Great many people may tell us that we are wrong—that numberless beings destroy themselves when they are fully aware that they are offending the laws of God, and placing themselves within the laws of men. We agree with them; but one in the full enjoyment of his mental capacities ought not, and should not, have recourse to suicide.

Death is the last step which we all take—death is the conclusion of all careers. But we are told that there is another world; that there is a supreme Being above who watches us, who listens to our prayers, and who, at a given day, will reward us for our deserts. He will not do so if we fling ourselves away from Him, and make no attempt to fight against the vicissitudes of the world.

Do Christians imagine that everything ought to be smooth with them? Do they think that they are placed here below to enjoy an existence deprived of all cares?—that they are brought into

[LYDIA AFTER HER RESCUE FROM THE WATER.]

the world for no purpose except to live and to enjoy themselves—to be continually draining the cup of pleasure, and to be as happy as the day is long?

Where then would be their merits? What right have they, or would they have, to expect a reward in that sweet place where cares will not be, where the highest bliss will be found, and where the centuries will glide on in the enjoyment of the most delicious ecstacy, where the good father will find a good son, where true hearts will meet never to part again?

Anyone that seeks relief in a sudden death, we say, is afflicted in his mind; and we must be correct in our assertion, for the coroner at every inquest—ninety times out of a hundred—

passes the verdict to which we have given expression.

Lydia, then, must have been mad.

Whether she was or not the story will show.

When she opened her eyes, she found Poll was by her bedside. She saw five or six strange faces, and she fancied herself indulging in a dream.

"Where am I?" she inquired of Polly, to whom she took a kind of fancy at first sight.

There is something extraordinary in human nature. It is strange, indeed, how likings and dislikings are first engendered! She contemplated Poll, and, although she half-guessed that she had sinned, still, she liked her appearance.

"You were very nearly drowned, miss," Poll said, in reply to Lydia's query.

There was a tone of respect and of friendship in Polly's words which, in a moment, went to Lydia's heart.

"Oh! I remember it all," she said; "I threw myself from Westminster-bridge. I hoped I should have died, but they would not let me. Oh! I have a frightful headache, my dear," she said, taking the coster-girl's hand.

Polly reclined by the bedside.

"I am a stranger to you," she whispered into her ear, "but I will help you, if I can. We are both victims; we should be friends. We have no one in the wide world to care for us; why not love each other like sisters?"

"Do not talk thus," Lydia pursued; "I am awfully weak, and to speak is more than I can bear."

Polly bowed her head, and remained silent. She had met with a rebuke which she expected not, and her foolish pride was too acutely offended to allow her to utter a syllable.

Lydia noticed her new acquaintance's despondency.

"I beg your pardon," she said; "I did not mean to thwart you; but you must excuse. What is your name?"

"Polly."

"Any other?"

"I don't remember."

"Well, Polly, here is my hand," Lydia said; "shake it."

Polly took it, and placed it to her lips.

There was something so odd in these two girls meeting each other, that they could not help thinking over it. Lydia muttered to herself, "I come to life again; I meet a friend." Polly, on the other hand, was saying, "I fall out with my Charley, and something good turns up out of it." For the latter could not but notice the beautiful style of dress of the dashing girl before her, and she compared her own attire to hers. She knew that Lydia's garments were made of the purest silk; she was not at a loss, either, to reckon the price of her cotton gown, and, whatever may be said to the contrary, although the clothes do not make the gentleman, still, it contributes greatly towards it. Thus it is also with ladies.

For dress, in itself, inspires a kind of respect.

What must be the feeling, I ask, of those unfortunate wandering girls in London, living by the price of their own charms—of their short-lived beauty—when, walking on the wet pavement, during the winter's nights, they see the happy and successful horsebreaker dashing out of her elegant and well-apparelled brougham?

They do not think that there are "many called, and few elected," in all spheres or professions, but they know that they are as bad and as depraved as themselves; they know that they are selling their smiles like they are themselves; that the former do it heedlessly, for a temporary happiness, while they have to do it to earn a pitiable and dreary living.

And they feel it, too, poor things!

And where do they show their bitter disappointment?

Do they mention it to the careless passer-by? or do they bury their own thoughts over the counter in so many half-quarterns of gin, which lead them to the station-house?

Reader, answer not, but draw your own conclusions.

It was what Polly thought.

There was Lydia!—there was she!

She fancied herself as good as Lydia—as bewitching as Lydia. Nobody had yet told her who she was. Still, a something induced her to think that that interesting girl—whose rescue from the water she had witnessed—was some fashionable West-end gay woman, driven to madness, gulled to despair by a terrible story unknown.

We deem it right that, when we are writing a tale for the enlightenment of our readers, we should be most precise in entering into the most trifling details. Here we are as particular as we can; and we always acquaint those who condescend to peruse us with the various feelings which must actuate those who, from time to time, are called upon to play a part in this true drama of life.

Some women would have felt an indescribable envy against Lydia, and would have wished that she should have perished; others would have been delighted at the conclusion which had taken place.

Polly was one of the latter.

Under any other circumstances she might have been jealous of Lydia's attractions, of her style of dress. Now she was not. She loved her, and she kept her hand closely pressed within her own.

"And how came it that I was saved from the water?" Lydia inquired of Polly. "I thought at the time that no one except a stranger witnessed the step I took; and he would not, I should have thought, taken any further trouble about a girl he knew naught about."

"I am sure I do not know," Polly pursued, "what took place. When I came within a few yards of the arches of Westminster-bridge, the alarm had been given, and boats were already searching for you."

Lydia now noticed the scar that Poll had upon her cheek.

"Why, what's the matter with you, girl?" she ejaculated, softly and slowly. "Somebody has been cutting your face all to pieces."

"Oh! it's nothing."

"You take it very easily," Lydia began, astonished. "It is a frightful wound!"

"Oh! it's nothing," Polly pursued; "it is only a trifling scar, that will soon get well. I do not mind it a bit; but I cannot help thinking of him that gave it to me."

"It was a he, then?" Lydia inquired.

"The man that I had lived with for years was the man that did it. You see before you the result of four years' kindness and of devoted love. Charley, indeed, had become very violent lately; but I would not stand it, so I left him."

"Left your husband! Why, you are a happy girl to have been married! If I had been fortunate enough to get a companion to share my destiny, I would not have done what I did."

"He was not my husband," Polly pursued, silently, "although I loved him dearly."

"And will you never see him again?"

"Never."

"Perhaps he will repent."

"He may."

"And yet you will not forgive him?"

"That I will not, for I think that he who strikes a woman is a coward. I am not a raw girl from the country. I am pretty, I think, and I will try what I can do at the West, having lived at the East-end ever since I was born."

Lydia hid her face within her hands.

She had tried to seek in death an entire forgetfulness of her past conduct. She made a friend in a strange, singular way, too; and the first words that she heard contained an amount of immorality which she could scarcely realize.

She contemplated Poll mutely and silently.

"How steadfastly you are gazing at me," Polly began. "Do you think that I am not on the right side?"

"I do not know. I will not pass an opinion."

"Well, I will, and here it is. A poor girl is decoyed away from her home; numberless promises are made to her by unprincipled individuals that never intend to carry them out; she is young, she believes all she hears, and it is all up with her once she has yielded."

"Was that your case, then?" Lydia inquired.

"To a certain extent it was. Charley courted me—he loved me, I believe. I loved him. We lived together. One day I asked him to marry me. 'Poll,' he said, 'don't talk nonsense. Ain't we happy as we are, and as contented as if we were to go and put a crown or two in the parson's pocket?'

"'Certainly, says I.'

"'Never talk about that bosh again?' says he.

"And I never did; and we managed to get on pretty well together, until he took to drink. He became irritable; and he used to blow me up and hit me. To-night the crash came, and he threw a beer-jug at my face, of which you still see the marks."

"Oh! the villain!—the cruel fellow!" Lydia muttered.

"But I'll take my revenge against him some day, unless he tries to apologize for what he has done."

"How will you find him out, if, as you tell me, you have quitted him?"

"Rightly enough. A lover can always find his sweetheart when he likes, were she at the end of the world—at least, such is my opinion."

"Do you think so?"

"I do."

At that instant a voice was heard without, and a slight knock followed.

"Who is there?" Polly inquired.

"Can I come in?" a voice asked.

"I suppose so," Lydia pursued.

And, ere the last words had died upon her lips, a man entered the apartment.

It was the individual who we saw had followed Lydia from Piccadilly to Westminster, and who had been the means, by his exclamations, of bringing to her assistance that help without which she must have perished.

Lydia recognised him at once.

"I saw your face before, sir," she said. "You besought of me not to carry out my design; yet I did so. I have had no opportunity to thank you before; let me do so now."

She pronounced this phrase in a slow, lady-like manner, that the new comer noticed in a moment.

"I came here," he said, "to see whether you were quite recovered, and whether you wanted anything. Besides, I have a bracelet of yours; and I wish to return it."

"Keep it, sir, for the present," Lydia pursued; never inquiring how the stranger got possessed of it. "You saved my life. You deserve a reward, which I would willingly give you were it in my power to do so."

"You can do so."

"What is it? Why do you wait? What do you solicit?" Lydia inquired, coaxingly.

"The favour of an interview."

"Most willingly. My name was Lydia Wilson yesterday: it will be so to-morrow. If, in three days, you like to call at my place, you can, and I will be happy to receive you."

She pronounced these words in a studied, slow tone.

"And who have I the honour of asking as my visitor?" Lydia inquired, after a while.

"Leonard."

"Leonard—Leonard?" Lydia muttered, as the stranger bowed and retired. "Why, there is a Captain Leonard that courts one of Lord Vineyard's daughters. Could it be the same man, I wonder? Oh! if it is, I, too, will show what a woman can do!"

In this brief interval she had made up her mind.

Mankind had proved deceitful to her. She would wage war against it.

This was the resolution which gradually sprung within her brain; they were rather harsh ones. Whether she altered them time will show. She was too admirably suited to perform the *role* of a demon. She looked so innocent, so heavenly, and so bewitching, that no one would ever have ventured to give her credit for harbouring any guilty design.

It is nigh incredible what a few days—nay, a few hours—will operate in human nature.

One would fancy that, after the miraculous escape that Lydia had had of being drowned, she would have turned her thoughts towards heaven, and offered to the Omnipotent her heartfelt thanks for her having been prevented to die in a state of sin; that she would have endeavoured to reform her career, to become a good, honest, and well-behaved woman.

It was quite the contrary.

Had she been by herself, perhaps she might have done so. But the words of Polly had produced a terrible effect upon Lydia; they had kindled within her heart a feeling of vengeance, of which the terrible consequences will be fully described as the story proceeds.

CHAPTER VII.

ONE OF LYDIA'S FUTURE ADMIRERS QUITE AT HOME—LORD VINEYARD'S TWO DAUGHTERS—A FEW STRAY THOUGHTS.

Two sweet girls were the daughters of Lord Vineyard. The eldest was twenty, the youngest barely entering into her nineteenth year.

They had never left their mother's roof, where the greatest attention had been paid to their education by talented and accomplished governesses.

They were both highly educated, and in every respect suited to give happiness to those who, in the course of time, would become their husbands.

Lady Vineyard was a kind, good mother to them, and had always been a faithful wife to Lord Vineyard; and yet, notwithstanding the comfort of his family circle, Lord Vineyard had, nevertheless, launched into a series of immoral pleasures, of which we have already spoken in the course of this story.

Since their childhood, the ladies Wester—for such was the family name of Lord Vineyard—

had always enjoyed all kinds of luxuries, the natural attributes of wealth.

No wish of theirs had ever remained ungratified.

They had had their ponies to ride when children; and now that they were merging into womanhood, they had been provided with the finest cattle that ever grazed on his lordship's property.

Constance, the eldest daughter, was considered by all to be one of the most skilful and graceful lady-riders who displayed her faultless figure in Rotten-row in the gay afternoons of the season.

Adele, the youngest, was, on the contrary, rather shy on horseback—not that I mean to imply that she was a coward, but her nervous system had been so shaken from a fall she got when very young, that ever since she had remembered her accident.

Lady Vineyard had never been allowed to know the state of her husband's fortune. A thing she knew was this, that it had been left entirely under Lord Vineyard's control; that he had squandered the best part of it, if not the whole; and, further, she knew also, that when he came to his uncle's title, he entered into full possession of his large personal property, and of his immense estates, of which the entail ceased with the present owner.

This was the extent of Lady Vineyard's knowledge. She had often endeavoured to coax his lordship into making her his confidant; but on that point he had always shown himself inexorable; therefore, she was at a loss to guess what provision was, or would be, made for her two daughters in the event of their happening to fall in love with some suitable party, who would be inclined to lead them to the altar, with a respectable dowry, but who would be reluctant to marry them penniless.

This was a business-like view to take; but still, under the circumstances, it was the most reasonable one to adopt.

The ladies Wester had been considered the belles of a ball, which was given by a foreign ambassador at the court of his Imperial Majesty Napoleon III.; but I do not think that the same flattering compliment was paid to them when they appeared at the court of St. James's on their return from the Continent.

Constance was, beyond doubt, a fine, dashing woman. She realized to an eminent degree the Saxon type, so much admired. She was extremely fair. Her blue eyes, her golden hair, her white teeth, her snowy neck, could not have been found fault with by the boldest critic.

Adele offered a striking contrast to her sister. She was dark, and would have put you in mind of a Parisienne, with her hazel eyes, her little *nez* slightly *retroussé*, and her wavy, auburn hair. She was also excessively witty. She had read, *en cachette*, nearly every fashionable French novel, and she had drawn from her voluminous readings a smack of originality which was very pleasant to listen to.

If the ladies Wester had never pondered very deeply over their future prospects, Lady Vineyard had done so for them.

Happen what might, she was resolved to break the subject to his lordship, and find out from him how matters stood.

Contested elections are not so expensive nowadays as they were in former times.

Lady Vineyard was aware of that; still Lady Vineyard could not conceal to herself the fact that Lord Vineyard must have got rid of a good deal of money when he had paid his nephew's expense to represent that English county which he thought ought to have a Conservative representative.

The contest had been a hot one, and gossip had been busy in spreading reports about intimidation, coercion, and bribery, and in naming a fabulous sum as that spent by the successful candidate.

His lordship had, in answer to his wife's query on the subject, replied, that a parcel of idle fellows at the Reform, annoyed at their defeat, had amused themselves in propagating idle rumours in which there was not a particle of truth. Every man, he would conclude, knows his own affairs best; and Lady Vineyard, fearing a scene, would apparently be silenced for the time being.

It was difficult to know how Lord Vineyard managed his affairs.

He used to allow Lady Vineyard a certain sum every quarter to defray the expenditure. That sum had always been regularly paid.

A certain number of horses were always kept in the stable, so many male and female servants always composed the household, and there was every reason to hope that these things would last for ever.

If Constance or Adele wished any increase to their wardrobe, Lord Vineyard, as a kind father, bid them order what they wished, and cause the tradesmen to send in their bills.

He never had taxed his wife with extravagance, who deserved, perhaps, now and then, a little censure on that head, albeit she could not be accused of deviating from the right duties of a mother and a wife.

In both capacities, let it be said, Lady Vineyard had always acted well. But who will not, at times, be guilty of a little piece of extravagance?

It is very difficult to help it in many cases. Mrs. White wishes to rival Mrs. Browne; Mrs. Jones thinks that she will surpass in elegance that vulgar-looking Mrs. Robinson; Lady Darwin has got a set of diamonds from Emanuel's which throw the countess's *parure* in the shade. She will buy something better.

The petty jealousies which exist among women are bad enough, but not worse, indeed, than those which reign among the lords of the creation.

Those things are too well known to make it necessary for me to dwell now at any length upon them.

But let these few remarks be brought to palliate what is done every day—namely, living beyond one's income.

That it is necessary to do so does not follow, as a matter of course; but there are instances when to act otherwise is simply akin to impossible.

Perhaps Lady Vineyard and her two daughters were of the same opinion; but how they would have reformed their expenditure had they known the rapidity with which Lord Vineyard was squandering his fortune.

Lydia was an expensive toy to keep.

Another item which I have forgotten to mention, Lord Vineyard was a sporting character.

He had a stud of his own, and, like all men similarly situated, he thought his horses were class enough to beat his neighbour's mare; and hence great winnings, and hence, more frequently, great pecuniary losses.

Lord Vineyard was not the only one belonging to this class. He was, to a certain extent, universal.

That he was a clever statesman had been amply proved by the favour in which he stood with the ministry, who had bestowed on him—while they were in power—a situation of trust; to discharge the duties of which not only required influence, but also great discerning powers, and high political attainments.

No doubt, when his administration would hold the reins of the Government, Lord Vineyard would again obtain some influential post; but in the meantime he had to wait, and this he did very patiently indeed.

His *liaison* with Lydia was one of those many ties in the life of a man which linked his destiny to her for a certain time.

It was rendered more serious from the very fact that he felt for the girl a deep affection.

Up to the time when I write Lydia's name was unknown to Lady Vineyard; but the secret could not be kept much longer, as she would draw upon my lord's exchequer with such unremitting perseverance that, ere long, it would be sadly diminished.

Once my lord should be in want, Lady Vineyard would get acquainted with the fact, for how could the daily expenses be met unless there was cash forthcoming?

Then for the great tug of war!

The time had not yet come when his lordship would be coerced to make sad revelations to Lady Vineyard.

His extravagance had known no bounds, and of late he had implicitly gratified every request of Lydia, of whom he was gradually getting fonder.

This state of affairs was, indeed, likely to entail a great deal of ill-feeling between husband and wife, when the whole truth would come to light.

Lord Vineyard was aware of this, and, nevertheless, he continued heedlessly to lead a life of dissipation, regardless of the fate of his darling children. Poor girls! their hearts were noble, generous, kind, and good; and, although Adele knew that men were wicked, she would not bring her mind to think that anyone belonging to her would open himself to reproach.

Lord Vineyard was a bad-tempered man at times, it is true, but his anger did not last.

When he would be vexed he would compress his lips, and remain silent; but an affectionate kiss of Adele would soon put him in good humour again.

Lady Vineyard always indulged his lordship; for he was one of those individuals who, when they take a dislike to anything or anyone, become spiteful—nay, cruel—to the object of their antipathies. The world is full of them; and—I am sorry to say it—Lord Vineyard belonged to one of them.

At the moment I write, Adele and Constance Wester had just entered the drawing-room, attired in their afternoon costume—that is to say, ready to receive visitors.

May be Constance expected someone, for she seemed rather pre-occupied; and, from time to time, she listened, as if to catch the sound of some visitor's steps ascending the staircase.

She was in that mood, when a powdered footman boldly opened the door and announced Captain Leonard.

When he appeared, the ladies Wester rose to greet him, and a scarcely perceptible blush rose over the countenance of Constance.

When the three personages were seated, Captain Leonard was not long in drawing the two girls into conversation.

"I hope her ladyship is well," he said, questioning the eldest daughter. "I saw her yesterday at the park, and she told me that she had been suffering from a *migraine*, and that you had both gone to Richmond to visit your aunt, Mrs. Ramsworth."

"Oh! mother is much better," Constance now replied. "She has, however, been confined the whole morning to her bed-room, and I do not think she will move out to-day. By-the-bye, I met your fair cousin walking in the terrace, and she was kindly inquiring after you."

"Ada is a nice girl," answered Leonard, like a man who was accustomed to no small amount of flattery on the part of the fair sex—who was young and comely, sang beautifully, held a company in a guards' regiment, and had entered this life with very good odds, having been lucky enough to be born with a silver spoon in his mouth.

Leonard had a good income, and, what is more, he knew how to manage it. He never got into a scrape, always paid his way manfully and honestly, and was a general favourite with all those who knew him.

Constance had been smitten with his courteous manner, and she would have so liked to become Mrs. Leonard!

Leonard had in his coat button-hole a most beautiful camellia.

"What a pretty camellia you have!" Constance said. "Who gave you that flower? Some charming young lady, I suppose."

Constance knew perfectly well that Leonard was wont to be daily supplied by his "gentleman" with this addition to his toilette—considered by many to be etiquette—but she only spoke to induce him to make some answer, by which she might detect some little secret she wanted to know.

"No, indeed," he replied; "I am not fortunate enough to meet young ladies kind enough for that. They may sometimes pick a small bunch out of their bouquet, but I do not treasure those things so much as, perhaps, they would expect me to."

There was a flippancy in his conversation which Constance greatly relished.

"And do you place great value in that?" inquired Constance.

"Yes, to a certain extent I do," was the reply.

"Explain yourself, pray," pursued Constance, in a queenly tone.

"If I happened to lose it, I would feel uncomfortable, as I am accustomed to it."

"Then I fear it would be asking too much of you to make me a present of it?"

"You are certainly speaking in a way which could leave me no doubt as to your whim," replied Captain Leonard, good-humouredly smiling; "but I will comply with your wish."

And he pulled the flower from his coat, and he gently placed it on Constance's lap.

"How very kind of you, Captain Leonard!" Constance said, as a beam of pleasure brightened her lovely eyes.

"You may well say that," Leonard pursued, "for you are the only one to whom I would give it."

"You are indeed complimentary—very complimentary," Adele said, who had remained mute during the dialogue, occupied with her own thoughts.

"I am very sorry. I beg pardon—thousand pardons!" retorted Leonard; and, as he was alone with two girls, he became bolder. "Let me," he said, "apologize for my want of courtesy in the gallant style adopted by our worthy ancestors."

Thus speaking, he fell upon his knees, and he seized Adele's hand, which he drew to his lips.

"Oh! this puts me in mind," Adele said, laughing, "of a passage I read in one of Charles de Bernard's tales—I do not remember the title of the book, but I know that there is some swain who apologizes for some little mistake in a similar manner. Unfortunately, the lady is busily occupied with some interesting work of tapestry. While our gallant hero is on his knees, he happens to pick up some wool which is lying on the carpet. The husband, or the future intended of the lady, enters the apartment a few instants after he has risen, and by the trifling incident which I have mentioned, he detects a great many things which he otherwise never would have found out."

Leonard, who had paid great attention to Adele's little story, closely inspected every article composing his dress.

"I feel confident," he said, "that I will not meet with the same fate as the French hero."

From what I relate, the reader will perceive that Captain Leonard was rather on familiar terms with the ladies Wester.

He had known them for a couple of years, and they liked him very much.

The captain's shooting-box was adjacent to my Lord Vineyard's establishment in the country. Many a time Constance rode side by side with Leonard in the hunting-field; many a time Lord Vineyard and the captain and party set out on shooting excursions; and many a time Adele was piloted by the gallant captain through the rapid whirls of the dizzy waltz.

These details will doubtless account for the intimacy which existed.

Lady Vineyard always welcomed Captain Leonard under her roof with pleasure, and he never was left out of a party, or of any entertainment, given by her.

In common justice to him let it be said, that he always did great credit to his guests; for, being rather fond of music, he used to sing and accompany himself on the piano, in a way which would have led people who were not personally acquainted with him to mistake him for some professional of unquestionable celebrity.

Lady Vineyard, as a mother and as the natural guardian of her children, had a right to watch closely an intimacy which she hoped would ultimately result in marriage. But the captain had never given the slightest hint of his wishing to ally his coat of arms to that of the Vineyard family; and even if he had, it would have been difficult to say when; for Lady Vineyard up to the present had been unable to find out which of her two daughters had made an impression upon Captain Leonard. He was the same to both—had been so ever since he had first been introduced to the family.

For a fortnight he would be all attention to Adele, and she would naturally fancy herself the lucky one; but her anticipations would soon be dashed to the ground a few days afterwards, when the captain would act towards Constance in a way which would induce the latter to think that the feeling he had for her was akin to love.

Great many mothers would not have tolerated similar behaviour, but Leonard did everything so quietly and so good-humouredly that it would really have been dangerous to interfere, for every day a proposal of marriage might emanate from his lips.

Constance of late had, perhaps, been a greater favourite with Leonard; but how long this would last was a problem which could be solved by no one except himself.

If Leonard had received kindness at the hands of Lord Vineyard's family, he had returned it by every means in his power. There were no obligations on either side; and, were they to discontinue each other's acquaintance, no one could have had any reason to complain.

Captain Leonard had always acted, and, indeed, intended ever to act through life upon this principle—that you should look upon your friend as one who might turn your enemy.

It was a good plan of his, and one by which he had made up his mind always to abide.

Those who knew the ladies Wester were inclined to think that, ere long, they would throw off their maiden garments; while, on the other hand, those who knew Captain Leonard were, on the contrary, inclined to think that he would remain a bachelor as long as he could.

The world is full of those characters—of those fortunate individuals, who move in the best society all their lives; who are always affable with the pretty ones, attentive to the dowagers, and irreproachable in their manners towards every one with whom they are brought into contact. They enjoy themselves in their own fashion; court *la brune et la blonde*; go everywhere; and to whose mind the idea of uniting their precious life to that of another is a thought which they have looked upon as likely to occur at some period or another; but who, from their behaviour, lead their acquaintances to think that celibacy possesses for them too sensible a meaning to allow them to take a decided step without mature consideration.

I knew, and I know still, two Irish gentlemen, who are bachelors; they are brothers. The eldest has a very good income, and was, for many years, a Member of Parliament for a southern county; the youngest is in the receipt of a thousand a year.

It was not the occasions which they needed, for they had both travelled all over the continent; had been introduced to the highest families of the land; and yet, up to the present, they are single.

The eldest had been paying his attention to a lady of some rank and fortune. All the preparations for the marriage had been made; the future bride and bridegroom were visiting some tradesman, to settle about some furniture, with which they intended to furnish their house in town.

The bridegroom thought this a very nice pattern, the lady objected to it on the plea of its being too gaudy. They had a few words about the choice, and they quarrelled.

"Thanks be given to heaven that I see you in your true character!" the future husband said.

" If we cannot agree before marriage, what will it be afterwards ? " So he left his fair partner in a state of extreme excitement, which showed her that between the cup and the lip there is sometimes a slip.

The marriage was broken off.

The younger was walking in the Bois de Boulogne, close to Paris, with a fair damsel belonging to a very good family in the Faubourg St. Germain — the hot-bed of that legitimist aristocracy who will not recognise in the great man who sways the destinies of France that immense genius, extraordinary talent, that public opinion cannot deny and has already acknowledged in him.

While strolling in a lonely path he heard the cuckoo—that wayward, unsettled bird, so fond of visiting other nests besides its own. He thought there was an unmistakeable warning in the incident above described ; and, next day, sending a few lines to his fair intended, he left Paris — kindling in the family's mind those natural feelings of annoyance and disappointment which such an eccentric mode of proceeding could not but have given rise to.

I have jotted down, then, these little anecdotes, which I think will not be deemed out of place, to show to my readers that, if Captain Leonard, after many years' acquaintance, was yet uncertain how to act towards the ladies Wester, his case was not so extraordinary as many might fancy it to be, and is to be met with every day in the course of life.

Were not my words sufficient to insure belief, a glance over the newspapers would soon show that the numerous breaches of promise—which so frequently are left to judicial arbitration—are ample guarantees to testify to the truth of my remarks.

Now, to enlighten those who may do me the honour of perusing this work, I may as well inform them that Leonard was gradually and steadily beginning to look upon Constance in a different light than that of a friend. He was beginning to believe her to be an " uncommon nice girl," who not only would procure happiness to the husband who would unite his destiny to hers, but still do him credit.

Leonard had learned to study the character of the young creature.

As far as he could judge, he had come to the conclusion that she was endowed with those genuine, precious qualities of the heart, that refined turn of mind, those enticing manners, so necessary to a woman — and which, if she is already interesting and a fit subject for love, render her, in my opinion, still more attractive.

Leonard was no exception to the rule, and, although he was not a selfish man, he looked for a great many things in a wife.

Youth, beauty, birth, education, and wit were the necessary requirements which he thought ought to be possessed by the woman of his choice.

Whether he will find these attractions in Constance, whether he will seize the opportunity when it offers of becoming master of them, the story will show.

It is certainly very flattering to man's pride to be the owner of dazzling objects ; and a certain thrill of pleasure, of happiness, and of self-satisfaction must run through the being of him who enters a ball-room with the loveliest woman to be found in the whole assembly congregated around him leaning on his arm as his legitimate and faithful wife.

I do not say that Constance was such. She was anything but so accomplished a member of the fairest, loveliest, and gentlest portion of humanity, if my readers form an opinion from my previous description.

But there is one thing to consider—love.

If Leonard really loved Constance, would he take her to pieces, as we sometimes do when we wish to persuade ourselves that some one or another is not worthy of our love, our friendship, or our interest ?

Do we look upon those who have touched our *corde sensible*, with a critical, severe, harsh, and catechising eye, ready to find fault with every little fault, however trifling that fault may be ?

Do we not, on the contrary, look upon she who has made an impression upon us, as the prettiest creature in the whole world ?

Are we not ready to cover her silky eye-lashes with a succession of warm kisses ? Are we not ready to keep her soft, white, smooth hands within our own ? Are we not so much engrossed in the contemplation of her attractions, be they few indeed, to forget everything else for the time being ?

And, were she to remain dumb to our entreaties, should we not weep like children ?

Now, mind, I am talking of real love—not of that kind of so-so feeling which means nothing, and throughout which a certain amount of interest is often, if not always, to be traced.

The highest pith of love is not attained in a few hours—is not the work of a few weeks, with certain creatures ; while, with others, it springs within their hearts within a very short period.

Under the denomination of love at first sight, may the latter feeling be assigned.

A few—nay, many—people deny that there is such a thing as love at first sight—that such a sentiment can be kindled in a momentous exchange of the gaze of two beings.

Generally speaking, we do not become enamoured of a person in a day. Those who have loved feelingly and deeply will, I doubt not, agree with me.

But some do, as the tale will show.

How contented, then, must those be who possess within their hands their own happiness—the means of realizing what they seek and long after.

Leonard was thus situated ; and, doubtless, had he proposed for Constance, Lord Vineyard would have been delighted to grasp the opportunity of securing for his daughter a desirable husband, with a good income, a good position, and, moreover, a man whom he thought knew how to control his actions, manage to steer clear of the many temptations which beset the path of the "golden youth," and who would certainly endeavour to make his child happy.

Captain Leonard's affection for Constance had not yet reached that *ne plus ultra* which only ends in matrimony.

Would it ever come to that ?

Would Constance ever become Captain Leonard's bride ?

And would the two meetings that the guardsman had with Lydia—the first one on Westminster-bridge, the second in the tavern where the girl recovered her consciousness—have no bearing upon the events which are about to occur ?

Did not the expressive eyes of Lydia make a deep impression upon the gallant captain ?

Did not her lovely state upon her couch, after her rescue from the water, remain deeply rooted in the mind of Leonard ?

Was he not anxious to become acquainted with the girl's strange story, with the cause which had induced her to have recourse to the rash step she had taken ?

Was he aware that the father of Constance would have had to answer for the death of a charming, innocent girl, had her body been discovered too late, and when the last spark of life would have already fled from her lively, budding heart ?

Had he not felt an unaccountable interest for this girl ? Had he not shown it by soliciting an interview ?

Had she not granted it ?

And was war to be the result of an acquaintance so strangely made ?

CHAPTER VIII.

LYDIA AND POLLY AGAIN—THE STORY GOES ON—THE CHILD OF THE WEST—THE FOUNDLING OF THE EAST—RESPECTIVE CHARACTERS MINUTELY DESCRIBED.

I HAVE often thought it strange, indeed, to witness the rapidity with which bad habits are acquired, to see how quickly one seizes hold of anything calculated to interfere with his spiritual welfare, as any deviation from the path of honour, virtue, and Christian behaviour naturally must.

This illustrates what has been said over and over again, and which is wafted forth to the ears of those who, on Sundays, are induced to go to a neighbouring church, to listen either to the mad rantings of a fanatic preacher, the sober theology of a well-paid rector, or to the enticing and spontaneous eloquence of some fashionable clergyman—namely, that man's nature is naturally wicked.

To woman's character, also, can the same unflattering truth be applied ; as they, too, will sin, and fight with their Maker, remain dumb to that whispering, heavenly voice which He ever breathes to us in a variety of shapes and forms, ever tending to induce us to reform our evil ways, to become good, and to find in the grace of God that peace and quietness without which we cannot thrive in this world, without which we cannot be happy.

We have often, I daresay, noticed among us individuals who possessed but very little religion—whose ideas concerning the same were so originally ridiculous as to induce us to shrug our shoulders with silent contempt, or, to express ourselves more accurately, with feelings of sadness at finding that there is a black sheep not far distant who will not be saved—who will keep his mind in a state of guilty Atheism, his heart closed to those who, by a praiseworthy attempt to endeavour to show him the right path, the way wherein he should tread if at some future period he wishes to obtain forgiveness from Him to whom we never apply in vain.

Those characters to which I have just alluded are too numerous not to be recognised at once by my readers ; but if their careers have been watched, their end looked into (provided they have been called away from the earth), have they ever prospered ?

A few—very few indeed—have been successful, for success must attend some, however bad they may be, and however addicted to the pernicious ways of the world ; but what has become of the greater number ?

Ask the hopitals ; ask the workhouses ; ask all the refuges for the destitute, and hear the heart-rending answer which will be given ; whereas, if a human being is conscious of a future state—possesses some kind of religion, however trifling—he is not irretrievably lost ; he knows when he does wrong ; he knows when he does good ; and that knowledge, indeed, is sufficient for him if he possesses a mind amenable to occasional religious impulses.

What keeps up the broken spirits of so many deserving, starving people in the city of London ? Is it the paltry pittance, too often grudged by the bloated officials who are entrusted with the dispensation of public charity, or is it the inward satisfaction which they have of knowing that misfortune is not their work ?

That, after the storm, there must come a sunset ; that the star must shine at some time or another over their path, although hidden for a weary, long period by dark clouds — hitherto obscuring a youth which should be happy and buoyant, or an old age to whom the cruel pangs of hunger are too new to be borne with that resignation obtained only by an early apprenticeship in the career of poverty and of privation.

Unfortunately, Lydia was too young and too careless to think over what had taken place within the few days which had elapsed since that evening during which she had flung herself from Westminster-bridge into the dark, rolling, deep water of the Thames.

Thoughts of religion never entered her brain.

It is exceedingly probable that had Lydia found some kind, good-hearted soul by her bed-side, instead of dissipated Polly, who was too young and too depraved to reform herself, or to induce anybody else, the line of conduct which she would have adopted would have been quite different to that one which she was resolved to take.

If she had been told that she had sinned ; that many had done so before her ; that they had found a lenient pardon, not only from God, but from the world, a wholesome repentance might have dawned upon her, and she might have become an honest, respectable member of society.

Now she was an " outsider," and she meant to remain one ; only she would take a striking revenge against the world, because one had acted towards her in a guilty manner—because he had taken an unfair advantage of her attractions.

Where such youth and such beauty were blended together, was there no excuse for Lord Vineyard ?

As the question is rather a ticklish one, and there must be a variety of opinions respecting it, we will not expatiate upon it.

There are many busybodies in this world who are ever ready to find fault with every one besides themselves. I am not one of them ; and if there was a law more stringent than the present one to punish seduction—and if I sat on the jury I would willingly add my voice to that of the other twelve—a majority, of which the effect would be to bring in a verdict which would cause the accused to remember to the longest day of his life that there is a justice in the land.

Up to the present period, however, if a girl is over fourteen years of age, and enticed away, I am not aware of there existing any law by which the delinquent can be punished according to his deserts.

[CAPTAIN LEONARD AND THE BELGRAVIAN LADY.]

But we live in a fast, go-ahead century. Civilization is rapidly hurrying on towards higher and better ends with unremitting wide strides; and, ere long, let us hope that this glaring defect in our legislation will be remedied by the wise heads that, doubtless, will spring forth from the rising generation.

I need not tell my readers that Polly and Lydia became great friends.

Although their natures were different, indeed, they felt an unaccountable sympathy for each other.

The world lives by contrast; hence the reason of that friendship which sprung within two young hearts—one yet innocent, the other already rotten to the core.

Talk about the West-end!

What are the "Yelling mansions of Pimlico?" (I reproduce this expression, which some years ago I read in one of Mr. Shirley Brooks's tales. I thought there was a volume contained in these few words at the time. Hence I write them.) What are they, indeed? What is the Haymarket? What is Leicester-square, where vice reigns supreme, when compared with the City, the Borough, where the London poor live and swarm? See vice there! See the want of religion there! See the immorality that peeps through broken pewter jugs, that reels from the ignorant, besotted drunkenness of the vulgar, low natures in their bacchanalian revelries.

Lydia was the child of the West-end!

Polly was the foundling of the East-end!

We will follow them both through their wayward careers. We will analyze, with the minutest accuracy, every feeling which actuates the hearts beating within their respective breasts. We will dissect them like the student, with his scalping instruments, working upon the human flesh that comes within his study.

Why, then, I ask, had destiny permitted that those two beings should meet?

Why should Polly, after having left her home, wander towards the very spot where Lydia was about to be rescued from the muddy stream?

Why did Polly encourage Lydia in her war with society?

Because she was of a wicked nature.

Because she loved licentiousness.

Because she loved all that is bad, guilty, sinful.

Because she craved for strong emotions.

Because she worshipped gold, and the many luxuries that wealth produces.

She had seen Lydia; she had gazed with envy upon her rich dress; she had longed for the day when her charms, sold to the first purchaser, would place her in possession of that cash which she needed — without which wicked, depraved natures, like that of Polly, look upon life as so many irksome hours, which should fleet away faster and faster, to hurry them on—

Where?

To old age, with its wrinkles—with its bitter, piercing remembrances.

Polly is not a character that I have fancied myself; she is not one of those extraordinary beings whom writers delight in picturing, and whose original is not to be found.

This character exists.

Is it in London still?

Why be too premature? Why unravel in a few words years of debauchery, of sin, and of dissipation? Why throw at once the veil over scenes which we will be most accurate in describing? Why allow the curtain to fall over the last act of the drama without having first witnessed the representation from beginning to end?

There are many unknown tales in this life which never come to light; which either remain hidden in the solitude of a country village, or are silently performed in the house of our next-door neighbour.

Our duty, however, as writers is to bring forth scenes of which the hideous details might make us shiver with disgust; to portray, without partiality, virtue and vice; to show how the best ends are attained by the most unlooked-for means; how the worst conclusions are sometimes the reward of many who, to obtain something in view, labour for years in vain.

Yonder, before my window, the country stretches forth in luxurious fields; close at hand a picturesque bridge runs over the railway arches. I have left the whirl of London city—the bustle of the large metropolis, to seek, far away from the British capital, that quietness which I need after a career of pleasure, and now of hard toil.

But I have it not. While writing, the thread of my narrative is disturbed by piercing shrieks emanating from a woman's lips; and I find that, were I inclined to do so, not a few steps from the place where I dwell, ample materials for a heart-rending exposure of matrimonial life are to be found.

I inquire of a neighbour what the whole story is about.

I have no time to hear his answer, ere a man —a gentleman, indeed, to all appearances— rushes out of a neighbouring villa with a dagger in his hand.

He threatens all those around him; he swears that he will give four inches of his shining steel to the first one who raises his voice—who dares to call him to account for the harsh manner with which he behaves towards his wife. He confesses that he beats the poor woman morn, noon, and night with a riding-whip that he ever keeps by his bed-side; and he takes God to witness that he will continue to do so, and that the happiest day of his life will be when he will contemplate his female companion writhing with the agonies of death.

The crowd begins to get thinner; the peasantry return to their homes; the pot-boy of the neighbouring tavern disappears in the distance; the ostler of a wayside inn thinks it high time to have his supper; and, to use Gray's words in his "Elegy in a Country Churchyard," they all

"Leave the world to darkness and to me."

Guilty eaves-dropper, I listen. Something warns me that, although public opinion is hard against the man, there are no natures so bad as will not at some time or another be softened by womanly tears.

There must be reasons which have made him as he is.

I am repaid for my watch. I hear sad revelations—hear a conversation unfit for publication. I learn that the man is hurried on to madness by the constant sight of a woman whom he loathes; whom in days gone by he married when pure, and who has used the cloak of matrimony to shelter the vilest purposes.

I pity the husband, I feel for the woman. The first has recourse to constant libations, to drown his sorrow; the latter is afflicted with epileptic fits, which render the drunkard's home an unbearable hospital.

And I begin to think of the little use there is in producing another book, to write what occurs every day, when the remembrance that the public always feel interested in becoming acquainted with new characters compels me to return once again to the "Outsiders of Society."

*   *   *   *

It was about two o'clock in the afternoon.

Lord Vineyard, having been compelled to run down into the country, had not been able to see Lydia for a few days; hence, he was not aware yet of the sad incidents which we have related in the previous chapter.

The very morning that his lordship had been conveyed from the railway-station to his home, he had paid a visit to a fashionable jeweller of the west, and there he had made a few purchases, which he intended to bring to Lydia, to atone, we suppose, for the dastardly advantage he had taken of her youth.

Little, indeed, did he expect that he should witness a home deserted, that he should be welcomed by a servant, who would be unable to give to his lordship any particulars relating to Lydia's whereabouts—who was as unconscious as himself of her behaviour, of her rash step which was to be productive of terrible results —and who could assign no clue to the girl's prolonged absence.

He walked rapidly along the pavement which lay in the neighbourhood of Belgrave-square, where he lived; and, ere he had stepped very far, an anxious cabman hailed him from his seat; and Lord Vineyard was soon hurried on, with that rapidity which a driver always displays when expecting an extra fare, towards the place where Lydia's residence stood.

With a quick step, he ascended the flight of steps which was in front of the house, and rung repeatedly the bell-pull, which he was not slow in seizing in his feverish hand.

Kate answered the call.

"Is your mistress within?" Lord Vineyard inquired.

"No, sir."

"Never mind, I will step upstairs and wait until she returns."

"I cannot tell you when that will be, sir."

"At what o'clock did she go out this morning?"

"She did not go out at all this morning."

"She must be in, then."

"No, sir; she has been away from here for the last few days, and I am sure I cannot make out where she is gone."

"What do you mean?"

As Lord Vineyard uttered this last sentence he stopped short upon the landing and catechized the girl from head to foot.

"Miss Lydia went away four days ago," the servant resumed. "The evening which followed the night you slept here she left this place without saying a word. I am sure she must have done something very extraordinary, for she seemed very excited; and the last time I laid eyes upon her"——

"Truly, girl," Lord Vineyard pursued, "you must be dreaming! What are you talking about? How could she leave here without, at least, telling you where she intended to go? Perhaps she has been asked on a visit to Mrs. Haltering?"

"She has not, sir."

"How do you know?"

"Because Mrs. Haltering called here herself yesterday to inquire after her, and she was very much astonished to hear the same tidings which I have just given you."

"Did she make any remarks?"

"She did."

"What were they?"

"Common-place enough, my lord."

The girl now began addressing the nobleman by an appellation, which, up to the present, she had totally disregarded.

She muttered to herself—

"Just like him; he has taken the girl away in the country with him; thinking, perhaps, that she was not safe enough in town to suit his fancy."

Lord Vineyard bit his lips. His curiosity was great, and he was at a loss indeed to account for Lydia's disappearance.

"Anyone else been here?" his lordship inquired.

"Yes, sir. A gentleman and a lady."

"Who were they?"

"The lady was Mrs. Leicester. I remembered her quite well; and the person who accompanied her gave me his name—I think it was Major Williamson. They came here the morning after Miss Lydia's departure, and they could make nothing of her absence."

While the servant was still speaking, Lord Vineyard opened the door of the drawing-room and walked in.

It was easy to perceive that the mistress had been away, for two or three emptied bottles were standing upon the cupboard. The ashes of a cigar lay carelessly upon the chimney-piece, and the whole appearance of the apartment was far from being irreproachable.

At that moment the letter struck Lord Vineyard's attention.

He rushed towards it, and, breaking nervously the seal, he glanced over its contents.

They were as follows—

"VINEYARD,—What did a poor girl do to you to treat her as you have done? Sooner than to live in disgrace, a woman has a right to have recourse to suicide. By the time you will have read this note I will be no more. Ask the Thames for that body upon which you have satisfied the cravings of a lustful passion. Tear from it that heart which you have broken; and may the contemplation afford relief to your fiendish soul! But remember that you will have one day to answer for that existence which you have blighted—for the madness of a girl driven to despair—and who would curse you from the pith of her heart, were she not to think that one about to die should first forgive, if she wishes to hope for forgiveness from above.

"UNFORTUNATE LYDIA."

His lordship took a long time ere he could decipher the words above written—which Lydia had scrawled in too great a hurry, as we have already seen, to enable her to do justice to her caligraphy.

She had jotted down the ideas as they had flowed from her over-excited brain; her pen had ran heedlessly upon the paper, and she had in a few lines conveyed to his lordship's mind all the sadness of her thoughts.

When he had perused its contents, the letter dropped from his hand.

Overcome by feelings which our pen would be powerless to describe, he fell upon a seat which stood immediately beneath him, with his face buried in his hands.

His anguish was intense; his sorrow too great to be realized.

"Lydia, poor Lydia!" he muttered; "Lydia, whom I worshipped like no being could have done, has been snatched away from me for ever! No longer will I listen to that silvery voice which went so keenly to my heart; no longer will I gaze upon her expressive bright eyes, whose sweet expression I cannot forget. Now, her features—a few days ago so commanding and so prepossessing—are rendered hideously repulsive by the hand of death; those pretty lips, which I embraced so often, are now parched and of a violet hue; cold is that heaving breast, where love ought to have reigned; and altered, indeed, must be the finest model that destiny ever threw in man's path."

And the old man wept, and he fancied he saw Lydia's corpse lying stiffly upon a wooden stretcher, being conveyed to the hospital.

Truly, indeed, Lord Vineyard—at one time the fashionable roué, the reckless and unprincipled fast man, whose society, nevertheless, had been courted by the proudest families of the land, who had been a favourite among the golden élite of London society, who never met a frown, and who was always welcomed with sweet smiles—began to know what sorrow was.

He who had gone through all the phases of a gay life, whose existence had been a constant succession of excitement, and who, from the man of pleasure, had sobered down to a politician's lot, was at last looking forward to the morrow with feelings of awe.

Now the days would be long and dreary to him; without his idol, life would be incipient; and, without Lydia, he already felt a blank in his existence that his imagination thought nothing could fill.

The proud nobleman, the descendant of an old stock, whose wishes were orders for his followers, whose speeches were listened to in the House of Lords by his peers, ever ready to lend a willing ear to the flowing of a cultivated mind, to the result of occasional study, had been stung to the quick by the silent reproaches of a poor girl.

The extensive landlord, the reputed wealthy aristocrat, the father of a beautiful family, felt a feeling of disappointment, so keen, so bitter, that he felt now cowed and prostrated by the news which he had just heard. Thus subdued, he kept his features bent downwards, as if he trembled to face the walls of that room, which, could they have spoken, would have revealed the slow progress of a systematic villainy; which could have told of a bright night, when a poor girl had been shamefully drugged with sparkling wine; which would have, perhaps, revealed many unknown dramas, consigned by their silence to everlasting oblivion.

Meanwhile, let us leave his lordship—plunged in all the reveries of a disappointed and of an embittered mind—to revert our attention to fresh scenes, to become acquainted with new characters, who will have to perform rather an important part in the course of this tale.

CHAPTER IX.

WHEREIN WE MEET OLD FRIENDS—POLLY RELATES HOW HER ACQUAINTANCE WITH CHARLEY BEGAN—SHE GIVES HER REASONS FOR LEAVING HIM, WHICH ARE CONCLUSIVE ENOUGH.

LYDIA is lying upon a sofa; Polly is in an inner room, trying a dress which Lydia has lent her some money to purchase; and Mrs. Leicester is sipping a glass of liquor, puffing from time to time a Russian cigarette, which she holds in her taper fingers.

The conversation runs on as follows:—

"My dear Mrs. Leicester," Lydia begins, "I must really think of going away. I have been on a visit with you for the last four days, and I daresay you would like to see me at the bottom of the sea."

"You mean t'other side of Jordan?" Mrs. Leicester inquires. "Not at all, my dear. You are welcome to remain here as long as you like, and your friend, too," she continued, accentuating her words rather loudly, and meanwhile leaning upon Lydia's shoulder, to whom she whispers, "although, mind you, I think her too fast, considering her short apprenticeship at the West-end."

It is useless, we suppose, to inform our readers that Lydia had not yet returned to her house in Piccadilly; and that, when she had sufficiently recovered her consciousness and her strength of body to be able to move, she had made up her mind to leave the tavern where she had been conveyed.

When the moment arrived for the departure, the parting scene was moving, indeed; and, if all the blessings which were bestowed upon her by the publican, his wife and daughters, and the whole staff of people employed in the establishment—which was pretty numerous, as, at times, it did a rattling trade—were likely to have any effect upon her future career, in truth, happiness for ever would be on her side.

Unfortunately, so many idle words are not likely to be productive of any very satisfactory consequences, as, in the first instance, they were provoked from the innkeeper's girls by her youth, her beauty; and the mystery which surrounded her arrival among them had not a little to do with the interest which the good people felt for her.

On the other hand, the generous manner with which she behaved towards the latter portion of the community, in making rather free with her money—of which, perchance, she had found a pretty good stock in her dress—had kindled within their hearts those exuberances which some people will display when rewarded for things far beyond their deserts.

Be the matter as it will, Lydia quitted the tavern in the vicinity of Westminster-bridge in company of Polly, leaving the brains of all those who had had occasion to see her rather puzzled as to her rank and real calling in life.

Many thought her, perhaps, some future heroine, about to figure in some startling tale published in the *Halfpenny Miscellany*, but they never dreamt of the possibility of Lydia being "a pretty horsebreaker," notwithstanding the strange and low appearance which Polly presented, and which proclaimed her what she was—a common coster-girl.

They thought of her at the time, and they may think about her still; but while they are doing so, Lydia is already far away, and, accompanied by Polly, was rapidly approaching the neighbourhood of Mrs. Leicester's villa, at Fulham, which had been bought and settled altogether upon her by her friend, Major Williamson, and to which latter place, we have seen, Lord Vineyard's mistress had taken her quarters.

What was her reason for her not returning at once to her abode in Piccadilly, we are at a loss to fathom; but if she acted thus, she was, perhaps, justified in doing so, as a natural feeling of revenge against her seducer might have induced her to remain away from him, to prolong the sorrow which she knew he could not but experience in reading the note which she had left behind her.

Now, ere I proceed, I will inform my readers that I do not intend to exhibit in its naked, filthy truth the mysteries of midnight, which would make of a sensational and everyday-life story a fit production to be exhibited in the windows of the shops in Holywell-street, Strand.

I will not delight in bringing them in low coffee-shops, in cheap divans, where occur scenes which are only enacted by snobs, by nobodies, by needy clerks, and perhaps by thoughtless, brainless youths, who think that, to see life, they should ruin their constitutions in drinking adulterated malt and corrupted spirits; and, to appear great in their estimation, render themselves ridiculously conspicuous in the opinion of others.

I do not wish to bring them in contact with the lowest classes of unfortunates in the lowest haunts of vice, although occasional allusions to the latter, and a closer acquaintance with the former, might become necessary, and make it incumbent upon me to do so, to show " that such is life."

I fear, however, that if I wish to be truthful I will be compelled to unravel a great many things which many may think ought to have been left in the background, if, faithful to my task, I wish to portray high and low life.

For does not high life offer great scope for the description of racy details, as money mainly sways society? And if we believe what many of us, doubtless, have found to be true—namely, that one half of the world lives upon the other—the poor must needs exist at the expense of the rich; and if the rogue and the sharper thrive for a while, it can only be at the expense of the wealthy initiated.

Mrs. Leicester and Lydia had been already talking for a while when Polly came in from the inner room with the dress, the utmost satisfaction plainly perceptible upon her features.

"What do you think of my dressmaker, Polly?" Lydia inquired. "Do you fancy her style?"

"I do," replied Polly, in a bold voice, which Mrs. Leicester by no means relished. "I think she will do me justice. I am anxious, indeed, to have the dress completed, and I daresay I will look right well in it."

As she uttered the last words, her eyes fell suddenly upon Lydia, who, reclining upon the sofa, seemed wrapped anew in deep thought.

"Lydia," Polly began, "why will you keep on everlastingly fretting? What's done cannot be mended, and if you have been deceived once, it is now your turn to begin."

Mrs. Leicester, on hearing Polly, who made herself at home, and no mistake—perhaps a little too much so to suit a woman whose ideas had already been refined by the numerous thoroughbred gentlemen with whom she had come in contact—looked upon her new acquaintance with renewed amazement.

The coster-girl was intrinsically suited for the *role* which she had chosen herself.

Had she been taken out of an unknown world by a mysterious being, in a position to accomplish miracles, and had she been asked the following questions—

Will you be one of those women who from time immemorial have existed, and always been held up to public scorn?

Will you be one of those whose motto is heartlessness, dissipation, plunder, immorality, lewdness, and mercenarism?

Are you contented to be deprived of all feelings, to have a heart which will not be amenable to any sentiments of charity, love, and purity?

Will you be satisfied to be endowed with an everlasting want to sin, with a feverish longing for guilty enjoyment, with a constant craving for enervating pleasure?

Will you undertake to hurl on men to ruin, to blast the prospects of the hopeful, of the young, and the inexperienced?

Will you promise not to be softened by any tear, by any entreaties, however genuine; to play, like a clever actress, with the most sacred feelings, and to be deceitful in the extreme?

Will you be a heartless, wild beauty? Will you endeavour to refrain, within your breast without a heart, whatever spark of generosity, honesty, the One above might try to instil within your wicked frame?

Will you be a female demon placed upon this earth for man's perdition? Will you enter into a bond with the evil-doer to become solely the instrument of his bad ascendancy?

Will you be a tool in his hands?

Will you promise to gloat over your sins upon your death-bed; to die alone, without friends, without even having ever known what is the meaning of that sweet word, "home?"

Will you swear that you will not, or never try to, repent; that you will never make any endeavour to save your soul from a terrible chastisement of everlasting wringing pains?

Polly was the girl who would have answered—

"If I am allowed to swim in wealth; to wear thousands upon my wrists; to dress in all that is sumptuous, extravagant, and costly; if the world will treat me well; if my career is devoid of cares; if all my whims are gratified as soon as conceived; if no request of mine ever remains unanswered, I will do what you require of me."

And such was Lydia's new companion.

Can one, then, be surprised that, whatever good sentiment Lydia entertained, however generous her nature might have been, ere long she could not but get her own self corrupted, her mind vitiated, by the contact of such a woman as Polly?

Mrs. Leicester had fast achieved smoking her cigarette; she threw the remaining bit in the fender.

"And what do you propose to do, Lydia?" she asked, in a sympathizing tone.

"I don't know yet," Lydia replied, weakly. "I will never see Lord Vineyard again. I will try to earn an honest living."

"Nonsense, nonsense, girl," Mrs. Leicester replied. "If you take my advice, you will do nothing of the kind. In the first instance, the idea is preposterous; and in the second, it is not practicable."

"Not practicable?" Lydia ejaculated. "Why not?"

"Because of too many things I could not describe. But will you listen to me?"

"I will."

"Do you give me credit for being your friend or your enemy?"

"My friend."

"And do you imagine that I would advise you wrongly, Lydia?" Mrs. Leicester inquired.

"I do not," Lydia replied; "still, I should like to become a good girl."

"And where would that lead you to?"

"To respectability."

Mrs. Leicester was not prepared for a similar answer; but, emanating from one who, if she was not one of her class already, would become one shortly, if she had the management of the girl's destiny, she made no remark upon the propriety or impropriety of giving expression to the above sentiment.

After a short interval, during which the three wild beauties spoke not, she resumed—

"Would respectability keep you, Lydia?"

"That it would not!" Polly ejaculated, putting in her spoke. "I met many a respectable party while in the Borough—thriving tradesmen, whose families sickness surprised one day; shortly afterwards they got laid up themselves. At first they were barely enabled to get 'a crust;' but, when disease set in, they soon began to want food. Darn respectability, say I!"

Thus speaking, Polly walked towards Lydia, and snapped her fingers, as if she wished to convey to her friend, in a more forcible manner, the opinion which she held relating to a substantive which, in the case in point, had given rise to no small amount of discussion.

"I know this," Polly continued, "that when I used to walk through the streets of London barefooted in summer, with big, heavy clumps in winter—although, to tell the truth, I would rather at any time be 'padding the hoof,'* as far as comfort and ease is concerned—pushing on my 'worrab'† before me, or with only a basket in my arms if I could not raise sufficient 'dust' to pay for the hire of the former, from the neighbouring 'dolly-shop,'‡ the yennom did not emoc ni easy."

"What's the meaning of these last words?" Mrs. Leicester inquired. "I understand the other ones, but"——

"What!" interrupted Polly, quite astonished, "do you not understand that 'yennom did not emoc ni easy' means that money did not flow in so easily?"

"Certainly not," Mrs. Leicester replied; "I never heard such expressions before."

"Go on, go on, Polly," Lydia pursued; "I am getting quite amused."

The coster-girl did not allow her new companion to repeat her request, for she soon resumed the thread of her story.

"Well," said she, "we got on rightly enough, it is true, in the beginning; and, what between what I and Charley used to bring home of a night, we could always have managed to keep clear of the 'big house,'§ had he not lately taken 'to lushing,' and to keeping company with a parcel of 'bludgers.'‖

"'I am blest,' says I to myself, 'if I'll have it any longer.' No, I would not; I was not going to put up with his 'crab.' He was going wrong, I knew; and, in course, if he would keep on 'hanging about,' one day he must be 'done for a rump,'¶ and, although he was up to a 'move or two,' at length find his master in the 'everlasting staircase.'* He had no conscience of late; no, he had not. I was not bound to him by any ties. We had no kids while we lived together, so I did not see why I should 'blue'† all my things to give the 'blunt' which he ever wanted to go and 'blow it' at the first 'booze' he came to."

Mrs. Leicester and Lydia quite liked the girl's story; and, although Mrs. Leicester's beginning in life was not much superior in a worldly point of view—as we will soon see ourselves when she will relate her own first steps in the career of vice—yet she could not but feel interested in the narrative of Polly's "first start."

"However," Polly resumed, "I rather fancied Charley, for all that; and, if he had only kept his 'bounce' to himself, I might, perhaps, have given him the chance of 'burrying his moll'—namely, running away from me as soon as he would have got tired of my companionship. But, may be," Polly pursued, "you would rather have me 'shut up' than to annoy you with details in which you take no interest?"

"You are wrong there, Polly," Lydia interrupted. "I am quite amused at your graphic descriptions, and would like to know how you first met your Charley."

"So would I, too," Mrs. Leicester echoed.

"Well, then," Polly went on, "I'll tell you how it was that I first made Charley Wood's acquaintance. It was on a Monday night; it was rather dusky; the business with me had been rather slack; and I was standing at the corner of the New Cut, Lambeth. You know where that is, I suppose?"

"I do not," Lydia pursued. "But never mind about that."

"Yes, I was moping about, looking for a flat of some kind or another, with which I might make a little 'blunt,' when this here Charley Wood comes up to me, blowing a cloud as dense and as thick, that a yard around the place was filled with smoke, although what I am relating was occurring in the open air.

"'Have you made a "doogheno hit"* to-day?' he asks, in a jeering way, scanting my stock on hand.

"'Who are you talking to?' I replies. 'Mind your own business,' says I, 'and leave me alone, will yer?'

"'That I won't,' he answers, quite boldly. 'Blow me, if I will, my tulip. You do not seem to be a "dab tross," although you can tell your mind with anything but civility.'

"I wheeled on my barrow, and he keeps on talking to me.

"'Will you stop annoying me, Charley Pitcher?'† I says.

"'Why,' he says, 'you are right, "enif elrig;"‡ my name is Charley.'

"'What!' says I; 'are you Charley Wood?'

"'The very man,' he replies.

"Now, I had heard a great many girls talk about this chap, and constancy to women was not one of his main attributes; so I turns round to him, and says—

"'Well, Mr. Charley Wood, what do you want with me?'

"'To give you a "mop up." I ain't proud; I will give you whatever you like to drink.' And so he takes out a purse. He shows it up to me, and I see a lot of "long-tailed ones"§ in it.

"'Nantee palaver,' says I to him, 'I ain't a nincumpoop; and, as I have always lived honestly up this, I ain't going to be made a "nymph of the pave" through you, Mr. Charley Wood.'

"'You misunderstand me, my tulip,' he answers.

"'I only want to keep company with you in a honest way, in course. I would not take such a pretty one as you to the "Nanny-shop;" and, if I were to buckle to you, I would be straightforward, you know, and all square, too.'

"'Cheese your barrikin,'‖ I says, 'and leave me by myself, do yer hear?'

"Although I spoke as I had done, I would have been taken quite aback had Charley taken me to my word and 'obsquatulated' in consequence; but he would not go. He was an off-and-on kind of chap; and, as luck seemed to

---

* "Padding the hoof"—walking without shoes.
† "Worrab"—barrow.
‡ "Dolly-shop"—illegal pawn-shop.
§ "Big house"—workhouse.
‖ "Bludgers"—thieves and housebreakers.
¶ "Done for a rump"—convicted for thieving.
* "Everlasting staircase"—treadmill.
† "Blue"—pawn.

* "Doogheno hit"—to be successful in selling.
† "Charley Pitcher"—a low cheat.
‡ "Enif elrig"—pretty girl.
§ "Long-tailed ones"—bank notes.
‖ "Cheese your barrikin"—hold your noise.

have set in with him, he would muck-up to some one that night.

"His manner towards me had been rather bluff at first, and I once thought that, if not 'lumpy,' he was at least 'flatch-kennurd;' and, if it had been so, I would not have kept on talking to a 'lushington' of his kind; but I soon found, when I entered into further conversation with him, that I had made a mistake, and that he was right as a nail.

"He had apparently been doing no work that day, for he was rather 'kiddily togged.' So I looks at him, and, in a 'jiffy,' sees what he is made of.

"On his nob he had rather a tasty fur cap; he was quite a buck, and, what between his blood-red fancy Billy, his Benjamin, and his red Benjy, he was 'bang up, and no mistake.'

"'Kool him,' says a girl, looking at Charley; and, in an instant she exclaims, scanning him from head to foot, 'I would be surprised indeed if that 'ere chap had not enough chinkers 'to square the omen for the flowery,' thereby implying that he had quite enough money to pay for flash lodgings.

"What would you have done under the circumstances, Mrs. Leicester? How would you have acted, Lydia," the coster-girl inquired, "if you had been situated as I was at the time—without any family, any friends to help me, and only getting a few shillings occasionally from what I earned, and from what I got by an old chap of seventy years of age who lived in the alley where I dwelt, and who used to "yappoo yenep"* a time for every kiss I gave him? I was afraid of the old monster, with his old face all covered with pimples, with his old nose as red as a strawberry. What would you have done, I ask?"

"This requires consideration," said Mrs. Leicester; "wait a bit; I'll soon tell you. Was Charley Wood young?"

"About two years my senior."

"Do you think he could make a lass happy?"

"He looked like it."

"In short, did you fancy him?"

"That I did."

"Well, then," Mrs. Leicester replied, after a moment's silence, during which she seemed to be thinking on one thing or another, "shall I tell you what I would have done?"

The coster-girl replied in the affirmative.

"Let me see, then, what are the exact words?" and she mused for a while as she spoke. "Why, I would 'have tumbled to his barrikin' like you did yourself, and like ninety-nine girls out of a hundred would have done, and no blame to them."

"'Come on, my tulip,' Charley Wood says to me. 'I'll give you a blow-out like you never got before. Leave the worrab behind; there is no fear of dragging, and your stock is as safe there as it would be were you keeping watch by it.'

"It may seem strange," Polly pursued, "but still it is true—pilfering from each other is a thing unknown among costers. Whether male or female, they will look after each other's barrows—or whatever materials which they may have—and the thought of robbery among themselves occurs so seldom, that, although it is surprising to think so, it is, nevertheless, true. While I was among them I never heard of an occurrence

of that kind, and one may fairly say that it is as rare as the apparition of the 'blue moon,' which means an unlimited period."

"Did you go with Charley Wood that night, then?" Lydia inquired, casting her pretty blue eyes upon the coster-girl, her gaze portraying, in its penetrating glance, the amazement which she felt from the true story she had heard.

"After all the particulars which I have given you," the coster-girl replied, "I will leave you to form your own opinion. I left my worrab behind, and when I came to him, 'You need not trouble yourself,' he says. 'I'll give an ounce of occabot and rouf yeneps to a yob to wheel it to my place, where you will find it in the morning.'

"'I ain't a going with you, to-night, Mr. Charley Wood.'

"'Tush pu,' he says; 'I have got lots of "swag," and you may as well help me to spend it.'

"This was, he thought, a conclusive answer; and he made me think so too. Where he got his 'haddock' so well filled I do not know. He thought nothing about 'half-a-tusheroon,' and he must have spent at least a pound that night, flashing it away as if he were the Bishop of London."

Whether the last idea was an appropriate one we do not know, nor will we pass any observations upon it; but Polly had heard, probably, that there was such an individual as the Bishop of London, and,—ergo, fancying that he must have had a good deal of money—she fancied that, like her coster-friend, he spent it in a similar manner.

"So I allowed Charley Wood to take my arm," the coster-girl began, resuming her narrative, "and in we went to the first boozing-ken which we met.

"The place I shall never forget it. Charley, however, seemed to be well known there. They all received him, and scraped and bowed to him as though he had been some great gun. There, standing behind the bar, were 'blue-fakers,'* 'blackberry-swaggers,'† 'brown-papermen,'‡ 'bug-hunters,'§ 'chive-fencers,'‖ 'buzzers,'¶ 'buz-nappers,'** 'chaunters,' 'crack-fencers,' and a great many molls; some of them apparently flash, and others lamentably hard up; some even without a 'commission'†† to their backs.

"'What will you have?' says my Charley to a young knuckler, of which the togs were so old and shabby that they shone like waterproofs.

"'Ain't particular, governor,' he answered. 'I'll have a go of blue ruin while I am about it.'

"'Have it hot or cold?' inquired the landlord of the place, whose features were indeed too repulsive to enable anyone to gaze upon them long without feeling frightened.

"He was, as Charley told me, one what would have got swung up long ago had he been punished according to his deserts.

"'Hot,' replies the knuckler; and, with a cool impertinence, he began to address me as if I were an old acquaintance.

"Charley, meanwhile, was polishing up the

---

* "Yappoo yenep"—give a penny every time.

* "Blue-fakers"—low sporting characters.
† "Blackberry-swaggers"—a person who hawks tapes, boots, and laces about.
‡ "Brown-papermen"—low gamblers.
§ "Bug-hunters"—low wretches, who rob drunken men.
‖ "Chive-fencers"—hawkers of cutlery.
¶ "Buzzers"—pickpockets.
** "Buz-nappers"—young pickpockets.
†† "Commission"—shirt.

blue ruin as soon as it was served up, and inwardly I could not but think that, ere long, he would get so boozy as to be unable to take care of himself; and that, if I wanted to cut from him, I would easily have an opportunity to do so.

"'My tulip, gemmen,' he says, presenting me to the company. 'What thinks you of her?'

"'Give us a bell.'

"This would have been the last thing in the world to which I would have thought the company would have placed me, and I was about to object to the request when I heard a voice saying—

"'That's right enough; come out strong, and give us a good one.'

"'Twas Charley Wood who had just spoken.

"I saw no way to get out of it, and so yielded. I gave him some 'bawdy' story that the old covey, about whom I already have spoken, had taught me, and it made the walls of the ken ring with the loud laughs and exclamations from the company present.

"Charley Wood," Polly continued, "was getting 'boozy,' and no mistake. I saw a 'doxy' * 'trisking his cly,'† and, ere I could say a word, his fogle had been eased from him, and passed away to the other end of the room.

"They were a 'flymy' lot of customers, and I began to think how rash I had been in placing myself in a position of mixing in such a company. I had seen lots of roughs, but such characters, by the jumping living Moses, I had never seen before.

"I squeezed Charley Wood's arm, and asked him to come away.

"He growled in reply; and I saw at once from his look that, had I said another word, he would have soon put a stop to my 'patter;'‡ he would have given me 'a cant over the kisser,'§ quickly followed by another one upon the chops, and I held wisely my jaw.

"He would keep on treating everybody around, and flashing his 'dlog' about; and, when I would say anything to him, he would reply, 'Shut up, my tulip; one good turn deserves another; in more occasions than one has this 'ere chap, and this other chap, helped to sell my stock by "chucking a jolly."'‖

"'He is right—he is right, you 'ere, Square Moll. What, do you interfere with Charley Wood the first night that he picks you up?' exclaimed a crack-fencer, standing by my side. 'The dunops belong to him, and he has a right to blow it; and, sooner than to stand your d—d patter, I would soon draw your claret, or give you a fister upon the mug, which would close that 'ere tongue of yours.'

"'To whom are you speaking like that?' Charley Wood inquires, who, although 'kennurd,' would not mind getting up a 'barney' wherein a mill would be involved.

"'Beg your pardon,' the chap says; 'I meant no harm.'

"'For the future, then, hold your jaw; if you only open them to drab my elrig "Brown Jo!"'"

"Do not loose your temper over it, mate,' says

* "Doxy"—female companion of a thief.
† "Trisking his cly"—emptying a pocket.
‡ "Patter"—speech.
§ "A cant over the kisser"—a blow on the mouth.
‖ "Chucking a jolly"—when a coster praises the article that a comrade is trying to sell.

a sailor, close by. 'The lad only spoke as he did for a bit of fun.'

"'What say you to bring out the broads and have a turn with me?' asks another, forming a group around us two.

"'I am blowed if I don't now, come,' says Charley. 'But I ain't going to play with you. I'll have no "carney;" unless you got the flimsies I won't go.'

"'I got them as well as y'self mate,' the sailor replies.

"'Flash them, then.'

"'Here is a tiung. How many more do you want to see?' and the sailor took a five-pound note out of his 'inside hip.'

"'Here is the swag; but first let us have a slag of blue ruin.'

"'For all round?' says my dlo yob.

"'In course,' says the sailor; 'I ain't half-seas-over yet, and I can stand a go or two.'

"'Who is going to pay for the peep at the ceiling?' inquires a chap, entering. He was a coster, and he evidently knew Charley Wood, for the two shook hands together as soon as they recognised each other.

"'Who loses yappoes.'

"'My crown is down,' says the sailor.

"'I'll bet it's a "case,"' replies Charley.

"A few words followed this crabbing remark of Charley; but the sailor, having been blarneyed over, his temper soon recovered its usual joviality.

"'Two out of three?' asks Charley, 'or sudden death?'

"'Sudden death.'

"'Here goes, then.'

"'What is it?'

"Charley took up a 'yenork' out of his jacket, and, having looked at it, exclaimed, 'I'll best you, my friend.'

"'No, yer won't.'

"'Yes, I will.'

"The sailor kept his hand upon the coin. 'Sing out, mate,' he says; 'I'm getting quite thirsty.'

"'What will you bet I do not cry right?' Charley asks.

"'All the dlog I got in my inside hip,' and, thus speaking, he takes out four couters, and flashes them upon the bar.

"'Four pounds, mate? All right, I'll cover them,' says Charley.

"'Hold this dlog, will yer, Bill,' says Charley, 'until I win them from this 'ere cove.'

"The whole assembly, attracted by the last proposal which had been made, were gazing anxiously over the two men's shoulders to see the result of the existing wager. I was myself in the greatest anxiety, and I feared that Charley would lose.

"'What is it going to be, mate?' the sailor inquires. 'You are a d—d long time making up your mind.'

"'I say it is a head,' says Charley.

"'It is a woman, then. Where are you now?'

"Charley Wood said not a word.

"'Was it fair playing, my friends?' he asks.

"'Yes, yes; could not have been fairer. You lost your money; say no more about it.'

"He took up the crown that the sailor had been tossing with.

"'You d—d scoundrel,' says he, 'it is a counterfeit coin. You will not get the teb of me,

[LYDIA AND MRS. LEICESTER.]

I'll tell you. I will keep your money, and fight you, if you like.'

"While he spoke, Charley Wood's eyes had sunk within his head, with a feverish, cruel expression; and, doubtless, the sailor knew that; for scarcely had his words died away from his lips, than he looked up, but his antagonist was nowhere to be found, and had already 'back slang it,'* and, doubtless, by the time he recovered his consciousness, the sailor—who turned out to be no other than 'a barker,'† disguised in seaman's clothes—was already far away, having taken along with him the four pounds that the publican had given him, as soon as the verdict of his having won the money fairly· had been given by the assembly of sharpers, who, doubtless, were in the swing, and who would rob a foolish coster, encumbered with swag, just as well as any other inexperienced individual.

"To this little incident succeeded a general banging; and, it being closing time, the 'Barney' thinned gradually, and I found myself with Charley Wood in the streets.

"He took me to his lodgings, and I lived with him ever since.

"This was, my ladies," the coster-girl pursued, "the manner in which I first made the acquaintance of Charley Wood."

* "Back slang it"—get out of the back way.
† "A barker"—a man who stands outside penny gaffs and low public-houses, to induce people to go in.

While we have endeavoured to relate, as graphically as it laid in our power, the incidents above described, we have occasionally reproduced, with all their peculiar technicalities, the expressions in currency among the low classes with whom we have made our readers acquainted.

We have not omitted to give the "slang," as used by such beings as Polly and Charley Wood for instance, whom we will have occasion to see again in the course of this story; but we have been careful to abstain from giving whole sentences in a language which must be unknown to many, and which would have compelled those of our perusers who may be less enlightened than others, familiar with the Billingsgate and wild tribe vocabulary, to have occasion to refer too often to the notes at the bottom of the page—a step which would entail great inconvenience, and, thereby, reverting their attention from one thing to another, tend in a great measure to lessen the interest of the romance.

"From what I have heard you say," Mrs. Leicester renewed, reverting to Polly's story, "am I to understand that a great many other girls act as you have done, and, once tired of their companionship with a man who they no longer care for, they leave him to seek fresh acquaintances?"

"As a rule they do not," Polly replied. "Coster-girls hold rather curious notions upon certain things, more especially upon matrimony. If the men were only less brutal, less abrupt, and as faithful to their wives as the latter are to them, the morals and ideas of the costers would, I think, become greatly improved. But, unfortunately, they do not. The women, however, think that to act as they do is all fair and square, and the children which spring from these unions, contracted in the same manner as mine with Charley Wood, are just as well considered as those born in wedlock. There is no opprobrium attached to bastardism in the Borough; and children, whether legitimate or not, generally look after themselves, and behave as their parents have done, as soon as they grow to man's estate —sometimes before. It is all one with a distinct class, who are cut off from the rest of the civilized society by the curious ideas they hold upon honesty, religion, and who, in fact, possess a code of morals entirely their own, and which they will not mend, notwithstanding the endeavours that are daily made by praiseworthy, good men to reform a state of demoralization which is really disgraceful in the heart of a great city."

It would have been difficult, indeed, for a person who might have been present during the previous narrative of Polly, to realize to his imagination the possibility that a girl, who had expressed herself as she had previously done, could have brought forth—without a moment's prevarication, without being at a loss for a syllable—so true a statement of ideas entertained by the class to which she so lately belonged.

Mrs. Leicester and Lydia remarked, as well as ourselves, the great improvement which the coster-girl had suddenly made in the way of expressing herself.

"And why," said Mrs. Leicester, "did you leave Charley Wood?"

"Oh!" said she, "that would be too long a tale to tell you."

"You told us nearly all. Why omit the rest?"

Polly soon saw the justice of this remark; and so she replied to it at once, by acquainting Mrs. Leicester and Lydia with the details which we have given in our previous chapter.

"No," the coster-girl continued, in conclusion, "I was not a going to waste my youth and my beauty—if I've got the latter, which I suppose I will have to find out myself—upon a worthless chap, who took to lushing of late as dreadfully as he had done, and who, if he took it into his head, and had seen some other elrig that he might fancy better than myself, would have left me at a moment's notice, as the only tie which could have kept us together was children— a thing we never had."

Polly spoke like a girl who knew what she was about; and she seemed to be perfectly satisfied, as far as she had gone, with having ran away from a home where, of late, she would, as her portion, get more kicks than halfpence.

Time, however, will show whether she had been wise in leaving the East for the West, and whether she was destined to find, among a more civilized portion of the community, that wealth, those comforts and pleasures which she longed for, and to obtain which she had made up her mind to walk fearlessly and boldly through the low steps of the degraded life which she had been leading; which, taken at the very worst, could not have been more irksome to a wicked mind— inclined to evil, yet promising certain refinements seldom found among coster-girls—than the existence of immorality and of improvidence which she had gone through for the last four years.

CHAPTER X.

CONSULTATION BETWEEN A COMPARATIVELY OLD STAGER, A YOUNG BEGINNER, AND A FRESH IMPORTATION.

MRS. LEICESTER, after her smoke, seemed to be relieved.

She had listened attentively to Polly's story.

When she had heard the whole of the curious details which we have given forth, she opened her lips at last.

"Polly is your name, ain't it?" she asked.

"It is," Polly replied.

"You wish to come among us, don't you?"

"Well, I think I would like to do so," the coster-girl answered.

"Have you thought over the 'ups and downs' of a gay woman's life?" Mrs. Leicester retorted.

"I don't know what they may be," Polly answered.

"Would you like to try them?"

"I would."

Lydia, in the meantime, was gazing earnestly upon the two women who stood before her.

She was good—yes, Lydia was good.

This is an adjective which means a good deal; yet she could become "bad" all in a minute.

She had done so, we have already seen.

She would take a revenge against society.

Was she fitted for it?

We will see.

Was Polly the real type of a *Lorette*?

The story will show.

Lydia gazed upon Mrs. Leicester with amazement.

She had been seduced, it is true. She looked forward to the life which it would be her lot to follow with awe—nay, with fear.

There was Polly, and she longed for it.

Very few women could have understood, with the very short experience which Lydia had, the pith of the minds of the two females whom she contemplated.

Polly was "vice," in its original and primitive form.

Polly wanted lewdness; Polly wanted pleasure; Polly wanted everything that is sinful—to gratify the wicked promptings of a young, yet corrupted mind.

"Do you know," Mrs. Leicester continued, "that to get on among us fast women it requires a good deal of talent?"

"Do you call it talent?" the coster-girl inquired.

"You mean 'tact,'" Lydia pursued, joining all at once in a conversation which was in its birth.

"I call it 'talent,'" Mrs. Leicester continued.

"I think I have got that 'talent,'" Polly said, coolly.

Mrs. Leicester again gazed upon Polly.

There was an amount of self-possession — of boldness—in the coster-girl's late remark which she could scarcely realize.

"Now," said Mrs. Leicester, "you are a coster-girl. You were, were you not, but a few days ago?"

"I was," Polly replied.

"And where did you get all your ideas, pray?"

The coster-girl looked at the questioner.

There was a good deal of revengeful spite in that look.

"Where I got my ideas?" Polly asked. "I am sure I do not know. I have talked to you before, as only we coster-girls can talk. I'll try to speak English if I can."

"You may try," Mrs. Leicester pursued; and when speaking, she indulged in a satirical, quiet, slow, composed smile, which annoyed Polly more than if the woman had indulged in a loud laugh, from which she could make her own conclusions.

Mrs. Leicester's smile was too reserved to be fully understood.

"Do you think," the coster-girl asked, "that I cannot be as good as you, any day?"

"I am certain you could," Mrs. Leicester replied. "I do not doubt it for an instant. I feel convinced that, standing in the New Cut, or by London-bridge, or by any other place—I don't care what it is—looking at the passengers going by, with your feet wet in winter, with your arms bare in summer, you saw a good deal of life. But that won't do here."

"It won't?"

Polly accentuated that question in a manner which was spiteful, bitter, and to the point.

"What are you aiming at?" Lydia now asked. "What has Polly been doing to you?"

"Nothing," Mrs. Leicester replied.

"Why be too hard upon her, then?"

Mrs. Leicester was about to reply, when Polly prevented her doing so, by exclaiming suddenly—

"Because she can take her part."

New astonishment on Mrs. Leicester's part.

"I hope that dress which you are trying on will suit you," Mrs. Leicester pursued. "You seemed to fancy it."

"I did," the coster-girl replied.

"I suppose you never wore silk before?" Mrs. Leicester inquired.

"Now, look here," Lydia began. "Why are you so bitter against Polly?"

"Darn it all!" Polly began. "She does it for want of anything else to do. I do not take one-half of what she says for what she might mean. If I did"——

"What then?" Mrs. Leicester inquired.

"It would be a case of a fight," Polly pursued. "I ain't a going to be humbugged or bamboozled by a woman like Mrs. Leicester. She is no lady; if she was, she would not insult one who is beneath her roof, and her visitor."

Mrs. Leicester held out her hand.

"I beg your pardon, Polly," she said. "The smoke made me tight. I have been wrong; will you excuse me?"

Polly and Mrs. Leicester were both handsome girls. They flew towards each other, and they kissed one another's lips.

Whether these marks of affection came from Mrs. Leicester or from Polly, we know not.

We should say the former.

She was a West-end girl. She was a woman who had graduated in all the steps of a gay woman's life, and she liked to make a friend.

"Polly," she said, after a while, "I'll love you, and tell you what you should do, if you will only leave aside those extraordinary notions which you have."

"I got no extraordinary notions," Polly retorted.

"All serene," Mrs. Leicester pursued. "If you were turned out upon the streets now, what would you do?"

"I do not know," the coster-girl replied. "Try what I could do; and if unsuccessful, return to my barrow in the Borough. The first step may lead to something—the other leads to the hospital."

"Great ideas, those," Mrs. Leicester pursued.

"Do you think so?"

Lydia was amazed.

Never in her life had she learnt so much in so short a period. Why, had you told her beforehand one-half of what she heard, she would not have believed it.

At present she saw what we have related, and she could be under no misapprehension about what she witnessed.

"The taste is vitiated now," Mrs. Leicester began. "When that kind of thing will stop, I do not know.

"I have seen a good deal of the world," Mrs. Leicester continued; "but, somehow, I like Polly's style and her ways. That girl is original, and she will do. Now the taste is morbid. I am a gay woman—I ought to know; I see human nature in all its phases—I can judge. Go to our theatres, to our music-halls. The former, perhaps, are as bad as they ever were; but, at the latter, one will hear expressions which no respectable person would have condescended to listen to when morals were less corrupted People may talk about the days of the Regency, but they were not worse than the present ones. Now it is all for "painted smut." It is all for far-fetched ideas — extraordinary sensational tales; and people now-a-days do not seem to care "a row of pins"—to use the expression that Sir Robert Peel is so fond of quoting— about the Queen's English, provided they give you a good story, with a fair sprinkling of love and murder. If a crime is committed, see how eagerly the public rushes to newspaper-stalls to read an account of what has taken place. They must know what the murderer or murderess is made like; what he or she drinks; the amount he eats; and they go mad about it. No, nothing tame will go down, unless one is taken by storm."

Lydia kept her beautiful features held upwards; and her hazel eyes were riveted in a steadfast glance towards the speaker.

She had been listening attentively to Mrs. Leicester.

Polly, in the meantime, was drawing her own conclusions.

She was one of those intelligent girls who, although born in a humble sphere of life, possess a mind of which no one could fathom the pith.

She was an incomprehensible being.

Towards one end she had bent her whole thoughts, but, we are sorry to say, that it was anything but a laudable one.

Mrs. Leicester ceased speaking.

When she had finished her long-winded sentences, she allowed her well-made form to rest voluptuously upon the easy chair upon which she was sitting.

Her pretty, well-shaped foot was plainly perceptible as it now and then became uncovered by the soft, silk folds of a tasty-made dress, and her taper fingers ran heedlessly across her eyebrows—which she was rubbing for want of something better to do.

Mrs. Leicester knew that she had said something true, from the attention which Lydia and Polly had bestowed upon her words; she guessed that her sentence had attracted, and, furthermore, engrossed the attention of her two companions.

Thus musing, she remained silent.

"What do you mean by saying that people must be taken by storm?" Lydia inquired, breaking the silence which had reigned since her host had stopped her conversation.

"That anyone who is surprised by something out of the way will be caught in a net, which he would have certainly kept clear of had it been set in a pool of stagnant, undisturbed water."

"Devilish good idea that!" Polly exclaimed.

Mrs. Leicester took no notice of the coster-girl's remark, but she looked at Lydia, as if to try to detect what she thought.

"If what you say is true, Mrs. Leicester," Polly began, "it is just the right time for me: I am on for any game."

"You forget one thing."

"What's that?"

"You omitted a clause."

"I do not understand you."

"You call yourself a 'cute girl?"

"I think so."

"Why, you can't be; you are up to any game—that is to say, provided it pays."

"Of course—of course!" Polly replied; "it is so simple, that it would be unnecessary to allude to it."

The two women bowed their heads, as if they wished to confirm, by this mark of assent, their approbation of the opinion which Polly had just given way to.

Yet Lydia was gradually beginning to think that Polly was far from being in the wrong. Her mind fleeted from one thing to another—so uncertain and so wayward was it, that it came to no final conclusion.

"Lydia," Mrs. Leicester resumed, "I am sure that, now that I have given my opinion to your friend Polly, you would like me to put you up to a thing or two?"

"What is that?"

"Would you like to be like Kate Hamilton?"

"Who is Kate Hamilton?"

"Rather a dashing woman. She's getting old, though."

"I never saw her—never heard of her; tell me about her, will you?"

Lydia pronounced these words like a girl who was getting very interested, and who wished her request to be complied with.

"She keeps a night-house."

"Oh! I would like that," Polly exclaimed. "Lots of champagne. I hear champagne is a very nice thing. I never drank any of it; still, I know it must be uncommon nice."

"Would you fancy keeping a night-house, Polly?" Mrs. Leicester inquired. "It is exactly the same thing as a public-house, only gentlemen stand behind the bar, instead of less unfortunate individuals."

Polly's eyes sparkled, and she shook her head.

Lydia contemplated her new friend.

"Well, I would not," she said. "I would so delight in becoming 'somebody'—to drive in the park during the season; go down to Brighton or Scarborough, and astonish the natives; take a tour on the continent, when tired of England's foggy climate; be the queen of a ball; and be taken for a lady wherever I go, except when an *incognito* could not be kept up."

"That would never do in England. That style of thing would not pay in this country. We English people are too moral for that," Mrs. Leicester pursued.

"Are they?" Polly inquired.

"But, look here, to attain what I say I would like to," Lydia asked of Mrs. Leicester, "what should I do?"

"Know how to ride right well."

"I am up to that."

"Talk slang."

"I will learn that—you will teach me, Polly, won't you?"

The coster-girl smiled, with a wicked, cunning smile, and she answered in the affirmative.

"What else will I have to do?" Lydia pursued.

"If you find anyone in love with you, hate him."

"I do not think I could do that."

"If he is rich, I mean," Mrs. Leicester continued.

"If he is poor?"

"That's another consideration."

"What do you mean by that?"

"Why, that you should rather love a poor fellow than a rich one. You could keep the former at the expense of the latter, and that's quite the cheese among us fast women—I mean the *élite* of the outside world. I do not imply by the *élite* a gaudily-attired unfortunate, who starves half the week to shine in the light at night; I mean the women like me and you, Lydia. Williamson keeps me well—I know the fellow would marry me if he had not got a pretty young wife; you are kept by an old nobleman, who would do anything for you; and Polly is cheeky enough to carve her own way in the world."

"And she knows it, too," a bold voice replied.

"What else should I do?" Lydia pursued.

"Go to the heads of any of the West-end theatres—the Strand, the Haymarket, or the Olympic might do—and give fifty pounds or one hundred pounds a month to the stage-manager to let you walk the stage. You will get a kind of smack then; otherwise you won't get on."

"Is that all?" Polly asked.

"Quite enough, too, I should say," Lydia continued. "Why, bless my soul! I could never face a thousand spectators looking at me. Why, I would faint!"

"I would not," Polly pursued. "It would take a deuced good audience to make me faint."

Mrs. Leicester again looked at Polly.

"You are a cool one, too," she muttered.

Lydia was about to speak, when she thought it better not.

Polly got up, and walked towards the end of the room.

The two women turned round to see what the coster-girl was on the eve of doing.

"Do not mind me," she said. "I am rather thirsty, and I want a drop of brandy. I see it there, and do not see why I should not help myself."

"Now, remember, Lydia," Mrs. Leicester said, "what I told you. If you do not look out, Polly will take your place with Lord Vineyard, and where will you be?"

"I do not care," Lydia replied, and she shook mournfully her pretty head.

"But you must, Lydia," Mrs. Leicester replied.

At that instant the sounds of glass against the crystal struck Lydia's ears.

Again she turned round, and she looked towards Polly.

She shook Mrs. Leicester by the arm, and bid her to follow the direction of her finger.

Polly was just in the act of draining another glass of brandy.

"Decidedly, I repeat it," Mrs. Leicester pursued, "that girl will do."

No more was said for the present; and Lydia dozed, and the coster-girl drank, and Mrs. Leicester went away to see about some household matters which she should attend to.

Meanwhile let us revert our attention to others who have already been made familiar to our readers in the early part of this tale.

CHAPTER XI.

WHERE THE AUTHOR TAKES THE LIBERTY OF CORROBORATING, AMONG OTHER THINGS, THE OPINION PASSED BY MRS. LEICESTER IN SAYING THAT THE PRESENT STATE IS EVERY DAY GETTING MORBID, AND THE IDEAS OF THE PEOPLE BORDERING UPON IMMORALITY—AND MORE SO NOW THAN EVER, WE MAY ADD.

HAD Lord Macaulay's famous traveller from New Zealand lately dropped in amongst us, he would, while waiting for the broken arch of London-bridge, from which to sketch the ruins of St. Paul's, have doubtless many and important subjects to occupy his thoughts, and prevent him from dying of *ennui*.

He would have marked our bustling streets, our stately edifices, our solemn temples, the noble ships that crowd our docks, or the panting "fire-horse" that bears us swiftly on, as the arrow that cleaves the air.

All these he would have noted as one takes in the various features of a landscape; but one fact, or rather one name, he would have marked as cropping out with special significance from all others.

That name is Müller.

On every wall, in every journal in London, this name would have stared him in the face.

He would have found all minds pre-occupied about it, all tongues busy with it.

He would, therefore, doubtless ask himself what could have given such marked and exceptional prominence to this name.

In his ignorance or innocence, he would naturally suppose that it referred to some conquering hero, some Alexander or Cæsar, coming amid the spoils of conquered nations, and with the names of one hundred battles inscribed on his victorious standard, to receive the highest guerdon that awaits the warrior's sword—the gratitude of a free people. Or, he would probably connect it with some illustrious orator, some great poet, some modern Petrarch, advancing, amid the applause of an enraptured nation, to receive the immortal crown of laurel in the capitol.

What, then, would have been his surprise on learning that this wondrous and ubiquitous name was neither a soldier's, nor an orator's, nor a poet's, but simply that of a vulgar criminal flying from justice, of a murderer (or presumed murderer), whom the blind goddess had summoned to her bar after having, not unnaturally, sought to place the ocean's wide expanse between himself and the hangman's deadly grip?

Here is really a splendid subject for a new chapter in Mr. Carlyle's "Hero-Worship."

When shall we cease to place our criminals on a pedestal, and burn incense before them?

A few weeks ago, and the name of Müller was unknown to fame, having been completely buried in the appropriate obscurity of the tailor's shop.

He commits, or is supposed to commit, a great crime; and, lo! two continents immediately ring with his name. His features are reproduced by the busy fingers of the artist, his every act recorded by the fertile pen of the journalist, while locks of his precious hair are anxiously coveted by sentimental young ladies, as a suitable addition to their collections of sensational curiosities.

Si tanta sunt premia victis.

If such be the reward of guilt, what place, pray, shall be assigned to innocence?

Here we have a result entirely disproportioned to the cause.

A murder, clumsily executed, for a paltry motive, and speedily detected, can scarcely be said to afford the elements of a very startling melodrama.

And yet so it is.

It is a phenomenon which is worthy of some attention at the hands of the psychologist, and might suitably form the subject of a chapter in a new theory of the moral sentiments.

In the meantime, the public will naturally await with anxiety the report of the commission appointed, during last session of Parliament, to inquire into the expediency of modifying or altering the laws relating to the punishment of capital offences.

The question is an old one, but not the less interesting for that; and the problem still remains, whether, in taking away that which he does not and cannot give, man does not arrogate to himself the privilege of God, in whose hands alone are the dread issues of life and death?

Looking at the question even from the less lofty ground of mere human prudence and expediency, it is still to be seen whether capital punishment does not tend directly to defeat the principal object in view—namely, the security of human life.

When the law seizes on her victim, and, with her venerable hand, squeezes him to death, the spectator of this edifying scene may well exclaim—

"If you wish me to respect life, pray add to your precepts the weight of your example. Respect it first yourself, by proclaiming its absolute inviolability, at all times, and under all circumstances."

Si vis me flere flemdrum est tibi primum.

When John Wilkes once said that the worst use to convert a man to is to hang him, he expressed, without, perhaps, meaning it, a truth which was destined, at no distant day, to occupy the thoughts of grave and earnest men.

As the whole subject, however, is now *sub judice,* we shall take leave of it for the present, merely reminding our readers of Voltaire's remark, that capital executions are profitable only to the executioner.

The present is emphatically a travelling age. The wandering mania seems to have invaded all ages and classes, from the school-boy to the sage; from the babe in arms to the lean and slippered pantaloon, whose footsteps are already awaking the echoes of the grave.

Does any one doubt it?

A glance at our streets or parks will soon convince him of the fact.

Take, for instance, Hyde Park, lately so gay.

What a desert!

All the fine birds that usually flutter on the upper branches of the social tree, have unfurled their wings and fled to sunnier climes—to climes where—

A wind ever soft from the blue heavens blows,
And the groves are all mytle, and laurel, and rose.

Diogenes might now roam through the West-end, and look in vain there for a man—at least, if man were to be found only among the upper ten thousand, among those whose fathers came in with the Conqueror, or whose names are enshrined in the elegant pages of the "Court Guide."

The nomadic propensity, however, is not the appanage of any class, for it is as old and as universal as humanity.

The earlier travellers were certainly not embarrassed by any difficulty as to the choice of means, and yet they seem to have enjoyed a very large measure of the spirit of enterprise and adventure.

This is abundantly testified both by sacred and profane history, and it is, as may be expected, the theme of many a brilliant narrative both in song and in story.

Prompted by various motives—by the love of pleasure, of knowledge, of glory, or gain—man has been a wanderer from the beginning; and, as the same causes will always lead to the same results, a wanderer, we may presume, he will remain to the end.

Happily, in more modern times, he has been able to summon to his aid a most valuable auxiliary, which never tires, and whose speed outstrips that of the swiftest steed of the desert.

By the aid of a little fire and a little water, time and space are annihilated, and the rapidity of the whirlwind eclipsed.

Such are the triumphs of steam; but we must not forget that there is yet reserved for it,

in the opinion of many, another victory, more important than any which it has hitherto achieved —its victory over man himself, by leading him back into that path of unity and harmony from which he once strayed at Babel.

Let conquerors indulge their dreams of universal empire; peace has also its victories and its empires, and among the greatest of these would be the restoration of one common, universal language, to be spoken by all the children of Adam, from Indus to the Poles.

This is the grand fact which, looking to the constant and ever-increasing intermingling of nations, we may already discern dimly looming in the distance.

"Impossible!" some will say; but why impossible? The fact has already existed—nay, exists. Did not all Europe, meeting in Palestine at the period of the Crusades, end by speaking one language, known in history as the Lingua Franca?

Then, have we not at present more than one universal language—the language of music, for instance—the language of numbers, or algebra— not to speak of the language of the eyes, or of that of flowers, so much more eloquent, according to Byron, than that of words?—

"All those token-flowers that tell
What words could never speak so well."

What, after all, is language but a set of signs or sounds for the expression of our ideas? and where is the philosophy of being wedded to one set of signs, if we can have another more generally useful? Demosthenes (notwithstanding Dr. Johnson's opinion) was, after all, very near the truth when he said that all eloquence consisted of gesture.

It is, no doubt, quite true that such a consummation would aim a serious blow at that endless variety which Guizot ("Hist. de la Civil.") tells us is the characteristic feature of modern, as distinguished from ancient, literature.

But, then, we should assuredly gain in energy and strength what we may lose in variety.

"I would rather," said the Empress Catherine of Russia, "find a man who could give me two things with one name, than one who could give me two names for one thing."

This practical sentiment was worthy of the bold mind that planned the destruction of Poland.

Poor Poland! Bleeding, martyred Poland! Once more the hopes of thy sons are trampled out in blood. The Cossack is again supreme within thy gates, and the Russian bear, as he gnaws thy noble and chivalrous heart, growls his defiance in the face of indignant Europe.

But let him beware.

The day may soon come when Europe will not content herself with vain and impotent remonstrances; and,

"Freedom's battle once begun,
Bequeathed by bleeding sire to son,
Tho' baffled oft, is ever won."

But enough of this discursive matter. The reader waits, and wants the story.

Will he excuse me for having deviated from it, for once in a way carried away by my pen?

I hope and trust he will; and I will endeavour to make him do so, by sparing myself no trouble to amuse or interest him.

Having apologized thus far, let me resume the thread of my narrative.

CHAPTER XII.

WHEREIN A WHOLE CHAPTER IS TAKEN UP TO DESCRIBE THE CHARACTER OF A MAN WHO IS TO BE SEEN EVERY DAY FROM TEN TO FOUR.

MR. GORGES was a queer specimen of humanity.

He was an Israelite, every inch of him: even had he been born what the world generally denominates by the name of Christian, his very nature, his grasping disposition, his "grab-all" inclinations, would soon have induced those who knew him to call him what he really was, a heartless scoundrel—a filthy Jew.

He dwelt in the neighbourhood of the Adelphi.

In a lane branching off one of those streets of questionable character, of seedy appearance—and there are many such in London—stood a broken-down, old-fashioned house, with a brass plate outside the door, with Mr. Gorges' name upon it.

The neighbourhood of the Adelphi is "queerly" inhabited. Queer people live here and there, around and about. There are houses—dwellings where pettifogging attorneys hold offices to have a business-place.

Where scheming promoters of ephemeral companies—bonâ fide speculations, of course (see Times, and newspapers of the day)—plot the ruin of foolish, indiscreet, well-to-do capitalists.

Mr. Gorges was a bill-discounter by taste, a solicitor by profession.

He never undertook but highly respectable cases.

A similar individual would have a myriad of respectable clients.

Gorges never embarked in large speculations.

He was—nay, he is—a careful man; and all the blarney, all the big talk of the cleverest Irish leg in London town, would not induce him to lend a farthing on Irish estates. The property should be in England, or he would not entertain any proposal.

He did a £100—nay, £200—nay, £300: that was about the extent of his figure—that is to say, if he thought that the money was as safe as the Bank of England, if he had two good names—even one "good one" besides your own on the stamp—he would not mind letting you have £75 upon a £100 bill at three months, holding, in some cases, the acceptance in his own hands for a few days previous to "parting."

As a rule, however, small amounts were Gorges' "forte."

He lent small sums—£25 to £50—and with him the heavier transactions constituted the exception.

But my readers would like, I fancy, to know how this gentleman looked.

What were his features like?

Whether he dressed well?

Whether, in seeing him walking in the street, his demeanour bespoke his calling?

Well, read on.

The following is an exact carte-de-visite.

Five-feet-eight was about his height.

He had a sharp, hooked nose, putting you very much in mind of the noses which are sold during Lent, and mostly exhibited during all the year round in the shop windows of theatrical hairdressers and costumiers in the regions of Covent Garden.

His dark eye was like that of a hawk—cruel, merciless, and piercing—with an expression of low cunning not easily described.

His hair was jet black; his forehead low and wrinkled; his mouth large and sensual; his teeth long, yellow, and badly set.

His manners were rude and coarse, something similar to those of a Whitechapel pickpocket.

His hands were large, and greatly in disproportion with his body; and upon his forefinger he always wore a big diamond of the purest water, which he was very fond of displaying, by always curling his whiskers when he happened to be addressed by a stranger.

He always walked with a brisk, nervous step, as if he had something in view, some appointment to which he should punctually attend. To see him standing still was a feat that his most intimate friends never saw him accomplish.

Even in his office he received you, entered into conversation with you, and the greater part of the business was done, while he stood upright.

Another feature I forgot to mention.

Beneath Mr. Gorges' chambers there was a snug little room, where clay pipes and bitter beer were constantly used and consumed.

There was the great rendezvous of Mr. Gorges' staff.

Men about town—of Langdon's style—who had fallen so low as to become emissaries of that vile member of society; sheriffs' officers waiting for an order to pin some unfortunate debtor; young gentlemen looking out for cash; hungry, half-starved, well-dressed commission agents—all in the discounting line, "pals" of Gorges'—waiting for "pigeons," for raw muffs to fleece; and wild boys, curing their spirits with libations of malt. A great many outsiders dropped in and out; while a few others—at a loss to employ their time, too lazy to walk, too stupid, not intellectual enough to read—spent there the hours of a life, irksome to themselves in many cases, and burthensome to the people whom they might happen to be living upon.

The last time I saw Mr. Gorges, it was early in the day in the city.

Doubtless he was about to discount some bill at about two to three o'clock in the afternoon, when my noble swell, in want of a few pounds, would make his appearance from his West-end resort—having got up at noon with a frightful headache, and unable to get right again, notwithstanding his having drank nearly a bucket of brandy and soda.

What "my friend" Gorges was doing in the city is best known to himself.

I did not ask him, but he seemed busy, very busy. So I concluded that if he was there he had business "there."

Now, a great many people go to the city for business and on business, but how many go to the city to look out for business?

If, at one o'clock in the day, when London at the east-end of Temple Bar is so full—so crowded with a multitude of moving beings—some unearthly creature could read the minds of one-half of the people, who appear so palpable and so honest, what extraordinary revelations, what "racy" confessions would come out.

Then or never would be the time to start a public company, any amount of directors, unlimited capital for the rapid publication of heart-rending, moving, touching, soul-stirring, highly-interesting, harrowing romances, for the immediate publication of original perfectly new tales.

After consideration, however, I thought that if Mr. Gorges went into the city, it was because bill-discounters generally, previous to parting with their money, always "must send to the city"—*ergo*, the money must have been in the city, is in the city, and he went and fetched it himself.

Mr. Gorges, on that particular day, wore a white hat, with a huge black crape around it.

Now, I wish someone would tell me why a certain class of sons of *perfide* Albion will wear black crape round a white hat ?

Do they think it becoming ?

I remember once I strayed down Holborn. It was about five o'clock in the day, and I had nothing—no business, I mean—to bring me there; still I walked on.

Out of curiosity I strolled into one of the passages which abound all along its pavements.

I wound my way through a crowd of ragged Hibernian Paddies, looking healthy and blooming, with bright eyes, with wicked looks, with rosy cheeks ; through haggard, pale, sickly mothers, suckling their babes while sitting on the uneven steps or doorways of filthy, inhabited dwelling-houses ; through crowds of low, vulgar ruffians, standing outside pot-houses, with a black yard of clay in their toothless jaws ; some with besotted, but still handsome faces ; others with repugnant features, covered with scars and scratches, furrowed by the worst of diseases.

And I wondered how the children appeared so healthy, and the mother so sickly. How and where all those people lived, and how they died ; when, behold before me, in an old battered white hat, with a huge black crape around it, I recognised the broken-down remnants of a once blooming and successful prizefighter.

Then I understood the white hat, with its characteristic mark.

Poor Jem ! he drew the blood of his antagonist fearlessly, boldly, and for money.

Gorges does not draw the blood, but he draws all that is pure and good from the young, inexperienced, and foolish, who come within his clutches ; who begin with a fifty-pound bill, increase the amount as they get on in life, and, if they have any entailed estates, any reversionary interests to step into at some period or another, live ever to repent.

Scions of old families ; merchants' sons, with fast ideas ; youngsters with a commission ; clerks in government offices, with good prospects—who are doomed to lose their respectability—to drag their name in the gutter ; bound to go through the Queen's Bench — now Whitecross-street prison, or Horsemonger-lane gaol ; and to pass through the shameful stages of the bankruptcy courts ; thus to wind up a few years of recklessness, and to live disappointed men.

The money-lender had on a white hat, we have said. Let us finish him up. He had a brown lounging-coat—anything but good taste—a black vest, upon which hung loosely a heavy gold chain, with about fourteen or fifteen charms hanging thereto—of which the aggregate weight, without exaggeration, must have been at least half a pound of gold ; a pair of tight-fitting trousers of rather a showy black and white plaid ; and, finally, of Wellingtons, which, to give Gorges his due, fitted him, we must admit, like a pair of French kid gloves.

This is the portrait of the bill-discounter. This is a true description of the man who, the day which followed the one I saw him, was quietly standing in his office looking over the card of a gentleman who had sent word that he wanted to see him as soon as he would be disengaged.

CHAPTER XIII.

WHICH GIVES A WRINKLE OR TWO TO THE READER ABOUT THE WAYS AND MEANS OF FAST MEN— INTRODUCES A NEW PERSONAGE, IN COMPANY WITH AN " OUTSIDER " WHOM WE HAVE ALREADY SEEN — FURTHER DESCRIBES AN INTERVIEW, WHICH LED ON TO ANOTHER.

WHILE Gorges was scrutinizing the pasteboard which his clerk had conveyed to him, it may be as well here to revert our attention to two men, who, waiting outside, were closely engaged in a little chit-chat conversation, perfectly careless of the moment when Gorges' pleasure would show itself by his coming out of his dingy office to ask them to step in.

One of the individuals was Patrick Langdon, the other was a "gentleman" who went by the name of Captain Hogan.

As we know Langdon from an earlier date than his companion, and as we always take a clear interest in all those with whom we form some kind of acquaintance, we will dispose of our friend in the first instance.

Once this done to our satisfaction, we will attend to his companion.

The last time we saw Patrick Langdon, it will be remembered by our readers that he had some coin in his pockets, in the shape of four sovereigns, and a little silver over it.

After he had slept the sleep of the just—that is to say, as soundly as most unprincipled men do—he awoke quite fresh in the morning ; and the very fact of his having funds to rely upon, tended not a little to place his spirits in no trifling good humour.

He rang for his landlady, ordered a substantial breakfast, paid her one-fourth of her bill, to show her that, " if poor, he was virtuous and honest," and to instil, if possible, into her mind, a confidence which his total want of cash had hitherto been unable to give to the good woman, notwithstanding Langdon's numerous stories relating to his Irish estates.

Langdon, then, began to think about what he should do.

While so musing, the middle of the day came, and then, the weather being fine, the pavement dry and inviting for a walk, he strolled towards a second-hand clothes shop.

There he bought an exceedingly swell suit, doubtless, built by Buckmaster in days gone by— for some would-be swell, gone by too. He got his hat ironed afresh, and, bearing in mind the striking truth that a gentleman should always be well shod, he purchased a pair of Balmorals, which he thought looked extremely well.

Thus equipped, he resolved that he should make his appearance at the opening of the International Exhibition, and, by a *coup-d'etat* of his own, become master of Laura Wylde's heart, in as clever a manner as the Emperor subdued the French nation but a few years ago.

After attending to the details of his toilet, Langdon returned to his lodgings in Tottenham-court-road ; and, as the day—to use his own expression—was still young, he reclined upon his bed, and he took to smoking and to drinking bitter beer, until he very nearly rendered himself quite sick.

[THE INTERVIEW.]

He felt his head growing heavy, his brain getting thick, and he jumped up and looked at himself in the glass.

"Egad," he thought, "people will say that a good coat does not make the man. They must be mad who speak thus," he soliloquized. "Look at me now; what a difference between Langdon of yesterday and Langdon of to-day! Egad—he kept on talking still to himself—Langdon, you look uncommonly gentlemanly, and no one will ever dream that A. Moses rigged you out. Why, if Poole had taken my measure, he could not have turned me out better. Eh, old boy, you are not so bad looking after all!"

Thus speaking, Langdon paced up and down his room, curling his mustachios, and playing with his dark, huge, bushy whiskers.

Now that he was quite another man, Langdon resolved to show himself about town. He might meet some old friend, and, may be, clear another fiver; hear a good thing—a tip for some coming race—and back some of Scott's dark ones at forty or fifty to one when the day would come.

It was under this impression that the broken-down gallant officer wound his way down Oxford-street and had reached Regent-circus, when he found his shoulder warmly shook by an old acquaintance, and, turning round, recognised the companion who was now with him—namely, Captain Hogan—waiting outside Gorge's office.

"My dear fellow," Hogan said, on meeting unexpectedly an old acquaintance, "I am all right now."

"What do you mean?" Langdon inquired.

"That I am in luck's way," Hogan continued.

"You can tell a good one now and then," Langdon quickly retorted, biting his nails all the while ; "but I really believe that what you say is true ; you are looking first-rate."

"Can get any amount of money done?"

"What, on your bill?"

"Yes."

"Nonsense!"

"You will see."

"And how did you work the oracle?"

"You must not be too impatient; everything in good time. Come and have a glass of sherry and bitters—do you good, Langdon ; nothing like it in the middle of the day—prepares a man for seven o'clock ; he is quite at home with the ladies, then ; he is racy without being coarse, and slyly amusing without being at all ungentlemanly."

Standing behind the bar, sipping his sherry and bitters, Langdon was looking in amazement at his new friend.

He knew that Hogan had never been in the army in his life as an officer ; that he had been a private in a hussar regiment, and that he was the son of a city merchant who would have nothing whatever to do with him. And he wondered how a man like Hogan could get on so well as he appeared to, when he (Langdon) had all the difficulty in the world to make what is vulgarly called the two ends meet.

"Have a weed?" Hogan began, placing before Langdon a case full of eightpenny Havannas.

Langdon took the cigar, and lit it up.

"Good tobacco," he said, "that. What do you give a box for them?"

"I don't know, exactly," Hogan replied. "My valet pays the bill ; but I think they are rather expensive."

Had one of *Punch's* caricaturists been close at hand he could not but have noticed Langdon's physiognomy, and turned it to account in the next issue.

The cool bragging of Hogan had produced such an effect upon him that the usual expression of his countenance altered all in a moment.

"Do you go to such a man as Gorges?" Langdon inquired. "Why, he is no use. The first thing he will ask you is five shillings towards inquiry fees ; the next thing, he will tell you that he cannot entertain your proposal, and, with a grin, show you the door, leaving you to carry away with you the consolation that you have been done out of a crown."

"He may do so with those who are not up to a thing or two ; but, when he meets a fellow who knows just as much as he knows himself, he will part if he thinks it worth while."

"How much are you going to get?" Langdon inquired.

"Not much ; only forty pounds, at three months."

"Is it on your own note of hand?" Langdon asked.

"No," Hogan replied, "I have a fellow in the service at the back of the bill. I played pool with him the other night. I won a lot from him, and he gave me his signature and a note dated from the club to authenticate his autograph."

"And do you think you will get it?"

"Not a doubt about it."

"Trash—trash," Langdon replied ; "of what use is a fellow in the service to you?"

"A great deal, my boy."

Hogan accentuated these words like a man who knew what he was about.

"And do you mean to say," Langdon inquired, "that Gorges is going to do a bill for you?"

"Not much, old fellow."

"I thought he never parted."

"Sometimes."

"Queer customer."

"He is."

The two men had been talking for some time.

"What do you think he said to me one day when I wished to get some tin from him?" Langdon inquired.

"I don't know," Hogan pursued ; "tell us, will you?"

"Yes. I went to him one day—I happened to have been recommended to him by a clerk, a fellow in Somerset House ; I told him I wanted some money. Says he to me, 'Go to Gorges ; he will give you any amount if you are good, and if your representations are genuine.' I went to him"——

"Well, what about it?" Hogan inquired.

"Well, he would not stump up."

Hogan was a man of the world. If what Langdon had told him was true, a man should not starve in the city of London ; and if bill-discounters were such "*an innocent lot*," why, there would be no necessity for a chap to be in want of a crown, like so many of us sometimes are.

"And do you think you will get the cash now?" Langdon pursued.

"We will see."

At that moment Gorges—big Gorges, contemptible Gorges—came out.

"I beg your pardon," he said, addressing Hogan ; "will you step in?"

Hogan made no reply, but, followed by Langdon, he walked in.

"Good day, sir," Hogan said.

Gorges made no answer.

"I have done a bill of yours before," Gorges began ; "it is standing at the present moment."

"I know that," Hogan replied ; "will you cash the other one?"

Gorges reflected deeply.

"You gave me some references two months ago," he pursued ; "I have inquired there—they are all right. Will you excuse me, sir, for speaking to you as plainly as I do?"

Hogan held his tongue.

Gorges expected an answer.

He found a man who knew as much as he did himself, and he would not reply ; and Gorges did not repeat the query.

Gorges, however, did not know that Hogan was as cute as himself.

Had he known so, not a farthing would he have parted.

"I am fully aware," Hogan replied, "that you have a good deal of men coming here to ask you to lend them a little money, but that's no business of mine. You have already done a bill of mine ; will you do another?"

Patrick Langdon looked at Hogan and looked at Gorges.

The proceedings which he saw were so new to his old way that he could make nothing of them.

"Well, Mr. Hogan," Gorges began, "you only want forty."

"That is all."

"Do you wish to have it now?"

"I do."

"On the London and Westminster Bank?"

"Any other bank you like; say Rawson and Bowering, if you have got multifarious accounts. The latter is as good a concern as any, and as I was hard up once I would like to show them that a fellow sometimes can scrape a few pounds together."

"Strange remark, that!" the bill-discounter thought.

"Here is a cheque for forty pounds."

"All right," said Hogan.

He looked at the dill-discounter, and he saw the latter taking out his book, and drawing a leaf thereof.

"If you like to take a cab," Gorges said, "you will just be in time before the closing of the bank."

"All right," Hogan said, and he quietly walked out of the office.

"I have given over eighty pounds to that chap in two months," Gorges thought, as the two men left his office. "The references which Hogan gave me are satisfactory enough. I wonder whether that man is genuine."

CHAPTER XIV.

WHERE THE AUTHOR TAKES THE LIBERTY OF ASKING THE READER WHETHER THE FOLLOWING REMARKS ARE TRUE OR WHETHER THEY ARE NOT?

I do not wish to hold up to public opinion those frail creatures who, from a diversity of circumstances, have brought themselves to the lowest ebb of social degradation; some of whom deserve our pity, while others could not be too severely punished or despised, were their antecedents and their own behaviour brought to light.

I say this because, from what I have written, and from what will follow, the reader perhaps may feel inclined to think that I intend to place upon a pedestal of glory and worship women who, in a multitude of cases, some of them known, and others unknown, have an immense influence upon society, and interfere in more ways than one in swaying the destinies of men's career.

In my opinion, "unfortunates" should be kept where they are; and, as such as they have always existed, they should not be induced to come to nightly religious meetings in the hope of saving their souls—of retrieving their lost reputation; for, if one fallen beauty disapears, her place will be supplied with twenty.

But, if we look into the lives of all great men—of kings; of clever politicians; of bold sailors, who have been the glory of the land which gave them birth; of experienced, brave generals who have led the English banner through the fields where England's honour had to be defended—we will find that, at one time or another, women have been the means of inducing them to do that which they would never have done had they been left to themselves; while they have also been instrumental towards effecting, in a few exceptional cases, results which the most sceptical and bitterest judges would have found themselves unable to condemn.

Look at Charles II., with his numerous mistresses. Look at Louis XIV., of France, surrounded by all the beauties of his court. Look at Nelson, with Lady Hamilton.

Nelly Gwynn, in the first instance, did good.

Chelsea Hospital, as long as the cement and stone will hold together, will be there to proclaim to the world a gay woman's act. Madame de Maintenon founded convents, charitable institutions, and did perpetrate many praiseworthy deeds; and, but for Lady Hamilton, the great Nelson might never have acted in the manner in which he did.

These are a few cases which I have taken out of a myriad of them.

Were I not too conscious of the reader's interest, which should be kept up; were I not, also, aware of the great duty of an author, which is not to encroach, more than he can possibly help, upon a peruser's patience, I could give many quotations—bring forward a myriad of examples, which would tend, in the long run, to show what many know already—namely, that if there were many gay women, during all reigns, at every period of man's history—from the earliest age to the present day—out of a large number, a few creatures, more privileged than their companions or their predecessors, have, from time to time, endeavoured to turn their reign to some account; to use their ascendancy towards high, noble, and, what is more, to profitable and lasting purposes.

These women are not worse than guilty married women, who break that solemn word which they have given to a reverend official, when they have united their destinies to a male companion.

The latter, in my opinion, should be dragged to a public spot—the more crowded the thoroughfare the better—and, if decency did not forbid, and the laws of man prevent the accomplishment of an original idea of mine, I would like to see these women stripped of all their garments, by the hands of the executioner, and—as they have broken a solemn pledge—the blood copiously drawn, with sharp-cutting birches, from a body which they have prostituted.

For to sin these women have no right; nothing can palliate their guilt.

Disclosures coming under the above head will be related by me as the story proceeds; and I will show how a woman—the wife of a baronet—left her husband, who had always behaved well towards her; left a clustering family of loving, beautiful children, to rush madly into the arms of a worthless, dissipated sinner, now gone to pay his last tribute to Him before whom we must all appear.

She, also, the woman, is dead.

But what a change had taken place in her who lay on a drunken bed of sickness; whose fine features were rendered hideously vile by the course of vice; whose mind raved in its last agony, when she swallowed the deadly draught of poisoned brandy, which rid her of an existence rendered unbearable to her by the cruelty of the man with whom she had lived; who had forsaken her in disgust, to leave her to ponder on her guilt, and, with a mind which could not forget—although often distracted—that she had acted in a way that man will not forgive—that God must punish.

And then there are the women who have been divorced.

"Unfortunates" are not more to be blamed than they who have managed to play their cards sufficiently well to bring to bear all the political and acute ways of an intelligent woman, to ensure to themselves a social respectability, which some are successful enough to keep all their lives, which others are powerless to preserve except for a certain period.

With the latter it lasts until the day when, their characters being minutely inquired into, show them forth in their true light; exhibit those nervous and voluptuous cravings to which they have ever pandered, immediately procuring an immediate gratification to the promptings of desires, which constantly spring forth in certain women's breasts.

After some years, or a few months, their lives are brought forward, and all their movements are fully illustrated in the reports of the Divorce Court.

And then they are not allowed to sink into oblivion, if the parties happened to move in the higher spheres of life.

From their own vice springs forth a terrible and shameful notoriety, which all the Christian virtues—combined in one being—would fail to procure to them.

If their cases display any " spicy " incidents—thereby showing extra cruelty on the man's part, over-ingenuity displayed by the woman in endeavouring to baffle suspicion, meanwhile losing no opportunity to indulge freely in that which comes within the limits of Venus' dispensation—these racy, scandalous revelations will be taken up by the press, and extra publication given to a narration which, from its concocted filth and shamelessness, ought to be carefully hushed up by such moral people as we English pretend to be.

The *Times*, the *Daily Telegraph*, the *Standard*, will have leading articles thereupon. The writers of those widely-circulating journals will sip their sherry—take an extra allowance of alcohol—to work themselves up to that excited pitch which some talented natures require, to do justice to that skill which they possess in wielding their journalistic pen.

With that masterly genius with which leader-writers are endowed to such an eminent degree, they will study themselves to bring into a column or two the most expressive thoughts that their fertile imaginations can suggest. They will scan the whole of the British language to do justice to their theme; and, in a few nervous, well-put-together sentences, endeavour to convey as accurate an idea as they can of the cruelty or vice of the parties concerned, whose career is shamefully laid bare, although—I repeat it—private matters should not be inquired into, and they should not be digressed upon, as they are not in any way connected with any topic which comes under the province of journalism.

When a dashing horsebreaker, with wicked eyes, with sandy hair—who will, perhaps, be personified in the course of the tale—who possessed but one thing to recommend her—an original smack of beauty, which she knew how to turn to the best ends; who was intellectual enough to use blandishments to enslave the admiration and worship of a few idle and wealthy patricians, by knowing excellently how to indulge the vitiated age and tastes of successful humanity—when that creature was sold out of a tasty residence in Park-lane, what did we do?

Did we remain silent, and not expatiate upon the bold little woman who used to drive so well the gamest, finest, and most valuable pair of ponies that ever entered Hyde-park during the gay season?

No; we made it a subject of public discussion.

Letters were written to the most influential organs of the present age; and when a "Racing Calendar" and a "Burke's Peerage" were found to be the only literature indulged in by that little impertinent woman, did we leave the subject alone?

We had *cartes-de-visite* printed during her short-lived reign, and books were subsequently written purporting to tell a good deal relating to a pretty horsebreaker known only by a limited, privileged few.

And, after fashion made her the queen of the day, she left us for a while to go to another modern Babylon, where the foul English language emanating from that little mouth with brittle white teeth, where that woman-made demon was not so well understood, and where her reign was thrown into the shade by some ballet-girl taken up by some Russian prince, who began to think that it was a great pity not to give truffles and velvet-cushions to she who had lived mostly upon green apples, and dwelt in a garret, until her star shone forth.

Sic transit gloria mundi.

We want sensations, we want fresh descriptions, we want to force our way into my lord's drawing-room—to pay, unheeded, a visit to the "alcove" of a fashionable star; there to see her in her morning attire, and to tell the reader how her time is occupied.

What between her voluptuous lounge in the morning; her philosophy between the sheets, as a clever, amusing, and somewhat bitter fashionable writer describes it; what between her talking to her bullfinches—in coquettish cages—"ever saying will you feed me ;" what between reading a scurrilous translation of a French novel, receiving her visitors in a peignoir, beautifully embroidered, she found that a joyful and pleasant existence flew away.

From our description, we want to make the reader exclaim—

" Oh! what a pity so much youth and so much deception can be blended together, and why should such creatures be allowed to live in woman ? "

Because men are the first to blame; because wavy, glossy hair, an indignant little nose, a row of well-set teeth, expressive blue or black eyes, pencilled eyelashes, and dark and long lids, voluptuous lips, tiny hands, tiny feet, taper fingers, rosy nails and a soft skin, and everything else to correspond, will always make way in any large town where vice and wealth pull together—where a woman, endowed with a certain amount of blandishments, knows how to turn them to the best account, and, if favoured by circumstances, bear this in mind—if she sins, why not go the whole hog or none—excuse the vulgar expression—and, as Polly thought—

" If the mistress of a churl, why not that of a noble; if the toy of the vulgar, why not of the patrician ? "

And now for our next chapter.

CHAPTER XV.

WHERE HOGAN AND LANGDON, WITH THE CASH IN THEIR POCKETS, BEGAN TO THINK ABOUT DISPOSING OF IT, AND WHERE A GENTLE HINT TO THE HORSE GUARDS IS RESPECTFULLY GIVEN.

IT was about three o'clock in the afternoon when Captain Hogan and Patrick Langdon emerged from Gorges' office—the former with the cheque in his pocket for forty pounds.

Arm in arm, and as friendly as if they had known each other for centuries, and if between the two men there existed an affection which nothing could have lessened or shakened, the two "swells," for the time being, walked quickly onwards.

Being within a stone's throw of the Strand, it was not long ere they reached that always very crowded thoroughfare, which leads to different places, indeed—to the West End and to the city.

To the seat of pleasure, of frivolity, of dissipation, of extravagance, of constantly-lavished wealth. To the stronghold of hard toil, of deep thought, of carefulness, and hardly-earned, and mostly well-expended, riches.

"Cleverly done, that last tack of yours," Patrick Langdon began, alluding to Hogan's late success. "I did not think that Gorges would have parted with the coin."

"I knew he would," Hogan replied; "that 'spec.' of mine required no deeply-laid plans. There are some things, for instance, which need 'a deal of working,' but the case in point was as clear as the moon at noonday; and I feel convinced that, as sure as God made little apples, Gorges would accept my bill, and give me a cheque, which I hope will be duly honoured; but you should remember that I have an officer's name in active service at the back of the paper, and a military man can always get any amount of paper done."

When Hogan had spoken Langdon had pricked up his ears.

He knew that his companion would not deceive him, whatever he might do with regard to others; and the very fact of his hinting at the probability of the bill being dishonoured was a conclusion which, although very probable, did not afford him much satisfaction or inward pleasure to ponder upon.

"Surely," Langdon began, "bill-discounters would not give you a cheque likely to be dishonoured."

"Would they? As a rule they do not. It would not serve them; but sometimes they indulge in that little kind of amusement. But the other day, a fellow that I knew something about got his bill done for twenty-five pounds. The amount was not large, you see. He just wanted it for a week's time. The man he went to is a good one; he does a lot that way, and yet he gave him a slip out of his bank book, which was duly dishonoured by the banker to whom my acquaintance took it. The following day he got his money all right somewhere else; but even that shows you that there was something wrong somewhere."

Thus speaking, the two men strolled on.

They had reached the spot where the West-end branch of the London and Westminster Bank stands.

They entered the building, and we need not say that the money was paid within a few instants.

The time had elapsed since the moment that Hogan and Langdon had left the dirty office of old Gorges; and, what between their conversation—which had lasted some time—and what they had to do, it was very nigh closing time when the two friends found themselves again in the street.

The evening's darkness was spreading fast; a chilly March wind was sweeping everything before it, and causing everybody to say, "It is getting deucedly cold;" and night, coming on, was giving full scope to the West-end shopkeepers to display their goods, artistically laid out in their front windows, blazing forth amidst the refulgent sparks and bright glare of the numberless gas-burners.

The club-houses, abounding all along Pall-mall, were getting quite lively, and the Hansom cabs and four-wheeled carriages rattled over the pavements; and everything proclaimed the awaking of the fashionable world which dwells at that part of London town in the midst of which our two friends happened to be situated.

Langdon had no club to go to—five years had already gone by since he had to drop the payment of his yearly subscription—which, for a comparatively small annual payment, gives to a man that which very few other memberships can procure him—namely, a kind of social standing, a somewhat substantial guarantee of respectability—a handy place to step into in bad weather—a comfortable resort wherein to spend a few hours when time hangs heavily upon unoccupied, idle hands.

Langdon and Hogan halted at every step they took while in Regent-street—a locality which they had reached, and carelessly their glance fell upon all the dazzling objects which they saw.

Before jewellers' stalls they made the longest stay, and there contemplated with envy or with curiosity the substantial yellow gold, refined workmanship, and valuable precious stones, all glittering in gorgeous array, to attract the attention of—and induce to buy—the wealthy loungers who swarm in every large capital.

"What's to be done now?" Hogan inquired of Patrick Langdon, as soon as the wind's sharp blasts made themselves more strongly felt, and produced upon Hogan's constitution the effect of inducing him to think that one is better in-doors than out-of-doors on a chilly autumn night.

"Anything you like," Langdon replied. "It is too early to have dinner: let us take a stroll up and down the Burlington, and look at the women there—may be meet some value there."

The suggestion of Langdon was evidently looked upon by his companion as being a good one, for he hurried on his step and crossed over the way.

In two or three minutes after they had spoken, the two friends found themselves walking up and down the Burlington-arcade.

There are some places where a man does not mind walking by himself—where, indeed, he looks upon companionship as a bore, as many whom one gets acquainted with have nothing to say for themselves, and even if they do, that same is not worth listening to—but you must always be accompanied by two or three in the Arcade, if you do not wish to be the object of extra watch by the many who congregate there from six to seven in the evening in the first weeks subsequent to the opening of Parliament.

The shooting season is then partly over; hacks and roadsters are brought up to town; hunters are sent to grass, to recruit in the green fields that strength which they need after having had their exertion so severely taxed as it is in so many cases.

The country is, comparatively speaking, deserted for awhile.

Town life, with its unceasing renewal of pleasures, of gorgeous, expensive entertainments, succeeds the healthy recreation across country, over the heath, amidst the briars and furze of the forest.

The bloom of youth—which sets so beautifully upon the handsomely-made countenances of our aristrocratic English girls—gives place to the interesting paleness which ever attends unceasing sleepless nights, too great an indulgence in the dizzy whirl of "fast dances," the inhaling of the corrupted, perfumed air, which is freely breathed by the motley crowds huddled together in the Belgravian *salons*.

For a few months composing the London season everything is forgotten.

The excitement and mad pursuits of the horsemen after Mr. Reynard ; the final meeting of the hounds, when the reward is given to the boldest equestrian ; the danger attending the fearless clearing of deep hedges, high fences, stubborn, solid stone walls, are obliterated by new scenes, by the extravagant entertainments of the wealthiest metropolis in the world.

Langdon and Hogan were walking leisurely and quietly up and down, turning round occasionally to glance upon some little *nez retroussé* —some dark-eyed beauty, on for a dinner at "Verey's," a box at the Strand or the Haymarket Theatre, and a supper after that, or anything else ; not even too proud to accept a pair of gloves or a French bonnet from any of the tempting milliners' shops scattered here and there ; and indulging in a weed, notwithstanding the regulation which prescribes that no smoking shall take place within that selected spot—that fashionable rendezvous—when a fresh individual joined the two friends.

The new personage was a short little fellow, and placed you very much in mind of a French dancing-master as he swaggered along, fancying that there was great style about him.

"How d'ye do ? " he asked, in a lisping manner, contracting "How do you do " into a shortened sentence that few would understand.

Hogan looked at the young gentleman.

He did not seem to care much about making his acquaintance.

Something told him that the new-comer could be no use to him ; and, furthermore, that an introduction might end at a few hours' notice, with a very ingenious request for the loan of a sov., which, as a matter of course, would be declined.

By his manner, Hogan showed to the little fellow that he was not wanted ; so, after saying a word or two to Langdon, which might be resumed in this — "Confoundedly slow people coming up to town ! "—this short, clumsy little man strutted away in an opposite direction.

"That's a very clever little fellow, that," Langdon began, as soon as the individual had disappeared from his gaze ; "he belongs to that large family whose name begins with an O. His name, if I remember right, is Matthew O'Bryan. If he had sufficient brain to pass his examination for the army—and he has been up about a dozen times, at least—he would have done the Horse Guards."

Langdon pronounced these last words like an individual who was perfectly *au fait* with his subject, and who was too well aware of the truthfulness of his statement to fear any contradiction from anyone.

"Done the Horse Guards ! Explain yourself, young man ; I really do not understand you."

"Well, I will tell you. If Matthew O'Bryan had had any education at all, he would have passed his examination for a direct commission. Do you see that ? "

"I do not see it," Hogan replied ; "but, to be more accurate, I understand it."

"Well, his father is a clerk in some Government office, with about three hundred pounds a year. Matthew O'Bryan never had a sixpence to rub one against the other, and yet the fellow was blabbing everywhere that he was about to enter a cavalry regiment. Nothing but a heavy dragoon would do for him. He was frigtfully small, but that does not matter. The brain makes the man, not the muscular power. Louis Napoleon is a little man ; Wellington was a little man also."

"What has that to do with it ? Langdon, you are an awful chap for spinning yarns ; you ought to write a book, I am sure you would make a living by it."

"It requires brains to do that, and I have muddled my own too much with brandy-and-water all my life, and now with stout and bitter beer, and I feel that I should be powerless for the task. But now to return to that interesting little Irishman whom you just saw. He got his father to apply to the Horse Guards for a commission for his son. You have to deal with gentlemen there, who suspect no shuffling, no nonsense, and look upon such applications as fair and square. But the father of Matthew O'Bryan never could have raised sufficient to purchase an outfit for his son—much more a commission."

"And suppose he had passed his examination, how would he have managed about lodging in the purchase-money ? "

"He would have raised it by his own bill upon his worthless commission, and, in fifteen or sixteen months, have been compelled to sell out with a couple of thousand pounds in debt. Any young fellow appointed to a cavalry regiment can do any amount of swindling if so inclined, and what I tell you is done very frequently. As it is, he did not succeed, and he just managed to kick his heels about in the west of London ; and but the other day he went through the court of bankruptcy for about six hundred pounds of debts, assets *nil* ; passed his examination and obtained his discharge ; and now he is going upon the old tack again—back to his old game ; and if he does not look out will bring himself to Newgate,— as he has no friends, no family, nor any means to back him up. In two years he managed to victimize two or three swell tailors in Bond-street ; and, between you and me, I think he deserved the money, for he acted very cleverly throughout. Had he remained with us to-night, he would have greatly amused us ; he would tell you, for instance, that he was thinking of putting up for an English borough, and that the governor was ready to stand two or three hundred to meet preliminary expenses."

Langdon had scarcely spoken, and he was about to listen to a few remarks, which would doubtless have been brought from Hogan after the curious and novel revelations which he had just heard, when his companion dragged him towards the entrance of the arcade in Piccadilly.

At that moment he had seen a pretty bonnet in the distance.

"By Jove ! Hogan," he said, " I will introduce you to rather a stylish woman if you promise to behave yourself. Do you know a Mrs. Leicester?"

No answer was given to the query made by Hogan, but he hastened his steps, and just reached Piccadilly in time to be introduced to the lady in question, who was just entering a brougham.

CHAPTER XV.

WHERE THE MURDERER DASHWOOD MAKES THE ACQUAINTANCE OF A GIRL WHOM HE WILL NOT MANAGE SO EASILY AS HE THINKS HE CAN—AND WHERE A NOBLE DUKE, A YOUNG BARONET, AN OLD LORD, AND TWO OR THREE HORSEBREAKERS ARE ALL BROUGHT TOGETHER WITHOUT WISHING IT— AND WHERE HOGAN SEES A CHANCE WHICH MAY LEAD TO SOMETHING GOOD BY-AND-BYE.

MRS. LEICESTER was not sorry to find herself accosted by Patrick Langdon.

Owing to that pecuniary help which he had received from Mrs. Haltering, he had operated in the whole of his attire a change for the best, and although he was not strikingly got up, still he looked clean, respectable—nay more, gentlemanly.

Mrs. Leicester noticed the transformation which Langdon had undergone, and, to be candid, she was very happy to see it.

Not that Langdon was anything to her, or that she cared a straw for him. She had only met him once before, and being hard-up was no recommendation—at least we should say so—to such a woman as Mrs. Leicester.

Hogan was duly introduced to Mrs. Leicester.

"Allow me to present you my friend, Captain Hogan," Langdon had said.

A bow had been made by the lady.

Hogan had endeavoured to return the compliment in as courteous a way as he could, and the vehicle had driven off.

Why should we be nearly as particular towards gay women on the first introduction—if acquainted with a friend of ours, and known to be *bona fide* stylish girls, living under tip-top fellows' protection—as we are towards ladies?

This is an anomaly which exists in the purest code of society, and which ought to be looked into.

Never mind it, though; let us proceed.

"Have you seen Miss Laura Wylde yet?" Mrs. Leicester began, addressing Langdon.

There was a good deal of quiet chaff contained in the tone of voice with which Mrs. Leicester made the above inquiry.

"Not yet; how could I? The days do not fly so fast as you may think, my dear madam," Langdon replied, insinuatively. "The opening of the Exhibition will not take place before the first of May. We are close upon it, it is true, but still a few hours will elapse between the present time and the moment when I am to be introduced to the heiress of Onslow-square."

Hogan had not yet spoken.

"Speech is silver, but silence is gold;" and perhaps the *soi-disant* captain acted upon this wise saying.

"You took me quite by storm," Mrs. Leicester began; "I don't know whether I can take you both to the place where I am invited to dine. Do you know, Mr. Langdon, whither I am going?"

"I have not the slightest idea," Langdon replied; "but if you fancy for a moment that I have intruded my company upon you, allow me at once to alight."

At that instant Hogan placed his hand outside the vehicle.

"I have taken the liberty of entering your brougham without being invited," Hogan pursued, "but I was certainly not aware that you had matters to attend when a stranger might be in the way. I beg to apologize; and if you will permit me, I will avail myself at once of my friend's suggestion."

Thus speaking, Hogan kept on rattling the sovereigns in his waistcoat pocket, so as to show in a silent manner, of course, to his new acquaintance that he had a good supply of "yellow boys" with him, and that, if thrown upon his own resources, he could easily spend a pleasant evening that night without being in any way discountenanced by the lady's rebuke.

We should be sorry to let our readers think for a single instant that we wish to impress them with the idea that Hogan's style was the right one, and that to act as he did came within the province of a man of birth and education.

Not so, indeed. Hogan was not such as we would bring in in a novel as a type of good breeding, or of polished, refined manners. Such as he is, such as he was, we will describe him; and it will be seen that, notwithstanding a certain amount of that vulgarity which is peculiar to bagmen, he managed to win the good graces of an individual whom we will shortly see.

"You misunderstand me," Mrs. Leicester began; "I am asked to take tea this evening with a Mrs. Major Haltering. She is a lady well known to Captain Langdon, but she is rather extraordinary at times, and she might object to me if I brought any stranger to her."

"I will answer for her," Langdon pursued; "I feel convinced that Agnes will not be annoyed at making the acquaintance of my friend Captain Hogan. He is a first-rate fellow, and I would never have given him what one calls the 'devil his due' had not your late observation provoked my remark."

"Be it so, then," Mrs. Leicester continued; "I will chance her displeasure; and if she seems annoyed, why, you can come and spend the evening at my place."

While Mrs. Leicester was speaking Hogan never put in a word. He contented himself by listening to what he heard.

"Mrs. Haltering has a kind of party to-night. I dare say she will play on the piano. Are you a good waltzer, Langdon?"

Mrs. Leicester pronounced these words in a familiar sort of way, which left no doubt to Hogan as to Mrs. Leicester's rank in society. At first he had his doubts about what she might have been, but there are so many women in London who take it into their heads to become occasionally "giddy," that it is really a puzzle for one who has a knowledge of the world to say which is which.

I am certain that it is no easy task to pass at once a definitive opinion relating to many of those loving women whom we meet sometimes, be it in town, or more so at watering-places—say Brighton, Torquay, Tenby, or Scarborough. We are sometimes introduced to ladies whom we believe in our own hearts to be inclined to be rather fast. We accordingly pay our attention to them—stroll by the fine summer evening to hear the sonorous sounds of the band wafting forth its melodious tunes over the rippling dark waves, foaming against the rocky shore; and when we think we have a good opportunity to say a thing or two, and avail ourselves of it, we find, to our discomfiture, that we have made a great mistake, that we have been addressing one of the modest, pure, and well-behaved mothers —or future mothers—of England, and that unless we pay our hotel bill, or settle up our landlady's reckoning next morning, we stand a very good chance of being horsewhipped, or snubbed by our circle of acquaintances at no very remote period; while, in other cases, the winding-up is far different.

We take Mrs. A. or Mrs. B. to be a chaste creature of the highest stamp, and we find that here again we are in the wrong, and that she is mad for flirtations—mad for love.

Reflections similar to those crowded themselves before Hogan's mind, and hence, although he had put down Mrs. Leicester for what she really was, he, nevertheless, could not—in one moment— have pronounced a definitive opinion concerning her, had he been asked to do so.

"Here we are at last," Langdon exclaimed, when he found that he had reached the outside of Mrs. Haltering's house, which was situated somewhere in Brompton—but the exact spot of which it would be anything but wisdom to give here—and the brougham stopped, and Hogan, and Langdon, and Mrs. Leicester alighted.

The coachman ran up to the door; and, ere he had sufficient time to ask the servant whether the lady was within, Mrs. Leicester glided into the hall, followed by Langdon, who lost no time in introducing his friend, Captain Hogan, to Mrs. Haltering, who was too much a woman of the world to betray before anyone the contraiety which she experienced at a stranger being brought in within her roof.

Patrick Langdon had a good deal of tact about him, and he was fully aware that nothing is more awkward for parties who are unknown to each other than to remain face to face without either venturing to say a word.

When Mrs. Leicester, Mrs. Haltering, and the two gentlemen were all sitting together in the drawing-room, which was situated upon the ground-floor, the conversation ran upon the weather.

It is astonishing, though nevertheless true, that a topic which relates either to the warmth of the temperature, or to a total absence of rain, should be the first one which people who have a slight acquaintance of each other should revert to.

There were among the company two ladies and two individuals who could talk when they wished, and the dialogue which soon took place assumed a more spirited turn.

"I did not think you would come after all," Mrs. Haltering began, addressing Mrs. Leicester. "I am expecting a few friends—a few gentlemen and two or three ladies."

"Has Lydia accepted your invitation?" Mrs. Leicester inquired.

"She has," Mrs. Haltering replied. "I am expecting her here to-night, and someone else besides."

"Who is that?"

"Lord Vineyard."

"I thought Lydia would not see him."

"Nonsense, nonsense! A girl like Lydia, who has nothing to rely upon but her beauty, knows when to be silly and when to be reasonable."

"Have they made up their little difference, then?"

"I should say so," Mrs. Haltering replied. "He is ruining himself for the girl. He is awfully fond of the girl. I never saw, in all my experience, such infatuation. But she has got a very bad companion in that Polly."

Mrs. Leicester smiled.

"Who was she? Do you know anything about her? Do you know who brought her out?"

"She is not out yet, but she will soon be," Mrs. Leicester replied, slowly. "I know more about Polly than many people; still, for all that, I do not think that I have a right to speak."

"Who else is coming besides?" Mrs. Leicester inquired again.

Mrs. Haltering, as her answer, took out of a small pocket which was hidden in the folds of her dress a diminutive golden watch, beautifully enamelled and surrounded with precious stones, and she looked at it.

"It is getting late," she said. "I am expecting Mr. Martin Dashwood. He is, generally speaking, very punctual. I wonder what could have detained him. Do you know him?"

"I do not," Mrs. Leicester replied, "but I think Williamson does. They are members of the same club, I believe."

When Mrs. Haltering had mentioned the name of Dashwood, Langdon's blood ran cold in his veins. He was about to sit around the same table as a murderer; and, although there was something exceedingly romantic and out-of-the-way in such a meeting, he by no means relished the perspective which was in store for him.

He had a great mind to plead some excuse and to go away; but curiosity ruled the point with him; and he remained, standing motionless before a small fire which burnt in the grate, and contemplating the burning embers, amidst which his gaze lost itself.

Hogan was looking on the newspaper of the day, which lay carelessly upon the table; and, although he appeared, to all outward appearances, to be deeply interested in the matter before him, his ears were wide opened, and he was listening attentively to the women's conversation.

"I am glad," Mrs. Leicester began, "that Lydia and Lord Vineyard are friendly again; but she is one whom one cannot help feeling a certain interest for; she is so young, too, and so innocent, that she will never do for the life which she is called to lead, unless she finds some fellow to take great care of her."

"I expect her to-night, and, if she comes, she is sure to bring Polly with her. The latter has fastened herself upon Lydia, and she has not the courage, I think, of bidding her to leave her. She has already lent her lots of money, which I fear she will never get."

At that moment the sound of a firm, erect step ascending the stairs was heard, and a gentleman shortly afterwards made his appearance.

It was Martin Dashwood.

The abigail pronounced the name in a clear, smart tone of voice, which caused the whole of the company to rise.

"I hope that you will excuse me if I have kept you waiting, my dear Mrs. Haltering," he said; "but I could not come sooner, being detained in town by an appointment which extended far beyond the limits which I had assigned to it."

Mrs. Leicester and Hogan knew not Martin Dashwood's real character; but one individual did, and this was Langdon. He contemplated

[THE MOCK DUKE.]

the new-comer—to whom he, and his friend, and Mrs. Leicester had been introduced with indescribable amazement.

There stood before him Martin Dashwood.

He was dressed in a tight-fitting, blue frock-coat, which displayed to advantage his slim and well-made figure; and upon his left hand he wore a signet ring, enamelled in black, which contrasted strikingly with the white hue of his small hands; his features, though haughty and disdainful, wore a strange expression about the mouth, and were remarkably handsome and well-formed; his forehead was covered with a profusion of jet curly hair, and his step was as firm as a young man; his eye as keen and as bright as that of an eagle; his whole appearance was more prepossessing than otherwise.

Patrick Langdon could not but think that the revelations which Mrs. Haltering had made to him, had found their birth in her imaginative brain, and could never have occurred, for Martin Dashwood's deportment was such as would have alienated from a casual observer the thought even that he could have been guilty of the crime which he had perpetrated.

The dinner soon followed and passed off quietly, and without an incident worthy of our notice.

Dashwood spoke but little, and the greater part of what he said was addressed to Mrs. Haltering and to Mrs. Leicester, with an occasional word or two with the gentlemen present.

The evening succeeded, and the drawing-room began rapidly to fill with visitors.

Lydia came, accompanied by Lord Vineyard,

and immediately upon her footsteps followed Polly, leaning upon the arm of a diminutive individual, who was, at the utmost, five feet eight in height.

This insignificant little nobody, to all outward appearance, believed that he was known by no one present, except by Lord Vineyard, who had unwisely introduced him to Lydia.

Lord Vineyard had said to his friend that he kept a pretty girl. The latter had intimated the wish that he would like to see her, and both men had shaped their course towards Lydia's residence.

Then Lord Vineyard had met Lydia.

Then the other personage had met Polly.

For want of something better to do, he had remained in her company.

Polly knew not at the time that this little man with a hooked nose, and with a constant stooping gait, was the Duke of Ellingtoun. Had she been made aware of his real rank how differently would she have played her cards from the manner in which she was now doing, for she took no great notice of the duke, and as soon as she entered the drawing-room her gaze fastened upon Martin Dashwood, who was standing with his back to the grate, and upon him it finally rested.

But she did not allow her moves to be witnessed by any one.

She was too politic to compromise herself. Yet, as her eye wandered from one being to another, a sudden spark of inward satisfaction lit up her countenance, and her breast heaved with some indescribable sensation which bid her to hope.

She looked up again, and she beheld Martin Dashwood advancing towards her, and she listened to his talk for upwards of half an hour.

His conversation was strange, his manners original.

Polly appeared to take no heed of what he said, but contented herself to smile significantly.

Meanwhile, Hogan, who knew more about the little man than the latter thought he did, was engaged in close conversation with his grace, and entering into long details about some battles which were supposed to have been won by a general of the same name as that borne by the late private.

While the personages we have taken some trouble to describe were engaged in those little and insignificant chit-chat which form the life of a party, a sound of voices was heard without, and a young girl, accompanied by a youthful gentleman, stepped into the drawing-room.

Mrs. Haltering at once got up.

She walked towards the female new-comer.

"What, Laura, brings you here so late?" she said, addressing the lady. "Why, you are quite a stranger."

"I found it so confoundedly slow at home," the girl replied. "My father is gone asleep for the last two hours in his easy-chair, and my young companion, who is staying a night with us —Sir Percy Hugent—found it so dull—he did not say so, but I knew he did—that I thought I would come and look you up. I had no idea that you had so many friends here, otherwise I should certainly have stopped away."

Laura pronounced her words with a quick overflow. There was such an amount of genuineness and of truth in what she said, that the whole assembly was at once interested by her speech.

Laura was no "horsebreaker"—she was no "outsider."

She is now living in Grosvenor-square. I tell you the truth, reader. Will you doubt me?

At the time we see her she was careless, not innocent; for rather a depraved girl she always was, although, mind you, an acknowledged member of that society which includes all those who have a good income, a good house, respectability, and birth to back them, and she wanted to get married!

A good deal of ambition had Laura Wylde.

Although her father was only a clerk at £800 a year in a Government office—for what is a scribbler but a *clerk*, in all its meaning, be it good or bad?—although he was a red-tape official, gloating in all the *parvenu* conceit of a self-made man—although he stood well with the chairman of his board, still she was but an *employé's* daughter.

And Laura Wylde knew that, felt that, and acknowledged that.

Will I describe her to you, reader?

You may see her now that her dream is accomplished—now that she is married. Driving in the park in an elegant open carriage, of which the cushions are covered with blue satin, with her husband by her side, a stingy, fat, vulgar-looking man, who had nothing to boast of beyond having been born a gentleman, and having lived sufficiently long to drop into over £4,000 a year.

I insist upon those trifling details because they are true ones.

If any of my "fair readers"—let us hope that the greater number will be fair; of course they would read my book *en cachette*, and not openly—have been enjoying wealth's attributes, and, after a long anticipation of an expected crush, found themselves without every-day comforts, will they feel the loss of it?

But we began purporting to describe Laura Wylde; we may—or, at least, I may—just as well do so as not.

Fancy a loving, expressive blue eye, with a deal of vivacity in it.

Surmounting silky eyelashes, a bold high forehead, of which the expansion proclaims intelligence, of which the smoothness, deprived of any wrinkles, bespeaks youth.

Over the forehead lots of wavy, abundant hair, tastefully combed, although apparently straying away anyhow.

Rosy, pouting lips, just shaving "coarseness."

An "idea" of hair just covering lips above described.

White teeth, polished like enamel, which could bite anything, from a nut—a hard nut—to something less hard.

A little chin.

A budding bust, well shaped, slightly, only slightly, protruding.

Small hands, always feverishly warm; nails— we won't say rosy—that is rather a hackneyed word, and although a very good one for authors at a loss for an adjective, we will not use it, and say nails beautifully trimmed.

A small foot, tastefully shod.

From the head we have reverted to the foot.

We once head a story, which goes to this effect. It will not be a long one, so excuse us.

A father and his son were once strolling in the street. The son noticed rather a pretty foot, perhaps too much exposed to man's gaze to suit a governor's taste who always used to attend "Methodist meetings."

"What are you looking at so hard, my boy?"

"The girl's foot, father."

"And why so, child?"

"Because looking at things below, father, places me in mind of things above."

Wise child that!

The above anecdote, we hope, will be a sufficient explanation to our readers for our not explaining, more minutely, Laura Wylde's attractions.

Such was the girl to whom Langdon was to be introduced.

There exists among that species of animals— we are all animals in the creation—a kind of intuition which is occasionally felt by some, and which any pen would fail to describe.

That kind of intuition was felt by Langdon.

When Mrs. Haltering spoke to the new-comer, and called her Laura, Langdon's heart beat high.

That was the girl whom he was to marry.

Nice thing for him to get hold of.

A young wife, some education, rather good looks, a good deal of "winning beauty," a girl upon whom you could get "spooney;" when another, combining the features of one of Raphael's "Virgins" with the model of one of Canova's busts, would produce no effect, all for the want of that sly roguishness, of that *je ne sais quoi* which would cause a man to do for a woman what a woman would have been ready to do for a man. (We forget what it was, something great, true, sublime.) If we refer to the Right Hon. Mr. Whiteside's speech, M.P., in the Irish law courts, when standing before a full bench—before one of the most crowded audiences which ever filled a court of justice—he defended the honour, and compelled public opinion to bestow upon a woman that reward which the dry substance—the plain meaning of the law—has, after many weeks, many months, many years of protracted trial, at length denied to her.

Langdon looked at Laura Wylde.

The meeting at the Exhibition—that rendezvous upon which he had set up his mind—would not have to be undergone.

He thought so, yet he was mistaken.

Frightened, abashed by the numerous guests around her, Laura Wylde did not stop long.

She went away before Langdon had had an opportunity of being introduced in a legitimate, proper way.

She left, accompanied by young Sir Percy Hugent.

He thought he had no chance—it was all up with him.

Yet that evening at Mrs. Haltering's was productive of a great many results.

It was the means of beginning a great many adventures which we will describe.

It began the acquaintance between a noble duke and "a rank outsider."

That night Polly, while driving home, was muttering to herself, "This Martin Dashwood, I think, has taken a great fancy to me. I am very much mistaken if he has not. Where can it lead me to, I wonder? I will think of it."

On his side, also, Martin Dashwood was thinking a good deal about Polly.

Poor Langdon was annoyed, vexed, disappointed.

He had had a chance of hitting upon a girl with some money, and then she was already caught in the nets of an Irish baronet.

What is to follow—what was to follow?

CHAPTER XVI.

WHERE A WORTHY TRADESMAN IS INTRODUCED TO OUR READERS, AND WHERE WE MAKE THE ACQUAINTANCE OF THE WHOLE FAMILY, AND HEAR SOMETHING ABOUT SOMEONE WE ALREADY KNOW.

SINCE Mrs. Haltering's party, a few weeks had elapsed.

During those few weeks a great many events, which it will be our duty to describe in due course had taken place.

Availing ourselves of the privilege which authors possess (and which dramatists have abused by compelling the reader to fancy that, during the short space which occurs between the fall and the rise of the curtain, thirty years have or can elapse), we intend not to make of our novel a daily journal of the deeds performed by the characters of it, as many would, doubtless, be devoid of interest, and thereby be burthensome to the perusers.

We all know that Rome was not built in a day.

We all know that everything requires time, and that, in a few hours only, Polly could not have risen from the condition where she was to the lucky part which, we shall see, she was called upon to perform.

The following may seem improbable to our readers; yet it is, nevertheless, true.

Dashwood had felt for Polly an unaccountable craving; and it would be odd, strange, miraculous indeed, if, out of Dashwood's fortune—out of the money which he had obtained in the manner which he had done—out of the blood and the lives of his wives—she was to carve her own precarious fortune.

If Murder was to help Prostitution, and the former be means of raising the latter to an altar of demoniac eminence, before which the dissipated golden youth of the day were to pay their homages. Some of those who read this romance may not believe the story which we have related in a previous number,* concerning the cold-blooded way with which Dashwood had rid himself of many wives, whom he had only married for the sake of their dowry.

But as quietly and truly as the incident is told was the deed perpetrated.

Perhaps some of my readers may remember Palmer.

When strolling on the race-course, or shaking hands in a friendly and gentlemanly way with all the wealthiest patrons of the turf, to whom he was well known, could anyone have believed that he was guilty of the foul charge which was subsequently brought against him?

And yet it is generally believed that one-half of Palmer's crimes were never found out, and that he carried to the grave with him many a deep secret, which the warm lime which was poured on his inanimate form destroyed for ever.

Doubtless, could there have been a prophesying gipsy, who could have read the brain of man as well as some of them are said to read the careers of others from a close inspection of the hand, and had this gipsy sawed the top of the head from the culprit's body, and minutely examined the cerebrum, would not the revelations have been worth the highest price that can be given for detection of crime?

* See No. 4 of OUTSIDERS OF SOCIETY.

What we have related is true—after this we will say no more.

At the period at which this chapter begins, there was in existence, and there is still, in Bond-street, a jeweller's shop, which was patronized then—and may be so now, for aught we know—by the "world," and which, if reference is made to the Upper Ten Thousand Glossary, will be found to mean the circle of fashionable people when in town.

In that shop, generally speaking, were to be found two men.

They were constantly at work, indefatigable in their business.

The oldest of the two was Mr. Webster, jeweller, and proprietor of the whole stock on hand, which was worth thousands of pounds. He was about fifty-two or fifty-three years of age, and his countenance, which was blooming and rubicond, displayed those outward marks which are to be traced upon the features of a thriving tradesman, who was, to use a common phrase, the architect of his own fortune; and who, in his own way, of course, was thoroughly happy, being satisfied with himself, with the rattling trade which he did, and the commercial standing which he had attained.

The other person, who seemed to be as careful of his appearance as if he had to make half-a-dozen morning calls upon the fashionable inmates of the mansions which surrounded his place of business, and who was the identical reproduction of his father thirty years ago, with the exception that he knew a good deal more at fifteen than his father did at twenty-five, was Mr. Webster, junior.

Mr. Webster, senior, was the kindest of men whom you could meet, with a heart which was ever opened; he was also of a very weak character, and it was a wonder to all those who knew him how, considering everything, he had got on so well.

Alike all men who are aware that they are deficient in certain things, he wished, if possible, to make all those who surrounded him think that he was quite the contrary of what one would have taken him to be.

He thus endeavoured not only to belie his own nature, but also he wished others to believe him of a very strong mind.

The morning we see him it was about nine o'clock in the forenoon.

He was standing in his back parlour, with a frowning brow, a mouth slightly compressed, his left elbow holding up his head.

In his right hand he held a pen, so as to be ready to take a copy on flying leaves, which were close to him, of any particulars which were written in a ledger or commercial book, which he was pondering upon.

Mr. Webster had been turning the pages of his book for some time; occasionally he would give a sigh, which sounded very much like a grunt, while his son was giving orders to a young assistant to brush this and to brush that, to make this glass more shining, and to dust the chairs which were here and there.

"Arthur," the father began, after he had concluded his inspection, "I see that we have a good many old, standing accounts; you may look them up by by-and-by."

Arthur—or, at least, Mr. Webster, junior—replied in the affirmative, and took up the book which his father had just been handling.

"Are you aware, father," he said, "that Lord Vineyard's account is getting every day more heavy? Do you wish him to be supplied as long as he desires with goods, and am I to understand, father, that he is supposed to have unlimited credit here?"

To this question, Webster, senior, knew not what answer to make.

He wished, we have already said, to convey to people who did not know him the idea that it was only by the most unflinching severity that business could be carried out; and, habitually, he was wont to reply to his son's queries in a rough and abrupt manner, thereby endeavouring to show him that he should display his fatherly authority if necessary to do so, and if he thought fit.

He looked at his son.

The latter was a young man of twenty-five years at the utmost; he was of a height above the average; his manners were those of a West-end tradesman; and, let it be confessed, education goes so much towards remedying the vulgar tendencies inherent to humble birth, that a great many assistants could give some of our young swells—some of our young blood—who will take no valuable hint, many a useful lesson.

His features, although in no ways regular, were far from inducing a stranger to look upon Mr. Webster, junior, as a bad-looking fellow; and any one who would have seen him would have taken him to be one of those honest, candid, and upright individuals who think that honesty, uprightness, and Christian virtues are the necessary acquirements for one to get on in this world, and who accordingly abide by such principles.

"I would not have mentioned the matter to you, father," Arthur began, "did I not think that of late his lordship has, perhaps, no idea of the amount to which his bill is running up. His lordship has been in town the greater part of the winter, and now that the daughters are coming up to town again, it will still run higher and higher."

"Arthur," replied Mr. Webster, senior, "I am bery grateful to you, my boy, for having brought the matter forward, but you know, my boy, that it is not without a few losses that I have attained my present position."

While Mr. Webster spoke his son never said a word—never, even, ventured to pass any opinion, for he was too confident in his father to know that no one could speak to his worthy pater-familias in anything which related to matters of business, and more particularly relating to a concern in which he had embarked all that which he possessed, his intelligence, and whatever capital he had.

Although Webster, senior, wished, we have already said, to induce his son to believe him of an austere disposition, the manner in which he pronounced "my boy" at two different intervals was quite sufficient to convince him that he had a parent who would have gone through fire and water for his son.

"Is the amount a large one, then?" the father inquired.

Many people may fancy that it should sound rather curious that the principal should not know to what extent those against whom they have any claim are indebted to them.

They may have some vague knowledge about it, but when that is said it is about all.

But, as we wish to throw light upon everything, we will show from what source such ignorance springs.

Tradesmen who do a large business, and who are freely patronized by those who have a good deal of money to lavish, are so much taken up with the details of their special calling, that they can very seldom spare sufficient time to dive into accounts, about which many would not understand much were they to inquire into the credit, debit, sundries, profit and loss, cash, and all the multifarious books which form part of a merchant's book-keeping.

The consequences are, therefore, these—that they trust entirely to hired book-keepers, and rely upon them for accurate and detailed statements of all they have spent and earned at the end of the month or year.

Mr. Webster, junior, in this instance, was the book-keeper, and, although the father looked over the accounts, he might just as well have never touched them for the good he did.

In reply to his father Arthur Webster had gone to the parlour as he was in the act of searching the page where he would find the whole of Lord Vineyard's account minutely detailed.

In less than two minutes the son came forward with a big, heavy book, which he held in his hand partly opened.

"Lord Vineyard has given orders," the son said, looking over the book which he had brought, and which he laid open upon one of the glass cases which stood beneath him in the shop, "to have two separate accounts."

"Two separate accounts ?"

"Yes, father."

"Are you sure you are not mistaken ? "

"Here it is, father. Figures are stubborn things, and error is impossible."

This answer caused the old jeweller to think.

"See," he said, after a while, "what the respective amounts are."

"The first account is over eighteen months' standing. No, it is not," Webster pursued, turning over one leaf and then another, and referring to three or four small entry-books that he had under his hand. "The first account extends beyond two years back."

"How much is that ? " the father inquired, with authority.

"Two thousand, seven hundred, and eighty-two pounds, and sixteen shillings and no pence," the son replied, with the quickness and confidence which business people will assume when giving an answer concerning that which they are perfectly certain of.

"Did you ever send in the bill for that amount, Arthur ? "

"I did not, father. Your instructions to me were plain enough when I entered into partnership — which were, to wait our customers' pleasure, and never to annoy them by dunning them for what they owed."

The worthy tradesman bit his lips. He was uncertain whether he would blame or praise his son.

It was evident that he had fairly no cause to call him to account for any carelessness.

"And what is the other account ? " his father pursued, peremptorily.

"Would you see to that now, father ? It has been but very recently opened."

"Never mind about that. As we are looking over Lord Vineyard's liabilities to us, we may as well, while we are about it, go through it all, and have done with it."

Less than an instant sufficed to the young man to carry out the last part of his father's injunctions.

With that rapidity which is inherent to those who are accustomed to calculation he glanced over his ledger.

"I make the last account seven thousand pounds, father."

"Seven thousand pounds on one side, and how much on the other ? " the father inquired, anxiously.

"Two thousand, seven hundred, eighty-two pounds, and sixteen shillings," the son replied coolly, glancing again over another page in his book, not venturing to trust to his memory when an important matter like the one in point was at stake.

The father mused for a while.

"Arthur, look again ; you must be making a mistake," he began slowly.

"I am not, father."

"Will you obey your father when he speaks ? " the jeweller exclaimed, in a tone which showed that, although his worthy offspring was in noways to blame, the information which he had received was anything but calculated to smooth his temper.

"Nine thousand, seven hundred, eighty-two pounds, and sixteen shillings, eh ? " Mr. Webster muttered to himself. "By George ! I could not believe —— Why, I will never get that amount. Lord Vineyard is scarcely worth that income in two years ! "

"And are you sure, Arthur, of what you state?" the jeweller ejaculated. "Let me see the book myself."

The young man complied with his father's request.

"And how long since the last account is opened ? " the father inquired.

"Not above two months."

"Did you sell him the goods, Arthur ? "

"I know this, father," the son replied, "that yourself sold him the tiara of diamonds for which you refused two thousand pounds. I attended upon him myself on several other occasions."

"So did I, father, another voice pursued. "And I sold him the remainder, father ; at least it was not for him, but for rather a pretty girl, who has often driven with him here of late."

The person who had pronounced the last words happened to be the tradesman's daughter.

"It was one of his daughters, I suppose ; very dashing girls they are, too, the ladies Wester," Mr. Webster pursued. "But lately they must have been taken with what the French would call *un vertige d'extravagance*, to run in two months a bill three times as large as that which they incurred in two years."

"It was not any of the Ladies Wester who came here with Lord Vineyard," another voice pursued, "and the sooner you send your bill in the better for your sake and that of your children, Mr. Webster. Lord Vineyard lately has gone mad, and he has become quite enamoured with a little vicious creature who is anything but good-looking, and who came here the other day with a girl she called Polly. You were out, Mr. Webster—oh ! of course, instead of attending to your business—out galavanting somewhere or another. Lucy was in the parlour, and I strongly forbid her to have herself contaminated by two girls whom they now call 'horsebreakers,' or some name of that kind, and instead of attending to his mother, instead of allowing me to induce them to buy, why, Mr. Arthur was smiling at them; yes, he was bowing and scraping, and I am sure if it had been the Duchess of Cambridge, of the Duchess of Argylle, or the Duchess of Sutherland, or any other of our proud aristocrats, he could not have been more civil to them."

Here the lady drew her breath, and went on quickly for fear of being interrupted in her rapid discourse.

"And you complain, Mr. Webster! Well, you may do so. I hope that you will never get a sixpence, sir; no, not a sixpence, sir! Serve you right; yes, it will; and you will bring us all to the workhouse, at the rate at which you are going, I know you will; yes, I see it all. Allowing £7,000 debt to be incurred here, without any certainty of payment; oh!"

"Do not be too nervous, my dear Lotty," replied Mr. Webster, in a calm, collected manner; "we have not sent in the account yet, and I do not see why it should not be paid."

"Well, I do—I do," the lady replied. "No luck will ever attend a man who keeps a girl like the one I saw here the other day. Why, I am sure she is younger than Miss Adell Wester—and the old man ought to be ashamed of himself."

Mrs. Webster, who had just spoken in the manner described—her temper causing her tongue to give way at once to a great many remarks which she should not have pronounced before a girl of her daughter's age, whom we will shortly describe—was a woman of about forty years of age, for whom the quietude of a laborious and of an honestly-spent life had still preserved many of her youthful attractions. Although, if she had not on her soft cheeks that rosy tinge that sets so well upon the features of a girl of eighteen or nineteen, and which render women so attractive, she possessed, in all its bloom, that majesty of mature womanhood which has also its admirers.

But for the absence of youth, Mrs. Webster—who in all respects was nearly as pretty as her daughter—they would have been taken for sisters; and, had it not been for a very bad temper—of which we have seen a specimen—she would have been a very amiable woman.

Her eyes had lost nothing of their former brilliancy, and possessed a warm, loving expression.

Her forehead was still surmounted by a fine head of luxuriant dark hair—her waist, it is true, was not so slim as it was years ago, but the faultless symmetry, and her hands, feet, and ankles had not altered.

Many women in society are considered good-looking, and pride themselves upon their beauty, but it would have been an insult to compare Mrs. Webster to any of them.

It was, however, easy to perceive that Mrs. Webster had no pretensions to appear handsome; and that she owed entirely her "style" and her personal attractions to the immense care which she took of herself, and not to any wish to captivate the attention of the motley mixture of nobility and vulgarism—of fashion and frailty—which daily visited her shop.

Had Mrs. Webster been one of those coquetish women like there are so many—clinging to those charms which the steady course of time will snatch away from them with a merciless hand, with all the pertinacious stubbornness of the bitterest disappointment—she would have found in her daughter a dangerous rival, whom she should have sent far away from her if she did not wish to be gulled by the daily performance of that which she knew—that, however handsome a woman may be, if she has to contend with her equal in beauty and her superior in youth, the odds on behalf of the latter are too great to fight a battle, where the most studied cleverness would not ensure a success, and which the rival has already gained beforehand.

CHAPTER XVII.

WHERE WE ARE STILL WITH MR. WEBSTER'S FAMILY—WHICH DESCRIBES LUCY TO OUR READERS, AND ACQUAINTS THEM WITH THE CHARACTER AND IDEAS OF THE MAN WHOM SHE THINKS SHE LOVES—AND WHICH TELLS ONE OR TWO THINGS WHICH CANNOT BE OMITTED.

FOR, in truth, Miss Webster was what we would call man's dream of female beauty.

Tall, slim, superbly modelled, she combined in one being the majesty of a queen with the gracefulness of a nymph.

Her countenance possessed that faultless rigidity of design which is too often but a splendid mark to deceive the observer, and which hides beneath reproachless features a hollow mind; a heart as cold as ice, out of which the noblest feelings can be squeezed as easily and as quickly as the drops of water out of a damp sponge.

With the tradesman's daughter it was not so.

Her fertile and thoughtful imagination was betrayed by the expansion of her forehead. The first budding of woman's passions could be traced in her fiery and superb glance. The pure thoughts which occasionally she indulged into enlivened her smile. She was an angel; she was more than an angel—she was a woman, beautiful and lovely!

Could we call her a woman?

She was only entering into her eighteenth year.

For one of that age she was an unfathomable mixture.

When occupied, when engaged in some task set to her by her parents, she would take fits and starts of an unaccountable buoyancy.

In the morning, she would run with all the innocence and carelessness of a pensioner out for a week's holiday; at night, she would be all deep thought—her mind would be wrapped up in her own reveries.

Had she been asked, "What are you thinking of, my girl?" she would have replied, "I do not know; I am not thinking of anything very particular, father."

And the conversation would be ended there; and the girl would have thought again, and the father and mother, the former would have read the evening's paper, the latter would have looked with deep love upon that daughter whose fate she knew not what it was to be; while Arthur Webster would be smoking his cigar in Regent-street, and occasionally dropping into one of the night *cafés* to have a glass of liquor previous to returning to his father's home at a steady hour.

But Lucy was, perhaps, in love.

"Eighteen! glorious eighteen! blissful eighteen! Golden period of life, where hast thou fled?"

Then life is not irksome; then one looks forward to the many years which await the hopeful minds of those who, at eighteen, fancy that they will never grow old. The world is before them—the wide, wide world is opened to them—to walk either to glory, to fame, to wealth—to disgrace, to naught, to poverty.

At eighteen, the cares of a family are never dreamt of.

At eighteen, everything smiles before us.

Lucy was happy; but there was constantly before her eyes the picture of a young gentleman to whom her brother, with the parents' consent, had introduced her.

He was an artist.

He had studied in Rome.

He had exhibited portraits—likenesses of noble scions of old families.

He had obtained a golden medal at one of the French Exhibitions.

He was a member of the Royal Academy of Paintings.

The photographing system had, it is true, done a good deal towards destroying the prospects of his profession; still, he was but a beginner, and he was doing remarkably well.

Her brother was wont to tell her that he made three hundred pounds a year, which, for a young man, is a very good income.

How had he managed to do so?

Had he toiled hard?

Yes; nights and days, without ceasing.

Had Providence helped him?

Providence!

Does the world acknowledge that Providence will help a man to fame, to wealth, when he has principles? when he has a good heart? when he believes in One above, if he does not go to church, to listen to the neighbouring clergyman—to lend an attentive ear to the reverend and fashionable Mr. So-and-so, who preached so well last Sunday night?—Oh! you should have heard him!—such flowing sentences!—he makes such an appeal to the heart! I expect he collected a very round sum; but what a bore (everything one dislikes, *see* Fashionable Vocabulary) it is that the place is so crowded! Why does he not build a larger place? I will mention it to him. If Lady —— would only exert herself, I daresay she would manage to have the money he wants subscribed. It would be very considerate if she did. I hope she will; and so on.—If one does not wish to go to church, to act at variance with what the world bids us to do, it is, to a certain extent, all up.

Therefore, it could not be Providence who helped the artist to comfort.

It was Luck.

What's luck? I wish some one would define it to me.

Luck means success. Luck means everything which goes to show that one successful being has baffled the opinion that others held of him.

If a sportsman, with a horse apparently not up to stay the course, whose public form has been on the decline, wins a good handicap, to the great astonishment of all, at some unexpected moment.

If a man, in a few years, makes a fortune where others have failed.

If a solicitor of parliamentary favours obtains some good appointment under the Crown.

If a pauper marries a woman with money.

If a broken-down publisher starts a good thing.

If a stupid author without any education—whose phrases are full of grammatical errors—earns about thirty or forty pounds a week in writing penny numbers.

If a designing swindler goes through the Court of Bankruptcy to wipe off his liabilities, and obtain protection and a first-class discharge.

If a son of an old family is suddenly rid of incumbrances in the shape of living parents to whom he must pay off certain annuities, by their dropping off one after the other.

If an officer obtains his company through the death of a superior in command.

If a husband loses a wife who he is sick of.

If a man does a little swindle, and gets out of the scrape, and is discharged "without a stain on his character."

What then?

These individuals who have acted, or are acting, through too great a respect for "Mammon," and whose different little games have been slightly hinted at, are called "lucky."

Lucky is the word; but "luck"—what does "luck" mean?

The above relates to men.

Was Lydia?

Was Polly?

Was Lucy, the jeweller's daughter, lucky?

She thought so within her own mind as she gazed upon a pretty bracelet around her soft, snowy wrist.

She was looking at it, and her eye was riveted upon it, when her attention was attracted towards the door.

She was alone in the shop.

Messrs. Webster and Son had retired to make up Lord Vineyard's account, which they would forward to him, with a very polite request to pay —one of those civil epistles which West-end tradesmen only can write.

I remember once I received a letter from one of the fashionable Sackville-street tailors in Piccadilly.

It is, perhaps, no recommendation to say that within it there was a very well-written intimation to a little bill which had been standing for over three years.

I read it, and I must admit that if the author had not been a tailor, one of the same as Muller's, about whose guilt or no guilt the world may be said to use Shakspere's words—

"With open mouth swallowing a tailor's news,"

he might very probably have aspired to the same well-deserved reputation which Madame de Sevigné obtained by her perfect style of correspondence.

But to conclude. Was it luck, or was it Providence, that had helped the artist, the painter, to whom Lucy Webster had been introduced by her brother?

To this we will reply. It was mainly Providence; it was his "luck," which, backed by his own exertions, had enabled him to obtain an independence which, with his talents, would solve for him the highest dream of a young artist, the crowning pinnacle towards which all those that labour by their brain look forward to with unceasing ambition—namely, honour and fame.

But the portrait-painter had that which many cannot obtain—an intellectual head, bespeaking intelligence; a gray eye, which spoke volumes; the gait and demeanour of a gentleman, which can be acquired by those to whom a continental education has thought the immense superiority of the English system; who have freely mingled in all societies, where their talent, if not their birth, gives them admission, and who have known how to behave themselves when again opportunity has been offered them to improve themselves.

The artist's name was not a very aristocratic one. He belonged to a stock which must have been rather prolific in former days, for there were many bearing the same name as himself.

Mr. Browne was the painter about whom Lucy thought so often.

He had known that he had his way to make in the world.

He had seen many of his schoolfellows, with talents which none could deny, with abilities which could be called universal, who would take a sketch, and make up two or three sticks of matter for the printer to fill up a page at the last moment.

He could not have done so; he could paint, and that was all, but he flattered himself that he could do that, and do it well.

Everything requires study—he had studied.

Rarely did Browne spend a few of his precious hours to the life which he dreamt of—seldom did he go to any public place of entertainment.

He felt that the corn should be mowed when it is ripe, and he would not let the product of his harvest be destroyed through his own procrastination and delay.

Frequently he received invitations to balls and parties, tea-fights, routs, where the commercial community will take the greatest pains to ape the aristocracy by which they live.

What people call society had been up to this present period but a name to him. But it was a name which he wished to blend with his own—to awake one morning to find himself famous. He looked upon it as a wide arena, where, alike the Roman gladiators of old, he would fearlessly fight, and, by the sweat of his brow, if not by shedding his blood, receive the reward which public opinion will bestow to fame, in a voice which sounds much louder, which lasts much longer, than the loud acclamations of the thousands and thousands of eager spectators in the circus.

But let it not be thought that he studied not as deeply without as within; that he sought not knowledge everywhere he could find it; among the proud families where his profession called him; in the drawing-room when occasionally, but seldom, he delighted to put in an appearance; in the theatre, when with some of his literary friends he would stray forth.

From all these he wanted but a few things, a few well-earned plaudits, an acknowledgment that he was clever. Wealth he heeded not. This was a secondary consideration, which the artist never thought of; provided he had sufficient to keep him like a gentleman, he was satisfied.

Ideas, praiseworthy, noble promptings of a youthful heart, of an anxious aspirant to honour, which would also soon dwindle away when thirty would come—when mature age, a warning of gray hair, a warning of decrepitude, of sickness, which make one then long for something more substantial than was the artist's dream at the time when he became acquainted with Lucy Webster.

When Lucy had first met Mr. Browne—anything but a romantic name—although Sir George Browne in *La Dame Blanche*, one of the prettiest operas we have—plays rather a noble and prominent part there—although the name of Browne with an *e* is borne by some of the highest Irish families of the land, namely, the Sligos, the Kilmaines, the Oranmore, still it was not one which would have suited a wayward and romantic imagination like that of a pure girl ought to be.

Well, then, to resume.

When Lucy had first met Mr. Browne he had come to visit her brother.

"In one minute," had replied Mr. Webster, junior, "I will be with you, Browne;" and without saying another word he had gone to fetch his hat, and had joined his companion.

It was evening when Browne called upon Webster.

Nevertheless, in the semi-darkness which reigned, the artist had thought that he had seen a sweet vision, who appeared and who had disappeared swiftly and rapidly, causing the painter to muse about angels' visits and such like as he took his companion's arm.

The next thing which had occurred had been a sly offer on Mr. Browne's part for an order at the opera. Some fellow had promised one to him, a private box at Her Majesty's Theatre; would he, Webster's father, accept of it? was Mrs. Webster fond of music? His sister might like to spend an evening there. It was under new management. Next Saturday was to be a great night.

We need not say that the offer was accepted, and the artist requested to favour the worthy family with his company.

All this had been done in an off-hand manner, and no more was thought about it—except by the artist—except by Lucy—who many a time remembered the pleasant evening which she spent—treasured in her tastefully-decorated bedroom the faded flowers, which she had preserved from the new bouquet which Mr. Browne had so respectfully offered to her.

The artist remembered his travels abroad; he had rather a memory which served him, and he never forgot any incident.

He had contemplated with a student's earnestness the features of some of those sublime Madonnas—of some Weeping Virgins—masterpieces which had been delineated by great Roman masters, inspired by their religious feelings, their pencils guided upon the canvas by the invisible power of genius.

He had pondered on Dutch landscapes.

He had seen life in pictures. Life in reality.

Yet all these things dwindled away from his mind; and, while he mixed his pencil in the oil, he thought of a girl. From his recollection he had made this portrait of Lucy. He had presented it to the mother, and refused haughtily a remuneration which had been offered.

Lucy had thanked Mr. Browne.

In reply, he had said that he would give her a little miniature of herself.

She had willingly accepted it.

It was a tasty design; and, although small, the minutest delineaments of her handsome countenance had been minutely and faithfully reproduced.

That likeness of her own self had been set in a bracelet; and, as Lucy as yet had had no token of friendship, or, perhaps, a softer feeling from the artist, she always wore that "bracelet."

Yet they had never told each other that they loved each other.

Mrs. Webber was an extraordinary woman.

She had her prejudices against artists.

She believed that they were a "bad set;" and, although the idea that Mr. Browne's intentions could not be but honourable—from the few words

["I WILL NOT GO WITH YOU."]

which she had said relating to Mr. Browne—Lucy had never dared to rush into her mother's arms and to tell her, in her innocent language, the deep impression that the painter had made upon her young heart.

Matters rested thus.

The monotony of the shop was Lucy's lot.

She dreamt of the artist more than once.

Would she ever be his?

Although darkness would surround, she would feel her cheeks heated with a powerful blush; and in the morning she would appear to breakfast like one who has spent a restless night, and she would fear to encounter her mother's gaze.

Meanwhile the door of the shop had opened.

A lady and a gentleman entered.

It was Polly and Martin Dashwood.

It would have been difficult to recognise in the stylish girl now before us, accompanied by the handsome "woman-killer" (we do not wish to give to these last two words their facetious meaning, but we hope our readers will remember their terrible and ghastly signification), the coster-girl who, but a few weeks ago, had to put up with the insults of her companion, Charley Wood—of that drunken, besotted, low, drunken churl, whom we will, perhaps, see again when the time comes.

Beautifully attired was Polly, and in contemplating—

"That form, replete with loveliness and mind,"

to all outward appearance, of course, but with a

vicious, wicked, demoniac imagination, now a worthy child of Satan, strange thoughts would have occurred to those who, like ourselves, know the gutter from which she sprung, had been led through the vile, filthy, poverty atmosphere where she formerly dwelt, to see her again appear radiant, blooming, gloating over her success, systematically graduating through all the phases of a gay woman's career.

Lucy, the pure, lovely, innocent tradesman's daughter, was struck with an undefinable feeling when she allowed her limpid eye to rest upon that girl, who was doubtless about to make some extravagant purchase, and who she soon remembered when she heard Dashwood addressing her by the familiar name of "Poll."

CHAPTER XVIII.

WHICH SHOWS POLLY'S TASTE FOR EXPENDITURE— AND WHERE SHE IS INTRODUCED TO MARTIN DASHWOOD'S HOME—WITH A DESCRIPTION OF SAME.

WHEN Polly had entered the shop, she looked around, scrutinizing everything she saw, in the hope that her gaze might rest upon some expensive ornament which would gratify her fancy.

Unable to make up her mind as to what she would buy within so short a period, she walked towards the spot where Lucy, standing in a noble attitude, was awaiting the horsebreaker's commands.

Dashwood placed a chair by Polly's side, and the girl soon sat upon it.

"I wish to see," Polly began, "some of your newest and latest patterns in the shape of rings and bracelets. Price is no object, and the better finished the articles the better will I like them."

Dashwood smiled when he heard his companion speak; but, as he had brought the girl with him, he was perfectly willing to allow her to place him to whatever expense she thought proper.

It is extraordinary what a pleasure those who are born in a higher sphere of life take in mingling with those women who are thrown before their path—and as numerous instances tell us, the lower their origin, the more dissolute their habits, the greater will be their success—the mightier their triumph.

It was only on very rare occasions that Lucy was called to wait upon the customers who visited her father's establishment. Had she acted as he would have wished her to, she would at once have gone to warn him of the presence of two strangers, so as to make him and her brother to come and attend to them.

But we are told that forbidden fruit is sweet to the taste—that had it not been the case the first woman that ever lived would not have allowed herself to be tempted by the serpent, and thus it was with the tradesman's daughter.

She had seen Polly before, accompanied by Lydia and her mother. Mrs. Webster had been so particular in wishing her not to be contaminated by breathing the same air as that inhaled by the two horsebreakers, that now that she had found an opportunity to look fixedly at Polly, she gladly availed herself of it.

She was pure, Lucy was!—and although we may fairly say that her innocence was that of a spotless virgin, yet she found an indescribable interest in waiting upon Polly, whose character was known to her.

So without delaying more than she possibly could, Lucy opened the glass-case which stood immediately beneath her, and from it she withdrew some of the tastiest ornaments that one could have wished to possess.

"This is the latest thing out, madam," the tradesman's daughter began, presenting a very beautifully ornamented bracelet to the horsebreaker.

It was a bracelet beautifully chased. Upon the front part of it there was designed a horseshoe with two large, sparkling diamonds in the middle, surrounded by pearls, turquoises, and other precious stones.

"What is the price of this?" Polly inquired, taking the article in her hand and examining it carefully.

"A hundred guineas, madam," Lucy replied, in a cool, business sort of way.

Polly placed the bracelet upon one side.

"I think," she said, "I will buy this; I rather fancy it."

Lucy bowed respectfully, like she always did when a bargain was concluded.

"You also spoke about some rings, did you not? What kind would you like?"

"What is most worn now."

The tradesman's daughter required no further information.

Swiftly she wound her steps to another corner of the room, and in an instant came back with a variety of rings.

It would be useless here to dwell too minutely upon the common-place conversation which ensued. Let it be sufficient to state that Polly chose one thing and then another, and that after she had been in the place about twenty or thirty minutes Dashwood found himself minus of a hundred and seventy pounds, which he duly paid to Mr. Webster, junior, who happened to enter the room when the reckoning had been presented to him.

Polly was about to leave the shop with the parcel in her hand, when her gaze rested rather fixedly upon the miniature of Lucy's portrait, which we have already said she ever wore.

It was a tasty design, and could not but attract notice.

"I beg your pardon," Polly began, ere she went, "if I make rather a strange request to you. During the time which I have been here I have been looking at that very pretty likeness of yours. Would you mind letting me look at it?"

Lucy felt proud to see that Mr. Brown's talents were acknowledged by all, and within her own mind, she was certainly resolved to tell him, when she would see him again, that one and all coincided in admiring his paintings.

"This is not the first time," Lucy began, her eye sparkling with a beam of natural pleasure, her cheek flushed with an innocent blush, "that a similar request has been made to me. A great many ladies have already asked me to show them this bracelet, and some of them have been so struck with it, that the artist who did it has received, by this out-of-the-way means, many an order to paint portraits, which he doubtless otherwise would never have got."

Thus speaking, Lucy was handing the ornament to the horsebreaker.

Dashwood glanced at it also.

"This is very well done," he said. "Is the artist to be seen daily?"

"Mr. Brown is a friend of mine," Mr. Webster

now exclaimed, stepping towards Dashwood and Polly; "and I have no doubt but what he will be very happy to attend to any order which you might give him."

Polly looked at the speaker.

"Give me the artist's address, will you?" she said, after awhile. "Dashwood, you and I will go and pay him a visit. What say you if I get my likeness done? I think he is clever." And as she spoke, Polly returned the miniature to the tradesman's daughter, who was too gratified at what had taken place to be able to say a word in reply.

Mr. Webster again, in the meantime, had ran to his clerk, and he soon returned with a slip of paper upon which he had written the artist's direction.

Polly thanked Mr. Webster for his information, and having taken Dashwood's arm, the two beings emerged from the shop into the street, where a handsome brougham awaited them.

"Where shall I drive, sir?" the servant in livery inquired.

"Home," Dashwood replied, and the vehicle rattled onwards.

The distance was soon cleared, and the brougham stayed its course before a large four-storied house, of which the outward appearance was bleak and dreary.

It was situated in the outskirts of London, and it stood prominently in the midst of a large field which was totally uncultivated.

A carriage drive, apparently recently made, led to the door.

"Oh! I wish," Polly said, "you would leave this horrid place, Dashwood, and go and live more in the centre of the town. Although I have never been here before, the sight of this place frightens me already, I do not know why."

"What reason have you got to complain?" Dashwood inquired, peremptorily; "have I not told you that I will furnish a house for you shortly, and take you away from those lodgings of yours in Pimlico? You are never satisfied. I spent nearly two hundred pounds upon you to-day, and you are grumbling already. This is encouraging, to be sure."

There was something so mysterious, so cool, and so determined in Dashwood's manner that although Polly believed herself to be strong-minded, instinctively she said not another word.

When Polly and Dashwood entered the house they found themselves in a large hall, at the end of which could be seen a flight of handsomely carved steps, which led to the upper apartments.

Polly looked at the hall-porter who had received them. He was deaf and dumb, and he bowed nearly to the ground when Dashwood appeared.

"I have now known you for some weeks, Polly," he said, "and you ought to deem it a great favour, on my part, to admit you to my residence. Not a living soul ever enters here except my servants, who are all deaf and dumb, and my victims."

Dashwood pronounced the last word in a sinister tone of voice, and if Polly had looked towards him she would have perceived that his lip curled suddenly with a sarcastical, cruel smile.

CHAPTER XIX.

WHERE DASHWOOD'S RESIDENCE IS MINUTELY DE-SCRIBED—WHERE SOME LIGHT UPON HIS REAL CHARACTER MAY BE THROWN—AND WHERE POLLY SEES A GOOD DEAL MORE THAN SHE EXPECTED.

PREVIOUS to ascending the staircase which led upstairs, Dashwood shook nervously Polly's arm, and conducted her through a pair of baized folding doors into a large waiting-room.

While there he remained motionless and silent, listening attentively only to endeavour to detect any sounds which might reach his ears.

Having found that all was still, he began thus:—"Polly, you are the girl of my choice. I can read through you. You are young, vicious, depraved, and you will repay me for the manner in which I have acted towards you with the most infamous ingratitude. You have no feelings; you never had beyond than to satisfy the cravings of the most brutal passions. Although you tell me that you love me, I know inwardly that you hate me. Am I right?"

Polly looked boldly in Dashwood's face.

"You are!" she said. "But who are you? What are you? What can you be to read thus in woman's mind?"

"You want to know too much all at once, Polly," Dashwood replied. "I will, however, give you a chance of betraying me, if you like; but if you do, your punishment will be instantaneous death."

"You threaten?" Polly asked, endeavouring to suppress a feeling of undefinable awe, and which she felt inwardly. "Ah! ah! what next?" and she gave way to a forced sarcastic laugh.

"I only warn you," Dashwood replied. "Do you doubt my power?"

Polly attempted to speak.

"Will I tell you the answer you were about to make?" Dashwood inquired.

Polly shook her head in the affirmative. She opened her lips as to give him a reply, but her teeth rattled and her frame shook nervously.

"I cannot speak," she muttered after a while, in a half-audible whisper. "What have you been doing to me?" she pursued, in a still undertone. "My head reels! I feel an awful pain close to my heart!—oh, do not kill me!"

Dashwood held out his hand, and placed it upon the girl's forehead.

In an instant she recovered her consciousness.

"Am I awake? or am I asleep?" she ejaculated. "Dashwood, where are you?"

"Do you doubt my power, now?" he inquired in a slow tone.

"No; what must I do to satisfy your wishes?"

Dashwood placed his finger upon his lips.

"You will see strange things within this house to-night. Never must you divulge them to living soul. Secrecy is all I want from you. Will you promise it to me?"

Polly remembered the strange sensations which she had experienced but a few minutes previously, and clinging close to her strange companion she whispered into his ears a total submission to his request.

"'Tis enough," he replied; "now you may come with me."

Willingly would Polly have rushed into the open air had she been certain of finding safety in a hasty flight. As the idea entered her mind, longingly her eye rested in the direction of the door.

"My dear Polly," Dashwood began, "I can read the meaning of your eye. You want to go away from me. Let me not stop you. Go, by all means—go; but, if you act thus rashly, remember that this day three months, day for day, hour for hour, you will die upon a dunghill."

This last remark seemed to shake Polly's resolution.

"You are getting wise, I see, my beautiful demon," he said; "I am happy to find you have altered your mind."

Thus speaking, Dashwood conducted Polly into a spacious gallery, slenderly enlightened by a long series of lofty windows, and from thence into a magnificent suite of apartments, which it may be as well here to describe.

All that wealth can procure was to be witnessed in the room where Polly now stood.

The first place in which she went was hung with crimson damask with gold ornaments—with French flowers and artificial moss laid artistically upon the chimney-pieces of a most expensive white marble, and interspersed with innumerable beads and shells of the most varied description, surmounted by a heavy looking-glass.

Close by her side Polly saw, what struck her as being the sleeping apartments; they were divided from the rooms where she was by two twisted pillars, adorned with wreaths of flowers, intermixed with shell-work.

There was a large French mahogany bedstead, which stood in an alcove, at the top of which were painted Cupids strewing flowers and sprinkling perfumes; and a group of syrens just issuing from the bath, with their beautiful forms, their snowy busts, and their luxuriant wavy hair falling into clusters upon their soft skins.

Here and there were great jars, with sprawling dragons upon them, filled with flowers of all kinds, which were evidently renewed every morning.

The next thing which Polly saw was a small boudoir, which was evidently intended for a dressing-room. A tiger-skin covered the carpeted floor; under a magnificent Chinese canopy stood a toilette, supplied with boxes of gilt plate, paints, pastes, pagodas of perfumes, bronzes having pastiles, bottles of Hungary scents of all descriptions, rice powder, and all the apparatus for creating female beauty.

"What do you think of this place, Polly?" Dashwood inquired, looking proudly upon the splendid furniture which surrounded them.

Dashwood now went and sat down upon a voluptuous sofa close at hand.

He bid Polly to come by his side.

Alike the lioness which is subdued by some clever animal tamer, Polly, the wicked Polly, answered her master's call.

She reclined into Dashwood's arms, and his lips met hers.

"Do you know, Polly," Dashwood began, "that you are a very handsome, dashing girl? If your features were not so marred by the previous dissipation which you have led, you would be the finest woman in the world, in my own opinion."

A smile of pride enlivened Polly's lips, and the sweet perfume of her breath alighted upon the features of Dashwood; he squeezed the girl close to his breast.

Polly placed her hands into Dashwood's hair, and there was in her glance that extraordinary,

feverish, undescribable expression which betrays the longing desires of a youthful, anxious, budding heart.

"Is it not odd," Dashwood began, in an ecstasy of bliss; "is it not strange that I should have felt a craving for you at first sight?"

These words had scarcely been spoken, when Polly fancied she heard a groan, which warned her that some dying inmate was seeking assistance.

"Listen!" Dashwood repeated. "Listen!"

The same sound reached again Polly's ears.

"One of my victims sighing, sighing, sighing again," Dashwood began. "Polly, you know what you promised me."

"Secrecy, I remember; and I will keep my word."

"How long that woman lives, to be sure," Dashwood muttered. "She will not die. I will go and give her a beating. Will you come, Polly? I wish Captain Morgan had chosen another keeper for his cast-off mistress."

"What—what did you say, Dashwood?" Polly inquired. "Are there any women beneath this roof?"

"Women!" Dashwood exclaimed. "If you think you can witness the most abject cruelty, you will soon see whether there are or not."

"I can," was the quick reply.

"Follow me, then," Dashwood pursued.

Thus speaking, he proceeded upstairs.

Polly and Dashwood had now reached another landing.

CHAPTER XX.

WHERE POLLY GETS STILL MORE ASTONISHED—WHERE SHE WITNESSES THE AMUSEMENTS, DELIGHTS, AND OPERATIONS OF HER LOVER—WHERE LIFE IS SHOWN IN ITS MOST HEART-RENDING NAKEDNESS.

"STAY here for an instant and look around you," Dashwood began, addressing Polly.

The horsebreaker acted in accordance with the speaker's injunctions.

She was now standing on a landing more spacious than the one she had just left, distinguished by a noble balustraded stone staircase, and feebly illuminated by an immense stained glass window, through which the light of day cast but an uncertain and flickering glare.

Alabaster statues and bronzed candelabras and tripods were arranged about the place with elegant profusion, and the atmosphere was alternately rendered fragrant by the perfume of flowers scattered here and there in rich golden vases, and white with the incense of consuming pastiles.

"I am rich," you see, Dashwood exclaimed exultingly; "it requires money, and a good deal of money, to buy all that surrounds you."

The greatest astonishment was depicted upon Polly's features.

"This door leads to a suite of apartments wherein I will conduct you," Dashwood began, pointing with his finger to the right; "the other, with its mean dimensions, is the one through which we will have to pass to witness the last place which we will visit to-night."

Polly opened her eyes wider and wider.

"Come on, Polly," Dashwood muttered, "and do not say a word."

She was about to obey, when she heard the sounds of voices.

They were musical, refreshing, and sweet; and could only be uttered by women.

"I wonder what I am going to witness?" Polly thought inwardly, and mechanically she walked close on the steps of Dashwood.

Less than thirty seconds brought her behind a small door.

"Remain at a stand-still, and look through that small glass plate as I go in. You will see without being seen, and I daresay you will see something worth your attention."

Polly did as she was desired, and beheld two handsome girls.

They were dressed in a light costume, which enabled the symmetrical form of their bust, the faultless shape of their hands and feet, to be seen to advantage.

The oldest could not have been more than sixteen, and the other was barely a year younger.

Within the room the prospect was beautiful and inviting.

Crystal chandeliers—doubtless lit up at night—sparkled like diamonds, and the light which peeped into the apartment displayed the beauty and richness of the furniture, and the glittering delicacy of the ornaments. Long windows of pale pink glass were thrown open, and their transparent, gauzy shades drawn back, to admit the perfume which hyacinths of every scent and hue, fresh budding roses, the pale star of the Narcissus, and the brighter-tinged bell of the jonquil, arranged in China vases, exhaled from the balconies, where they were tastefully laid out.

Everything in that room bespoke wealth and luxury.

As soon as Dashwood entered the room the two girls rushed towards him, and kissed him affectionately.

They clung to him as if he was a kind father, and, surrounding him on each side, they laid their bare arms upon his shoulders.

Both girls were handsome, but an apparition of greater beauty than the youngest never burst upon man's gaze.

Her exquisitely fair complexion, her blue, large and bright eyes, the silken fringes which softened their intense radiancy, the slight incarnadined hue of her cheeks, were the details of a countenance on which an equisitely languid melancholy, which seemed to tell of such reminiscences as Plato dreamt of, conferred an expression which might well be called the music of the soul.

As to her figure, 'twas faultless; and the Florentine Venus must have yielded the palm to her had she been placed on a par with her.

Her hair would have placed a man in mind of heaven, would have made him long for a Mahomedan paradise, and could be compared to nothing but the full moon's rays on a pure marble pavement.

The other was also pretty.

She was, however, of a different kind of beauty. Her features, faultlessly modelled, needed that expression which her sister possessed; and, although many a peeress of the land would have given half her dowry to possess her attraction, still, for all, she could not have been compared to her younger companion.

"Why did you not take us out for a drive?" the handsomest of the two inquired, with a longing that no one could have resisted. "What is the meaning of keeping us here, as you do, dear Mr. Dashwood? This place is frightfully lonely, and in the middle of the night we hear sometimes groans and shrieks which make our blood run cold."

"My dearest girls," Dashwood replied, in a systematic, political tone of voice, "do not say that I do not think of you. See what I have brought you both. Will you find fault with me again?"

With her eyes riveted through the aperture, Polly gazed fixedly into the room. She saw Dashwood taking some golden trinkets out of his coat-pocket, and making a present of them to the girls.

One seemed delighted; it was the oldest.

The younger still clung to Martin Dashwood.

"Take me out of this lonely place, and keep your presents," she muttered, sullenly.

"What is that? Do you wish me never to come and see you again?"

"Oh! what does all this mean, I wonder?" Polly thought, inwardly,

After Dashwood had spoken, the two girls seemed cowed.

"Good-bye," Dashwood said; "good-bye."

The older shook the hand which he held out, and scarcely had he departed from the room than he heard the suppressed sobs of the youngest of the two creatures. She wept bitterly and loudly, and her sorrow was heartrending to hear.

When Dashwood stepped out of the room, Polly rushed towards him.

"Who are those two children, for they are not women yet?" she inquired, anxiously.

"Two orphans, whom a doting, but absurd father left to my care on his death-bed. They are fine girls, are they not? They are already bespoken; one is intended for Lord G——, the other for the Marquis of D——. I will get a great price for them, Polly; but I will not appear in the transaction. Mrs. Haltering has got a female friend who will help me in the matter."

Polly could scarcely credit what she heard.

Could it be true? could so much villainy exist in the world?

Had the things which she witnessed occurred to her in a dream, she would have looked upon them as impossible; and now to doubt was out of question.

"I have a large fortune, Polly," Dashwood pursued. "People think that I am worth thousands more than I am really; but that does not matter. In these days, when we have such murders as the Waterloo-bridge, and when returned convicts are presented at court by illustrious peers of the realm, everything is done and carried out. I act as I do because I like it; because, instead of trusting in God, I trust in Satan; because I want excitement of all kinds to live, because we are living in a free country; and because, on the principle that a man's house is his own castle, no one dares to interfere with him.

The coster-girl—the fashionable horsebreaker—felt her own inferiority. Because he was her superior in sin, she resolved to love him.

"And now for the last thing which I will show you to-night, Polly," Dashwood said.

Through the small door already described did he wend his way, accompanied by Polly.

In breathless suspense did the girl follow her leader.

What else could she see?

They both ascended a staircase, and so narrow

was it that there was scarcely room for one single being at the time.

"Whither are you taking me, Dashwood?" Polly asked.

The girl was beginning to think that her own safety was endangered.

"What do you fear, you foolish girl?" Dashwood inquired. "I will not hurt you; I love you too much to do so now."

Dashwood gave the word "now" such an intonation that more than once during the evening Polly thought over it.

As they ascended the steps the groans of a woman were repeatedly heard.

More and more audible did they become as they reached what appeared to be, and what was, in fact, the top of Dashwood's house.

CHAPTER XXI.

WHERE WE THINK IT NECESSARY TO DEVOTE A WHOLE CHAPTER TO A SCENE WHICH DID OCCUR—AND WHICH WE HOPE FERVENTLY WILL NEVER TAKE PLACE AGAIN.

SOME people are extremely fond of contrasts.

Had any one of them been in Dashwood's company on the night during which the events we have related occurred, he would certainly have had no occasion to regret having been an eye-witness of that which is to follow.

Dashwood had now reached the top of the staircase.

He turned round to see whether Polly had followed him.

A beam of satisfaction enlightened his countenance when he perceived she had.

The two personages were now close by a large, dark room, which emitted a musty, disagreeable smell, which told of its being seldom aired.

The passage where they both stood was plunged into a semi-darkness.

Although it was not yet evening, yet a faint light could be traced into the room when Dashwood was about to enter.

"Stay here, Polly," Dashwood said, "and through this eyelet-hole you will see and hear all." . .

Polly's heart began to beat.

She looked through the aperture for a second or two, and could discover nothing; for though the room into which she looked had not the shutters closed, the window being close barred on the outside and covered with dust and cob-webs, prevented the access of anything like a comforting, bright light.

Dashwood entered the room, and struck up a lucifer.

Shortly afterwards he lighted up a candle which stood upon the chimney-piece.

Then Polly could with ease contemplate the sight before her.

What a contrast between downstairs and up-stairs!

Wealth and extravagance could be witnessed below, abject poverty where she was now.

The apartment where her gaze wandered was deprived of the slightest article of furniture.

She saw a heap in a far away corner, the most distant part from the place where she was standing.

It was a collection of straw and rags, which formed the bed of two miserable objects, namely, a woman and a child.

Their countenances were so emaciated that

life, to all outward appearance, seemed to have fled from their bodies, which were so lean that it is no exaggeration to state that the bones of the child's back could have been reckoned.

Although there was a sudden light, the two creatures remained motionless.

They were asleep, doubtless.

The child, five years at the utmost, reclined gently in his mother's arms.

For it was mother and son now before us.

Dashwood approached the two bodies, and with a dark and ruthless countenance he gazed upon his sleeping victims.

"Awake! awake!" he whispered harshly into the woman's ears.

No heed was taken of his words.

Annoyed at the silence which reigned, Dashwood gave the woman a strong kick, and the sound of his heavy boot against the frail creature's back resounded loudly a few yards away.

The woman thus awoke, rose suddenly.

She must have been handsome; but her beauty now was vanished, and it was heartrending to witness a face so woe-begone with wretchedness and misery.

She looked liked the ghostly picture of them appearing among the living.

"Ah! ah!" she shrieked, shrillingly, recognising Dashwood's features. "What on earth, man, have I done to you? You have murdered my child! He has been dead since yesterday morning, and his cold body has been lying by my side ever since. See, monster, whether I speak to you true."

A sarcastical laugh was Dashwood's only answer.

"Is your brat dead?" he asked, suddenly. "Well, the sooner you join him the better. I am come here to settle you to-night."

The woman ran away from Dashwood.

In a crouching attitude, she went and buried herself within the shattered blankets.

"Rise up, woman, rise," Dashwood continued, pursuing the woman all round the room.

"You have killed my boy, my poor boy," the woman shrieked, embracing meanwhile the cold forehead of her departed son; "but I will forgive you if you give me bread—only a morsel of bread!"

Thus speaking, the creature, with all the agonizing despair of a starved creature, rushed towards Dashwood; and, clinging round his knees, implored him to have pity upon her.

"What do you say you want?" Dashwood inquired again, his eyes gloating upon the sufferings of the woman now before him.

"Bread! bread!" she exclaimed, but the last word trembled away in her throat, which rattled horribly with the parched convulsion of inaction.

A dark smile passed over Dashwood's lip.

"Sign, sign away your right to the property in the county of M——, settled upon you by Captain Morgan, and you shall have bread, liberty, and affluence again. You are a young woman yet."

The poor woman looked at her tormentor.

"I would rather die here," she whispered into his ear, "sooner than yield to you, monster! coward! wretch!"

And the starved woman held her fist in a threatening attitude towards Dashwood.

Dashwood's face grew livid with passion, and his lip quivered.

"I will conquer you yet. Infamous harlot!

you are not going to make me hold my tongue before you."

Dashwood's features were terrible to behold.

Had Satan appeared to Polly, she could not have been more frightened than she was by the appearance which her lover's features suddenly assumed.

"Oh! mercy—oh! mercy," she muttered, folding her arms on her bosom, while her long, matted hair fell in its clotted irregularity on her neck and shoulders. "Oh! mercy—oh! mercy."

But Dashwood heeded not the woman's imploring looks.

He caught her by the hair; he dashed her unmercifully to the ground. Subsequently he struck her with a heavy, knotted stick, which he picked up in a corner of the ground, where it was kept for the purpose.

The shrieks of the woman were appalling to hear, and it was only when Dashwood's arm was tired that he ceased beating the woman.

Once she attempted to return his blows, but exhausted by the exertion which she had undergone, she fell heavily upon the ground; her throat rattled, she breathed rapidly, and in an instant afterwards the most profound silence succeeded.

"Thanks be to Satan!" Dashwood exclaimed, "she is dead."

And having proceeded to ascertain whether he was right in his anticipations, he rushed out of the room.

"Polly," he exclaimed, "come here."

Panting, out of breath, her features as pale as those of the corpse before her, the girl approached Dashwood with trembling limbs and a half-distracted mind.

There was something so peremptory in his order, that to refuse was akin to impossible.

"Help me to fold these two bodies in these blankets," he said.

Through this gloomy task Polly had to lend an unwilling hand; once it was concluded, Dashwood carried the two bodies upon his shoulder.

It was not of a very heavy weight, for the woman had been starved ever since she had been confined in the room, and so had her child.

With his burthen Dashwood went out of the apartment and entered an adjoining closet.

"What are you going to do with the bodies?" Polly inquired.

"Destroy all traces of this murder."

"How will you manage that?" she asked, anxiously.

"You will soon see."

As he spoke he laid mother and child on the floor. Having done so, he moved two or three pieces of heavy furniture, which were in the way, and loosing a spring, half the wainscoting drew aside.

"This leads to a well," Dashwood said; "you will soon perceive how I will settle the mother and child."

Polly looked downwards.

Everything before her was dark, and she could distinguish nothing.

"And now for the _dénoûment_, as the French say," Dashwood pursued, sarcastically.

Not a word more did he speak, but he dragged the two bodies by the side of the aperture, and allowed them to fall.

A heavy subdued sound was heard.

It was like a distant splash of something heavy dropping in the water.

Dashwood closed the wainscoting, replaced the furniture from where he had taken it, and thus, having removed all traces of the fate of the unfortunate creature and her child, he descended the flight of steps which led below.

And when he and Polly found themselves again together and seated in the drawing-room, he began thus—

"Would you wish me, Polly, to tell you something for your safeguard?" he asked.

"Certainly," Polly replied, not knowing what Dashwood was about to say.

"Well, remember this—you are one of the parties to this day's work."

"How so?" Polly inquired, the blood running cold within her veins.

"Why, you saw me do it, and never took any steps to stop it. . . I know what I am about, you perceive, Polly; I have implicated you in my guilt."

The horsebreaker was too thunderstruck to say a word in reply.

"And what are you going to have now, Polly?" Dashwood continued, in the same tone of voice, and as coolly as if he had, all his life, led a career irreproachable in every respect; "do you say champagne?"

"Anything you like, I am not particular."

"Ring the bell, then; and meanwhile, I will relate to you the life of the woman who has just gone to her last home; you might like to hear it."

After what she had witnessed that day, it is only fair to state that Polly was very anxious to become acquainted with the antecedents of the creature whom we have introduced to our readers —whose sad end we have witnessed—and accordingly she replied in the affirmative.

The servant soon appeared, bearing in a tray a variety of wines and liqueurs, which he uncorked, to leave Polly her choice.

As soon as he effected his exit, Dashwood went to the door, and having assured himself that he was certain not to be disturbed, he began in the following terms.

But as the story is likely to be a pretty long one, we will take the liberty of concluding this chapter to begin another one.

CHAPTER XXII.

WHERE LADY FLORENCE'S LIFE IS RELATED BY ONE OF THE CHARACTERS OF THIS TALE.

"POLLY," Dashwood began, as soon as he felt satisfied that he had concentrated towards him the whole of the girl's attention, "I promised you that I should relate to you the antecedents and life of the woman whose sad end you witnessed to-day. Now, ere I proceed, it is necessary that I should tell you that she was the daughter of a French gentleman; that, although betrothed to a young officer, she married an English baronet with a very large fortune. Do you understand?"

"Perfectly," Polly replied.

"Well," Dashwood continued, "when she was comfortably settled in a tasty mansion in an Irish county, the officer whom she loved returned from India, where he had been rusticating. It was not his affection for the lady that brought him back, but the very fact of his having stepped into his grandfather's property—£3,000 a year— showed him the wisdom of giving up the service, and he sold out like a sensible man. And what do you think occurred?"

"I am sure I do not know," Polly replied, in a winning tone of voice, which Dashwood greatly relished; "how am I to answer that question?"

"This is what occurred then, Polly," Dashwood pursued. "The fellow with the £3,000 a year met the baronet's wife; a little flirtation took place between the two, which ended in the latter eloping with the cavalry swell, leaving her husband and half-a-dozen children behind, and giving to the country residents a very good opportunity for indulging in a little scandal for the next six months. The consequence was what it is generally; the two people soon got sick of each other, and one evening the captain offered me a thousand pounds if I would get him rid of a woman whom he loathed. 'Go ahead, my boy,' he said to me; 'there will be nobody to thwart you; I have settled some money upon her. Keep her closely located, and I will put her death in the papers. Her family is sick of her. The husband will not inquire after her, as it will be all fair and square.'

One evening I had Lady Florence — never mind her family name—closely watched, and she exclaimed to the man who brought her hither over and over again, 'No, sir! I won't go with you.' I was successful enough in getting her under my roof—the rest you have seen . . . . . Now I will begin my narrative; but, as I intend to publish it at some future day, I will speak as I would write. And now, attention.

It was on a winter's day.

The weather was boisterous and dreary, and the sun, which was hidden by dark and heavy clouds, was casting from time to time, but at very rare intervals, its weak and uncertain rays upon the windows of one of the most fashionable houses in Queen Street, Mayfair.

In the drawing-room of that house sat a young lady whose features were very lovely then, and whose physiognomy was in every respect identical to that of the woman who died here to day—minus twenty years of debauch, of dissipation, and immorality. . . . . .

The suite of rooms were very tastefully decorated, and the walls, covered with a rich and lively pattern, were ornamented with masterpieces belonging to the Italian school, and with modern pictures owed to the genius of the living celebrities.

When we first see the young girl she is deeply engaged in finishing a little embroidered collar, which she held in her tiny hand.

Suddenly, as if she had been guided by some unknown power, she relinquished her work for awhile, and began to unfold, with her pretty fingers, a letter which she had withdrawn from her breast, not inferior in shape or snowy whiteness to that of the Venus of Medici.

After she had read its contents she sighed heavily, and cast towards the ceiling a pair of beautiful eyes damped by some secret sorrow.

Apparently, the Divinity which she implored did not listen to her prayer, for she shook mournfully her pretty head, and marks of the utmost consternation still remained depicted upon her features.

She was about to resume her task when a gentle tap was heard outside the drawing-room, and the door was thrown open to admit a smart looking maid, doubtless the lady's "femme de chambre."

She made her appearance, conveying to her mistress a visiting card, on a little metal salver.

"Madam," the menial said, presenting the card to her mistress, "the gentleman is below, and wishes to see you if disengaged."

The lady glanced upon the name, and replied, with formal civility—

"Please tell Mr. Morgan that I will be happy to see him."

The servant swiftly retired, and the visitor entered the apartment.

He was a fine, handsome young man, endowed with intelligent and aristocratic features, and he had but a few days ago received his cornet's commission, and he was now waiting with a soldier's anxiety the moment when he should be called upon by the Horse Guards to join the headquarters of the light cavalry regiment to which he had been appointed.

His soft, blue eyes, of that almond shape which is so often to be remarked in paintings representing the Italian type of physignomy, displayed, when he spoke, a melancholy and thoughtful expression.

The forehead, of noble height, was surmounted by a profusion of jet black hair, and he possessed, besides, those distinguished manners, that upright gait, which denote at once the man of high character and of patrician birth.

The nature of his look, as it set upon the young girl before him, conveyed too many things for us to attempt a minute description of them.

For a long time the two personages talked carelessly of different matters, but had a close observer been there he would not have been at a loss to see that both were anxious to begin a subject which neither of them had sufficient strength or boldness to allude to.

After a while, however, the young man said—

"Florence, it is a long time since we were playmates. Eighteen months have elapsed since the gates of the convent where you were brought up, where, I may say, you spent a life deprived of all cares, have been thrown open to restore you to society, to bestow you upon a gay world in which you are destined ever to shine. Now, Florence, that you belong once again to mankind, will you forgive me if I am so bold as to recall to your mind a promise which you so often made to me, and which I hope you have not already forgotten?"

A moment of silence followed these last words.

This was rather an abrupt way to begin a serious and rather critical subject.

The speaker felt it, and he very soon perceived that his speech had produced on his fair listener an effect for which he was at a loss to account.

To a brilliant vivacity which the young girl's features had assumed there succeeded a frozen look of ceremonious disdain.

That such an alteration in Florence's manners could have taken place in so short a period was an unfathomable mystery to the young officer.

When last he had seen her, she had been graceful—nay, kind to him; now her demeanour was that of a perfect stranger.

"Florence," he said, in a measured tone, "I am afraid to think that I am speaking an unknown language to you—perhaps I am intruding—perhaps I had no right to come here—to force my way into your drawing-room without an invitation."

The young officer pronounced the last words in a manner, which he studied himself, to render as bitter and as cutting as he fairly could.

But his feeling was not a bitter one.

FLORENCE, PREVIOUS TO HER INTERVIEW WITH CAPTAIN MORGAN.

He loved Florence deeply; and the suspicion that his love might not be returned by the object which occasioned it, caused him to feel his heart beating with unknown and terrible sensations.

"Robert Morgan"—the young girl resumed, apparently grieved at the sad tone of her lover's voice—"there is a secret which I fear to reveal; but with you I must—I will be candid."

The young man's gaze was riveted upon Florence as she spoke, and the fiery glance of his beautiful eye conveyed too many things for us to dwell upon its expression.

No. 11.

Perhaps Florence noticed it, for she quietly went on,—

"To let you remain under the impression that that dream of our childhood can ever be realized, would be a cruel and treacherous behaviour on my part of which I will not be guilty. It would have been far preferable," she continued, "had we never known each other. For it was Fatality which made us wander along the same path— it was Fatality which made us exchange vows and promises, that the future was destined to dash to the ground. Two years ago fain would I have believed that events would have passed as they did—that I should be obliged to make you the present confession."

As the girl spoke there was an unmistakeable trembling in the tone of her voice—and it was evident she would have longed to withdraw every sentence which she uttered—could she fairly have done so.

"Oh, Florence," the young officer replied, "speak! but do not let me remain in an uncertainty, which is worse than death itself. Oh! do not let me entertain thoughts injurious to your feelings—to your character as a woman."

"Robert," the girl paused, heeding, when not wishing to heed the young man's last observation, "since we parted sad events have occurred; the whirl of life has blown over my destiny, and to it, like many others, I have fallen a victim."

Here Florence paused.

"Do not," she continued, "entreat me to speak to you any longer about that which cannot be remedied. I can only be your friend now: as your betrothed I am lost to you for ever."

And her eyes shone with uncommon lustre— her breast heaved—her hand trembled—and she appeared as if she were struggling against nature—as if she were restraining within herself the warm promptings of a youthful heart.

But the storm of her feeling was soon appeased by her anxiety to hear her lover speak— and she listened attentively.

What answer was she to receive from the young officer? she wondered, as she had perceived that her last words had sadly moved him—that in hearing her he had turned as white as a sheet.

Like the hurricane on the wide ocean, during a wild, stormy night, subdues for a few instants only the mad howlings of the storm—causing the waves to rise—the ships to sink—to burst forth anew with renewed strength, so the young cornet remained silent for a brief interval, and suddenly exclaimed, with a frenzy which filled Florence with awe,—

"What! is it you, Florence, who hold to me so terrible a language—'as your betrothed I am lost to you for ever'? What is the meaning of this phrase? Am I not wandering under some horrid hallucination—am I not dreaming? Can it be you, Florence, whom the world has already stamped with its impure and universal stigma— answer me, Florence? But no! I was a maniac, to seek truth, innocence, candour, in a frame from which I shrink now with contempt! How unbounded—how foolish—how infatuated that love of mine, which placed you on a golden pedestal! How deceived—how mistaken I must have been when I thought you worthy of love— of admiration and worship! How blind I must have felt when, in the contrarieties of my short existence, I invoked your name, like the sailor calls a Providence to his help during a storm— when his vessel, beaten by the hurricane's tem-pestuous blast, is about to be engulphed in a watery grave!"

And as he concluded his last sentence, Morgan placed his forehead in his hands, and remained for an instant buried in his own thoughts.

Strange to say, Florence relished the accusations which were hurled against her by her lover.

Did she deserve them?

Did she love the speaker?

She reflected for a few seconds, as if she feared the moment when she would have to give utterance to words she dreaded to speak.

At length, as if she seemed to subdue a secret vow which bid her to remain silent, she said,—

"Robert, you are young, enthusiastic, and barely entering life—excuse me if I speak thus —why taunt about what cannot be undone?"

"To forget you, Florence, is impossible—I feel—I know it! Nay, I am persuaded that the sentiments which sprung up within me in my childhood are gradually becoming stronger. But tell me," he continued, in a mild and soft tone, "is there so terrible a knot that it cannot be untied?"

There was a deep anxiety in the tone of his voice as he spoke.

Subsequently he reflected for a few minutes, and suddenly—as if the momentary musing in which he had indulged had the effect of exciting his feelings—he exclaimed, with feverish excitement,—

"Florence—dearest Florence—I hope that you are still as innocent?"

A crimson hue overspread the young girl's countenance: she rose from her chair with a dignified look.

"Robert," she said, "I did not think that you would ever tax me with so harsh an accusation. If I am altered, alas! you are sadly changed!"

"Forgive me! forgive me!" exclaimed the soldier, falling on his knees. "Oh, forgive me, Florence! the idea that you love—that you could love another, renders me unconscious of the words I utter! But, answer me, your affections are not engaged, I hope?"

The young girl shook mournfully her pretty head, and two tears shone in her bright eyes.

"Florence, I am a monster unworthy of you! I was accusing you—your speech has maddened my brain!"

"Robert," continued the young girl, who thought it would have been a sin to prolong the young man's anxiety, "listen attentively, and you will hear a very sad story."

The young girl now bid Morgan rise, and take a seat by her side.

"Robert," began Florence, when her listener had complied with her request, "the story which you are about to hear, and the circumstances which have followed each other since our last meeting, will show you in a forcible manner how presumptuous must that one be who heedlessly builds plans, regardless of the powers above."

"Florence, you must have been very unfortunate. But let me not remain in bitter suspense: I am prepared to hear any revelation, however painful it may be to my feelings."

After a pause, during which the maiden seemed to collect her thoughts, she began thus:

"You are aware that, when we parted last, the affairs of my poor father were in a rather embarrassed state. The banking houses in which he had lodged the greatest part of his capital gradually and successively failed, and by their bankruptcy my father soon found himself on the brink of ruin. He required an immense sum to carry on his vast and extensive business, and maintain his splendid factories, of which you know he was so proud. In the hope of regaining what he had so unexpectedly lost, he entered into a sea of speculations, which might have been crowned with success, had not the fall of the monarchy — followed by the revolution of 1848—paralysed all his movements, and swept to the ground all his mighty plans. Not only did he lose his capital, but he ruined his credit. Misfortunes never come alone, they say, and I, alas! experienced the truth of it.

"The year 1848 was my father's death-blow. For then were scenes of horror and of pillage: artizans abandoned their work, and assembled en masse under the rebellious banner, and those same hands which were wont by their labour to obtain the daily bread for the support of their families, were employed in shedding their breth- ren's blood, and in destroying the monuments and buildings raised by their own industry. For such was the blind fury of an ignorant mob, that their sole aim was the overthrow of all social and rational laws! That fury—I may call it madness —that revolutionary spirit of a nation, awakened from its peaceable state by venomous and wicked pamphlets—calculated to excite a mob already too much inclined to rebellion—brought on the Revolution of 1848. Rising like the storm which darkens the brightness of a fine day, it was the first signal of those civil dissensions which pro- claimed for a while an end to honest labour and prosperous industry.

"At that epoch my father and I left Besancon, amidst the bullets of the insurgents, the terrible and yet innocent songs of the "Gamins," and the mournful roar of the cannon, leaving death and ruin in its rapid and merciless track.

"We soon reached London, where the damp climate of the metropolis did not agree with my poor father's health—which had already received so terrible a shock by the unexpected loss of his fortune. He became every day weaker; and his mind, formerly strong and resolute, gradually sunk under the remembrance, ever present to him, of the failure of his commercial pursuits.

"I will not recall," continued the young girl, in a melancholy tone, "a sad picture, which my voice would be powerless to describe: suffice it to say, that about that time my father made the acquaintance of Mr. Kennedy, attaché at the English Embassy, who, at his father's death, was to become possessed of an ancient title and a fine estate."

When Florence murmured the last words, the young officer felt his heart gradually wringing with despair, and the demon of jealousy entering his mind, led him to guess part of the truth. In that young man of the name of Kennedy, he in- stinctively saw a powerful rival. As we proceed, we shall see whether he was right in his moment- ary foresight.

"Being a kind-hearted man," the young girl continued, "Mr. Kennedy became very intimate with my father, and owing to several important services which he rendered him, he secured his everlasting gratitude."

"Oh, Heaven! there is an awful meaning con- veyed in those last words!" exclaimed the young soldier, who feared his not being able to hear any longer the young girl's discourse.

"Robert," Florence replied, "I often led you to understand that you were the only one whom I ever loved deeply and truly—if a childish senti- ment can be called love."

"Why endeavour to convince me of a senti- ment which I always detected in you, beloved Florence? I ever thought that our two hearts were made to be blended into one. Without thinking of the future, earnestly I dreamt of happiness. To win a smile from your lips, I would have conquered the world, and lavished upon you that wealth which is so terrible an obstacle to our union!"

"Even now," he thought, "for thy sake, Flo- rence, would I encounter the most ignominious death!"

"But why," he added aloud, as if he feared to allow his thoughts play, "yes, why should I recall to my mind those happy—now miserable feelings, which you say cannot be realized? Oh, Florence! if you love me still, forget the world —forget all except the promise which thou hast made to me!"—as he spoke his eye brightened, and he grew more and more excited. "Let us fly to some distant shore, under a more grateful sun, where thou wilt become my wife! I will throw up my commission, which, to a poor man, is but an irksome position. Night and day will I toil, until I can give you happiness and comfort —until I can bestow upon you all that fortune can procure. Then, far away, we will live toge- ther, and spend an existence which, although dreary at first, will soon be brightened by the sweet hours spent in mutual affection!"

"That which you ask of me is impossible," replied Florence. "What I am about to relate to you will palliate my conduct, if not justify it in your opinion, I hope—but listen throughout to a sad tale, I repeat."

This last sentence was pronounced in so impe- rative a tone, that obedience was its natural answer.

"During his friendly intercourse with us," Florence continued, "Mr. Kennedy's kindness to me was gradually increasing, and under the cloak of his apparent brotherly affection, I inwardly guessed and feared that there was hidden a stronger feeling. Women's anticipations in that respect are seldom deceived, and unfortunately I had hit upon the real state of things. A few days had scarce elapsed when he told me, in the most subdued and respectful manner, that he solicited the honour of my hand."

"Oh, this is too heart-rending to hear, Flo- rence! oh, what a fatal love!" muttered the young cornet, his features displaying marks of the utmost grief and despair.

"This was but the beginning of sadder events," the young girl continued. "Notwithstanding my efforts to hinder a conclusion which I had foreseen, a sad tragedy was enacted, by which I was pledged to Mr. Kennedy as his future wife. My father was seized with fainting fits, which caused so great an anxiety to his doctor, that he begged me to prepare myself for his loss. The attacks came so quickly upon him, that I had scarcely time to convey the sad news to the limited circle of acquaintances who took an inte- rest in his welfare. In England we were looked upon as emigrés; and our circumstances being far from prosperous, we were known but to a very few. The numerous relations and friends who were wont to congregate in my father's salons in his days of opulence, had one and all forsaken us in our hour of need. Such is life! and I learnt the terrible ways of the world when I was but a child.

"In the room where the doctor was attending my sick parent I stood weeping, deeply buried in my thoughts, when who should come in but Mr. Kennedy. After having shaken hands with me in a friendly manner, he approached my father's bed-side. As far as I could judge he appeared to be sadly and sincerely moved. After some words of condolence on his part, I left the apartment to prepare some calming potion, and during my absence, it appeared, Mr. Kennedy made a full declaration of his love for me, assuring my father that, in the event of his being so ill-fated as to be torn from in his child, he would make it his duty to protect me in this world.

"Seeing that his plans were so much in accordance with secret wishes my father had harboured, he openly expressed his satisfaction; and as he seemed sincere in his request, my father followed the dictates of his own conscience.

"Without consulting my feelings, or ascertaining whether my heart was not already engaged, he replied to Mr. Kennedy by saying that he would feel happy and proud to receive him for the future as his son-in-law.

"While this last sentence was pronounced, I entered the room. 'Come, my beloved child, come nearer to me,' my father said. 'I fear that it is the will of God that a father should be parted from his beloved child. Oh, my beloved daughter! oh, Florence! I feel that my sufferings are rapidly drawing to an end, but I should die happy, were it not for the great anxiety I entertain for your welfare. Take Mr. Kennedy for your protector, for he loves you deeply.'

"I took my father's hand, trembling with fever.

"'For your dying father's sake,' he said, 'do return his disinterested affection. Without fortune, friends, or relations, what would become of you in this world? You might wander a long time in the rough and perilous path of life without reaching its weary end! Mr. Kennedy will watch your first steps.'

"It was in vain that, overwhelmed with grief by the sight of my father, I endeavoured to open my lips, to tell him that it was impossible for me to comply with his request; that long since my heart had been given to another, and thus the object of his choice could never become master of my affections. I attempted to speak, but when I listened to the words pronounced by his fatherly affection—when I witnessed his sunken eyes, from which life was gradually disappearing—my mouth was powerless to utter a refusal.

"He pressed me to obey, and—must I confess it?—I obeyed!

"By my assent, Mr. Kennedy and my father seemed to be excessively rejoiced—the latter particularly. I saw his lips murmur a prayer of thanks to the Almighty, and his eyes suddenly brighten with a radiant look that I had not perceived in them for a long time.

"Now that I think of it," Florence continued, "I wonder whether it would have been right or dutiful for a daughter to deny to her dying father his last pleasure on this earth?

"At that instant," she went on, "a priest who had been sent for made his appearance, bearing in his hand the cross, sacred emblem of his holy calling.

"He was a grave old man, from Farm Street Chapel, with a profusion of white snowy hair falling on the collar of his threadbare *soutane*. After he had administered the last comforts of religion to my father, and when the last rites of his pious office had been concluded, he remained in the room, praying for him whose soul was about to be launched into eternity.

"My father then beckoned me to his bedside, where I was led by Mr. Kennedy.

"In a scarcely audible voice, which was fast sinking, he muttered his farewell blessing; and, clasping me to his dying breast, pressed on my forehead his last kiss, holding still, in the agonies of death, the finger of one who in adversity had proved a staunch and faithful friend—Mr. Kennedy—who passed a few words to me.

"I heard him not. Overcome by the painful emotions which I had sustained during the last hour, I lost all sense of what was passing around me. I experienced a horrible dizziness—the blood suddenly rushed to my temples—and I fell senseless in the priest's arms! . . . ."

After having thus spoken, Florence remained silent for a while.

The affection that she had once entertained for one who was no more, had been too strong and too deep to be ever forgotten.

She sighed heavily, and tears were seen trickling down her sorrowful countenance.

"For several weeks after the melancholy event," continued the young girl, "I was confined to my bed with a wasting fever. Many a time, in the darkness of night, I longed for the moment when I should be relieved of my miseries in this world.

"A few days after my father's death, I perceived a lady stranger seated by my bedside. She spoke to me, in a friendly and soft tone, and informed me that she was Lady Kennedy, my lover's mother; that she came to visit me in compliance with her son's wish.

"I had a painful sense upon my mind of the kindness of Mr. Kennedy, and for all I was indebted to him I could not feel ungrateful. He was generous and noble-hearted: if one could command love, I would have bestowed it upon him.

"Lady Kennedy said to me that to be married I was, she thought, too young, and that she would act as a mother to me if I were to allow myself to be guided by her experience and knowledge of the world. She proposed that I should live for some time with her; and she assured me that if, at the end of a certain period, I felt reluctant to yield to her son's offer, he would certainly release me of my promise.

"I was in a dreadful perplexity. I knew not what line of conduct to adopt. On the one hand, I had forgotten your direction, and had no means of seeking your protection; on the other, if I refused to abide by Lady Kennedy's advice, not only should I have been reduced to poverty, but, what was worse, I should have disobeyed the promise I made to my dying father, upon which I looked as being sacred. Lady Kennedy further added that she knew her son to be endowed with those sterling qualities of the heart which a woman could not but admire.

"After a long conversation, it was resolved that, as soon as the doctor would permit me, I should take up my abode in her house in Berkeley Square. During my stay with that kind and worthy lady, I naturally frequently saw her son. Since then, his father having died, he has inherited the title of baronet, with the estates attached appertaining to it.

"What a dreadful sea of adventures you met with," murmured the soldier, who had been greatly affected by the narrative.

"Two years have now elapsed," she pursued; "I have learnt to appreciate the upright character of Sir William Kennedy. I love him now"—she could scarcely utter these words—"and it is finally settled that on Saturday fortnight my father's wish is to be fulfilled—Sir William Kennedy's happiness to be sealed."

"Ah!" ejaculated the young soldier, as if a dagger had been plunged in his breast; "ah, Florence, I saw your banns published. In the heat of the moment I wrote to you the epistle, but I meant not the hard words conveyed in it."

And he pointed to the note, which Florence had allowed to rest on the floor when the young man had entered.

"I read, indeed, your name, coupled with that of Sir William Kennedy, and I could hardly believe it to be reality. Now, alas! I perceive that it is too incontestable a fact to be doubted. So, good-bye!—good-bye!—and may you be happy!"

And Mr. Morgan, considerably moved, rose and presented his trembling hand to the young girl.

As he left her—perhaps for ever—he could not help gazing with a jealous eye on that voluptuous form — over which a happy rival would ere long sway with uncontrolled power. He was thus so deeply engaged in a contemplation which might have lasted for hours, that he did not notice the entrance of a third party.

Although the new comer was far from being handsome, he possessed that manly and open countenance which at once secures friends.

When he appeared, Florence rose from the sofa, and, endeavouring to suppress sad emotion, she said, with a melancholy smile,—

"My dear Sir William, allow me to introduce to you a friend of mine, Mr. Morgan."

While the two gentlemen were saluting each other, the lady continued,—

"Sir William, Mr. Morgan is one of my oldest friends."

"Sir," replied the baronet, in a becoming and friendly tone, "I bless the happy occurrence which procures me the opportunity of making your acquaintance. The friends of my wife are also mine. I say my wife," he pursued, after awhile, "for I consider Miss Beauprè as such, though we are, as yet, only united by the laws of the heart."

As he spoke, Morgan felt a chill spreading itself on his countenance, and he muttered some inaudible complaint.

"I am very sorry, Sir William," he said, in answer, after a moment's silence, "that I shall not be able to cultivate your friendship."

"Why so?" he curiously inquired.

Florence trembled. She dreaded some terrible explanation. However, her anxiety of mind did not last long, and it was soon relieved when she heard the young officer saying,—

"The reason is easily explained. I am about to get the Horse Guards to sanction my exchange in some regiment stationed at a foreign station. I am young, and anxious for promotion, and not having yet assisted at what we soldiers call the first smell of powder, I long to do so."

"This is the ambition inherent in every English soldier, I believe," retorted Sir William, with diplomatic gallantry.

The cornet bowed.

"I hope you will see us, nevertheless, before your departure."

"Your kindness overwhelms me," returned the young man, in a voice which, had it been well studied, would have been found to contain a world of bitter feelings. Happily, Sir William heeded it not. Having then shook hands with her former husband, the soldier cast a last glance upon his former *fiancèe*, made another bow, and withdrew.

Mr. Morgan walked thoughtfully home, and when he was crossing Piccadilly was nearly run over, by a dazzling carriage, hurrying swiftly onward.

He cursed the vehicle—not as a gentleman, but as a soldier naturally would—little dreaming that it conveyed in its swift course Lady Kennedy, his rival's mother, on her way to her residence, where she was staying with Florence previous to her marriage with her son.

"What a sad dream is life!" thought the young cornet, as he entered his lodgings. He immediately sat down to write to his agents, asking them to effect his exchange in a regiment abroad.

A few days afterwards, the following paragraph appeared in *The Times* newspaper, under the heading of "Fashionable Intelligence":—

"On the 20th inst., at St. George's Church, Hanover Square, by the Hon. and Rev. Douglas, who performed the marriage ceremony, was married William Kennedy, Esq., son of the wealthy and eminent baronet of that name, to Mademoiselle Emily Florence Beauprè.

"The lovely bride, who was given away by Lady Kennedy, was accompanied to the altar by a numerous and wealthy circle of friends and relatives.

"Shortly after the ceremony, the happy couple took their departure for the bride's town residence, where an elegant and fashionably attended *dejeuner* awaited the distinguished visitors."

The very morning during which the above was celebrated, Morgan was stepping on board one of the West India splendid and well fitted up steamers, about to sail from Southampton.

What a singular coincidence!

CHAPTER XXIII.

WHERE DASHWOOD GOES ON WITH THE STORY WHICH HE BEGAN—POLLY SEEMS TO HAVE TAKEN A GREAT INTEREST.

Deeply impressed with what she had heard, Polly remained gazing upon Dashwood's features, and endeavouring in her own mind to fathom the character of one whose strange ways she could hardly understand.

No sooner had Dashwood closed his lips than he rose. He walked towards the cupboard where the wines, which the servant had brought up, had been left; and, having poured a glass of liquor in a tumbler, asked Polly to join him.

We need not say that Polly accepted the offer.

Dinner followed; and, face to face again, the two beings were placed.

When, the meal being over, the cloth had been removed,—

"You have told me," Polly began, "the first part of Lady Florence's life. You have related to me in a very graphic and interesting manner a lover's interview; but the story surely does not end there?"

"No, my dear Polly, it does not," Dashwood replied. "I will conclude it for you bye and bye."

"Why not now?"

"Are you so anxious as all that?"

"Yes, I am, Dashwood," Polly replied, answering her lover's query; "although what you have related may perhaps be a solitary case. Still, for all that, it shows me what reliance must be placed in men. From your own account there is Captain Morgan, who at twenty would have worshipped the image of a woman — whose death he longed for at forty—"

"This is only a trifling detail," Dashwood pursued.

"What occurred in Lady Florence's instance is an everyday occurrence. Woman loves much longer than men can or will. She never forgets the first lips that has met her's; and, whether she is a fallen angel or an honest woman, there is a strange feeling which causes the heart of woman to beat, when she meets, after absence, the man she has loved—whether he has proved true or unfaithful to her. I remember once having made the acquaintance of a 'Wild Beauty;' youth was no longer her lot, and her loving eyes and attractive features, which were the means of encircling within her nets many a genuine worshipper, had not yet entirely vanished.

"At the turning of a street a brougham happened to dart by our side—she grew frightfully pale, and her hands shook nervously. I inquired from her what was the matter?

'Oh! nothing,' she replied; 'I just saw—I—the banker. Dearly he loved me once. Now he cares nought for me, and the last time I went to his office he received me as though I were a stranger—placed a five pound note in my hand, and, as a favour, begged me not to disturb him again, as he had business to attend to; and as his time in the day was very much taken up. This is the reward for woman's love. But I cannot forget him though,' and she pronounced the words with a pathos which well accorded itself with her narrative.

"Man is intrinsically selfish," Dashwood went on. "There are a few exceptions, of course; but I generalize matters, Polly, so as to be on the safe side."

Polly thought that there was a good deal in what Dashwood had said.

It contained in a few words what novelists delight to write about. What is daily performed—man's ingratitude after he has had what he wants—a woman's bitter disappointment.

"And will you tell me the remainder of the story?" Polly inquired coaxingly.

"I will," Dashwood pursued. "Only from Owen Street, May Fair, I will bring you to Ireland."

"Carry me to the end of the world in imagination, if you like," Polly replied, "but let me hear the end."

"Before such submission," Dashwood replied, "I would ill repay the bright anxiousness of your expressive eyes, were I not to comply with your wishes. So I will resume the thread of my narrative without any further begging on your part.

"When Captain Morgan, once a penniless sub, was on his way to England—when, standing on the forecastle of the noble ship which bore him home, he looked forward, his eyes scanning the deep blue waves, gently swollen by the morning's breeze—when he saw the white cliffs of his native shore glistening in the distance, brightened by the rising sun, he thought of that woman, of that French girl whom he had once loved. He wondered whether, with the position which his newly inherited fortune gave him, he could obtain admission into Sir William Kennedy's home.

"A man of birth, I will not say a 'gentleman,' because every tinker, every shoeblack who has a good coat on his back, and enough in his pocket to pay his current expenses, is dubbed with the name of which the real meaning is nowadays prostituted. Well, then, a man of birth—a man with £3,000 a-year, has very little difficulty in England to obtain admission anywhere.

"Captain Morgan knew enough of the world to be aware of that, and when he stepped from shipboard on to *terra firma*, he left his landing-place with a firm determination to see how the Florence of his youth looked after so many years' absence; to ascertain whether the feelings which he experienced at twenty had remained the same after the time which had elapsed.

"To London: to the great metropolis, where there is so much wealth and so much poverty. To London—where there is so much virtue and so much vice; where such immense fortunes are made, and greater ones still squandered and lost; where there is so much modesty, and such an amount of infamy—to the English modern Babylon Captain Morgan directed his steps after his sea voyage.

"At Long's Hotel he took up his quarters, previous to his interview with his family lawyers—there to learn how a father, who grudged him a sixpence when alive, had acted when he died; to become acquainted with the restrictions under which he entered into his patrimonial estate.

"London was the same as he left it—no perceptible change as far as he could see. The West was not altered; the same men were about town; people that one knows by sight had not disappeared—they lounged about as in days of yore. A few had gone, it is true; either to another world, or had been compelled to seek 'fresh scenes and pastures new;' but if not the identical ones whom Morgan had noticed, it was the same class of individuals.

"The captain was walking slowly along Piccadilly—he was just on the eve of hailing a cab—when, advancing towards him, he recognized the features of one whom he thought he had met before.

"The recognition was instantaneous.

"'By the Lord Harry! is that you, Mr. Morgan? Who would have expected to meet you here! I saw your father's death in the papers. Fine estate, that of yours, in Kerry; he improved it greatly, I understand, during his lifetime. Not sorry, I suppose, to have returned from India? Crack regiment which you left—they are coming home shortly. You look right well—still in the land of the living. No appearance of an impaired constitution—a diseased liver.'

"These sentences, pronounced one after the other, in a systematic, slow, gentlemanly tone, happened to be uttered by a middle-aged, aristocratic individual, who was the very person Morgan would have given anything to see.

"It was Sir William Kennedy—Florence's husband!

"'I have sold out, you may doubtless have perceived by the 'List,' heartily sick and tired of drill and constant parades. The military profession is a very fine thing for a youngster who likes to dazzle pretty girls with a dashing uniform—who delights to sport his spurs among tasty dresses in a ball-room, or at evening rèunions—but I do not see it now. Think of settling down in a year or two.'

"Those words could be said to have been Morgan's reply to the baronet's welcome.

"Thus the two rivals walked arm in arm; and from a casual meeting resulted an invitation on Sir William Kennedy's part, to the Indian officer, to come and stay with him at his mansion in Ireland.

"Strange, but true. The husband volunteered to place temptation in Morgan's way!

"When will people cease doing foolish things?

"But he—Sir William—never thought that a visit to his place could lead to what it did.

"Besides, English gentlemen have—or ought to have—an honourable code of honour, rather difficult to describe; and to fancy that Morgan would have made love to his wife was a thing about which he never dreamt—or, to be more correct, the idea never entered his mind.

"Doubtless, had he remembered the interview of former days which he had with Morgan, he would have acted otherwise. But he never knew—Florence had not told him—that Morgan had been on such terms of intimacy with his wife as would have resulted in marriage, had Morgan's father dropped off when he should have done so.

"Had destiny arranged matters for the best, instead of for the worst?

"The story will show.

"A few days after the common-place scene which I have alluded to, Morgan and the baronet were hurrying, with an express railway speed, towards the Emerald Isle—towards Sir Walter's place, where Lady Florence was much astonished to see her former lover entering as her husband's guest.

"Brought under her roof, as the family friend, it never occurred to her ladyship that Morgan would speak to her about sundry matters, which two beings had, or ought to have, entirely forgotten.

"The welcome which Morgan received from Lady Florence was not of that peculiar kind which needs a description of it. She did not betray, by any outward sign, whether the sight of one, for whom she might once have entertained a feeling akin to love, still caused her to experience the same feelings; or whether she was now proof against any attempt on Morgan's side to bring her to a guilty avowal of a passion, the indulgence of which would be a crime.

"'Did she love him still?' you may ask.

"Listen, Polly, and see whether I cannot moralize like a parson when I want to do so.

"I have so far acquainted you with the various details that it is in my power to give you, Polly," Dashwood pursued. "I will endeavour to sketch, as accurately as possible, a picture of the feelings which existed between Lady Florence and Morgan.

"After the latter had arrived at Sir William's residence, he was conducted through a marble staircase to the apartments which he was to occupy during his stay.

"When he found himself alone, with a 'matter of fact jug of hot water,' he gradually sank into a chair, and thoughts of a deep and excruciating nature presented themselves to his mind in rapid succession.

"He felt the palpitations of his heart, which told him that he still loved that sweet woman, whom he met again after years of absence.

"You will perhaps imagine, Polly, that Morgan ought to have been happy and joyful at seeing the object of his former love, in the full bloom of health and beauty. In this respect you would form a sad and erroneous opinion.

"Morgan's character partook not of ingratitude. He was endowed with a great estimation of that which is honourable and virtuous.

"He could not but feel convinced himself, that the sentiment which he entertained for Florence, who was a married woman, was far from being an innocent one; nay, he knew that it was a guilty and cruel feeling.

"No doubt you wish for an explanation of those two last adjectives; I will give it to you.

"It was a guilty feeling because, with all the tenderness and strength of his first love, he coveted a woman whom he had no right to desire.

"For was she not married? Did she not belong to Sir William by those sacred ties, consecrated by the disciple of God in this world? By those irrevocable ties, sanctified by divine and human power, had she not become her husband's legitimate property? Had she not sworn, on the steps of the altar, to remain for ever faithful to him whom she had chosen for better or for worse, and to whom she looked for protection in this life?

"Was it not, then, a guilty feeling? that of which the object was to inspire in Florence the forgetfulness of those principles of virtue to which she had so solemnly promised to adhere.

"On the other hand, I am fully convinced that it would have been cruel on Morgan's part, had he uttered words of love to Florence; hoping thus to revive in her heart a sentiment which would, perhaps, have been entirely forgotten, had not an amorous language given to it a new strength and vigour.

"Since her bridal day, had not Florence enjoyed a life deprived of all cares?

"To such a question, no answer can be found; for in whose power is it to penetrate in the narrow and entangled recesses of the heart, and fathom its meaning?

" She was—and had been—happy, doubtless. The image of her love of former days being far away, she might have struggled for a long time without success, and ultimately have been so fortunate as to stifle the feeling which she once entertained for the young officer.

" But if she had forgotten him. Would not her love be kindled again by the constant and prejudicial presence of the being who formerly occasioned it?

" Perhaps her strength of mind was such, that she could have listened with indifference to phrases uttered by the murmuring voice of an enraptured lover. Perhaps, if Morgan was to attempt to call to her remembrance scenes long gone by, she would answer him with profound disdain, and with sarcastic coolness.

" ' The mind is strong, the flesh is weak,' and some say, that when love sits in a virtuous breast, no reasoning—no interior fight—is powerful enough to prevent a lover from wandering from the right path. The proudest of creatures is sometimes obliged to yield, subdued by that indescribable and unknown power, which plays with human nature like a child with a toy.

" I deny that, where religion exists, guilt will seldom follow; at least, such is my idea. Would it not, then, be cowardly and cruel, if Morgan, who knew Florence like his own sister (for had they not been playmates in their youthful days?), tried to destroy her family happiness?

" Did she love Morgan still?

" They had not met for years, and she only could solve that problem.

" And yet, I repeat, we are not so certain that he had his own mind clear on the point. Suppose she did, what then?

" Shall I speak?

" My sight is horror-stricken by a bloody drama looming in the distance!

" For if Florence, conquered by the captain's accents of love, failed in her duties, and followed the impulse of a fatal love, some disastrous consequence would surely follow her guilty behaviour?

" If, while carrying on a guilty intercourse with him, Sir William, trusting in his wife's purity and faithfulness, would not allow the brightness of his mind to be darkened by a shadow of suspicion offensive to him—would she, as an innocent mother, dare to give to her children the kiss of affection, with lips stained by an adulterous embrace?

" Would she dare to sustain her husband's look, when her ears would be ringing with these words:—

" ' Cast down your look, adulterous woman; your eyes betray your guilt! Instead of possessing the expression of candour and truth, they dazzle forth with a hideous lustre of lies and wickedness!'

" And if her love was discovered and made known, would not the pure and innocent forehead of the angelic creature whom we have seen in the beginning of this story be covered with the parental shame and infamy?

" What would the jealous fury of Sir William lead him to do? when he should learn that he had been basely deceived—cowardly duped; that a man whom he invited to his house, had assumed the mask of friendship to become his rival under his own roof?

" Would not his self-offended pride, which seldom forgives, coerce him—drive him—to wash out, with his friend's blood, the injurious stigma stamped upon a coat of arms which had ridden unstained through many centuries?

" Would not such a knowledge plunge him into an awful and frightful rage, ending with a bloody vengeance?

" Woe! woe unto the woman who, by her frenzy to satisfy the guilty lust of her passions, forgets all ties of honour and virtue!"

When Dashwood had concluded the last sentence which he spoke, Polly looked at him with amazement.

" You are the most incomprehensible man I ever saw," she said slowly. " I've been a common girl, you know that; I have lived among the lowest dregs of society—even the world; I have existed among characters of the most extraordinary stamp, men without religion—without any idea of what's right and what's wrong; among women who think nothing about themselves, and yet I never saw such a character as you!"

Dashwood's eyes sparkled when he heard Polly speak.

" There is a good deal in that girl," he inwardly thought. " There is something yet to be brought out of Polly. As a gay woman she will never do; she ought to go on the stage—she would make a fortune there."

" There is such a place as Newgate," Polly now said, boldly; " and if ever what you have perpetrated to-night came to be known, what will become of you?"

" I know that I will not die a slow death," Dashwood replied, as if he saw looming in the distance some dark scene; as if he heard the iron bell tolling the hour of eight; as if he witnessed before him a living crowd, eagerly watching the culprit about to fall by the hands of the executioner; as if he could foresee, in the days about to follow, a punishment which he too richly deserved. " Yes, I have a presentiment . . . . "

He did conclude his words.

Dashwood feared to speak!

" You are as pale as a corpse!" Polly said. " What has come over you?"

" Never mind, Polly," Dashwood replied, taking the girl by the waist, " do not annoy me —do not bring me to think; for when I do—"

" What then?"

" I think of Providence."

" You?"

" Yes."

" I am sorry that I touched upon a ground which you seem to fear to tread upon," Polly pursued. " But after what I have seen here, I hope, Dashwood, you will excuse me. If you had been a clergyman, you could not have moralized better than you did just now. Where have you found all the bold and honourable sentiments you gave way to?"

Polly pronounced these words like a girl who weighed every word she uttered.

It was a strange conversation, that which was taking place. Held between two " Outsiders" of the most corrupt ideas—of the most guilty antecedents; two beings whose lives have been partly pourtrayed already; whose deeds would fall beneath the justice of men—for whom burning would be the only adequate and just punishment for the evil deeds which they had done.

LORD VINEYARD AND HIS DAUGHTER.

It was an exchange of words between two personages, who had been linked together by the wayward hand of destiny—who were fated to go, hand in hand, through many years of debauch and dissipation; who were to cause mothers to weep tears of blood; sons to deny a father's authority; brother to allow brother to die of want and starvation; to tear the sweet ties of family asunder; to cause men, hitherto honest, to become dishonest; to plunge several of the older youth in all the mad and drunken indulgence of all that is wrong and wicked.

Worthy children of Satan! eager and submissive worshippers of Mammon!

"You have now gone through two phases of Lady Florence's life," Polly began, after an interval during which neither of the two beings spoke a word; "you showed her to me as a girl, you have depicted her to me as a married woman; what is to be the next character she will perform?"

"That of a guilty married woman. That of a wife rushing heedlessly from a home of bliss and comfort, madly to keep the company of a worthless fellow who cares but little for her—to bring herself to the verge of starvation, and then to be—"

"Murdered in cold blood, by a man of the name of Dashwood!"

"You are right, Polly," Dashwood replied, exultingly, "you are right!"

"You seem to gloat on what you have done," the girl pursued; "you seem to delight in the death of one who never did you any harm—who never offended or insulted you."

"Offended me she never did," Dashwood replied, "but she has insulted me."

"How?" inquired Polly.

"Well, when Lady Florence was brought here by my emissaries, I thought her a very handsome woman still. It would have gratified my pride to have enlisted her affections, and as she was to be my prisoner, it struck me that we might just as well spend our time pleasantly together as not."

"Then you had no thought of making her undergo the cruel treatment which you inflicted upon her when first you saw her?"

"I had not," Dashwood replied, peremptorily.

"And how came you to entertain such a hatred against Lady Florence, for you were hard and bitter against her; and I must say that, however cruel a man may be, he would never have acted towards a weak woman as you did, had he not strong reason to do so?"

"She scorned my offer, with a look which fully betrayed the antipathy which she had to me. She coolly informed me, that under no consideration would she acquiesce in the bargain which I was proposing to her. Since then I have lost no opportunity of showing her that my meaning was good, and many a time she must have regretted the bold hardihood of her behaviour. Now she has gone to another world, I shall get my money from Morgan, and more about the matter I do not care."

From the words Dashwood pronounced, Polly drew her own conclusions; and she learnt, in a very short time, the severe blow which man's character receives when his self-pride is baffled.

She was too clever a girl to show by her manner the knowledge which she gleaned from her friend's conversation, and she resolved never to trust Dashwood in any way, as far as she could help.

Besides, if we are candid, we are bound to admit that she feared Dashwood, and that she could not forget the strange feeling which had come over her frame when he had extended his hand towards her.

Perhaps it was a sensation that she would have experienced at any other time, and Dashwood might not have had anything to do with it.

Still, she determined to be prudent and cautious in the extreme in whatever intercourse she might have with him.

In this little respect she was perfectly justified, as Dashwood was one of those who could not forget any insult which he might have re-sented keenly at the moment it was directed at him; moreover, he was without mercy towards the offenders.

She had seen sufficient of him, during the short time which had elapsed since she had made his acquaintance, to know what were the weak points which he possessed—how he could be pleased or annoyed.

Polly was a woman who had no heart; yet, notwithstanding the degraded state of her nature, she could not but feel for Lady Florence, who had been launched into eternity before her own eyes, and, however slight her sympathy was, as the remembrance of what she had witnessed floated across her mind, she shuddered inwardly.

"The course of true love never ran smooth, Polly," Dashwood now resumed, "and the consequence was, that when Lady Florence left her home, she did not find with Captain Morgan that happiness which she expected.

"I should be deviating from the truth, were I to state that the first months which they spent together were not of that blissful character experienced by those, who for many years have longed for the possession of each other.

"But the warmth of Morgan's passion soon dwindled down to a feeling of indifference, and he was very much astonished to discover at length, that although Lady Florence was a very loving woman, still, for all that, he had exaggerated to himself the real nature of his love.

"This is not by any means uncommon," the speaker continued, "and, as the mind mainly sways the body, many people fancy that they are endowed with certain virtues and certain vices—long for the indulgence of certain studies or recreations, of which the birth can be traced to their imagination only.

"Meanwhile, to improve matters, and to regain her lover's devotion, Lady Florence—not being able to dispel from her mind the rashness of her guilt, the loss of respect and consideration which her step had entailed, the hopelessness of ever being allowed to return to her husband—became gradually downcast, and she might be truly said to be afflicted with the "spleen."

"At the end of a year she was confined of a child (the boy whom you have seen this day, Polly), and, powerless to bear the awkwardness and shame of a position which soon became known among all those with whom she was formerly acquainted, she did what many foolishly do—to drown her sorrows, as some graphically describe it, Lady Florence launched heedlessly into drunken fits of the most uncontrolled dissipation.

"The scenes which I have witnessed would baffle the expectations of the greatest admirer of Hogarth's clever and coarsely brutal delineations of 'The Rake's Progress.' Suffice it to say, that Morgan at length felt for Lady Florence—whom he would have ever respected had she remained true to her husband—a loathsome and bitter antipathy, which went keenly to her heart.

"She could not forget that she had sacrificed consideration, if not happiness, for the man with whom she had eloped, and the ingratitude which he displayed was unbearable to her, emanating, moreover, from the father of the son she had borne.

"Captain Morgan, however, was not lost to

all sense of honour, and of respect for his character as a gentleman, and he settled upon his forlorn offspring a very fair sum, to which he will, as a matter of course, drop in by the death of the two parties concerned, and he is greatly in want of it too, as he is going it rather fast, to use a worldly expression, which is somewhat to the point.

"Need I relate to you, Polly, the incidents which followed each other during the criminal intercourse which was carried on between Morgan and Lady Florence. You would, doubtless, think that their love was such as could never have taken the turn which it subsequently assumed.

"Like two doves they first loved fondly together; but finding, doubtless, that at their respective times of life, all the romance and poetry of love ought to be looked upon as ridiculous, Morgan studied the matter-of-fact side of the question.

"It struck him that, after four years' intimacy with Lady Florence, after having had his and her name branded forth to public opinion in the Divorce Court, it was nigh time to get rid of an incumbrance, which was so irksome to him that he would have got rid of it at any price.

"In common fairness, I cannot blame him. To see that fair, and yet handsome woman, reeling through the streets of Dublin during the hours of night—having escaped the vigilance of her keepers—in a state of delirium tremens frightful to witness; to hear her sobs and her vain entreaties, beseeching Morgan to return to her feverish and anxious embrace; to contemplate that man's violent temper, exhibiting itself in its cowardly rage against a frail creature, would form chapters of a thrilling drama, to do justice to which a pen would fail. It would outrage the laws of moral decency—it would pander to a vitiated taste, which it would be criminal to gratify.

"And yet, supposing that one was to enter into all the minutest details of an everyday occurrence, where would it lead to?

"To show man's selfish ingratitude—his corrupted and base ways and means.

"Now to conclude the narrative with the description of the terrible winding-up which you have assisted at this day.

"If I acted as I did, I have some excuse," Dashwood went on. "Morgan asked me to become the executioner for him. He placed me in the way of securing Lady Florence, and partly from motives of love, revenge, and of thirst for gold, I became a tool in his hands.

"Whether I shall ever be called upon to account for the deed which I have performed—to give an explanation of my behaviour—I cannot foresee. You know, Polly, what I have already told you, and no more need be said now.

"You have now the whole of Lady Florence's history, and I hope it has interested you."

When Dashwood had concluded his story, Polly made no answer, but it was with a feeling of intense alarm and anxiety for the future that she gazed upon him.

The story she had heard—the scenes which she had witnessed—the death of Lady Florence, to whose fate she had been a spectator, filled her mind with a strange, unaccountable feeling, and when she found herself turning on the soft couch of the room, which we have already described, she wondered whether she had really beheld the terrible face and agonizing cries of Lady Florence, or whether she had been the victim of some unearthly and strange vision.

As soon as Dashwood had terminated his narrative, he went out of the room.

Previous to doing so, he wished Polly farewell, and said he would be back again in the morning.

Thus left alone Polly endeavoured to sleep.

But she could not do so; her efforts to have recourse to slumber were completely fruitless.

The haggard and supplicating features of Lady Florence beseeching mercy were too strongly impressed upon her mind. The piercing sobs of the youngest of the two girls, who apparently slept over her head, had made too deep a sensation upon her whole being, to allow her to forget, at a moment's notice, the several adventures which had befallen her.

Vainly she tried to explain to herself the mysterious character of Dashwood, but this was beyond her power.

More than once she thought of ascending the stairs which led to the apartment above, where the two young girls were confined, to explain to them the horrible doom which awaited them; but she remembered too well the ascendancy of Dashwood over her, and she dreaded to do so.

"After all," she muttered, "that which I have seen concerns me not. In the event of anything awkward happening, I should only have to explain what occurred to screen myself."

Thus, whatever chance she might have had of doing good, vanished from her mind before her own selfishness; and after having been turning about upon her couch for the greater part of the night, nature at length asserted her sway, and just when the first streaks of morning dawned upon the window of the room—a slight and uncertain ray peeping through the curtains—she fell into a deep slumber.

CHAPTER XXV.

THE INTERNATIONAL EXHIBITION OF 1862—A FEW WORDS THEREUPON.

THE first of May, 1862, had at length arrived.

Our readers can easily perceive that we are not relating things which occurred years and years ago, but that our tale may fairly be looked upon as a story of our own times.

This was to be, we remember, the happy day on which Langdon was to be introduced to Laura Wylde.

Who does not remember the Great Exhibition of 1862?

Who does not remember having glanced over this clumsy monument of architecture? built at so great an outlay, and which ultimately turned out to be a failure, owing to the lamented death of the intellectual and clever Prince who first planned it.

Doubtless, had our beloved Queen's consort been allowed to remain among us, the huge pile of buildings, which stretched as far as the eye could reach in that immense plot of ground at Kensington, would not have been pulled to the ground by a Parliamentary majority; and there it would have stood for centuries, to convey to future generations the spot where the International produce of all the remotest parts of the globe lay disposed in symmetrical array for universal inspection.

Industrious, far-seeing, and wise was the mind of that man who was the first to inaugurate International Exhibitions!

Shades of Prince Albert, let us bow before thee! Thou art no more! Snatched in the prime of life from a world, in which thy name will ever remain as that of a great benefactor, thou didst good for a country with which thou identified thyself, although it was not thy own.

Thy detractors while thou wert alive were many; now that thou art no more they are none; and, swelling the universal chorus of voices which acknowledge thy virtues, England is still loud in thy praise.

The sons of Albion sympathized like one man with their noble Queen's sorrow. They felt that a great blank in the country's history had been wrought by the decease of the Prince; and even an upright, honest, straightforward Opposition respected a sovereign's mournful privacy, and by a disinterested and well-timed forbearance, forbade the cares of her home to be disturbed by political struggles.

Readers, scan the annals of history, as far back as you wish so to do.

Can you find, during any previous reign, any such manifestation of a nation's gloom, which testified so strongly to the high respect—the deep veneration—a Queen was held by a great and grateful country, which knows how to love one who, as a sovereign, as a mother, as a wife, has been irreproachable during years of a prosperous reign; one who, in the former capacity, may be set as a pattern to coming queens; one who, in the latter capacities, may be said to be a standing example for the mothers and wives of Old England.

But everything must pass away! Gradually and slowly Time will do its work, and where, we may ask, is now that wonderful Exhibition?

Those colossal walls—that high dome—that mighty building has been levelled to the earth! No longer does that gigantic wonder of man's powerful industry stand prominently before our eyes.

All the glittering, showy, and sumptuous produce of British India, and of the Eastern world; land of warmth, of gold, of glowing vegetation, of silks, of cotton, and of sugar cane; of rich flowers, and of brilliant and varied and dazzling plumaged birds; of romance, of poetry, of mighty palaces, of unbounded wealth; source of England's colonial prosperity, land which has caused Britain to exult on her mighty sway, subsequently to weep over the loss of her brave sons' blood, spilt in the defence of her proud ensign, then clouded by treachery and fiendish rebellion.

All the produce of the North, land of the reindeer, of fishing, icebergs, furs, corn, hemp, flax, timber, iron, hides, and tallow.

All the unbounded vegetation of the South—the ever-renewing harvest of the Western soil—all the continental goods—have been conveyed back, in swift gliding vessels, to the lands from which they sprung, and of that mighty building nought now remains but an empty space, strewn with huge stones, mortar, and cement, which ere long will be appropriated by affluent speculators to more lasting purposes.

Everything is now gone, and where millions of money have been expended we see but a wreck. As we gaze upon that large plot of ground in Kensington, we may fairly exclaim that that wonderful international contest of trade and commerce, which induced so many thousands of souls to pay a visit to the English metropolis, from the remotest parts of the earth, is now, comparatively speaking, but a name!

———

CHAPTER XXV.

LANGDON AND HOGAN AGAIN TOGETHER—POLLY AND DASHWOOD—THE PICTURE GALLERY OF THE EXHIBITION.

IT was with a beating heart, with a mind full of the most sanguine expectations, that Langdon, accompanied by Hogan, forced his way through the motley crowd which was standing outside the main entrance to the International Exhibition.

On the strength of the " spec." which was contemplated, and which Hogan thought could be easily carried out, if proper precaution was taken to secure the prize, the latter had helped our friend with as large a donation as he could conveniently spare out of the remittance he had obtained from Gorge, the money-lender, to whom we have previously introduced our readers.

It is all very well to talk about pastorals; to talk about love in a cottage, and such like topics.

We say this as an apology to those who might feel inclined to find fault with us for alluding so often to monetary matters, for, although coin is a base, filthy metal (very much so indeed, no one can deny), can anything be done without it?

Willingly would we agree with the French fabulist, La Fontaine, that—

" Ni l'or ni l'argent ne nous rendent heureux,"

could we reasonably do so, but we fear we cannot, as, like our friend Patrick Langdon, more than once, I dare say, many of us have been placed in a very ridiculous position from the want of it.

All day long Langdon walked in the building, without being successful enough to meet Mrs. Haltering, who had doubtless forgotten her appointment; and our gallant swell was beginning to look somewhat crestfallen when, following the direction which Hogan's steps were taking, he allowed himself to ascend the steps which led to the picture gallery, where so many beautiful paintings were exhibited.

Langdon cared not about that which he saw around him.

The dark gloom of the Flemish school, the dashing beauty of the French artistic colouring, the mute but life-like landscapes of Landseer, attracted not his gaze.

There were many pictures around him; they were handsome ones, no doubt, but his eye rested not on them.

He was biting his nails, and inwardly cursing Mrs. Haltering.

We believe that the former way of showing his

annoyance was anything but good breeding, and we are convinced that the latter one would not meet with Mr. Spurgeon's approval.

Langdon, however, thought but very little about the code of etiquette; and the features of the eloquent Tabernacle enthusiast and worthy preacher were far indeed from his mind.

Where was Mrs. Haltering? Where was Laura Wylde?

Where on earth could the two women have got to?

Confound it all!

If they did not wish to see him—at least if Mrs. Haltering did not wish to meet him, why did she make an appointment in the German Court?

And why did she not keep it?

Perhaps some unlooked-for accident had occurred?

Perhaps Laura Wylde was unwell?

Perhaps her father, the crusty old clerk, had objected to his daughter venturing with Langdon's female friend?

It would have been as well if she had dropped him a note.

As it was he was done for.

He had paid his guinea for his entrance, to listen to some music — it was very good, of course—and to be crushed to death by a fashionable and wealthy world, which in his own heart he wished at rather a warm place, which novelists, as a rule, are too polite to allude to.

She might have foreseen all that.

Mrs. Haltering ought to have known by this time that Langdon—a man about town like him —could not afford to drop twenty shillings for all that bosh.

Had he got a ticket for nothing, he would not have minded the loss of time a bit; but considering the critical circumstances of his position it was really too bad.

Yes, it was!

The above thoughts were somewhat similar to those which crowded themselves in Langdon's preoccupied, disgusted mind.

Have any of our readers ever been disappointed by a lady fair at a rendezvous?

If they have, they know too well what it is to have to wait hours uselessly.

If, after a half day's suspense, they are gratified by the appearance of the face whom they are expecting, the annoyance received is soon softened by the pleasure experienced, in the reward of their impatience having at length been gratified.

But if it is not so? What then? Why, however bitterly I would dislike any one, I would not wish them anything worse than being disappointed in an appointment.

A mute spectator of the scene to which we allude could not have helped a smile could he have contemplated Langdon leaning on Hogan's arm.

"There is no one branch of the fine arts in which there is so much barefaced affectation and bad taste as a portraiture," Hogan began, addressing Langdon, whom he soon extricated from his deep reveries. "How do you account for it? Do you think it comes from the vulgar inclination and perverted taste of the town, or from the want of capacity and invention?"

Had any query purporting to ask Langdon to throw some light upon the date at which the first king of Dahomey came to life, he could not have been more puzzled or annoyed by his friend's question, and certainly he would not have been in a better position to answer it.

"My dear fellow," he replied, "I am no critic. I beg that you will drop the subject. I am thinking of something else besides a crowd of unmeaning, vulgar, staring portraits, which fill this gallery."

"You are by no means a pleasant companion," Hogan replied. "My dear Langdon, although you are vexed at the sans façon manner in which your friend Mrs. Haltering is treating you, that is no reason why you should be so surly now."

"I beg your pardon," Langdon replied, submitting to his friend's just recrimination, and fully acknowledging inwardly the truth of his last remarks, "but a fellow cannot help being bad-humoured sometimes."

"Granted! When you see Mrs. Haltering, tell her your mind, my boy. Nothing like having it out with any one you have a grudge against, albeit I, for one, consider that you should always keep what you think within you. Never let your neighbour know whether you like or dislike him."

"That might be a very good trait in one's character," Langdon replied, "but I am sorry to say that it is not mine. It partakes too much of Jesuitism or Priesthood, two religious orders which I hate sincerely, and no mistake, although I have been a good many years amongst them."

"That accounts for it," Hogan replied; "you have learnt to judge them, and you have thus been enabled to form your opinion of them according to their merits. I do not agree with you altogether, though. I think that there are some good men among priests and jesuits, but we do not see them. All the simple, kind, good-hearted natures are sent into the country-places, where their worth is found useful; whereas deep, plotting men are required in town, to suit themselves to the society in which they live, and work the oracle when a chance occurs.

The two men had been walking on in a slow, steady step, when Hogan suddenly left his friend.

"By the Lord Harry!" he said, "here is the Duke of Ellington. I must not lose the chance of shaking hands with him, he seems to have taken quite a liking to me."

Thus speaking, he quitted Langdon, to join the Duke of Ellington, whom our readers have already met previously at Mrs. Haltering's house.

Left alone, Langdon began to ponder on the uncertainty of woman, and he puzzled his brains to account for the non-appearance of Mrs. Haltering.

That she was present at the opening of the Exhibition this day he could not but feel convinced; but to go in search of her, among the thousands of people who surrounded him—who crammed every nook and corner of the building —was a task the ill success of which he could not but foresee, without attempting to carry it out.

He was thus thinking, when he heard the sound of voices.

They were familiar to his ears, so he quickly turned round.

Close by his side he saw Polly and Martin Dashwood.

He had met them before.

He had been introduced to Dashwood, it is true, by Mrs. Haltering; but, acknowledging the present worldly superiority of the man who accompanied the horsebreaker over himself in the social scale, he felt reluctant to be the first to address him.

The couple were standing before a lady's portrait.

It was really a masterpiece—what the French would call a *chef-d'œuvre*; and any one who had sufficient knowledge of the fine arts to pass an opinion thereupon, could not fail to be struck with its graceful touch.

It was Lucy Webster's portrait, which Mr. Browne, the artist, had asked the mother's permission to exhibit.

The mother's pride had been flattered.

The request had been granted.

And need we say that notwithstanding the recriminations of Mr. Webster, senior, who had strongly objected to have his daughter's likeness exposed in bold relief to the gaze of a criticising public — among whom there might be some friends or acquaintances, nay, some of his customers, who would not have approved of such assuming liberty on a tradesmen's part; notwithstanding the candid opinion which he gave that such a step was by no means a wise one; that it was by far too forward a proceeding to be countenanced.

Mr. Webster's, the head of the family, objecttions had been overruled. The canvas had been lowered from the prominent place which it had occupied in that worthy tradesman's drawing-room, and formally and duly hung in the picture gallery.

CHAPTER XXVI.

WHICH REVERTS TO SEVERAL PEOPLE WE ALREADY KNOW.—AND WHERE THE INTEREST OF THE STORY SLOWLY BUT GRADUALLY INCREASES.

LUCY WEBSTER was life itself.

Was it as a symbol of her innocence that in her picture she was attired in a white muslin dress, which fitted her to a nicety; and that in the midst of her budding bust, and fastened to her stays, a small bouquet of violets was her only ornament.

Had the artist suggested the costume as that which would most become a girl of eighteen; or had Lucy thoughtfully put on the dress, because she thought she looked well in it?

Had she been told so at the different sittings which she had made at the artist's studio, accompanied by her watchful if not suspecting mother?

The expression of the forehead had been minutely reproduced. The fiery and superb glance; the expressive blue eye, beneath which a dark circle betrayed a woman's budding passions.

The whiteness of the soft skin had been adhered to.

The small hand, with taper fingers and rosy nails; the well-shaped mouth, with slightly pouting lips, which displayed in a smile, illuminating the whole countenance, a row of dazzling white teeth, was masterly and faithfully portrayed.

Had Lucy been a fortunate daughter of a peer—had she possessed a handle to her name—had she belonged to an old county family, with broad acres (not mortgaged)—such a picture would have insured a rapid fortune to the talented author who drew it.

As it was, it only caused speculation to halt and admire.

There was a dash of talent in Lucy Webster's portrait, which accorded itself well with the original.

If the Royal Academy "hanging committee" would always place such pictures in the places which they ought to occupy, instead of in such situations as, from obnoxious associations or want of proper light, prevent the observer from discovering all the beauties of real masterpieces, the exhibitions would greatly resound to their credit.

If I am permitted to give an opinion, I will say that I deem nothing more irrational than portrait exhibitions. It displays the mass of pride, vanity, and self-conceit which exist in society, when year after year we find such swarms of weak heads trained to look rational upon canvas, which the originals seldom do on the shoulders of the proprietors; and which are, with as much stupidity as indelicacy, foisted on the public notice in the same rooms which are adorned by the rich, chaste, and intellectual productions of a Northcote, or a Wilkie, or a Landseer.

The photographic system has done a good deal towards lessening the mania which people have of having their likenesses exhibited. Where, years ago, they would have had to pay fifty or a hundred pounds to have a faithful reproduction of their own selves in oil, they will now have their cartes de visite, and confine them, and very wisely too, to their own circle of acquaintances.

The portraits of persons celebrated, and worthy of imitation for their talents or their virtues, such as eminent writers, distinguished singers, and first-class actors, bold and enterprising soldiers or navigators, politicians who, by the measures which they have endeavoured to bring forward, or have ultimately carried out, have benefited the country in which they lived, and are therefore entitled to the gratitude of the same, should be readily admitted, and a prominent place assigned to them; and also where such assistance as that of Lucy Webster is offered to a collection, it should be eagerly accepted.

But the admirers and supporters of painting should not be compelled to gaze upon the representation of a lot of "nobodies," fancying themselves great guns; women who have figured, or are about to figure, in the Divorce Court; females who have nothing to recommend them, beyond having been married to noblemen, who are known to us only through the *Court Guide* and the *Racing Calendar*. And why are the Joneses, the Smiths, and the Robinsons allowed to publish portraits of their insignificant selves?

These are the ideas which have suggested themselves to my mind when, walking through an exhibition gallery, I have referred to the catalogue to see the name of such and such a portrait as meets the gaze, fully expecting that the person who thrusts her or his face into yours is endowed with a name either known in the world of science, art, or literature. We have a right to feel disgusted at reading at the bottom of the catalogue, which professes to give us information, the words "a portrait," which in a few words means a lady or gentleman whom the world knows nothing about.

With Lucy Webster's portrait it was, however, not the case; for Polly, who was accompanied by Dashwood, stood looking at the canvas with a steadfastness which it would be difficult to attempt here to describe.

Uncertain how to act—whether he should should speak to Dashwood or not—Langdon, in his solitary mood, gradually forced his way behind the man whose character he knew too well not to fear him, so as to listen to the conversation which he held with his fair companion.

He might, by meeting him unexpectedly, address him, when he otherwise would not have liked to do so.

The crowd around him was moving on, and thus, unnoticed, he remained behind Dashwood.

"How very like that girl we met in that shop, Dashwood!" the horsebreaker was saying.

"I never saw anything to equal it."

"I should take her to be something better than a tradesman's daughter—shouldn't you?"

"She's very handsome, to be sure."

"What do you think that artist would charge me, Dashwood, for my likeness?"

"My dear girl, how am I to tell? I do not know what standing he may have. Some of these fellows stick to rather a high figure."

"Did you notice, Dashwood," Polly continued, in a winning tone of voice, "the deep blush which covered the girl's features when we looked at her miniature?"

"What? Do you mean Miss Webster?" Dashwood inquired.

"Yes, the very one," Polly quickly retorted.

"I cannot say that I did," Dashwood replied smartly. "You seem to take a great deal of interest in this picture; what do you see so wonderful about it?"

"Nothing, certainly," said Polly, "beyond that I would like to have my likeness taken as well as that."

Langdon was listening attentively to the conversation, but he could not as yet discover that he had been doing much good in undertaking the rôle of an eavesdropper.

"How do you manage when you want to have your likeness taken?" Polly again inquired, returning to the subject.

"Do not worry me, for Heaven's sake!" Dashwood replied. "Why, you go and see the artist, and ask him his terms. If they suit you, you enter into a bargain with him, and you find him just as civil as a hosier from whom you might buy sixpennyworth of tape."

"Oh, you are one of the most unaccountable beings I ever saw —"

And the horsebreaker was about to continue her sentence, when Dashwood interrupted her.

He had been gazing upon Lucy's portrait for some time.

"You had better, Polly," he finished, "get yourself taken in a white muslin dress, too."

As he spoke a derisive smile wandered upon his pale lips.

"What do you mean by that?" Polly asked, rather vexed, for she at once detected the cutting meaning of her lover's remarks. "Do you mean to imply that I am too pure to be taken otherwise?"

A silvery laugh, such as horsebreakers only indulge in, followed her words.

It was not a loud, coarse, vulgar laugh; it was a kind of free expression of gaiety, wished to conceal the effect produced by the insulting remark of Dashwood.

"The very thought which I had," Dashwood replied. "You are very sharp to-day."

"To be in your company any time would be enough to make anyone so."

These few sentences had been exchanged in much less time than we could have described them.

They had, besides, given rise to a feeling of anger which kindled within Polly's breast, and induced her to hate—like a fallen woman only can hate an honest woman—the pretty creature whose portrait she had so much admired.

Dashwood now begged of Polly to move on.

Do not go just yet?" she quickly ejaculated, "I should like to stay here a little longer."

"You may remain here altogether, and sleep in the building, if you like," replied Dashwood, ungallantly. "It is time to go, the place is closing."

"Is it?" Polly inquired, in a tone of voice which she endeavoured to render as coaxing as she possibly could.

"Look at your watch, and do not worry," Dashwood replied.

The horsebreaker now discovered that which she had not discovered before; namely, that Dashwood was in a bad humour. She accordingly acted as he bade her.

"You are right," she said, "we must take our departure."

As she passed by Langdon with Dashwood, she gave no sign of recognition to the late dragoon, and he did not seem to take the slightest notice of a gay woman's impertinence.

Langdon's eye now encountered that of Dashwood.

The latter took no notice of him.

To ascertain whether Dashwood really meant to offend him, Langdon walked once or twice before him.

Dashwood, however, turned his head another way.

"That man has cut me," Langdon thought, "I wonder what can be the reason of it? I suppose he does not wish to know me."

He was thus soliloquising, when he saw Hogan and the Duke of Ellington jumping into a Hansom cab.

The former waved his hand to him as a farewell.

"Lucky dog, that Hogan!" Langdon thought. "He has got a way about him. Shouldn't be astonished if he was to get the Duke's name to a bill, he can do it if any one can; and am I doomed to be always padding the hoof in this way?"

The remembrances of better days—remembrances of the time when he was wont to drive his four-in-hand down Sackville Street, when he sported a stall at the opera, and when he thought nothing of giving a hundred pound cheque to a "Wild Beauty," or St. John's Wood fallen angel—of hacking his horse for a cool "thou" in a match with Lord So-and-so—came across him.

Bitter remembrances were those!

He bit his nails over and over again, and a tear glistened in the corner of his intelligent grey eye.

He was now outside the Exhibition building.

The huge, motley, and apparently thoughtless crowd dwindled away before him—like ice melting before the scorching sun, and he was about to depart, to return to Tottenham Court Road—where his landlady, doubtless, who had at length seen the colour of his coin, awaited him with a bottle of the real stuff—when he thought he felt some one squeezing his arm.

What words could describe the immense bliss that this good pinch afforded him, when he at last saw Mrs. Haltering, accompanied by a large circle of friends.

Who were they?

Some of them we perhaps know, while the others may not have been yet introduced to our readers.

Under these circumstances, and as certain things must be told which require space, we will beg leave to conclude the present chapter and begin another.

———

CHAPTER XXVII.

WHICH INTRODUCES FRESH PERSONAGES TO OUR READERS, IN THE SHAPE OF OLD MISS HOOTH AND MRS. CHETWYND, THE MOCK DUKE—AND WHICH BRINGS LANGDON ONCE MORE WITH MRS. HALTERING, AND WITH HIS YOUNG FRIEND, LAURA WYLDE.

NOTHING could exceed the joy which filled the breast of Patrick Langdon, when his gaze rested upon Mrs. Haltering's features, and when, amid the circle of acquaintances which surrounded her, he discovered the pretty face of Laura Wylde, the dashing heiress.

The suspense in which he had been kept during the whole of the day—the bitter disappointment which he would have experienced at his journey to Kensington being productive of no happy result—were certainly relieved now by the pleasure which he felt at again finding himself in the company of Mrs. Haltering.

Who the persons whom he saw before him were, he was at a loss to know.

Their countenances were not familiar to him; with the exception of Laura and his old friend, he had never met them before.

If the truth must be told, it is only fair to state that Langdon would have preferred seeing a smaller number of strange faces, and that he would have relished far more a tête-à-tête interview with Laura Wylde, than to find himself suddenly thrown among the several beings, to whom, as a matter of course, he would be introduced in the course of time.

Men who have moved in society at some period of their life—albeit, from a concourse of circumstances over which they had no control, they may have found themselves excluded from it—must know that it is not always with pleasure that they are compelled to make fresh acquaintances.

As this book is written for the purpose of describing, rather minutely, several characters

—which I beg to say do not exist only in my imagination, and who are, at this present moment, "alive and kicking"—it may be as well to inform those who may peruse my work, what I really mean by "Outsiders."

Granted that ere now, in the first pages of this story, I have already said what I mean by "Outsiders;" but, as all those who happened to be with Mrs. Haltering come under the above denomination, to lay a little more stress upon the subject, and to enlighten them a little more, will not, perhaps, be deemed out of place by an impartial, intellectual, and often indulgent reading Public.

By "Outsiders," I do not mean only what a narrow mind might fancy, namely, gay women, and all the followers of that thoughtless and vicious tribe; I mean those who are actually shut out from society.

What is Society?

Some people call Society "The Upper Ten Thousand"—a large clique, which will admit within its intimacy none but those whose acquaintance is to be sought, owing to their rank, their talent, or their wealth, namely, the aristocracy of birth and the aristocracy of genius.

This is truly a faithful description of a class which ranks highest in the social scale, but how many have been admitted into society—either through their right to such admission, or through a cringing subserviency to those in whose power it is to open the doors of the select tabernacle.

But if the number of such is great, the name of those who have once seen life in good society—and who have been cast out of it, either owing to adversity, poverty, misconduct, dishonesty, or too great a wish to rival their betters—can, without exaggerration, be termed legion.

They are too numerous for us to try to enumerate them.

They would comprise railway kings in disgrace, stockbrokers high on "change" smashed and done for, successful and bold speculators, whom the chain of destiny had ceased to favour, well known sporting characters, against whom ill-luck seems to have set in, noblemen, who, through some disgraceful notoriety, are no longer known by their equals, women (no ladies?) who, bent upon having it their own way, have found that the world cannot be brought to think like them, financial men, who have figured in transactions that do not quite resound to their credit, noble marquises who have bartered ministerial favours, and been too prone to be the first promoters of some dirty jobs, superior officers who have dabbled in island speculations, tiptop men who have been brought to pay a visit to that well known building in Basinghall Street, and a great many others, whose inferiority is too striking to expatiate upon.

Now, although all these would not come under the denomination of that world which Alexander Dumas the younger calls the *Demi Monde* (because of the limited dominion of the latter), they are "Outsiders," nevertheless.

Dashwood — Hogan — Langdon — are male "Outsiders."

It need not be said that the general portion of our characters are such, with the exception of Lord Vineyard, who may hereafter become such, once he has "lost caste;" but whether he will

FATHER WILKINSON.

do so or not, it is not our province here to state at present.

Then there is all the "small fry," a catalogue of which we have given in our introductory pages.

When Langdon approached Mrs. Haltering, she curtsied and bowed; not one of those bows which would be indulged in by a good worthy lady "from the country," but majestically, and with that ease which women of the world possess in such an eminent degree, whether they are "Outsiders" or not.

"She was happy to see him. Thought he had gone back to his estate in Ireland. Never expected to meet him outside the building;" and so forth.

To these remarks, Langdon replied, like he could sometimes :—

"By rights I should have crossed over yesterday, if I had taken my agent's advice (every Irish gentleman has, or ought to have, an agent, whether his property is his own or that of his creditors); but London is getting so full and so gay—people are rushing up to town so—that I thought I would remain a few weeks longer up here."

As a sequel to this masterly speech on Langdon's part—which he had accentuated like a man does when he is not a bashful youth of twenty, and when he knows that he is catechized by more eyes than one—succeeded a general introduction, which our Irish friend looked upon as being his due—and nothing more.

There is nothing like putting a bold face upon everything.

Langdon knew that the slightest of his movements were watched by some of the party, and he felt that it devolved upon him to make the most of his introduction.

Besides, he was too delighted not to be all smiles and blandishments; and being now in a fair way of securing Laura Wylde's heart, he resolved that he should not have to blame himself if he failed in the result, which could not but turn out as he wished it.

We are all of us more or less conceited, when we meet a pretty girl, we think that we can do a good deal; but we should remember that there is some one else besides ourselves to consult, in a matter similar to that, the execution of which Langdon was fully bent upon.

With Langdon it was a case of pick and choose.

He was firstly introduced by Mrs. Haltering to a Mrs. Cherwynd; subsequently to Laura Wylde; afterwards to an old lady of the name of Miss Hooth, and finally to a crusty old gentleman, who was denominated by Mrs. Haltering by the glowing appellation of the Duke of Soubillon and Rohan.

Langdon bowed to the nobleman, and fancied that he was one of those sprigs of foreign nobility who invade this country for the purpose of fortune and wife hunting, on the strength of a title which, in ninety-nine cases out of a hundred, is not recognized by their respective Embassies.

That he should come at once to such a hasty conclusion respecting a noble Duke, about whom he knew but very little, having only been with him for a few instants, may be deemed by many very ill-bred.

But there is a certain feeling which exists among gentlemen, whether they are rich or poor, which enables them to detect at a glance those among whom they are brought; and to that far-seeing quality, which places them in a position to choose the genuine article from a smuggled one, we must assign Langdon's suspicions.

On this interesting topic however more anon.

And, as Langdon found himself among ladies, we must abide by what we heard a wise old gentleman once say; namely, when ladies are in the case, everything else must give place, and thereby begin a fresh chapter to that effect.

CHAPTER XXVI.

WHICH IS DEVOTED TO A FAITHFUL AND ELABORATE DESCRIPTION OF THE RESPECTABLE MEMBERS OF MRS. HALTERING'S FASHIONABLE PARTY.

WE remember having been told a story concerning a worthy squire, who, finding his hour drawing nigh, asked his son to step by his bedside, and, as a parting advice, made him promise that he would never squander the fortune about to be bequeathed to him in keeping a woman or a pack of hounds, as there are always in this world many fools to be found who will do so, for the benefit of the more enlightened ones.

Langdon would have discovered the wisdom of the story—had he been acquainted with it—when, scanning the party around him, he saw four ladies, who were by no means to be despised, and for whose company many would have been delighted to pay a good round sum of money.

As it was with him, he came in for a lot of good things, "Free, gratis, for nothing," as the saying has it.

He was at first most attentive to Laura Wylde.

A girl that has a good income in her own right, a wicked eye, a passable bust, and some style about her, deserves to be cultivated by a fortune hunter.

Being fully aware of this, Langdon came out as strong as he possibly could; kept walking outside the lady, and occasionally fumbled along the carriage road, for fear of being thought awkward.

Laura grinned—she was greatly amused at our Irish friend.

We have said somewhere that she was by no means a novice, and that she knew a thing or two.

Young ladies do nowadays; and, as bad luck will have it, the moneyed ones are the 'cutest.

Patrick Langdon at last had fairly, without any great difficulty, been introduced to Laura Wylde.

She was not what a good-looking fellow, difficult to please, would call pretty.

But there was a smack of originality about her, which would have pleased an old man of sixty (wishing for her and not her fortune), which a young one could not but have admired, considering the substantial appendages, which enhanced her attractions to a considerable degree.

Be her fortune ever so small, an heiress is never ugly, provided she is not a monster.

Laura Wylde possessed the beauty of the D . . . . !

Do my readers understand me?

No?

Well, she possessed the beauty of a certain nasty gentleman, who is sometimes represented with a pair of horns and a long tail, who is supposed to do all the mischief in this world; whom some people call Mephistopheles—others Satan.

She was plump also, and many people like plump girls—I do, for one.

Laura Wylde was not witty, or intellectual.

She could talk a lot of nonsense about her young lady friends, flirt like English girls who have been in Ireland a few years only can, and that is about all.

This so far settles the heiress's portrait.

And now for old Miss Hooth.

The party wound their steps towards Hyde Park.

Mrs. Haltering, the Duke of Soubillon and Rohan, and Mrs. Cherwynd walked foremost.

Laura and Langdon brought up the rear, and were perfectly satisfied to all outward appearance with the post they occupied, when an addition was made to the young couple.

It was the old spinster, who took it into her head to join them.

Miss Hooth was an old girl of fifty at least.

She liked her drop of whisky hot, when, funds being low, wine could not easily be got.

She was on terms of close intimacy with Mrs. Haltering—to be candid, she was the identical female to whom Dashwood had alluded, when speaking to Polly about the two girls whom he was about to "bring out."

She was a "go-between," in all the meaning of the term.

Mrs. Cherwynd was her friend, and so was the Duke.

Where she had picked up the former we cannot state with proper accuracy; but we know for a fact that she had picked up with the Duke of Soubillon and Rohan at a boarding house at a guinea a week, somewhere in the neighbourhood of Fitzroy Square.

While the old Duke was using his fork as a toothpick, and cleaning his nails with his table knife, he had heard Miss Hooth, during dinner-time, talking about her friend Lord this and Lord that—about the Marchioness of L—— and the countess of B——, in whose family she had doubtless solicited admission as a governess; and fully convinced that to know so much about "Milor" and "Miladi" she must be somebody herself, he had made up to the old spinster.

It was even whispered that the Duke had ventured—had de facto taken—liberties with Miss Hooth, to which the latter did not, or had not, objected.

There would have been a great scandal among the inmates of the boarding house, had not the master of the establishment—who had hitherto received his weekly payment from the Duke with a punctuality which made him loth to lose so good a boarder—silenced the tongue of gossip, by saying that there could be no foundation in the report currently spread about, as he was ready to answer for Miss Hooth's known respectability, and the Duke was too good and too religious a man to commit himself.

For let us not omit to say, that the Duke was wont to go to early mass every morning, and that he went to communion regularly on the sabbath day.

For a strict adherent to the Church of Rome was his Grace the Duke of Soubillon and Rohan.

Miss Hooth would do "anything" for anyone who would ask her out.

And as her income was limited—and she took very good care to let every one, out of whom something might be got, know it—he helped her with the present of a dress or two, a suitable addition to her second-hand "shabby fine" wardrobe.

This is but a trifling sketch of Miss Hooth, but as we have two other persons to describe, we will, for the future—by their deeds and acts, allow our characters to speak for themselves.

Who was Mrs. Cherwynd?

Who was that dashing, handsome, fair woman, who did try hard to make people believe that she was a lady born, by her occasional generous impulses—by her hypocritical, scheming, wicked, guilty behaviour?

But let us first describe Mrs. Cherwynd—she is worth a few lines.

Fancy, reader, a skin as white as snow—such a skin as would induce a witty rake to call her "Snowdrop;" a pair of eyes—whose real colour one could not easily make out, but which put you in mind of the eyes of a weeping Virgin, with this difference, that the Virgin's sight is dimmed with sorrow, while the other is battered by dissipation. Not legitimate dissipation, but a dissipation which an everlasting indulgence of ever urging passions cannot gratify; red hair—no—say golden hair—of which the glossy waviness is very similar to la chevelure dorée of a reigning empress; most beautifully set teeth, the front part still intact, and threateningly brittle; lips which would be rosy, did not the woman live too fast to preserve any freshness about her; a bust which was once firm and well-shaped, but which has partly disappeared, and which, to be made to look like a woman's, is propped up by the tightest stays, and by some of those "sham" corsages, of which the valuable pattern is only to be seen at some of our fashionable French milliners in London; a ridiculously tight waist; a proud gait, such as Madame du Barry, Louis the fifteenth's French harlot must have assumed, when dragged from a den of infamy to be hurled upon the purple of a licentious and ephemral throne; a small foot; and a pair of hands, which no one would notice, were not the fingers crammed with gentlemen's rings of fabulous price; fancy all that, and you have Mrs. Cherwynd's likeness.

Mrs. Cherwynd was one of those women who could have loved a man deeply; but, if one offended her, could also hate terribly, and never forgive.

Curious to say, these were the identical feelings which anyone who had enjoyed her intimacy would have expressed towards her.

We meet namby pamby sort of creatures in this world, who produce but very little impression upon us—to whom we may lend an attentive ear while they speak, but whom we forget almost the moment we get out of their sight.

This could not have been said of the fair woman.

There was such an amount of deep thought, occasionally relieved by such naiveté; such a mixture of hollow show with such a substantial share of charity; her voice at times was so silvery—at others it vibrated so pleasantly, that she was greatly original.

She was such as a man would have loved as a mistress, hated as a wife!

She was one who would have indulged any whim which she took into her head, and if—like a fashionable lady, whose name it is not for us here to quote—she had taken a fancy to the groom who followed her to the hunting field, she would have gratified it, just as soon as she would have given herself up to the first nobleman in the land.

She thought that, because she had been married by a wealthy squire, who had a goodly hall, cared only for his bottle and his horses—occasionally for his wife, when taken with a "fit of the beast," who saw but little society, and who saw still less after his union, she could carry the world with an upper hand.

It would have been difficult to fathom the character of Mrs. Cherwynd.

Did she act as we shall see her doing out of show, or from true kindness of heart?

We read sometimes sad accounts in the newspapers — murders perpetrated by jealous and bitter men.

This dashing woman would have kindled such, had she, by that cutting impertinence which she possessed in an eminent degree, driven a rejected lover to the worst stage of despair.

She could be—and often was—disgustingly ungrateful, and would be exceedingly astonished to find that other people could be the same.

How many of those who peruse this work have read the Life and Confessions of Jean Jacques Rousseau, one of the greatest library geniuses that France ever possessed?

See how bitter—how vile that man was.

After having been loved, cherished, and petted by the finest ladies of the court, he turned round against them at the eleventh hour, and exposed their names in bold type in the books he wrote.

Was he a solitary case?

Certainly not!

And why and how was the woman ungrateful?

By turning round against the man who loved and married her; and by seeking to be divorced from him, after having received at his hands consideration and fortune.

To whom could this feeling of hers be ascribed?

Did it spring naturally within her, or was it the work of a crafty, fashionable Roman Catholic saint, who advised her to forsake the Protestant religion, and embrace eagerly the faith of the Church of Rome?

But all in due time.

The Duke of Soubillon and Rohan, with whom Mrs. Cherwynd was engaged in close conversation at the time at which we have taken the opportunity of describing her, was a short, stumpy, vulgar, fat looking man.

His features possessed a low, cunning expression, wherein it would have been impossible to detect the smallest shade of frankness.

His grey hair was closely cut, like a convict's; his eye leered villainously from under beetling brows; his nose was short and ill-shaped; his mouth was small, and his under jaw slightly protruded forward; his chin was sharp and lean, and he had the neck of a bull.

He was wont to dress in a costume which would really have made you mistake him for a wealthy stockbroker, who studied comfort, and when he went out to pay visits, to those among whom he had, by his political ways and means, managed to obtain the *entrée*, he was generally accompanied by a powdered footman, whose gorgeous livery accorded rather awkwardly with his master's whole demeanour.

There was something very comic in the appearance of his Grace the Duke of Soubillon and Rohan; and it was owing to Miss Hooth's advice, who strongly urged him to leave the boarding house where he liv d, to take stylish chambers at the West End, and to do the thing first-rate, that he had managed—no one knows how—to raise sufficient cash to carry out his plans.

We are strongly inclined to think that the Duke de Rohan, being in more ways than one connected with a number of secret and mysterious religious orders, was, at times, in a position to replenish his exchequer from sources which were known to a very few.

It was he that had instilled into Mrs. Cherwynd's mind the idea of becoming a Roman Catholic, and who had taken her to a reverend gentleman, to whom our readers will be introduced as the story proceeds.

It would have well repaid the attention of a spectator, had he been able to contemplate the annoyance exhibited by the Duke one day, when, walking in Regent Street, he was hailed by the conductor of a 'bus, who, in a caddish way, sung out to his grace—whose appearance seemed to strike him—"Only threepence, sir, all the way!"

CHAPTER XXVII.

WHICH RELATES MOSTLY TO A PRETTY GIRL, AND SAYS A FEW WORDS ABOUT HEIRESSES IN GENERAL—AND WHICH FURTHER SHOWS THAT AN IRISHMAN CAN OCCASIONALLY GO AHEAD.

THERE are certain periods in man's life, when the accomplishment of a longed for wish seems to him as a dream, and when he can scarcely realize to himself that he is in the midst of that which gratifies his most sanguine expectations.

Such might have been said to be the feeling which crept over Langdon's mind, when he found himself in the company of the beings we have described.

That he was now walking side by side with Laura Wylde—that he had at length found an opportunity of winning her affection—he could not doubt, and, like a clever general, who prepares his plans for the day of action, he firmly resolved that she should not escape, if he could possibly help it.

It has been often suggested that the stories of the present day contain such far-fetched incidents, that could certainly never occur in the course of every-day life; and that authors are too prone to indulge in descriptions of scenes which can only be found in a fashionable and successful novel.

I hope sincerely that such faults will not be assigned to me; and that if my readers take no interest in the welfare of Patrick Langdon, and the other characters who have already been introduced to them, they will at least give me credit for adhering to the truth—and that, also, with perhaps too much faithfulness and accuracy.

Langdon wished old Miss Hooth at the end of the world, and could he fairly have done so, he would have politely requested her to go back among those whom she had just left.

He endeavoured, by a gentle hint, to convey to her the gratification he would experience if she were to join the Duke of Soubillon, and that fair woman about whom we have already spoken.

Unfortunately, the code of our society is rather strict in certain things, and it is highly probable that, had he given way to the truthful expression of his thoughts, the spinster would have immediately complied with his request, and would have informed Mrs. Haltering, without a moment's delay, that her gentleman friend was a most vulgar individual, and that it was really a pity that people should be compelled to fall across such contemptible characters.

Fully aware of the consequences which could not but follow any expression of his disappointment, Langdon smiled and bowed at Miss Hooth, and, by his courteous behaviour, made a friend of the old girl.

Miss Hooth, although intrinsically selfish, was one of those women, whose day being gone by, always feel themselves flattered at any mark of attention, however trifling, paid to them, and, as it costs them nothing, are always willing—and in some instances volunteer—to say a good word or two on behalf of people about whom they know but very little; and, as such ones as old Miss Hooth have not often occasion to praise others, when they do, it occasionally turns out to be productive of more good than they ever anticipated.

The conversation which was held between Laura Wylde, Miss Hooth, and Langdon, as a matter of course, reverted to the day's show.

She had travelled all over the continent, and so had Langdon.

She could speak French a little, and so could our gallant friend.

Hence they both indulged in a *parlez vous* twang, which greatly delighted the old lady, and the meaning of which Laura could not understand.

For the latter was frightfully ignorant.

She could write a letter—long ones, too—with a good deal of sentimental exuberance; but though her sentences conveyed to the reader the pith of her thoughts, they were not always framed with that servile submission which educated people seem to entertain for Lindley Murray's English grammar.

These, however, are only trifling details, which it is, perhaps, indiscreet and very ill-bred of us to mention.

But as we are now speaking of a pretty blonde with a pretty fortune, we hope to be excused for laying bare those weak points which she possessed.

She was not educated.

And she is not the only one deficient in that respect.

When girls are bewitching, and entitled to some fortune, their education is generally neglected.

They are often spoilt children, and their parents think that to be able to play moderately on the piano, so as to set a giddy party of anxious dancers in motion, and accompany a singer through one of those tame songs, composed for those who wish to make people believe they can sing, are sufficient attainments for a girl who will only be called upon to do one thing when she grows up, namely, to keep her affections to herself, and not throw herself away upon any one who does not in every respect answer the expectations that pater or materfamilias may have indulged in regarding their daughter's worth.

Laura Wylde at present was "in the market" (see fashionable vocabulary, as indulged in by some of our young English blood), and it rested with Langdon to say how cheap, if the whirl of circumstances favoured his endeavours.

We know, by this time, sufficiently well how our Irish friend's private matters stood, to come, without any very mature reflection, to the conclusion that, were he to be successful in that which he had on hand, no one would buy her cheaper.

"There is an immensity of love in that girl," Langdon muttered to himself, as he found himself alone in Laura's company—having been deserted, to his great satisfaction, by the old spinster, who, finding no great interest in listening to Laura's twaddle, had returned to the side of the Duke.

Mrs. Haltering and Mrs. Cherwynd were also walking leisurely.

As the latter had not been let into the secret of the bargain which had been made between Langdon and Mrs. Haltering, she looked upon the meeting with the Irish gentleman as one of those casual occurrences which happen every day.

"Who is that gentleman to whom you introduced me?" the fair woman asked.

"Langdon? He is an old friend of mine," replied Mrs. Haltering. "I have known him for years."

"Is he in the army?" the fair woman asked again, "he looks rather military."

"He was."

"What regiment was he in?" Mrs. Chetwynd continued.

"The 14th Light Dragoons," Mrs. Haltering replied, with that self-satisfaction which a woman like her feels in praising the character of her acquaintance.

"He is not in them still, I suppose?"

"No."

"Has he sold out?"

"Yes."

"He is like my cousin, Lord Squandermuch," Mrs. Chetwynd pursued. "He also has sold out. But, to tell you the truth, it was always a puzzle to me how he remained in anything so long as he did, for he is really a perfect booby, and to be a soldier, it strikes me you require some energy."

"Oh, it cannot be said that my young friend Langdon wanted any of that," Mrs. Haltering replied. "He is a very clever, courageous fellow; he was acting major to one of the volunteer regiments in the Crimea. He had a very good fortune at one time, and he has nearly lost it all. He loved display a little too much, and ruined himself."

"Great many Irishmen's fault, that," replied Mrs. Chetwynd. "There are indeed few countries in the world which produce more spend-thrifts than the Emerald Isle."

"How is that, I wonder?"

"Because some of them have the heart of a king, with the purse of a country curate. Generally speaking, they are a thoughtless class of fellows, and never think of the morrow. And has he any property left?"

"A little."

"Good thing for him if he could make up to that young friend of yours."

"Yes, very."

"Do you think he has ever thought of it?"

"I cannot say," replied Mrs. Haltering, innocently. "I am not aware that he knows what a nugget he has fallen upon. But he seems very attentive to the girl, for all that."

Mrs. Cherwynd turned her head round, and quickly glanced upon Langdon.

A smile appeared upon her lip.

"Yes," she said, "he seems to be decided upon producing an impression upon your *protégé*. I wonder whether the girl likes him or not?"

"I will take good care to find out," muttered Mrs. Haltering, inwardly.

And she would, too, no doubt.

Mrs. Haltering was a woman who would sift matters through.

Moreover, we remember that she had a certain interest in seeing Langdon's flirtation end favourably.

He would not only benefit himself by the transaction.

By the above conversation which had taken place between Mrs. Haltering and Mrs. Cherwynd, it will easily be seen how very anxious people are to get acquainted with others' business besides their own.

We would be the last in the world to give the fair woman credit for being of an inquisitive nature, but when we make the acquaintance of persons we have never seen before, naturally we make inquiries relating to them.

When Mrs. Cherwynd had glanced towards the direction in which Patrick Langdon and the heiress were, the eyes of the former had met those of the fair woman; and from that look had sprung between the two one of those indescribable feelings which sometimes lead to something, and more times lead to nothing.

It should be remembered that Langdon was still a dashing, handsome fellow, and from the likeness which we have previously given of Mrs. Cherwynd, our friends may be inclined to come to the conclusion that she was one of those who would eagerly seize an opportunity of becoming acquainted with one who, from his present obscurity, would not be in a position to injure her reputation, as much as one of those fashionable, wealthy men she was in the habit of meeting occasionally, being the wife of a landed proprietor, and the bearer of one of the oldest names in the country.

Langdon never allowed anything to escape him, and in Mrs. Cherwynd's eye he thought he had detected one of those mute invitations, which only a few men will penetrate.

I do not purpose to write a book for children; and if I had been told, when I sat down to pen this story, that it would be read by perusers of religious publications, I would have wisely abstained from committing myself; but I appeal to men of the world.

What is a novel but a book to amuse us?

If a true one—if within it there is to be found a sprinkling of scandal—all the better.

But as all my characters are under assumed names, I am perfectly safe.

Although a married woman, Mrs. Cherwynd was one who looked upon the sacred rules of it as a mockery.

The old spinster will play her part when the time comes.

We shall see the Duke of Soubillon and Rohan carry out his little game, and all those whom I have introduced to my readers will defile, one after the other, in their respective turns.

There will be plenty of sensation, as there is sometimes in real life; and no trouble will be spared by me to fulfil an author's duty—namely, to amuse and interest those who read him.

Langdon had, during the few years of dissipation which he had led—during the few years which had ended in his ruin—met with more occasions than one to study the natures of various women.

He had been thrown among all kinds, and all classes; among the patrician lady, and the plebeian maiden.

Where wealth is to be squandered heedlessly, is not knowledge easily attained?

Unfortunately, experience comes when it is, alas, too late!

Thus he soon guessed the real character of the fair woman.

He had, indeed, come in for a very good thing.

We are all liable to make mistakes, and it was a query, indeed, to know whether Langdon was wrong in thinking that Mrs. Cherwynd was one of those dissipated creatures who abound in this moral metropolis.

The great thing is to find them.

Many might have spent a life without meeting the same; but among what society had the late dragoon found himself cast?

Surely Mrs. Haltering was a very useful member of society.

It could not be said that he was not among distinguished personages.

There was a noble Duke—a real Duke—the identical man upon whom Hogan had fastened his precious person.

There was a mock Duke, or at least Langdon took him to be such.

Was he mistaken?

There was a respectable married woman, beautifully dazzling, gorgeously handsome, although slightly *passé*.

There was an innocent heiress, the daughter of an official, holding a situation of trust in a government office; an old spinster, whose grey hair ought to be a guarantee of respectability.

There was Mr. Leicester; Polly the horse-breaker, who was not called "Skittles;" Martin Dashwood, who might have put one in mind of Palmer, the murderer; and Lydia and Lord Vineyard.

The two latter we shall, ere long, meet with again.

The party had just reached the end of that long road which led from Hyde Park to the northern entrance of the exhibition, and, uncertain what to do, the several beings halted.

"Will you come and take a stroll, and look at the people inside, Laura?" Mrs. Haltering inquired of the young girl, in a coaxing tone of voice.

"I promised papa," Laura replied, "that I would be in by five o'clock, to take a drive with him; and if he finds that I have disappointed him, he will perhaps be angry with me."

Now, to be candid, let us at once admit the following:

Laura was entering into her twentieth year, and she thought that to say "papa" sounded very prettily, and as there were many people listening to her, she wished to appear as attractive as she possibly could under the circumstances.

And she attained the end she had in view.

Langdon thought that Laura was killing—*charmante à croquer*, the old Duke of Soubillon and Rohan would have expressed it, had he been called upon to give an opinion.

"What a selfish gentleman your father must be!" Langdon said, in reply to the words uttered by Laura Wylde.

The heiress looked steadfastly at our Irish friend.

Old Miss Hooth and Mrs. Cherwynd thought this a rather queer remark.

Even Mrs. Haltering began to repent having introduced Langdon to Laura.

And it would have been impossible to state to what extremes his Grace the Duke of Soubillon and Rohan would have gone, had not Langdon settled the matter by pursuing, quicker than we could write it,—

"Yes, Miss Wylde, I maintain that your father must be terribly egotistical, if he persists in having you always with him. Other people, besides himself, ought to be considered; and if he does not, he ought to know, that wherever you go, you produce such a deep impression—that the charms of your company are so irresistible—that it is indeed cruel of him to snatch you away, from those who, like your humble servant, cannot but feel everlasting pleasure in admiring so much perfection united in one being!"

When Langdon concluded his long-winded sentence, it struck him that he had no idea he could so far follow the thread of his mind.

The gallant speech seemed to relieve Mrs. Haltering.

The fair woman smiled.

Old Hooth nodded her head, as if she highly approved of what he had said.

The Duke compared French politeness with Irish blarney.

And Laura Wylde, highly amused by Langdon's off-hand way, forgot her promise to her father, and, more at home with her new acquaintance than she remembered having ever been with anybody else, allowed herself to be persuaded to walk beneath the shady trees which led to Rotten Row, towards which the party now shaped their course.

CHAPTER XXVIII.

A STROLL IN HYDE PARK—LANGDON'S STAR IS IN THE ASCENDANT.

THE path which the party had been following led to the carriage drive which became fashionable during the Exhibition season, because it was a short thoroughfare to the building.

The loungers never could make out why the carriages should have altered their accustomed drive, and chosen a road which became so suddenly patronized, instead of the hackneyed one by the Serpentine.

The reason has been given above, so why expatiate upon so trifling a detail.

"You are very gallant, sir!" Laura said, as soon as the different personages whom we already know had moved on. "Why, I am not in the habit of having such compliments paid to me."

It must not be forgotten that this was Laura Wylde's answer to that exuberant flow of language indulged in by Langdon in the preceding chapter.

"I am not complimentary," he replied. "I am only speaking the truth, Miss Wylde, and if I have been bold in doing so, I hope you will excuse me."

There was in Langdon's way of speaking an indescribable amount of submission which Laura immensely relished.

At length she had met one who admired and loved her!

Such was the thought which crossed her mind.

Little, however, did she know that her interview with Langdon was one of those concocted affairs, of which the main object was to obtain possession of her own body, for the sake of her fortune.

Little did she dream that Mrs. Haltering, with a far-seeing policy, had prepared this meeting.

Had she assisted at that conversation which took place between Mrs. Haltering and Langdon, in the journey which they took from Swan and Edgar's establishment to her house, Laura would have fairly confessed that, although she thought herself clever—very clever—there were many besides herself who could teach her a thing or two.

Yet she liked Langdon—she liked his ways, altogether.

Place a bumpkin—a vulgar, coarse, ungentlemanly, sheepish-looking individual in a girl's way, whoever she is, and see whether she will be able to enjoy his company, if he has not a title, or a frightful lot of money to back up his absurdity, and tell us the result.

Whereas, if you throw a handsome, gentlemanly, courteous, and aristocratic individual in a girl's path, the conclusion is very easily foreseen.

The world is a queer mixture!

Had Mrs. Haltering told Laura Wylde the following :—

"I am going to introduce you to a friend of mine, who has his wits about him, who had once a good fortune, and who is now penniless; who has sufficient tact to make you believe that he is in love with you, when he does not care twenty straws for all the Laura Wyldes in the world, without a fortune; who will play his part in such a manner, as to make you believe all he says is genuine."

What would the heiress have exclaimed?

I am sure I cannot say; but I know this—she would have been most frightfully disappointed.

Ignorance is bliss! and as Laura looked upon

Langdon as a true admirer of her charms—if she had any—she did not once regret having failed to abide by her father's request.

Laura was a girl who went out a very great deal.

She had often been asked by some of her relations—distant ones—to go and spend a few weeks in the country, but owing to the selfish watchfulness of her father, she had been compelled to decline all the invitations which had been forwarded to her.

The old official was tenacious about his daughter's company, and he would not allow her to absent herself from him.

Thus her life was entirely confined to town, and, with the exception of a trip or two which she made during the course of the year, either to Brighton or to Scarborough for a few weeks, her whole existence might have been said to have been spent in London.

Amongst a certain class of people she did go.

She went out to balls and parties, met a great many handsome, dashing cavaliers; and yet she had seen no one yet whom she liked so much as she did our identical Patrick Langdon.

She had certainly, during her peregrinations, been accosted by some of her male acquaintances—beings of the male specie—who, having no mind, and a good deal of money to spare, were got up regardless of expense, and whom increased contact with could not but disgust any sensible woman, man, or child, and yet she had not met any one whose company she would have preferred to that of Langdon's.

Where should Laura's liking have sprung from?

Langdon had said but very little to her.

Beyond the casual remarks which one would make to another, nothing worth noticing had escaped his lips.

True, he had paid her a long-winded compliment.

That was about all.

But how many people can pay compliments to a girl—how many can recite poetry to the object of their love—without kindling any reciprocal sentiment from the fair inamorata?

It was Langdon's way.

It was his style which won him so many friends.

As a matter of course, he ought, and he should marry the heiress.

Mrs. Cherwynd—tired of walking, tired of listening to the very interesting and highly intellectual conversation of the Duke, Mrs. Haltering, and the old spinster—now came to a halt.

The fair woman would not be bored a moment longer than she wished.

If tired of a certain thing, she would try another.

She was the queen of that assembly which we have described.

She knew it, and she felt it.

"I am getting very tired," she said. "That walking about in the exhibition has nearly killed me, and I want to rest."

She was thus speaking, when two personages came close to Mrs. Haltering, and one of them, —Dashwood—leaving his friend, approached her, and—with that refined polish which gentlemen only possess—shook hands with her in a friendly way.

It was not a very well-timed step on Dashwood's part, to act as he did, considering the company which surrounded Mrs. Haltering; but knowing her character well, he acted accordingly.

Evidently he had something to say to her, for he stood talking for a few minutes, while her friends stood at a stand-still.

"Dashing fellow that is, standing there," Mrs. Haltering ejaculated, pointing with a glance towards the spot where Dashwood's acquaintance was.

"Yes," he said, quietly, "that is Captain Morgan, an old friend of mine."

"Do you mean the member for W——?"

"The member of Parliament that was, you mean?"

"Oh, it's all the same," Mrs. Haltering replied. "Bring him to me some day or other, will you?"

"I dare say I may have occasion to do so," Dashwood thought, and, bowing to Mrs. Haltering, he joined his friend, who soon disappeared among the crowd, which was every moment getting thicker.

Half-an-hour elapsed, during which our friends walked and strolled about.

They gazed upon those dazzling carriages, upon those sumptuous turn-outs, striking pictures of such wealth—such show—and such empty hollowness!

They saw Lord Vineyard and his wife and two daughters—Captain Leonard driving in a brougham with Lydia; and all the faces which were known to them appeared, as if in a living panorama.

Young Sir Percy Hugent, Laura's friend, bowed to the saddle of his steed, which he sat nobly; and all these things passed, and the stroll came to an end, and every individual of that party, to whom we have introduced our readers, separated.

Langdon wished good bye to Laura, "he hoped he would have occasion to see her soon again."

Mrs. Haltering went home with her *protégée*.

The old Duke took a cab to his quarters.

And Langdon found himself with Mrs. Cherwynd and old Miss Hooth, standing before the Wellington statue.

He would have wished them farewell also, doubtless, had not Miss Hooth given him an invitation to dinner.

The fair woman did not seem to object to it.

Langdon was "a knowing shot" so far, and he was fully conscious that if his company was not needed, the fair woman would have taken very good care to let him know it.

How he blessed his lucky star! and, giving credit to the old spinster for a good deal of kindness, he began to make friends with Mrs. Cherwynd.

Does not this incident show that one should always study old girls, and that, in more ways than one, they may sometimes be in a position to help others, if not themselves?

———

MR. BROWNE'S STUDIO.

CHAPTER XXIX.

WHERE WE MEET CHARLEY WOOD AGAIN, WITH HIS COMPANION, BRASSY BILL, ABOUT WHOSE CHARACTER A FEW WORDS ARE SAID.

"HAVE another pot, Charley?"

"No, I've had enough."

"You may as well."

"No."

"One more—It won't hurt you."

"I say I shan't."

"Why not?"

"I don't want it."

"Do you find yourself getting 'beargered' already?"

"I do not."

"Sure?"

"Yes."

"Then why not have another swig?"

"Because I ain't going to drink any more."

"You are not?"

"No."

"You will not alter your mind?"

"You have already had my answer."

"Is that understood?"

"If you like."

"Very well, good bye then. If you will not stand another, I will not remain a minute longer with you."

"It was that confounded drink that did it before! What became of Polly, I wonder—since that night when she left I never see anything more of her. However, I will not fall out with you, Bill; you and I have known each other some years, and so here it goes."

Thus speaking, the individual who had uttered the last words turned round to his companion, and calling the potman, who was standing behind the bar, he placed half-a-crown upon the counter, to meet the expense which the order he had given would place him to.

The scene we have described, and the conversation which had taken place, was occurring in the tap-room of a public house in Kent Street, Borough.

It was on a Monday evening, about nine o'clock, and, beyond a few people scattered here and there, the two beings who had just spoken were the only customers who happened to be within the walls of the tavern where we have just seen them.

One of them was an old acquaintance of ours.

He did not seem to be in very great stress for money, for his garb was such as to induce any one, who was acquainted with the means and habits of the tribe to which he belonged, to proclaim him in first-rate circumstances, and driving a very good trade.

On his head he had a close fitting worsted tie skull cap, and his hair, tastily arranged, fell in greasy ringlets upon his temples.

His waistcoat was of broad-ribbed corduroy, with fustian back and sleeves, and his coat—of a light sandy colour—was enlivened with plain brass buttons. Although we could not easily define the exact name of its cut, it put one greatly in mind of a shooting coat, with its two large pockets on each side, and its tasty and showy appearance.

Round his neck he wore a silk handkerchief, the pattern of which was a yellow flower on a green ground.

His trowsers, which were of dark coloured cable cord, fitted him tightly at the knee, and swelled gradually until they reached the boot, which they nearly covered, and upon which he must have placed a great deal of pride, for a wreath of roses was worked below the instep; and from the occasional glances he bestowed on his feet, it was evident that he felt happy, and felt confident that he was as well shod as any being of his class whom he might meet in his wanderings.

"That's the stuff, Charley Wood, that'll do a fellow good. I never drink spirits when I've got anything on hand."

And the speaker took up the pewter jug, and helped himself to a long draught of that vulgar drink, commonly denominated "Cooper."

Having already given our readers a faithful description of Charley Wood the coster, whom we have seen in the beginning of this story—and who, we remember, was the first love that Polly ever had—to turn our attention to his companion may not be deemed out of place here.

Whether we wish to do so or not, however, we are bound to devote a few lines to this personage, as he is destined to play rather a prominent part in the events which will follow, and who may be the means of bringing together several characters who are familiar to those who may peruse us.

To say to what profession, trade, or calling he belonged, would have been a puzzle to the most critical observer; and as we can only speak of him as we see him, we must allow our readers to form their own conclusions.

He was a burly, coarse-looking man, of about five feet eight in height.

His forehead was covered with a long scar, which stretched along its whole length; his sunken eyes, of a dark grey, possessed an expression so frightfully repulsive, that none could have ventured to stand the fierceness of his gaze, were not that expression partly concealed by beetling brows, of a reddish hue.

His upper lip was cut in two by a wound scarcely healed, and what remained of his nose—which, from the effects of some frightful disease, had been cankered away, thereby laying

bare the greater portion of his left nostril—was so red and covered with pimples, that it was no difficult task to conclude that Charley Wood's companion was fond of his "lush," and that he did not always rest satisfied with the comparatively inoffensive and palatable frothing half-and-half to which he had just helped himself.

This individual was known by the name of "Brassy Bill."

He did no work, but had always plenty of the "needful" about him, and did not mind paying for one or two "tops fo reeb" (namely, pots of beer) when he met old acquaintances hard up; and would occasionally lose a good deal of money with the costers, who were not too proud to take advantage of anyone.

At the gambling table he was looked upon as a good sort, and always welcomed by the members of a tribe, whose notions of religion and morality were not so deeply imbued as to cause them to keep clear of a rather suspicious character.

It was whispered among them, that Brassy Bill had paid more than one visit to the treadmill, and that he followed a course of life which leads to such a place as Newgate.

But they did not care much about a "cove's" antecedents, if he was a good fellow when among them.

Now, the object of Brassy Bill, in seeking Charley Wood's company, was rather a deep one; and as he had, before now, been entrusted with one or two sundry jobs by our acquaintance Dashwood, it may not be improbable that he wanted some strong, stalwart companion, to help him in some of those dark deeds where fresh hands are occasionally required to sound the way.

Bill wore a long drab coat, of a light yellow hue, such as cabmen are occasionally seen with, and the dark felt hat which stood jauntily on his head, had evidently never been manufactured ultimately to become the property of such a man as he.

He contemplated Charley Wood with all the fiierceness of his glance.

CHAPTER XXX.

WHERE THE COSTER AND BRASSY BILL ARE STILL TOGETHER—AND WHERE A CONVERSATION, WHICH LEADS TO A BARGAIN BETWEEN THE TWO MEN, IS FULLY AND MINUTELY DESCRIBED.

THE two men had been drinking for some time, when Brassy Bill resumed the conversation, which we have been compelled to break off to attend to the sundry details which we have given above.

"What a chap you are, Charlie," Brassy Bill said, "to be constantly thinking of that girl who lived with you, and who, after all, went away because she was tired of you."

"Aye. You mean Polly, don't you?" inquired the coster lad, with a slow, deep tone, which he endeavoured to render lively.

"They tell me," Bill continued, in an off-hand manner, "that since she has gone you are quite a different chap. That you never would keep company with any other."

"That's true enough, mate," the coster replied. "I thought, you know, that I did not care a jot about Polly, but when I go home at night I miss her, that I do. I should like to see her again."

"You would!" Brassy Bill exclaimed. "I suppose you are in love?"

"Not exactly; still, I should like to meet Poll. I have tried to meet others at the gaffs, but, bad luck to it, I cannot find her equal anywhere."

"You must be a muff, to be sure," Brassy Bill pursued. "You are a young one, too, and no mistake. Ain't there an old proverb, which says that there is as good a fish in the sea as was ever caught out of it?"

"I don't care about all the proverbs in the world. I know this," Charley Wood replied, "I would give anything—do anything—to see Polly."

Anyone who had watched the countenance of Brassy Bill, when the coster pronounced these last words, would have been powerless to refrain a feeling of indescribable awe.

Some subdued voice would have warned him, that Charley Wood's companion had some terrible design upon the youth, and that he was inwardly plotting the execution of some nefarious deed.

Bill's features had assumed a jovial expression, which contrasted strikingly indeed with its usual look.

As he drew out of his mouth a short clay pipe which he had been smoking, and opened his toothless jaws to imbibe some more of the beer, a fiendish smile appeared upon his thick lips.

"Had Poll any friends?" Brassy Bill inquired.

"She had not. At least, I never saw her with any."

"I dare say she has found some by this time."

"What do you mean?" the coster inquired, eagerly.

"You understand English, don't you?"

"I should rather think so."

"Can there be two meanings to my words?"

"I ask you, what do you mean?"

"I repeat what I said."

"What's that?"

"You ain't deaf, I hope."

"This is the first intimation I have had of it, if I am."

The coster pronounced these words in a vexed, annoyed tone of voice.

"Now look here, my boy," Brassy Bill resumed; "I asked you whether Polly had any friends."

"I told you she had not," Charley Wood replied.

"In reply to that, I further said, 'I dare say she has found some by this time.'"

"Yes."

"What is there in that for you to get vexed at?"

Charley made no answer.

"She was a pretty girl, was she not?" Brassy Bill continued.

This question filled Charley Wood with a bitterness which no pen could describe.

He was beginning to hate cordially that man Brassy Bill, who was playing so mercilessly with whatever spark of feeling he might have had, and his words were the more cutting to him, because he knew there was too much likelihood

of the insinuation which they conveyed having come to pass.

Now Charley Wood had found out, as soon as Polly had left him, that he really loved the girl.

While with him, she had often and often helped him to spend pleasantly the time which they had before them, after the market hours were over, and, as we never discover the value of that which we hold dear until we have lost it, so had the coster had occasion, more than once, to regret the brutal behaviour which he had exhibited towards her, once he had been deprived of her company.

"I should like to find out where Polly is," Charley Wood again muttered. "Maybe she went and drowned herself when she left me. She was in a state of great excitement. I think —that is, as far as I can recollect—it was a wild night, and if she did not meet anyone to help her, I am sure she took a rash step. She had no money about her, that I know; and what can a girl do without it in this here city, when she is, moreover, a total stranger to all? She never came among any of those who were acquainted with her, and it seems strange to me. I had some idea that, once her temper had gone down, she would have returned home, but she did not, and that's what I cannot make out, or anybody else. I waited all the morning for her, and then the next morning after that, and then finding, at length, that she was nowhere to be found, I gave it up."

Brassy Bill had listened attentively to the coster's conversation.

Over and over again the frank language of the youth caused him to smile, caring very little for whatever sorrow he might entertain, and when Charley had ceased speaking, he began in his turn.

"Let us give up this beastly stuff, Charley," he said, "and let us be on for a drop of 'blue ruin?'"

"No."

"Do?"

"No."

"You won't have a 'peep at the ceiling,' then?"

"No."

These last two negatives were uttered by Charley Wood in a peremptory tone, which would have induced anyone else besides Brassy Bill, to relinquish the task of attempting to shake a resolution which seemed, indeed, firmly rooted in the speaker's mind.

But the acquaintance of the coster was of a nature which would stop at nothing, and he would have his way in all things.

"You have become a teetotaller, I suppose, all in a minute?"

"I have not," the coster replied, "but, somehow, you wish to make me drink to-night, and I am not inclined to do so."

"But you will drink if I do."

Brassy Bill uttered these words in a tone which was still more determined than that assumed by the coster, and the latter evidently perceived it, for he looked at him in mute amazement.

"Since when do coster girls go and drown themselves, Charley Wood?" he asked, in a jeering way. "Did you ever hear of such a thing?—I did not."

And he indulged in a loud laugh, which

caused the company—which had gradually increased during the conversation which had been held between the two friends—to direct their attention towards him.

Charley Wood was getting more and more astonished.

"Let us have a quartern of your 'blue ruin,' and two glasses, governor," Brassy Bill continued, addressing the landlord of the tavern, and paying for the same on the production of the gin.

The coster now made no objection to drink with Brassy Bill.

Something told him that his companion knew something about Polly.

"No, Charley, Polly is not dead yet," the man said.

"Do you know where she is, then?"

There was a feverish trembling about the youth's fist, as he laid it upon Brassy Bill's shoulder, his breast heaved, and the glare of his glance had something unearthly in it, as his eye flashed with anxious scrutiny upon his companion's countenance.

Brassy Bill did not fail to notice all the incidents we have described.

"That chap is crazy about Polly," he muttered. "If properly handled, he will be a capital tool in my hands—just the chap that I want. He is not known by the crushers to be in my line, and such as he may afford me valuable assistance. There is a good day coming, and I shall make some money yet, if I am careful; if I don't, why, my name ain't Bill, that's all."

"Do you know Polly's whereabouts?" asked Charley Wood.

"If I did, what avail would that be to you?"

"I would try to meet her."

"You!"

There was such an amount of contempt in Brassy Bill's exclamation, that the coster's features became as white as a sheet.

"Yes, me!" he replied, with his lips closed, and with his clenched fists, which he kept by his side. "She is not so altered that she would deny to see me."

"She may be," Bill pursued, coolly.

"I don't think she would."

"It's very likely."

"Do you really know where she is?"

"Now, my friend, do not be too anxious. Drink off your stuff, and then I will talk to you."

The coster acted as he was bid.

"Now," said he, "I am listening."

"You are of an awfully excitable nature," pursued Brassy Bill. "Who told you that I knew where your friend Polly may be? A coster girl in London is not of such importance as to be so easily traced as you think. I may not be able to find her out."

This answer was unexpected.

In an instant Charley Wood became so crestfallen, that it would have been impossible to fancy that so short a space of time could have effected such a change.

He looked up, however, after a while.

Brassy Bill was smiling significantly.

"Oh, I feel," he said, "that you know a good deal more than you wish to let out. But do tell me, will you?"

However hardened some hearts may be, there is something so keen and so touching in the entreaties of a youth, however depraved that youth may be, that to prolong useless suspense—to withhold from his ears that which he must ultimately be made acquainted with—appears cruel to many.

Brassy Bill was moved by Charley Wood's prayer.

"You said, I believe," he began, "that to meet Polly again, you would do anything. Do you fully understand the meaning of those words? Can you realize to your mind the pith of their signification?"

"I can," Charley Wood replied.

"That it implies housebreaking — perhaps murder?"

The last sentence was pronounced by the ruffian in so low a tone that it was heard only by Charley Wood.

It had been uttered in an under whisper.

The coster hesitated.

"You fear?" asked Brassy Bill.

"Never mind," the youth replied, "I will keep my word."

"But the girl may not be worth seeking. She may have become a 'Nymph of the Pave,' as some of you chaps call women that barter their youth and beauty for gold."

"You can prove that, can't you?"

"Yes."

"Do so."

"I will, on one condition."

"What is that?"

"You help me in my endeavours to crack a crib."

"Yes, with all my heart."

"That's so far right," exclaimed Bill.

"And if I do my part well," the coster pursued, "you help me to find Polly?"

"I promise you to do so," Brassy Bill replied. And now, to cut matters short, is that a bargain?"

"It is."

"When will you be ready?"

"Any time you like."

"That is sufficient. And now, come on; away from this place we shall be able to talk more freely."

And as the two men emerged from the public house, for a few yards they heard a woman's voice, singing:—

"Duck-legged Dick had a donkey,
    And his lush loved much for to swill,
One day he got rather lumpy,
    And got sent seven days to the mill.
His donkey was taken to the Green yard,
    A fate which he never deserved;
Oh, it was such a regular mean yard,
    That, alas! the poor moke got starved.

"Oh, bad luck can't be prevented,
    Fortune she smiles and she frowns;
He's best off that's contented,
    To mix, sirs, the ups and the downs!"

"Let me listen to that song, it was a favourite one of Polly's. But, really, shall I ever see the girl again?" the coster said.

"Don't stay here," Brassy Bill replied, rather hastily. "There is more verses than one to it, as you are aware; and standing here in the cold is a state of things I do not see for the present. If you are ready to help me, come on."

And Charley Wood allowed himself to be led away by Brassy Bill.

The night being dark, and the heavens covered with heavy clouds which betrayed the approach of a storm, the two beings mingled among the crowd, and hurried on, with quick steps, towards a destination known only to one of those parties whom we have seen sallying forth together.

CHAPTER XXXI.

WHERE A FEW WORDS ARE DEVOTED ON BEHALF OF TWO PERSONAGES WHOM WE HAVE SEEN TOGETHER IN THE PREVIOUS CHAPTER.

IT would not be to our purpose, were we to describe minutely the various steps which were taken by Brassy Bill to insure, beyond doubt, the services which the coster youth had volunteered to give him, on condition that he would place him in a position to meet Polly once more.

From the frantic and wild state in which he was, Charley Wood did not emerge for a few days, as it was the aim of his companion—who was an adept in the career of vice—to keep him in a state of drunken unconsciousness, and not to permit him—until he had gone so far as to render retreat impossible—to indulge in such reflections as would show him the recklessness of his behaviour, and induce him to retract a promise which bound him to carry out some deed, the exact import of which he could not be said to have ever fully understood.

It was a deeply laid plan, that which was conceived by Brassy Bill.

He meant nothing less than the "cracking of a crib," as he would graphically have described it to one of his pals.

To do so successfully, he required the assistance of some strong companion, like Charley Wood appeared to be.

The scoundrel had lost no opportunity of working upon the feelings of his intended victim.

By occasional words which he intermingled with his speech, he played his part so well, and so cleverly, that he could not have found, in the whole of this huge metropolis, one who would have answered his purpose better, and who was, in every respect, so well adapted to help him to carry out the object he had in view.

It may seem improbable, perhaps, to some of our readers, to find that Charley Wood entertained still a strong affection for the girl who had forsaken him.

He longed for an opportunity to meet her again, and to gaze once more upon her features.

But this is not, by any means, unaccountable.

Those who have deeply studied the human heart, will willingly concur with us in admitting that, however base and degraded a man may be, he will occasionally act in a manner which, at some time or another, he will repent of; but he will not and cannot forget—if he belonged to life's golden period, youth—the first lip that has met his.

Charley Wood's acquaintance with Polly, it should be remembered, was not the acquaintance of a day.

For a few years they had faced the world together ; enjoyed life when luck dawned upon them, comforted each other when bad times had come upon them.

For they had not always led the quarrelsome existence in the midst of which we introduced them to our readers, at the beginning of this tale.

Although children of low parents, of humble, if not illegitimate birth, when young—very young—they had loved each other, in their peculiar way.

Polly had gone away from the Borough, as we have seen.

Amidst fresh scenes—amidst the glittering pomp of gilded vice—she had soon dismissed from her thoughts the coster lad.

Not so, indeed, with Charley Wood ; he had pondered over the blank which was caused by her departure.

Repeatedly did Brassy Bill notice the sullen and morose disposition of his young friend.

Instead, however, of endeavouring to subdue the burning fire of his blighted disappointment, he would keep it up by pouring oil upon it, in the shape of a few remarks which, instead of setting the youth's mind at rest, had, on the contrary, the effect of torturing it.

Thus the coster could not bring himself to think that Polly would ever condescend again to be his companion.

Although he was far from knowing her real position, he had heard sufficient from Brassy Bill to know that she was now meat for better than he.

"Wealth will buy Polly now, Charley, and you must become rich if you still fancy the girl, that's all."

To this remark of his companion Charley Wood had made no answer, but mused inwardly.

He would have risked a good deal—nay, his life—in his present state of mind, to be brought face to face with the girl, and having a suitable opportunity to tell her how often he had repented of his brutal behaviour, and to ask her forgiveness.

If he mentioned that idea to Brassy Bill, he would soon silence it by a sarcastic, hollow laugh, implying that Polly would care but little for such devotion on a pauper's part.

Brassy Bill had never, at any time, been endowed with any amount of feeling.

He had been brought up to a trade which he did not like, and, finding that money was not so easily got as it was spent, he took to picking pockets, and after having carried on this game for a few years, and having made sundry visits to some of the gaols in the metropolis, he tried housebreaking.

This, latterly, had answered very well, and he wished to make Charley Wood his accomplice.

Had the youth been permitted, on the morning following the night during which we assisted at the conversation which he held with Brassy Bill, to return to his every day avocations, beyond doubt he would have done so.

He would have seen the folly of entering into a compact with a man, whose character he knew sufficient of, to induce him to come to the conclusion that in his company he could do no good, and that if not on the present occasion, he would certainly on some other, find himself mixed up with some adventure that would not redound to his credit; nay, endanger his safety, and place himself within the pale of a law which he dreaded, but which, as yet, he had no reason to fear.

The old stager knew well enough the reluctance which Charley Wood would exhibit, once he recovered the full enjoyment of his mental abilities.

To prevent such a thing occurring, he kept him well supplied with as much spirits as he liked to drink.

During his lucid moments, the coster would frequently ask his companion to tell him where and what Polly was.

But to his question no answer had yet been given which had enlightened him upon what he wished to know.

Brassy Bill kept the name of Polly constantly upon his lips, as a bait for his young companion.

He felt convinced that it possessed such charms for Charley Wood, that where everything else would fail, that word alone would have the effect of preventing him from leaving his company.

Charley Wood on two or three occasions asked the housebreaker when and where he was thinking of requiring his services, and if so, to tell him.

"My boy, it is no use to do things in a hurry," Brassy Bill had replied. "The time is drawing nigh: it has not come yet, but ere long will be upon us, and then you will find that our assistance is needed, otherwise I should not have acted as I have done."

But as the hour has not sounded yet, we will for the present part company with Brassy Bill and his youthful companion, and revert our attention to some of our characters, to whom we must return, if we wish to follow slowly but steadily the course of our narrative.

CHAPTER XXXII.

WHICH TELLS A FEW THINGS WHICH HAVE NOT BEEN MENTIONED BEFORE, AND REVERTS TO LYDIA.

As if our readers were witnessing the scenes of panorama unfolding themselves rapidly and successively before their gaze, so they are led by us through various spots of the metropolis, and, as the case may be, they are called upon to make either a slight or an intimate acquaintance with the high or the low, the rich or the poor, the opulent or the destitute, as the story goes on.

They doubtless remember, that when Lydia—whom we have lost sight of for some time—hurled herself from Westminster Bridge into the deep waters of the Thames, she would have met with a certain doom, but for the alarm which had been raised by Captain Leonard, ere we introduced to our readers.

The latter had availed himself of the invitation which Lydia had subsequently given him to call at her home; and when, in due time, he brought back to the poor housebreaker the casket which he had so miraculously found,

he heard, from the girl's own lips, a story which he was far from expecting.

Naturally he felt a certain amount of sympathy for the poor girl, and as he met her over and over again, from his renewed interviews sprung an intimacy between him and Lydia.

As much as he had been astonished at Lydia's story, as much would Lord Vineyard have been could he have discovered that his rival was no other than one, towards whom he looked forward to one day or another for his future son-in-law.

The systematic, slow villany which had been resorted to by Lord Vineyard to carry out his ends, was fully described by the horsebreaker to Captain Leonard; and the consequences were that, with the feelings which actuated his noble and manly heart, he inwardly despised the old patrician.

At first, however, it must be confessed, Captain Leonard had not placed much reliance on the girl's statement; but as his opinion of her improved upon acquaintance, he no longer doubted the accuracy of what she had told him, in confidence.

One cannot be too cautious in believing what he hears.

To substantiate what I assert, let me give my opinion relating to the women of London—the "Wild Beauties," as they are called by some people.

Is it not a well known fact, that not one "Lorette" in Paris or in London, or anywhere else, ever falls through her own fault?

If we credit the stories indulged in by gay women generally, shall we not feel inclined to pity them?

Shall we not think that they have been awfully ill-treated, and that, without a single exception, they have all been the victims of the deceitful, selfish, and persuasive ways of men?

We hear that they have been decoyed from their homes by false promises; that they have been tempted to sin; and that, once they have done so, they are cast off, like an old glove unfit for any further wear.

This is the old "Rigmarole."

It is *toujours perdrix*—it is always the same song; and if it does not come out in weekly numbers, it does in monthly ones, with a few variations.

This is, of course, one side of the question only.

What is the other?

If any philanthropic, religious, and highly deserving men—like the author, for instance—have endeavoured to ascertain, from the girls' own mouths, the steps which have brought them in that wide arena of licentiousness and uncontrolled lewdness and vice, where they shine for a few years only, what will they hear?

That men are not to blame only?

Ask "Baby this," "Polly that," why they have gone upon the town?

Because one had too strong a liking for the footman at the corner house.

Because the other wished to leave the greasy butcher's stall for a well-appointed brougham.

Because cotton dresses did not suit the ambitious ideas of a viciously inclined humble maid.

Because the tradesman's daughter wished to "live fast" for a few months, and then repent.

These, mind, are the women's own accounts, rather coarsely reproduced.

Nevertheless, if the French proverb, "il ny a pas de fumée sans feu," is true, the following may be drawn:—.

That there is a good deal of vice in this wicked world in which we live, and that, if men are bad, women are sometimes worse.

Lydia, since the day when we introduced her to our readers, had greatly improved in every respect.

Lord Vineyard had carried out his idea, and very few could be said to have derived more benefit than she did from the masters that his lordship had provided.

She had availed herself of the opportunity which she had offered to her, and unanimously did her masters pronounce her perfect.

They might just as well have refrained from expressing such a flattering opinion; for when the horsebreaker was told that she required no more instruction, she very coolly dismissed all her preceptors.

The greater part of them had been civil and respectful to her, notwithstanding the knowledge which they had of their pupil being Lord Vineyard's mistress, with the exception of one man, who met with rather a harsh and unexpected dismissal for his impertinence.

This was "Mossieu Lapin," the French master, who took it into his head that Lydia was enamoured of him.

Instead of teaching her French grammar, he attempted to teach something else—threw out some very bold hints about certain wicked things which are frequently performed on the other side of the Channel; and Lydia, having not yet graduated into all the steps of a horsebreaker's life—who, however, was not so innocent as not to be able to guess Monsieur Lapin's insinuations—plucked up her spirits, and haughtily commanded him to retire.

The worthy preceptor having failed to abide by her request, and having fallen upon his knees to make Lydia believe that his feelings were genuine, was summarily kicked downstairs by Captain Leonard, who happened to effect his entrance while the ludicrous scene to which we have alluded was taking place.

Looking upon a woman's reckless career like that of Lydia, it strikes us that girls ought to pine, that the rosy colour of youth ought to fade from their cheeks, and that they ought to feel so deeply the loss of their innocence and womanly respectability, that the hours which they spend, and the wealth which they obtain, ought to be unknown to them.

How is it that they seem to thrive and look right well on it?

It would have been difficult, indeed, for any observer to recognize in Lydia—in the girl before us—that foolish creature who wished to have recourse to suicide.

She was truly handsome and beautiful now.

Owing to her rather short apprenticeship, Lydia lived very quietly.

She received a few lady friends—Mrs. Leicester, Polly, and Mrs. Haltering.

Between Lord Vineyard and Captain Leonard she dispensed also her favours.

Little did the former know that he was not the sole worshipper of that pretty, enticing girl, whose fortunes we have followed from the beginning.

Fools build houses for wise men to inhabit; ergo, Lord Vineyard had brought out Lydia for his acquaintance, Captain Leonard.

It may be as well to acquaint our readers with the secret which had preserved for Lydia her attractions, in all their freshness.

She kept good hours.

Whenever she remained up late, it was in her own house.

Night resorts she had not yet patronized.

In fact, she had not gone out much, except to the Haymarket Theatre, the Strand, and the Olympic.

Lord Vineyard did not like to show himself much in public with his young protégée.

But as Captain Leonard was a bachelor, and cared very little about Qu'en dira la monde? he was wont to take to Lydia a box and a pretty bouquet, which she seldom declined.

Lydia greatly enjoyed an evening at our westend theatres, where she found no slight amusement in listening to Buckstone's farces—some of those witty jokes which this popular actor can perform so well; or in gazing upon those scenic effects which are so remarkably wrought by his talented management.

She liked also to be early in her box—to arrive just in time for the rising of the curtain, so as not to miss any of the evening's fare. The Haymarket was her favourite place of resort, and she could not have been blamed for her taste for this last-mentioned theatre, as it is as nice a house as there is to be found in the English metropolis, and it deserves to be supported by the public, as it is, and has been for some years, in the hands of a clever actor and gentleman.

To the Strand she went some times—occasionally to the Olympic, and now the opera season was about to begin, and she had already hinted to Captain Leonard her wish to have a private box there.

These were the only entertainments which induced Lydia to venture out of doors. To the Portland Rooms, to Mott's, to Kate Hamilton's (now defunct), or to any of those places, she had not paid a visit yet.

And the reason is very simple. She had no need to go there, for men sought her, and she not them.

She had freely bestowed all her favours upon Captain Leonard, and she had called to her help all the blandishments which she possessed to get him to fall deeply in love with her.

In doing so, she acted out of a revengeful feeling, which can be easily understood.

She had heard, through what means we know not—perhaps from Lord Vineyard's own lips—that Captain Leonard was wont to pay his attention to the Ladies Wester, and she thought that it would be sweet for her to snatch from the daughters of Lord Vineyard one whom they could not help envying—considering his fortune, and his noble and gentlemanly ideas.

How very communicative to be sure men are towards their mistresses.

As they are not likely to meet with any sympathy at their hands, they are most eager to find it; and now, at the last interview which Lydia had with Lord Vineyard, the latter begged of her not to be too extravagant, as he could ill afford to gratify her whims, which were daily becoming more exorbitant; and he had begged of her to curtail her expenditure, as he was gradually getting into more straitened circumstances.

To this prayer Lydia had replied with a sarcastic and studied bitterness.

She did not mean to deprive herself of what she had already enjoyed, and that, if he was getting too poor to keep her, the best thing he could do was to vacate the place, to allow some one else to step in.

His lordship had been far from expecting such an answer from a girl whom he thought was far too simple and too innocent to give way to such a coarse idea, and, thoroughly disappointed, he had returned to his town residence with rage in his heart.

By the above words, it will easily be seen that Lydia had made the most of her time, and that, if she had fallen a victim to Lord Vineyard, she was resolved not to remain his idol longer than it would answer her purpose.

Trusting that we have said enough concerning Lydia to enlighten our readers with regard to the change which had been effected in her whole being, and in her mode of life, we will begin a fresh chapter to attend to matters of a different nature.

CHAPTER XXXIII.

WHICH REVERTS TO AN IRISH BARONET—AND RELATES WHAT OCCURRED TO HIM.

THE scene we are about to describe took place in Duke Street, St. James's.

It was about two o'clock in the afternoon.

In a room rather tastefully furnished sat a young man.

To say sat is indeed misappropriating the term, as it would be far more accurate to say that he was leaning upon a silken sofa which stood in one corner of the apartment.

Although it was in the month of May, a small fire burned in the grate.

The new personage was no less than Sir Percy Hugent.

His eye was fixed upon the ceiling at the moment that we write, and his meerschaum pipe, which was not yet smoked out, had escaped from his hands.

It seemed evident that he was plunged into very deep reflections.

Sir Percy Hugent was a young Irish baronet, of about nineteen years of age, whom we have already seen ere now in company with Laura Wylde.

His object in coming to town was to pass his examination for the army.

An old uncle, who studied his nephew's welfare to such an extent, as to let him have as little money as he possibly could, had provided the youthful and hopeful aspirant to military honours with a few letters of introduction on his departure from the Emerald Isle.

Those letters had been duly and carefully locked up by Sir Percy Hugent, and, with the exception of the one addressed to Laura Wylde, he had not made use of any of them.

When he came to town—his first visit to London—he had driven to Onslow Square, and had seen the rusty old clerk, about whose company he did not seem to care much after further acquaintance.

However, he had accepted a kind invitation from him to stay at his house.

This Sir Percy had accepted, until he found such quarters as would meet his requirements.

Laura Wylde was a very nice girl, to be sure, but she was not so enticing as to be able to restrain the wild exuberance of an Irishman, who longed to make the most of his stay in London.

Hence, after kindly thanking the old gentleman—namely, Laura Wylde's father—for the kindness he had displayed towards him, Sir Percy, after a week, took his traps from the worthy clerk's habitation, and entered into his new lodgings.

In his new lodgings it will be our province to pay him a visit.

Being under age, the young baronet laboured under the same difficulty as many others in the same predicament as himself, namely, he wanted money.

He had come to town with a hundred pounds, but that sum had dwindled away in a few weeks to a mere nothing; and between spending his evenings at night resorts, and his days with those expensive toys which come under the denomination of "Wild Beauties," he was now frightfully hard-up.

The object of his meditations was to consider how he could obtain some funds.

He had, it is true, sufficient cash to pay his current expenses, but he wanted a fresh instalment, to meet the craving desire which he had for pleasure.

Had Sir Percy written to his mother for some funds—his father having been dead for some years—it is very likely that whatever request he might have made would have been complied with, with a few recommendations to be more cautious for the future.

To write to one's parents is the advice we would give, but it is very seldom followed.

If it only was, what troubles, what subsequent difficulties would thereby be prevented.

Sir Percy Hugent had studied at a military establishment in Dublin, and as his passing the required examination was, in his opinion, a dead certainty, he had not opened a book since his arrival in town.

As a natural consequence, he had forgotten, in a few days, what it had taken him months to learn.

For the present, he was very quietly taking forty winks after his smoke.

On the table, close by his side, stood a decanter of sherry, half empty, and a beautifully embroidered silken pouch, in which, from its swelled dimensions, it was easy to perceive the narcotic supply was contained.

The young baronet had never thought of using his letters of introduction. He had used one, and the recollection he had of Laura's father was quite enough to prevent him using another, for fear of his again meeting a similar bore.

Sir Percy was meditating, when a letter was brought to him.

It was handed to him by a boy with a red face, who acted as page to the establishment.

He opened the paper, and glanced rapidly over it.

"By Jove!" he exclaimed, in a state of wild excitement, "here it comes, at last!"

The boy remained motionless, awaiting an answer.

"Is there anyone downstairs, James?" Sir Percy inquired.

BRASSY BILL AT WORK.

"Yes, sir."

"What are you waiting for?"

"For an answer, sir."

"Is the bearer of this note below?"

"He was when I came up."

"Well, then, go down and tell him that I will call myself in the course of the day."

"Yes, sir."

And the boy with the red face disappeared instantaneously.

When he found himself alone again, Sir Percy reclined upon the sofa, and looked on the paper which had been brought to him.

"Does not this beat Ireland hollow!" he exclaimed. "Why, I might be in Dublin fifty years, and I should never get such a letter as this."

And he read aloud the following:—

"Mr. Helchman presents his compliments to Sir Percy Hugent, bart., and begs to inform him that he will feel highly honoured if Sir Percy will favour him with a call, as he can be accommodated with whatever amount of money he may require."

The young baronet could not help smiling, on perusing the note for the third or fourth time.

"Deuced civil fellow that Helchman is, to be sure. But how did he find out that the yellow boys were scarce with No. 1? I never said a word to anyone about it, except Mike Hardy, and they seem to know all about it. But those things will come out sometimes, and that accounts for it, I suppose."

Thus speaking, the young baronet took the paper, and having folded it, placed it upon the chimney-piece.

He then opened a door which led to his bed-chamber, and immediately proceeded to attend to his toilet.

This is a very important item in a young gentleman's life at the West-end, and we have heard of instances where some of them have spent half the day in getting themselves up.

On the present occasion, however, Sir Percy was not long ere he had concluded it.

Half an hour was quite sufficient for him this time, and although, as faithful recorders, we are bound to admit that he was not one of the conceited puppies of the Dundreary style, it is only fair to state that never had he accomplished that most important task in so short a period before.

He did not tie and untie his scarf about a dozen times, to see whether the pin set better this way or that way; he did not pull off one coat to try on another; he did not think that light pattern trowsers would be more suitable to the weather than those dark ones which the tailor had just sent up; but he placed the cloth on his back anyhow, and having ascertained before the glass that he looked respectable, the young baronet sallied forth, to attend to the business of the day.

"I wonder," he muttered to himself, as he strolled down Pall Mall, "whether the fellow who wrote to me will part to-day, and will let me have some coin at once. I am frightfully hard-up, and must have some before night, and that's all about it. But did not this epistle just come in time? Were not London so full of obliging people, I should have had to write over to Ireland, and not got an answer perhaps for two or three days. As it is, however, everything turns out right, and if I succeed, why, I will confess, with Shakspeare, that "all's well that ends well."

Thus musing, the young baronet reached his destination.

CHAPTER XXXIV.

WHERE A WEST-END COMMISSION AGENT'S OFFICE IS DESCRIBED, AND WHICH RELATES WHAT A YOUNG IRISHMAN SAW THERE.

I DARE say that a great many of those who read my work would feel very grateful to me, were I to give them the address of Mr. Helchman—of that kind and interesting specie of humanity who sent the inviting letter to Sir Percy which we have already alluded to, as it would save them the trouble of looking out for similar characters when they come up to town, and want money as badly as our young friend did.

Now, for various reasons I will not do so.

In the first instance because, if I did, I should only be raising hopes which would be doomed never to be realised, as very few men happen to be young baronets with large expectations; and in the second instance, I would not give the address of Mr. Helchman on principle, as this is not a bill-discounter's directory.

I believe that somewhere in the Bible the words, "Seek, and ye shall find," are to be found.

But anyone without expectations might seek all his life a loan among bill discounters without finding it, were he young and inexperienced, and not so well acquainted as many old stagers are with West-end dodges.

Now, from the epistle he had received—which we have forgotten to mention was written upon scented paper — Sir Percy fully expected to alight at some respectable house.

His idea, that a man who could lend any amount lived in splendid style, was not a far-fetched one.

What was not his astonishment, then, when he halted before a small low-roofed kind of bastard shop, situated in an arcade at the back of some theatre.

Behind the windows there was a kind of green baize cloth, which hid the movements of the people inside from being perceived by casual observers, and upon the glass was painted, in bold letters, the following very high-sounding words:—

MR. HELCHMAN,
EAST AND WEST INDIAN MILITARY AND NAVAL
AGENT,
FOREIGN CIGARS IMPORTER,
WINE MERCHANT,
GENERAL COMMISSION AGENT FOR ALL THE EAUX
DE COLOGNE AND SCENTS IN THE WORLD,
&c., &c., &c.

Of course this looked like business, and Sir Percy boldly entered the shop.

It seemed that everywhere the young baronet went he was to meet boys.

One boy—a page—attended upon him; a boy in the shop answered him.

"Is Mr. Helchman within?" Sir Percy inquired, catechizing at a glance the whole of the shop.

He was very much astonished at seeing not five pounds worth of furniture in an office, the outside appearance of which seemed to promise so much.

"Mr. Helchman?" the boy replied—a lad of about fourteen, who put one greatly in mind of Dickens's fat boy, in "Pickwick." "No, sir, he is not within just now. He is only gone to the 'pub,' to have a drink with Mr. Mike, he will be back directly, sir."

The young aristocrat was thunderstruck.

"Mr. Helchman gone to have a drink at the 'pub' with Mr. Mike!"

What the deuce was the meaning of such an answer?

To be candid, it greatly puzzled Sir Percy Hugent.

Immediately on entering the shop called by Mr. Helchman an office, there was a desk, which was so high that the boy, who was perched upon a stool from which he could not have fallen without injuring one of his limbs, could scarcely reach it.

Sir Percy looked at the stool, the desk, and the boy.

Subsequently he glanced upon the furniture of the office, which we will now attempt to describe.

Behind him was a large cupboard, with glass doors, through which could be seen about a dozen glass bottles scattered here and there, which had once contained champagne, but were now empty and without corks.

"Doubtless some of Mr. Helchman's samples of wine," thought Sir Percy.

Facing him was a staircase, which led upstairs, and on his left there was a piece of furniture, of which it would be madness to attempt a description.

It was of the same shape as a sentry-box,

with the exception that there was a door at the front of it, that you could either close or leave open after you.

The peculiar construction of this sentry-box struck Sir Percy.

"What is this used for?" he asked, pointing to it.

"That box, sir?"

"Yes."

"I can't tell you, sir," the boy replied. "I know he keeps his papers there, and often hides himself in it when he don't want to be seen."

"Thank you," the young baronet said. "I will not wait any longer."

"You will not, sir?" inquired the lad.

"No."

"This is of very common occurrence here, sir; but perhaps you will leave your name, and I will enter it in the book?"

"Never mind about that," Sir Percy replied, "I am a stranger to Mr. Helchman, and may call again at some other time."

And as he spoke he moved towards the door, and was about to leave the office, but was prevented from doing so by an incident we must not omit to relate.

"You must not go out of this place without leaving your name," the boy exclaimed; "I have strict orders to enforce that rule."

And as if he wished to follow his words by immediate execution, the youth leant forward to seize hold of Sir Percy, to prevent him effecting his exit.

But, unfortunately, ere he could do so the chair slipped, and he fell heavily upon the lower part of his back, which he commenced rubbing with the palm of his hand, being evidently in great pain.

At this instant Mr. Helchman and Mike returned from their errand.

"What has my clerk been at again?" the former individual inquired.

Sir Percy was half angry, half laughing.

He felt greatly inclined to give way to that hilarity which he could not but experience in contemplating the critical position of the poor lad.

"Beg your pardon," the clerk—as he had been called—replied, in a humble tone of voice. "This gentleman came, and asked after you, and as he was going away without mentioning his name, I tried to detain him."

"And in attempting to do so," replied Sir Percy Hugent, "he met with his present fate. You ought not to blame him, as he acted entirely according to the orders you gave him."

"But which he endeavoured to carry out too strongly, I fear," said Mr. Helchman.

Now, when the confusion which followed the little incident which we have described had subsided, Mr. Helchman, with an eye to business, bowed very low, and turning round to the young gentleman, said, in a silvery tone of voice, which he was wont to assume for the purpose,—

"Pray, sir, whom have I the honour of addressing?"

"I have not given my name yet," the young baronet replied; "but now I will do so. I am Sir Percy Hugent."

"To whom I sent a note this morning?"

"The identical man," replied the young baronet.

"I am happy to see you, sir. What can I do for you?"

"Not a great deal."

"I do not exactly understand."

"Shall I explain?"

"I wish you would."

"With pleasure."

Sir Percy took Mr. Helchman's letter from his pocket, and was about to read it, when the latter prevented him from doing so, by exclaiming,—

"Oh, I remember, sir. You wish me to accommodate you with—"

"A loan of a hundred or two," the young baronet pursued, finishing the phrase. "I want a few sovereigns at once, as I am confoundedly hard-up at present."

"Do not let such a trifle stand in your way," Mr. Helchman answered, quickly. "I dare say that, before more than a few hours are over our heads, I will comply with your request far beyond your anticipations. In the meantime, I hope you will excuse me for a few minutes, as I have one or two letters to answer. Pray take a seat, and I will not detain you long."

We will profit by the few moments during which Mr. Helchman is busy opening and reading a number of letters, to revert our attention to his young companion, and subsequently to himself, when the first sketch has been attended to.

Sir Percy walked towards the fireplace, and sat down by the grate.

In a minute afterwards Mike advanced towards the young baronet, and entered into conversation with him.

Mike—for such is the name by which we shall know him, was a young man of about twenty years of age.

He was rather good-looking, and his intelligent blue eye would have induced people to give him credit for a good deal more brain than he possessed.

That he was a gentleman would have struck anyone who met him as extremely likely; but it is so difficult now-a-days to tell who's who, that we will remain silent on that score, and describe him in full.

How it was that he happened to be the companion of such a man as Mr. Helchman might have seemed odd to many, but when it is told that Mr. H. had been the means of getting him to borrow a few hundred pounds, upon some reversion which he was to come into at a certain age, it will easily be understood that the young man was grateful for the service rendered.

Like hundreds of others, who would do a great many things did there not exist in this enlightened century many impediments which are not to be got over, Mike had made up his mind to enter Her Majesty's service as an ensign, if he could manage to do so.

He went up to pass his examination about a dozen times, but finding that he would never have sufficient courage to undergo the very easy test laid down by the Committee of Military Education, one fine day he gave up the attempt as useless.

Yet he remained as friendly as ever with Helchman, and by his gentlemanly way and his off-hand manner, was the means of bringing the commission agent a great many recruits.

If a round sum was lent, he pocketed a certain per centage, which he never forgot to claim.

The worst drawback for him, however, was

that at certain periods of the year money-borrowing people were scarce, and how he lived during those bad times was a mystery to all.

On the particular day during which we introduce him to our readers, the money must have been in somebody's pocket—in Helchman's, if not in his, for more than one visit had been paid by the distinguished and worthy pair to the neighbouring tavern.

Mike was a young man about town, and would not shrink before any dirty job.

If he thought, by allowing the girl with whom he lived occasionally to be picked up by some young swell with a few pounds, he could draw some coin from her in the course of the next day, he would willingly have done so.

People did not suspect a young man under age to be so depraved and so corrupt as he unfortunately was, and hence they were led by him like lambs to the slaughter-house.

If, during an evening "on the loose," he heard some genuine young fellow expressing the want of twenty-five or fifty pounds, he would tell him that he knew where to get it for him.

"Meet me to-morrow, at such a spot," he would say.

An appointment was then made, and Mike would introduce the unsuspecting individual to Mr. Helchman's office.

The business being successfully carried out, Mike got paid for his services.

In this world we all want some reward for our trouble, and he got his, of course.

Now, one may imagine that this was a very good tool in the hands of such a man as Helchman.

Will it be credited by our readers, that Mike had no idea of the shameful *rôle* which he was playing.

He looked upon it as all fair and square, and would have felt very offended indeed, had he been told, by a conscientious, good, and disinterested party, that he was acting wrong.

He came from Limerick, and, as a matter of course, he was an Irishman in all its purity.

Mike was quite young at the period when our story takes place, so perhaps he has mended his ways by this time, and returned to old Ireland to seek renewed freshness.

Mr. Helchman was a very different kind of person to his friend Mike.

Had you dressed him in the most stylish clothes that could come out of the most fashionable tailor's shop, you could not have mistaken his low origin.

Formerly he had been a wine merchant, subsequently he became insolvent, went afterwards into some other business, on the strength of a little capital which he got from an old woman whom he married, was either unsuccessful or lived too fast—the latter is most probable—and became bankrupt.

As a *pis aller*, he then turned commission agent at the West-end, succeeded pretty well at first, managed to make a few pounds a week; elated by his success, he left his old wife, and lived with a servant maid who had been in his service.

If report spoke true he had two children by her, and was not likely to stop.

Mr. Helchman's features were repulsive in the extreme.

It could not, however, be said that he was ugly, but there was something so cunning and so low about him, that it was easy to perceive he had not mistaken his vocation, in becoming one of those land sharks, whose constant aim it is to live at the expense of the golden youth of the present day.

Such characters have always existed, and will always exist, as long as people in the same position as Sir Percy Hugent will have a craving for money, and for the pleasures which are purchased by its help.

Mike now leant over the baronet's shoulders. "Are you hard-up?" he asked.

"Frightfully so. Are you?"

"I am just now. I am about to get some cash."

"Is Helchman a good fellow to lend?"

"Yes."

"Is he wealthy?"

"Yes. His business is worth at least five hundred a year," Mike replied. "But he never lends, upon principle, he has been done too often, but he knows some very good men, who will part to any amount."

"What is his business?" Sir Percy inquired.

"Commission agent," Mike replied.

"Is that a good thing?"

"Why, it must be. He pays a very heavy rent for this place, and unless he coined gold, he could not do so."

Sir Percy thought that this answer was conclusive enough, so he asked no further question, but kept on puffing his cigar, anxiously awaiting the moment when Mr. Helchman would be ready to attend to what he required.

The commission agent was not long ere he had concluded whatever he had to do, and finding that his new victim was likely to get impatient, he came out of his sentry-box, which we have already described.

Approaching Sir Percy, he said,—

"Now, Sir Percy, I am at your orders. If you like to come with me, I will introduce you to some parties who will advance you whatever cash you may be in need of."

The young baronet rose, and followed Mr. Helchman out of the office.

Mike remained within, to await the result of their errand.

But as we have matters of more importance to look into, and as we must attend to other personages besides Sir Percy, who is, comparatively speaking, but a very fresh acquaintance of ours, we will leave them for awhile, and conclude the present chapter.

CHAPTER XXXV.

WHERE POLLY TAKES IT INTO HER HEAD TO ACT IN A WAY WHICH MUST PUZZLE EVERYBODY BESIDES HERSELF—AND WHAT OCCURRED IN AN ARTIST'S STUDIO.

WHEN Polly—whom we saw with Martin Dashwood at the opening of the Exhibition—had returned to the lonely house which was inhabited by him, and where the death of Lady Florence—brought on by the cruelty of the man with whom she had lived—had occurred, she pondered on the likeness she had admired of the tradesman's beautiful daughter.

A wish entered her brain to have her own portrait taken by the same artist.

There are some extraordinary whims which will creep into a girl's mind, and why Polly should take the one which we have alluded to in her head, is indeed beyond our thought.

The horsebreaker had noticed the sudden blush which had covered Lucy's countenance, and was it to ascertain whence it came that she decided upon the strange step of making the acquaintance of a man who was a total stranger to her?

Owing to a want of something to do, people will do most unaccountable things; will plot deeds which a raving mind only would indulge in, and they will choose for their victims those individuals whose names stand prominently before them in bold relief.

For, if the biography of all those who have attained some renown in the artistic world is carefully perused, it will be found that they have met with most extraordinary and most wayward adventurers.

Having said so much, let us proceed.

The morning which followed the day that Polly had paid a visit to the Exhibition, there was a large concourse of friends in Mr. Browne's studio.

They were just rising from a table, where a sumptuous luncheon had been laid.

Several of the artist's friends had heard the flattering reports made relating to the portrait of Lucy which he had exhibited.

It was only a picture of a young girl, it is true, but still it had been admired.

One and all acknowledged that it was a masterpiece of incontestible genius.

Browne was listening to his friends' remarks, and was smiling with pleasure at their flattering opinions.

They were all congratulating him, and Mr. Webster, Lucy's brother, was the loudest in his praises.

The conversation was at its height, when a packet of letters was brought in to the young artist.

With a quick hand he opened one after the other.

In a great many envelopes there were only insignificant words, expressing the casual observations of some of his acquaintances.

He opened another envelope.

That letter he thought was empty.

He was about to throw it aside, thinking that it was a trick which had been played upon him by some fool jealous of his success, when inside he felt something, which felt like a flower.

He was not mistaken—it was a Forget-me-not.

This silent appeal to his feelings caused him to think.

"Oh, I know," he muttered, "who sends me that. Dear Lucy, I will not allow thy sweet face to escape from my mind. Oh! I see, in this silent token, a stronger proof of thy love than if thou hadst written a thousand lines!"

For whom could it be but Lucy who had acted so modestly?

He had never yet spoken of his love to her: she also had remained silent.

He had remained away from her for a few days, was this a silent reproach?

Then he became sad.

He blamed himself for his coldness, and tore the envelope into a thousand shreds, and placed the flower in his bosom.

"Poor Lucy!" he muttered again, and he turned round, as if he had been frightened at his words having been overheard by Webster, who had come to pay him a visit.

Yes, truly this feeling of Lucy for him tormented him.

Browne was a strange mixture of love and worldly consideration.

Although he had never yet met any girl for whom he felt a deeper sensation than that which he experienced for Lucy, still, he thought that to marry would have stayed his future prospects.

There are some natures who are so egotistical, and yet so full of reciprocated passion at times, that to analyze them would really be a task which none would venture to attempt.

It is perhaps owing to such ideas, that he was induced to act as we shall see him doing.

Browne opened the last letter, which he held in his hand.

He read it over and over again.

He could not believe what he was reading.

"Gentlemen," he said, after a while, "I have more success than you think. Here is an epistle I have just received."

All the youths crowded round him, and he read aloud the following:—

"Sir,

"One who has admired the likeness of Miss Lucy Webster is anxious to see the artist who has combined so much genius and talent together. She is not a duchess, she is only a pretty woman, as she has been told so frequently. She is anxious to have that opinion corroborated by you, and if you do not fear to meet her, she will be happy to see you this evening, between eleven and twelve o'clock."

The artist was literally puzzled.

All the company joined in a loud laugh.

"What name is there to that curious note?" one asked.

"That's a secret, at present."

"Oh, do tell us?"

"Where abouts is the residence of the original writer?"

"Now, Browne, do not keep us in supense."

The artist made no reply.

What was he to do?

Then the likeness of Lucy crossed his mind.

"Should I be acting well towards that poor girl," he thought, "if I were to attend to this appointment? No, I will not go."

"What do you intend to do?" one of the party inquired, advancing towards the artist.

"I shall not avail myself of the invitation. Anyone who may wish to assume my name, may on this occasion do so."

The whole company were anxious for such an opportunity.

Eight voices asked Browne to favour them with the name and address.

Among those eight there was one who shouted louder than the others.

It was one named Mathews; he was the youngest pupil of Mr. Browne.

The latter put the letter into his hand.

"There," he said, "take it, only you must behave yourself."

"Thank you, I need not that advice," replied Mathews. "I wonder who could write such a letter? perhaps some old girl. It is doubtless a hoax. Never mind, we will see what it is, and we will try to enjoy ourselves."

This concluded the first part of the proceeding.

Gradually the company disappeared, and beyond the artist's pupils, no one was in the studio.

Browne retired to his private room, and gazed upon the forget-me-not.

Was it love which was awakening itself in his breast?

Did he begin to feel that craving which needs another's company?

Had he at last discovered, that a woman's love may sometimes urge on a man to fame and fortune?

Whatever might be the cause we know not.

Suffice it to say that he returned among his pupils appearing to be dull and annoyed, and cast, as it were, a cloud on the gaiety that had reigned in the morning.

In the evening he went to try and see Lucy Webster, but she had gone to take tea with a friend.

CHAPTER XXXVI.

WHICH DESCRIBES A JOKE CARRIED OUT BY ONE OF MR. BROWNE'S PUPILS.

THE next day, Mathews, having returned to the artist's studio, related to Browne the result of his interview.

He was rapturous in his praises of Polly—who we need not say had written the note.

Faithfully did he describe the residence of Dashwood.

He expatiated on the magnificence which was everywhere visible.

He described the features of Polly, and explained to Browne how the girl had come down and had waited for his appearance, and how she had opened the hall-door for him.

What she was he could not say, but there was something mysterious about her.

She had told him not to mention what had taken place to any living soul, as she would have to suffer terribly, were her conduct made known.

The girl had told him that she was not married, only kept by the man in whose house she lived, who was in the country for a few days, and she had profited by his absence to act as she had done.

She had made him promise that he would draw her likeness, and she would pay him handsomely for it.

"And what did this extraordinary creature say to you, when you told her you were not the artist she wished to see?"

"It was not likely I should have done so. I should have been afraid."

"Afraid?"

"Yes."

"How so?"

"Because I should, of such a woman."

"And did you allow her to remain under the impression that you were —"

"Mr. Browne? Of course I did, and the consequence was, I was welcomed like no one else would have been, I venture to say."

"It is beyond belief!" the artist exclaimed. "Well may people say, 'live and see,' or 'live and learn,' for every day one is fairly puzzled."

Browne was annoyed at the joke, to which he would not have attached much importance, had the writer been one whose acquaintance he did not care to make.

But when he heard the gorgeous description of Polly's handsome features, he really repented of having allowed the matter to go so far.

"I hope, Mathews, that you did not compromise me?"

"What do you mean by that?" the youth replied. "Oh, leave me alone for that, and I showed her that, as England expects every man to do his duty, when called upon you were not far behind."

We do not know how this coarse joke would have been received by the artist, had not Mathews pursued quickly,—

"But you need not fret over the chance you have lost of seeing the girl. I have made an appointment with her to meet me in my studio—at least, in my worthy master's—and she is sure to come in the course of the day. She is a woman I should like to bring down if I could, there is such a bold impudence about her, and I have thought of a very good joke which I will play upon her to-day."

"What is it?" several voices inquired, "speak out."

"Remember, I have nothing to do with it," put in Browne.

"You will not be mixed up in any way. Only remain as you are, when a messenger asks for Mr. Browne. The only thing you have to do is, not to deny yourself."

"I promise to do that, but I must know what it is all about."

"You will see me play my part. In the meantime wait patiently, and play yours."

Shortly after the conversation we have related to our readers, the wheels of a carriage were heard in the street.

Mathews ran to the landing, and looked out.

"Silence," he said, "it is she!"

And then he disappeared behind a large curtain, where all the artist's apparatus was kept which would be spoiled by being exposed to the open air.

Browne went into a drawing-room which preceded the studio.

A gentle knock was given.

The door was instantly opened by one of the pupils, who felt really dazzled by Polly's appearance.

Polly had on a veil which partly covered her face, and she was dressed with that gorgeous extravagance which proclaimed at once to the bystanders the lavish expenditure of her toilet.

She wore one of those pretty French bonnets, trimmed with velvet and lace. She had on a seal-skin jacket, and her silk dress, which fitted her to a nicety, was made of Irish poplin, of the most *recherché* pattern.

"I wish to see Mr. Browne," she said, in a firm voice, while the other pupils were looking upon her in mute amazement.

The individual who had been spoken to pointed towards the drawing-room.

Browne had heard the woman's voice, and while she was lifting her veil from her face, he turned round, so that when she stepped upon the threshold of the room where he stood, the eyes of both met in one glance.

"Mr. Browne?" she repeated.

"I am Mr. Browne," the artist replied, in a trembling tone of voice, so much had he been struck by the woman's appearance—by her dazzling beauty—by her catechizing glance.

"You, sir!"

There was such an amount of astonishment—such a deep disappointment—such bitterness in these two words, that for a moment the artist was cowed.

"Yes, madam," he said, "I am Mr. Browne."

Polly brought back her veil upon her face, and, turning round, looked around her in the studio.

Had anyone spat in Polly's face, she could not have resented it more deeply.

But this was not all.

That she had been duped was now apparent.

She seemed as if she was about to give way to her emotion.

"Bring in a seat here, some one," the artist exclaimed, terribly repentant of the part he had taken in insulting the woman before him.

Then Mathews came out of his hiding-place.

He had undergone a total disguise, and had put on a servant's clothes.

When he saw Polly he stepped back, as if thunder-struck.

No one could have performed his part better.

"What is the meaning of all this, sir?" the artist inquired.

"Oh, sir, you will excuse me, I hope," the sham servant exclaimed, in pitiful tones. "It was this lady who had written to you, and made an appointment, which I had the misfortune—oh, no! I mean the good fortune—to keep instead of you."

"Who is that man?" Polly inquired, pointing with her finger towards the servant.

"Unfortunately, I am only this gentleman's servant," replied Mathews, in as genuine a tone of voice as he could make it.

"That is one of my pupils, madam; and as he is young and foolish, I hope you will excuse him."

Polly got up, and leaning upon the artist, said,—

"Well, sir, had I been told that there were men vile enough to act the part which you have played, I would not have believed it. Good bye, sir, you are a coward, for none else would insult a woman."

Thus speaking, Polly left the studio.

In an instant she was in the street.

"I can believe anything after this," she muttered, and she bit her lip, with a disappointment which no one, except those placed in a similar predicament, can fully realise.

We have related this adventure in all its coarse truthfulness.

It was only a joke, but terrible results were to follow.

No woman could have forgotten it, and Polly did not, as the story will show.

CHAPTER XXXVII.

WHERE THE MYSTERIES OF THE CONFESSIONAL ARE UNRAVELLED—AND WHERE THE FAIR WOMAN AND HER PRIEST ARE BROUGHT TOGETHER.

AN adventure like the one we have related may seem beyond belief to some of our readers.

Many among them will scarcely credit that there could have been found a woman who would have acted as Polly did; that there could have been a man like Browne, who would have cared so little about such a letter as he had received, as to allow others to make the most of it.

And, last of all, it will be looked upon as really impossible that Mathews should have insulted a woman whom he had already deceived.

But it is, nevertheless, too true to be expatiated upon.

Now we must revert our attention to other scenes, and return to our friend Mrs. Cherwynd.

Under the cloak of religion, many things are carried out in this world.

We have said before that the fair woman was about to turn Roman Catholic.

What could have induced her to do so it is not in our power to fathom.

Suffice it to say that she was bent upon so doing.

Nothing of much importance had occurred out of Langdon's interview with her.

He had gone with her to her lodgings, in company with Miss Hooth, and returned home in the evening.

On the following day Mrs. Cherwynd went to see her priest.

Who that priest was it is here our province to state.

There used to be, and there is still, in London a small Roman Catholic chapel, which is highly patronized by all the old families who belong to that faith; it is situated somewhere in the West-end.

In the midst of fashion and wealth does this sacred building stand forth.

If you possess rank and wealth, you need not look out for priestcraft, it will surround you, and ever be at your beck and call.

But if you are poor, go not to them.

When you want help, seek it not at the hands of priests: but if you only want to throw your money away, or to give freely, they will ever be dancing attendance upon you.

That these sacred men have been the means of doing good, cannot be denied by those who will judge impartially; but the harm which they are guilty of is immense.

Mrs. Cherwynd's priest was named Father Wilkinson.

He was strikingly handsome, and in his garb he appeared truly like an angel.

He was so meek, so soft, and so mild in all he said and did, that to look upon him as being vicious would not have been tolerated by any one.

This was the man to whom Mrs. Cherwynd had applied for spiritual help.

She had been introduced by his Grace the Duke of Rohan to the reverend gentleman.

Mrs. Cherwynd had lived frightfully fast, and now that she knew she had sinned deeply, she sought to receive, at the hands of the priest, absolution.

By embracing the faith of the Church of Rome she could obtain that.

But let us describe her interview with Father Wilkinson.

It was not the first one she had had with him, hence they knew each other well already.

Unaccompanied by anyone, the fair woman left her lodgings at about twelve o'clock in the morning.

She walked along Berkeley Square, and then

along several streets which led to the Roman Catholic chapel.

Unnoticed she trod on.

There was the woman who had left her husband and children behind her—who occasionally came to town to revel in all the mad volupty of the most cynical lewdness—stepping in a quick, hurried style towards the House of God!

Was not that blasphemy?

Attend to your family, woman! Attend to your household—behave uprightly and honestly —do not forget a married woman's duty—remember what those duties are—and leave the church and the priests alone!

Do you think that, as a Protestant, you could not be saved?

However, onward—onward—to the chapel, and we will follow you.

She arrived at the chapel.

Outside there were many poor, destitute women begging for alms.

Money was no object to the fair woman, hence she gave the poor creatures half-a-crown each.

The beggars looked at her: "Good, pious woman that!" they thought.

Inside the building Mrs. Cherwynd walked.

A few people were engaged in prayers.

She went and knelt upon a bench, and then she prayed.

Her devotions did not last long. In less than five minutes she rose.

"Is Father Wilkinson within?" she asked of one of the chapel officials.

"Yes, madam, will you step this way."

Mrs. Cherwynd followed her guide, and in one of the sides of the chapel she was told to wait a minute.

"Father Wilkinson will see you, madam."

The fair woman felt her heart beating.

She was led into a small parlour.

Behind a desk sat Father Wilkinson. He held a pen in his hand, and had just been concluding some writing.

As soon as he saw the fair woman, he rose to meet her.

"I did not expect you this morning," he said. "You do not look well."

"I have been restless all night," she replied. "I cannot sleep at night, is not that odd? I feel very giddy sometimes."

"You should have prayed, and you would have been relieved."

Then Father Wilkinson took the fair woman's hands into his.

Eagerly he clasped them against his breast.

"You have been a great sinner," he muttered, "but you will find mercy still. Do you want to confess to me?"

"I think it would do me good."

"Kneel down, then, and let us pray."

The fair woman knelt by Father Wilkinson, and her head reclined upon his knees.

He muttered a few words in Latin, and having concluded, he thus began:—

"Have you sinned, either by thought or by deed, since I saw you last?"

"I fear I have."

"By both?"

"No."

"By which, then?"

"By thought."

"And what was that thought?"

"Well," replied Mrs. Cherwynd, "I cannot forget that I was married, when young, to a man whom I did not love, and often do I wish that I could be free to love the man of my choice."

"Do you think you have found him?"

Then Father Wilkinson made the sign of the cross.

"I fear I have."

"Why fear?"

"Because, if I was free, he would not be."

"Oh, stay your speech, madam!"

"Why so?"

"Because the temptation is sometimes too great."

A smile passed over the fair woman's face.

"I do not understand your meaning, Father Wilkinson," she continued, keeping gently her fine wavy glossy hair upon the priest's knees, and fearing to look the youth in the face.

For Father Wilkinson was not above twenty-five years of age, at the utmost, but he was really one of the handsomest priests that ever emerged from a seminary.

He seemed also to study his appearance with a care which would have been deemed ridiculously effeminate by those who might have known him.

His long wavy auburn hair was allowed by him to grow to a length which would have been more befitting a woman than one of the male specie, and his hands were beautifully soft and white.

Thoughtlessly, he allowed them to rest upon Mrs. Cherwynd's head, but he withdrew them quicker than could be described.

His whole frame trembled.

Many a woman, many a convert, had he seen before, but no one had produced upon the reverend gentleman the same feeling as the fair woman.

But this need not be wondered at.

How can nature ever be subdued?

The age of Father Wilkinson was the most dangerous period of man's life.

That is to say, when placed in the critical position in which he was.

But all these things must occur.

How, we ask, are they to be prevented?

If you place two beings like Father Wilkinson and Mrs. Cherwynd together, a great many unexpected incidents will occur for repeated interviews.

There was no one to watch or detect them; but, had a conscientious priest entered the confessional, what would he have said?

"I do not understand your meaning, Father Wilkinson," Mrs. Cherwynd resumed, "in speaking about temptation being too great."

And the fair woman rose, and looked around the small room.

There was a frightful amount of carnal longing in that woman's eye.

Her nostrils dilated, and her lip quivered, and she attempted to breathe.

If the following comparison may not be considered too strong, would it not suggest to one the picture of a bird of prey, gloating upon his victim.

For the fair woman knew she was irresistible.

She soon felt that, by the wild stare of her confessor.

A smile of triumph appeared again upon her lip.

"AN OUTSIDER OUT OF LUCK."

"If one sin by thought or by deed," she asked, "which is worse?"

Father Wilkinson knew not for awhile what answer to make. He had frequently indulged in that "spiritual flirting"—mind the words—that all young priests are guilty of.

But up to the present period, it could not be said that he had yet gone the whole length of the shameless wickedness which he contemplated.

Some women are bitter—some women are terrible.

Only a few words more, and Mrs. Cherwynd would have corrupted for ever a nature which hitherto was not so depraved as she was endeavouring to make it.

She had taken a strong liking to Father Wilkinson.

Something more than a liking.

It had gradually sprung within her frame.

It was not "love."

This is a feeling which should not be dragged in the mud.

It was a feeling, indeed, similar to that of Polly's.

One longed for the artist, who could attract public notice—because, from the very fact of her being what she was—unless she acted in the bold manner in which she had—never would she have cast eyes upon him.

The other longed for the priest,—because the idea was original,—intrinsically wicked,—and because she felt certain she would satiate the craving desire of a thirsty breast in the honeyed, pure, and freely bestowed drops of a new and uncontaminated nectar.

There was but little difference between the two women.

Polly and Mrs. Cherwynd were of the same stamp.

One was a kept woman—and the other had found some one to marry her.

This occurs every day.

There is nothing new under the sun. We all know that.

"You never answered my question," the fair woman said.

"Do not, I beseech you, speak thus," replied Father Wilkinson.

And he glanced upon the superb countenance of the beautiful demon before him.

But he could not sustain the lustrous gaze of the convert.

"When am I to be finally received into the bosom of your church?" Mrs. Cherwynd pursued, changing the conversation for awhile.

"When I inform Cardinal ——" (we must not mention names) "that you are worthy of the favour."

"Not before?" she asked, in a silvery voice.

The priest feared to speak.

He walked towards the door.

"Are you going to leave me thus?" she ejaculated, as if she dreaded being left alone—as if she dreaded that the only opportunity which she would have of seducing so handsome a priest was to be snatched away from her.

"I really believe," Father Wilkinson pursued, "that you have been sent here by Satan to corrupt my soul—to close for me the doors of a blissful place, where none but the good and pure are admitted. But there must be some allowance made when such blandishments are thrown before one's path."

"To make you confess the feeling which has existed in your breast for many a-day; but I was only playing with you, Wilkinson,—I knew that you had sufficient control over yourself never to sin by deed, if you do sometimes by thought.

"It is a gratification to know that if I am lost you will be too. I do not think that there can be any difference between the two. I have tried hard to retain within my breast what I felt for you. This last trial is too much for me. Fair penitent, I love you!"

The fair woman allowed her hands to be clasped by the priest.

Exhausted by the conquest which she had achieved, she sank upon the chair.

She was so pale, so loving, so enticing, that fair woman was—to such a pitch of excitement had she worked the brain of her youthful confessor—that she appeared not to heed him.

She remained—the clever actress!—in a state of unconsciousness.

She allowed the feverish and voluptuous lips of the priest to cover her superb forehead with the warm pressure of love.

She permitted him to unfasten her dress, so as to gaze rapturously upon her skin of alabaster.

She made no attempt to prevent him from indulging in those loving caresses which she had provoked by her speech.

She had conquered Father Wilkinson!

* * * * *

It is not in the province of authors, who are only relating, to dwell upon certain things which would be better omitted. But as we are only faithful chroniclers, and not novelists, we must establish the guilt of certain of our characters beyond the shadow of a doubt. We trust that we have done so.

Let it not, however, be thought that all priests are bad—all women like those whom we have brought before our reader. Sad, indeed, would this world be if such were the case.

But this is devoted to rather peculiar characters, and we show them forth in all their hideous truth and repelling nakedness.

A few days after the scene which we have described, Mrs. Cherwynd was duly and formally received into the bosom of the Church of Rome.

A cheque for £300 was given by her to some society for reclaiming fallen women from the path of vice, and she looked right well after her rather protracted interview with Father Wilkinson.

He preached on the following Sunday a very good sermon, and if any one had seen the attention which had been bestowed upon his words by Mrs. Cherwynd, he would have agreed that she was indeed a very good and religious woman.

Before we conclude this chapter, let us say a few words about the saint portion of humanity.

Women who could have acted like Mrs. Cherwynd and Polly, belong to a class of indescribable beings who exist in this present century, and who are dissatisfied with their lot.

For it must be admitted that the tameness of every day life is sadly wanting in excitement or sensations, and that, from the manner in which our laws are framed, women are deprived from joining in those exciting struggles where they could display that energy and strength of mind which some possess. We will not allude to the olden times of knighthood—not that we think a great deal now of those gone-by tournaments, when they were proclaimed Queen of Beauty; paltry way of killing time, which would not have suited them as well as it did if it did not give rise to some bloody contests, which ended in their being snatched away from their homes—carried away to fresh scenes by the successful warriors. And, if ill-treated occasionally, those times were not without many attractions for them.

Then they were betrothed when they were in their cradles, to unknown future suitors.

They were married and then divorced, without the trouble of all our law courts.

They were murdered, and afterwards the cause of constant bloodshed.

They were the means of establishing peace, or of declaring wars, and to be agreeable to one's mistress death was eagerly braved.

Then came the days of queens Mary and Elizabeth.

Woman's star was in the ascendant at that period; womankind reigned.

It was the fate of these queens to indulge in the whims which history has not judged too harshly.

It was in their power to revenge themselves, and to make the heads of those who would not, like slaves, worship their shrine, fall upon the block with the hatchet of the executioner.

But what are they to do now?

In these days of matter of fact—in this century of dry reality—to what purpose are they to use their minds?

We have the police courts, the divorce courts, and the myrmidons of the law.

If they sin and are found out, they are exposed

and dragged before the world, branded with shame and infamy.

What must they do now, then?

This is a query to which we are unable to reply.

And now to return to our story.

CHAPTER XXXVIII.

WHICH DESCRIBES AN IRISH BARONET AND A COM-
MISSION AGENT AT A LAWYER'S OFFICE—AND
WHICH RELATES TO THE FORMER'S FIRST INTER-
VIEW WITH "OLD NICK."

THE young baronet, accompanied by Mr. Helchman, was not long ere he was conveyed by a hansom cab to the place where he was to be introduced.

Sir Percy could not make out the facility with which Mr. Helchman informed him money could be had in London.

Although he was not one of those half-witted individuals who would starve in the streets were they not born to a title or a large fortune, he could not believe that his companion was strictly adhering to the truth.

His common sense enabled him to discern that the commission agent was, to obtain the good opinion of his new acquaintance, what is commonly denominated "drawing the long bow."

Like all people in straightened circumstances, and who, to make others believe that they swim in affluence, never open their mouths without uttering a falsehood, Mr. Helchman had, or was always about to borrow, thousands and thousands for noblemen, who existed only in his own imagination.

Notwithstanding all his big talk, it would have been a very fair query whether he was indeed worth five shilings, when the claims which stood against him were honestly discharged.

The social position of the commission agent was rather a low one.

His transactions being confined to obtaining money for doubtful parties, and for genuine individuals under age, it is not to be wondered at his being patronized by none except the young and inexperienced, out of whom he always took care to draw a commission, which would have been deemed rather high by those who, from experience, have been taught the real value of an introduction to a bill-dis-counter.

It may, perhaps, be thought strange that people in want of money should require the services of a go-between, considering the numerous advertisements of philanthropic men, ready to alleviate the wants of their fellow-creatures, daily appearing in the newspapers.

But when it is told that, out of twenty advertisements of that kind, there is not above one or two men—who are "good," it will easily be understood that an introduction is worth paying for, it being the intent of all parties that the money should be advanced, if the borrower be a safe investment.

This was about the extent of Sir Percy's reflection.

He knew all along that money could be got, and would doubtless have gone in search of it, had not the circular to which we have alluded—

and which is a practice very much *en vogue* among London jews and money-lenders, reached him at a most opportune period.

The place were the two men alighted from the cab, was situated in Raymond's buildings; in that hot-bed of lawyers, of honest men, and of rogues; of wealthy, upright solicitors, and of sharp, half-lawed practitioners.

Knowing full well that he had to deal with a gentleman, Mr. Helchman then paid for the cab.

This gave rise to a little discussion, which ended in the commission agent accepting two and sixpence from Sir Percy, to indemnify him for having volunteered to settle the shilling fare.

The hansom having been dismissed, Mr. Helchman and Sir Percy walked for two or three yards together, and finally, leaving the pavements entered into a small passage, which led to the lawyer's offies.

An officious old clerk, of about sixty years of age, with a snuffy red nose, an old office coat—threadbare and shining, like gutta percha, from the use which it had undergone—and his piercing eyes, hidden by a pair of green spectacles,—was sitting upon a high stool behind a desk, when the two individuals entered.

Behind this rusty amanuensis, at least four or five clerks appeared to be engaged in engrossing deeds, or attending to other matters connected with their master's business.

The lawyer to whom Sir Percy was introduced was evidently thriving in the world.

The old clerk, to whom we have alluded, who combined the post of cashier and confidential clerk, took no notice of Mr. Helchman.

But, seeing the latter approach towards him, he raised his green spectacles upon his forehead, and looked at him.

"Good morning, sir," he said, drily; "do you want to see the governor?"

Mr. Helchman replied in the affirmative.

"Can I attend to you?"

"No."

"Is it important?"

"Yes."

"You must wait then."

"Is he within?" asked the commission agent.

"Yes."

"Will you say I wish to see him?"

"I can't, now."

"Why not?"

"Because he's engaged."

"Will he be long?"

"I expect he will. There is a gentleman with him who always keeps him an hour or two when he comes, and I could not say when he will see you. Can you call again?"

Mr. Helchman now held a consultation with the young baronet, which ended in the latter determining to wait.

"You may please yourself about that," muttered the old clerk.

And his part being now gone through, he bent his head downwards, settled his green spectacles, and resumed writing a letter, in the penning of which he had been interrupted by Sir Percy's arrival.

He was not long ere he had concluded his task.

"I am going into the governor's room," he said, jumping off his stool with a young man's agility, "If you like to give me your card, I will leave it with him, and it might have the effect of hurrying him on."

The commission agent asked Sir Percy for one of his pasteboards.

The young baronet drew out his card-case, and complied with the request.

"Take it in," Mr. Helchman whispered in the clerk's ears, "and tell Mr. Nicholson that the young gentleman cannot wait much longer."

"All right, I understand."

And with these words the old clerk stepped into his master's room, which was situated at the back of the office.

The Irish baronet was beginning to get rather fidgetty.

Although he was anxious to obtain funds, he, nevertheless, was anything but pleased at the long time which he had already been kept waiting.

We do not know whether our readers are like ourselves, but, of all things which we abhor, it is waiting in a lawyer's office.

Sir Percy evidently was of the same opinion, for he walked about the room in a state of the greatest impatience.

At length the door opened.

The old clerk and the party who had evidently been occupying Mr. Nicholson's attention, appeared before Mr. Helchman.

"He is disengaged now, you may step in."

Mr. Helchman required no further bidding.

He beckoned Sir Percy to his side, and both went in to the solicitor.

Mr. Nicholson was a man of about sixty years of age, he was short in height, and extremely corpulent.

He had began the world without a penny, and never allowed an opportunity to escape him of telling you so.

His features were of that red hue, which proclaimed him to be perhaps a little too fond of his port wine after dinner, and his nose, which was covered with red pimples, put you more in mind of a potatoe, than anything else, it having, owing to some extraordinary process, lost its original shape.

He had a magnificent set of false teeth, which he was constantly showing, as he never failed to indulge in a dry laugh at the end of every sentence, which had won for him the nickname of "Merry Old Nick."

There was a brightness which was peculiarly striking in his intelligent orbs; and the whole of his phsiognomy made one come to the conclusion that, if Old Nick had made a tidy fortune by lending, it was not without a good deal of roguery and shuffling.

When Mr. Helchman had introduced the young baronet to Old Nick, he very politely rose, and, with that deference that all those who work for their living, entertain for the more fortunate part of the community, offered him a seat.

Old Nick now took up the card, and gazed upon it for a moment or two ere he spoke.

"Very old Irish family, that to which you belong, Sir Percy Hugent?" the attorney-at-law at last began, thus broaching the conversation.

"I had the honour of your father's aquaintance. Very clever man, your father, Sir Percy. I lent him some thousands upon Lumley's and Patrick Langdon's holdings, twenty years ago, for which I still hold a first class mortgage. When he contested the county of C——, at that

famous election which ruined his opponent. But in those days the estate could afford it better than it can now. You see, Sir Percy, that I know a little of your affairs; how very odd that we should meet, ha, ha!"

And here Old Nick indulged in his peculiar laugh.

Whether these marks of hilarity were appropriate, it is not our wish here to say.

But when our readers are made acquainted with the fact, that the young baronet was only four years old when this worthy paterfamilias, was lowered into the ancestral family vault, we hope that they will not misconstrue into an act of ill-breeding a little oversight, very excusable indeed, under the circumstances.

The young baronet remained silent.

With that dignified, aristocratic bearing which gentlemen assume when they allow themselves to be fleeced by such land sharks as Old Nick, he awaited an opportunity of speaking in his turn.

Sir Percy knew exactly how he was situated.

When twenty-one years of age he was to come into possession of all the ready-money which had accumulated during his minority, which was under his uncle's guardianship, besides a clear income of three thousand pounds a-year; which was the sum remaining of the yearly rents, after the interests on mortgages, marriage settlements, and various other items, some jointures to old aunts, annnuities to poor relations, &c., were discharged by the agent.

He therefore felt convinced that to borrow a few hundreds was only a "bagatelle," and looked hopefully forward to the end of the interview, to leaving Old Nick with a cheque for three hundred pounds—the amount which he had set his mind upon.

"Sir Percy Hugent," Old Nick began, eyeing the young baronet, "Mr. Helchman did not acquaint me with the object which brought you hither, but I can easily guess it. We have all been young, and obliged sometimes to replenish our exchequer from various sources, although I never borrowed a shilling in my life; and began the world without a single shilling. Ha, ha, ha!"

Sir Percy contemplated the old sinner.

It mattered very little to him whether he had began life with or without a penny.

He did not come to his dingy office to listen to the tale of a lawyer, who had been the architect of his own fortune, and paid his own fee out of his savings, to be sworn one of her majesty's attorneys; he came to get some coin, and that he wanted.

On the other hand, let us inform our readers that Old Nick was also becoming a very independent man.

Too often had he had to cringe and bow, for the sake of a few pounds, ever to forget it.

Besides, he had a boil, which was bursting, in rather an awkward place; occasionally, when its cutting pain was felt by him, his temper grew sour, and those around him knew to what source to trace his bad humour.

Alas! poor Nick is no more.

What between the boil and the port, he is gone where the good and the bad niggers go.

May he there rest in peace.

Beneath a cold stone, in a country church-yard, the money-lender now lays low.

Family he had none, beyond a wife, whom he

married because, without a woman to his table, the household seemed dreary and bleak to him.

His death caused no one to weep, and his disappearance was not even felt by that old beggar woman, who stands at the corner, and who, for twenty years, had asked him for a penny without meeting with success.

Yes, Old Nick, poor Nick, is dead now.

CHAPTER XXXIX.

WHICH SHOWS HOW THE INTERVIEW BETWEEN OLD NICK AND HIS NEW CLIENT CONCLUDED.

WHEN Old Nick had indulged in his peculiar laugh once more—his customary giggle had apparently relieved him—he apologised for the liberty which he had taken, adding, "really I could not help it," and reverted to business.

"Yes, Mr. Nicholson, your provisions are perfectly correct," Sir Percy began, alluding to Old Nick's last remark, "and althouth some say that, 'he that borrows, brings upon himself sorrows,' I nevertheless wish to borrow three or four hundred pounds."

"I should like to know the precise amount," interrupted the old money-lender.

"Say four hundred," Sir Percy replied.

"I would advise you to make the amount a trifle larger," added the lawyer; "it will be the same expense for a thousand as for four hundred, with a very few exceptions."

"Well let us say a thousand," replied the baronet.

"I make this suggestion"—the old solicitor continued—"because I know you Irish gentlemen too well—you would be sure to come again. London life is expensive: here is the gay season coming on, and one needs to have a good banker's account, without which it is impossible to do things " *comme il faut.*"

From the frequent opportunities which Old Nick took of quoting these three French words, it was once suggested, by one of his acquaintances, that it was the only phrase he remembered of a language, which he tried hard to learn in a trip that he made to Paris thirty years ago.

Whether there was any truth in this very uncharitable assertion, we will not venture ourselves to decide.

Moreover, we have too great a respect for dead men, to make any statement derogatory to their feelings.

Having seen quite enough of them during their lives, we naturally feel rather shy on acting in any way that which might have the effect of conjuring up their departed souls, in the shape of a spiritual apparition, " *à la Pepper.*"

"We will say—or, at least, Sir Percy, do I understand that you want one thousand pounds?" asked Mr. Nicholson, in a honeyed voice, assuming his part with praiseworthy promptitude.

"That's the amount upon which we decided just now, I believe," Sir Percy replied, in a cool, collected tone of voice.

It is extraordinary how very quick youth will become a man, when situated in the position of the young baronet.

He seems to know that this is the first step,—which must entail many others.

For, however large one's fortune may be, if you once begin to borrow you will never stop—whether you want to do so or not, you will be at it.

It becomes a mania—like a drunkard's thirst.

In this last sentence there is, perhaps, a little exaggeration; but we wish to be as pointed and as true as we possibly can.

"You have not told me your age, Sir Percy. Excuse the liberty which I take; but in matters of business, you know—besides, you are not an old spinster, and to speak about ages is not an unpleasant topic, I should venture to say. Ha, ha, ha."

"What a bore that man is, to be sure," Sir Percy thought, hearing the old solicitor giving way once more to his usual boisterousness.

It was not the laugh which was so unpleasant; but it was so dry, so cutting, and there seemed to be such mockery in it, that, to those who were not accustomed to it, it was obnoxious in the extreme.

"I am past twenty, and this day six months I shall be of age."

"Unpleasant! unpleasant! Very unpleasant that you are not twenty-one yet, Sir Percy. But we must struggle against the difficulties in our path, and overwhelm them. But what security do you propose to give? Do you think your uncle will be a guarantee for you?"

Old Nick knew that this was the last thing the young baronet would have consented to.

"We must manage without him, or anyone else," he said, quickly. "If you cannot advance the amount, why, there is an end to the matter."

And Sir Percy rose, like we all do, when we are on the eve of being disappointed.

"Don't be hasty, Sir Percy," the solicitor pursued; "we can easily arrange matters. I know sufficient of the property to be aware that your estate will bear such a trifling loan; but I must study my client's interest. If it were my own money I would not be so particular; but you will understand that the sums which I lend are entrusted to me—and that I must not part with them unless I see my way perfectly clear."

Here Sir Percy took a small gold watch out of his waistcoat pocket, and glanced upon the enamel dial.

"It is getting late, sir," he said. "Can you hurry the proceedings."

Old Nick had that confounded habit that most men have; namely, when he was about to advance money, he took a delight in keeping people waiting.

He mused for awhile.

"We shall have to insure your life, Sir Percy," he said. "That is the only way I see by which I can do business at present. But I do not wish to have made you come here for nothing: I will give you something on account, and you can call again, when we can enter into the matter more fully."

"Oh, that will do," the young baronet replied, who longed to be off. "This is killing work."

"How much do you want at present? Do not be too extravagant, Sir Percy; the more you have the more you want. You will excuse me, I hope; but as I began life without—"

"Let me have fifty or a hundred, and I shall

be in time to have it cashed," quickly replied Sir Percy, who dreaded a second edition of the bill discounter's early struggles, "and you may, between this and the next time I see you, see that you are not a loser by me."

Old Nick now placed his white, feverish, trembling hand upon a small book, which lay in the corner of his desk, amidst a heap of papers, surrounded with the usual red tape.

It was his bank book.

Carefully he opened it, and slowly filled in a cheque.

"Do not say that I am not a trump," he pursued, tearing the leaf upon which he had written. "I have made it seventy-five pounds."

And thus speaking, he bowed respectfully to Sir Percy, and held the paper towards his new client.

The young baronet rose.

"Can I get it cashed now?" he asked, not even condescending to thank the lawyer.

"To save you the trouble," Sir Percy," he replied, "I can send out my clerk, if you like. Meanwhile, please give me a receipt for the amount."

This part of the proceedings was very quickly gone through.

"No, I will get it myself," the baronet replied. "You will find this all right."

And as he spoke he handed his autograph to the lawyer.

Then, accompanied by the commission agent, he withdrew.

As he drove to Duke Street, St. James's, Sir Percy Hugent was in a state of the highest excitement.

"Houpla!" he exclaimed, jumping off the cab. "Helchman, come and have a glass of sherry, and here is your commission."

And he presented to the commission agent five sovereigns out of the instalment which he had received from Old Nick, and which had been duly paid by the bank upon which it was drawn, where he had called on his way home.

At the moment that the young baronet was stepping into his lodgings, had he been at the same time watching the countenance of Old Nick, he would have seen a smile upon his rubicund, pimply face, and have heard him mutter,—

"Fine estate, that of Sir Percy's; there will be some pickings there."

His musings were followed by the usual, "Ha, ha, ha!" thus illustrating Old Nick's satisfaction at his day's work.

CHAPTER XL.

WHERE A FEW WORDS ABOUT OUR ACQUAINTANCE DASHWOOD ARE SAID—AND WHICH BRINGS HIM IN COMPANY WITH ONE INDIVIDUAL WHO SEEMS TO KNOW HIM.

THE night was fast spreading its dark and foggy wings upon that huge city called London, which spreads itself far away upon the two banks of the river Thames.

A cold, chilly rain, emanating from the clouded horizon, was beginning to fall in torrents, rapidly submerging the pavements of the lonely streets with its overflowing streams.

The fog-lights shed but a flickering, uncertain light, and the wind which was howling from the river, was from time to time sweeping everything before it, in its steady and onward course.

It was a cold night, wet, and dreary, and if there were any human beings about, whom circumstances had detained out of their homes at this late hour, they were rapidly hurrying towards their dwellings like so many ghosts, who, fearing the light of day, glide swiftly and noiselessly back to their unknown resting places.

London seemed deserted and lonely indeed.

For it was indeed a terrible night.

From Westminster Abbey the bell had tolled twelve sonorous strokes, reminding the poor wanderers, who might be without shelter, that they would have to wait many a weary and long hour ere the morning would dawn upon them.

Long ago the last vehicle had returned to its destination.

No one was to be seen.

A death-like silence reigned, which was only interrupted by the sound of the rain falling upon the doorsteps of the neighbouring houses.

It was a wonder that any one should be bold enough to venture out that night.

Yet there was one individual who feared not the wet, nor the solitude of the dark, cold, stormy night.

Onward he advanced, leaving the Houses of Parliament behind him, and with a quick step making his way over the then newly built Westminster Bridge.

A large cloak concealed his features.

Scarcely had he appeared, than the rattle of a vehicle dying away in the distance, was distinctly heard.

The boots of the new comer were not damp yet, and he seemed as if he came out of a room, hence must have alighted from the cab, whose sounds struck the ear.

He never turned round, but still walked on towards Lambeth.

Through narrow streets and winding lanes he walked on, fearless of any one, when after twenty minutes walk he came to the extremity of a lane, from which he could see the river.

A small house stood on the right side.

He walked towards it.

With a stick which he held in his hand, he knocked gently.

For a minute or two no one answered his call.

"They are out, doubtless," he thought, "otherwise they would surely have answered me ere now."

And with his hand he opened his cloak, and his features could be plainly perceived.

It was Master Dashwood.

What brought him there?

What business had he in the small log house by the side of the river?

This was occurring on that night which our readers will doubtless recollect, when Polly was left by Dashwood alone in his dreary residence, situated in the outskirts of the town.

"Why," Polly had muttered, "does he leave me thus? What great mystery surrounds that man!"

Dashwood knocked again.

This time, the sound of footsteps answered him.

They came closer to his ear—clearer and closer.

At last the door opened, and a middle-aged man appeared.

"What have you been at?" Dashwood inquired. "I have been waiting here for the last hour. If you cannot be more punctual in the future, you may consider yourself disengaged, and the sooner you find yourself a new master the better."

"I did not expect you to-night, sir," said the man to whom Dashwood had spoken; "I am sorry to have kept you waiting."

He was a strong muscular man, the individual with whom Dashwood had the above conversation, and although it was evident that he did not like to put up silently with the words of his master, yet he would not quarrel with a man whose ideas seemed to coincide with his own in every respect.

"Manning, I do not want to blame you, you know that," Dashwood replied, "but, confound it all, to be in the wet at this hour is not one of the things which makes one's temper all the sweeter, if, like mine, it is already soured by disappointment."

The individual who had been called Manning bowed in assent.

"Do not mention names, sir. God knows who may be about."

"Too much caution is never amiss," Dashwood replied; "but the streets are deserted, and there is no one nigh."

"I am fully aware of that; but within we shall be safer."

"Of course we shall. Your advice is a good one."

Thus speaking, Dashwood entered the small house.

It was a broken down building, such as are to be found by the waterside.

Dashwood sat on a small wooden stool, and placed it by the fire.

Manning followed his master's example.

When the two men were thus resting, Dashwood began.

"Well, what have you done since I saw you last?"

"A good deal, captain."

"How many men have you got?"

"Only five; but they will die for me, and, of course, for you."

"Is that all?"

"Yes."

"Why did you not try to get Brassy Bill?"

"Brassy Bill!" exclaimed Manning with astonishment. "He would not come to serve you if you paid him like a king. You must have offended him, I guess, for he has a terrible hatred against you."

"Do you speak true?"

"If I can form an opinion from what he told me himself, he's your enemy for ever."

"Brassy Bill is?" Dashwood inquired once more.

"The identical man."

"I wonder what I have done to the man?"

"Shall I give you his version?"

"I wish you would."

"You will not be offended with me?"

"No."

"Well," Captain Manning began, "he said that he once did a job for you—spoke about a Lady Florence, whom he was the means of conveying to your house, and he said 'Dashwood behaved bad towards me. He promised me a hundred pounds for the job, and he did not give it to me.'"

"He lies!" Dashwood exclaimed, rising from his stool, and walking quickly across the small room, "he lies! I have given him a hundred pounds, and more than that, too. But the fellow was always dunning me for money, and one fine morning I told him that I would not give him any more."

"You offended him then."

"I do not care whether I did or not," Dashwood replied, angrily.

"Of course, captain, it is your own look out, not mine; but you know that men must be well paid; if not, why they won't work."

"Do you think that I am a novice, that I do not understand what I am about. Manning, you judge me wrongly. I am fully aware that the coin must not be wanting when a daring deed is to be accomplished."

Here Dashwood breathed heavily.

"I am sorry," he muttered inwardly, "that Brassy Bill is dead against me. He knows a good deal more about me than I like him to—and he may turn very annoying. Suppose he were to ask for the body of Lady Florence, where should I be?" and certain dark thoughts loomed across the mind of the fashionable murderer.

"Captain, you seem wrapped up in deep reveries," Manning now said. "This is not the way to carry out our plans."

These words had the effect of bringing Dashwood back to his consciousness.

"You have managed to get five men together, have you?" he asked.

"I have, so far, captain; but you must remember that it is not an easy task to get all at once such old blades as Bill together. Besides, we are not living now in the days when such a trade as ours could be followed upon the high road without fear of its being interrupted. We have to contend with great difficulties. Sir Richard Mayne is wide awake, and the London police cannot be bought for a song. I fear that I shall require at least two months before they can be brought to a state of perfection."

"Two months!"

"Not a day less."

"'Tis awkward," Dashwood pursued. "Two months is a long time."

"I know that; but it is better to wait and be certain of success, than to venture with tools that would not be fit to work with, and spoil a good thing all for being too hasty."

Dashwood mused for awhile.

"And when can I see these men who are to be the means of accomplishing my orders."

"When you like."

"At present, if I could."

"You are joking!"

"No."

"Come on, then, captain. I will show them to you without your being seen by them. Is not that a capital idea?"

"You're a jewel, Manning. But where are they?"

"Not far off."

"Have you given them an appointment?"

"I have done better than that."

"How do you mean?"

"Why, they are only one hundred yards from here."

"A hundred yards," Dashwood repeated.

"That's all."

"They have, perhaps, seen me coming," he said.

"Not they, and if they had, what then?"

"But I would prefer to keep my features unknown to them," Dashwood pursued.

"In course you would; and yet you do not mind looking at them."

"Can you blame me? I want to see whether they are up to their work."

"Very natural wish on your part, captain, that I will grant ere long."

And Manning rose, and directed his steps towards the small door.

Ere, however, he reached the open air, he turned backward and approached Dashwood.

"But, captain," he said, "if we were not to agree together about the terms?"

"Nonsense! nonsense!" Dashwood replied, in an off-hand manner.

"I have worked for you up to the present; obeyed your instructions implicitly," Manning continued.

"Who said you didn't?"

"That is not the question."

"What is the question, then?"

Here Manning looked at Dashwood, who, in the coolest manner possible, was lighting a cigar, which gradually filled the small room with its perfume.

"He does not seem to bite at it yet," he muttered. "Let us be more explicit."

Dashwood had taken a tremendous puff from his weed, and like a consummate smoker, was glancing upon the white ashes of the cigar, the quality of which he appeared extremely to relish.

"Do you want one?" he said, presenting his case.

Manning quicky availed himself of Dashwood's offer.

"I am thankful, captain," he said; "but after what I have told you, I meant to inform you that when people fall across each other, it is customary, under the circumstances——"

"For the employer to recollect that money is sometimes requisite."

"Exactly, sir. You have hit my idea upon the nail—or the nail upon the head, as folks sometimes say."

And having given way to what he considered an extremely good joke, Manning smiled pleasantly, in the expectation of the sum which he was to receive from Dashwood.

Dashwood, however, did not seem disposed to hurry business.

"Manning," he continued, "you are perfectly right to remind me of what I should do; but you know I have so many things to attend to, that somehow I forget what I have no right to forget."

And yet Dashwood did not comply with Manning's request.

"Extraordinary character, that!" Manning thought. "Is he, or is he not going to?"

And then, plucking up his courage he exclaimed—

"Do not trouble yourself; I know that you will make it all right now."

Manning pronounced these last words in so pointed, and so significant a tone, that no one could have misunderstood its meaning.

"Will two hundred pounds be sufficient for you to go on with now," he asked.

Manning looked at his master, and scratched the top of his head.

"If I had it all my own way, captain," he said, "I should say, that that sum would be plenty; but, don't you see, we have two young ones of about nineteen or twenty years of age, respectively, and they are fond of idleness, girls, and drink, when off duty, they like to sport fine clothes, and give the same to their molls, 'feed well and live fast,'—as they call it—while they are at it, and although I would not wish to encroach upon your good nature, I cannot but suggest that two hundred will not go far, and that if you wish to keep them with you."

It is impossible to say to what lengths of speech Manning would have allowed his tongue to carry him, had not Dashwood suddenly interrupted him.

Considering, that up to the present, you have as yet done nothing for me, I think that you ought to rest satisfied with the first instalment, but I will double the amount and make it four hundred, and, to conclude, I will give it you at once.

Then Dashwood took a portfolio out of his breast pocket, and counted to Manning the amount which he had mentioned.

The latter reckoned the sum afterwards.

"They are not flimsy ones, I hope, captain?" he asked.

"No, they are genuine enough, and I only wish I could afford to give you twenty times as much."

"No offence, captain, but don't you see, I study yourself in so doing, because, if they were bad ones, you would get us all in trouble."

"You may rely upon my straightforwardness with you."

"I knew that all along, captain, and I told Brassy Bill so too, but he won't have it, I know right well that you are not a 'nincumpoop'—a fool—and as it is bad policy not to pull well with such men as us, I cannot bring myself to believe that you are guilty of the charges that Bill made against you."

While speaking, Manning sewed the notes within his under garment, and having closed the door, walked by the side of Dashwood, who allowed himself to be led by his new companion through a variety of small streets and lanes, which led to a cross way, wherein stood a row of two storied houses.

We are arrived, captain, at the end of our destination," Manning said, "you will soon see all the little cherubs together."

CHAPTER XLI.

WHICH INTRODUCES THE READER TO A DWELLING
WHICH HE HAS NOT VISITED BEFORE, AND WHERE
HE SEES AND HEARS SOMETHING NEW.

WHEN Manning had spoken, Dashwood looked up, and perceived an old two-storied house, of which the shutters were hermetically closed.

No light was to be seen within, and to all appearance the house was uninhabited.

Manning placed a key in the lock of the door, which soon receded before him, and as it ran upon its hinges, he walked straight in, followed by Dashwood.

THE IRISH BARONET DOING TOWN.

The darkness around was dense in the extreme, and fear seized hold of Polly's lover.

Perhaps he had been tracked, and for the sake of his watch and chain, and whatever money he might possess about him, to be coolly murdered.

That help could be had was not to be dreamt of, and so he remained motionless, and when he heard the door of the house had been closed behind him, he dreaded to walk on.

"Where are we now, Manning?" he asked, quietly.

"You will soon see, captain; lay hold of my coat and follow my steps."

Now Dashwood thought that if he showed any symptoms of fear, it would give to his lieutenant an idea that perhaps he did not possess courage, and to remove from his mind whatever suspicion he might have, he whispered, in a cool tone of voice,—

"By Jove! this is a devil of a place to come to; have you got no matches?"

"In a minute I will set light to my bull's-eye," Manning replied; "but it would not do to do so now, this house is supposed to be respectably tenanted, and at this hour a light might attract the peeler's notice."

And along a narrow, dark, damp alley Manning creeped.

Close behind him Dashwood followed.

"Here we are at last!" Manning exclaimed. "We need fear no longer, as we have reached the back part of the house."

With these words he struck a lucifer against a tin box, which he always carried in his pocket, and soon applied the light to a small bull's-eye, very similar to those which are carried by the police in their nightly rounds.

Facing them Dashwood saw a narrow staircase, by the side of which dangled a greasy, thick rope, by which means one doubtless had to effect his ascent to the upper storey.

"This is a queer balustrade," Dashwood said, with a smile, to Manning; "but it is better than nothing, and if a fellow is careful he will not break his neck, which, it strikes, me he could not prevent were there no rope."

But Manning did not remain to listen to Dashwood.

With that rapidity which habit gives to all things, he ran up the flight of steps, and ere Dashwood was half way up, he saw his lieutenant grinning from the top of the stairs, and shedding the light of his bull's-eye after him, so as to help him in his ascent.

When Dashwood had reached the landing, Manning whispered to him,—

"Here, captain, here is a place where you can see without being seen, and you will then be able to form your own opinion concerning your men."

Scarcely had he uttered this phrase than he disappeared.

Dashwood, left once more in total darkness, grew still more puzzled.

This anxiety, however, did not last long.

Manning, with his bull's-eye, had effected his entrance into one of the adjoining rooms, and from the place where Dashwood was he saw a dazzling light.

In an instant he recognised the lamp, which Manning had placed close to a hole which happened to be in the partition.

Owing to this hole he now felt convinced that he would be able to see and not be seen, and to hear all the conversation that took place in the room.

Then he cast a cursory glance upon the furniture of the apartment.

It was that of an artisan with rather a good income.

There was a display of care which did not accord itself very well with the outward appearance of the house, and from the sofa, covered with old red velvet, and the wide, easy chair which stood by the fireside, it was no very difficult task to conclude that the occupant of the apartments was one who had some idea of comfort.

Old black pipes, remarkably well coloured, lay scattered upon the chimney-piece, and two or three likenesses, among which were those of Prince Albert and Queen Victoria, might have led one to believe that, whosoever he was, the inhabitant of that house was as loyal and faithful a subject as ever dwelt in her most gracious Majesty's realm.

This is the crib of my head-piece, my head man," Manning began, as soon as Dashwood had concluded his survey; "What think you of his taste? He passes in the neighbourhood for a well-to-do engraver, living with his wife like an honest British subject."

"Oh, he's married, is he?"

"Yes, and to rather a stylish woman, too."

"And what is she up to?"

"She helps him in every way she can."

"She was once kept by Brassy Bill; but they fought, and he left her."

"But you do not tell me what she does."

"Any mortal thing. She occasionally goes about from town to town, passing herself off as an Irish heiress, with immense expectations. She has a very good tale always on hand. She

is not above setting up a gay house in the Commercial-road when the sailors of the merchant ships come home after their sea voyage. She sometimes preaches upon teetotalism, and gives tea-parties to initiate herself with simple, poor people, whom she robs afterwards. She is not above taking a lady's maid's place, and tells us whether there is anything worth taking in the town house when master has left; and if she goes in the country she writes to us to let us know whether it is worth while taking a trip down to the part where she happens to be. Frequently she sallies forth to the Haymarket, and eases your fools of their watch and chain on their way home in the cab. If a young girl is to be decoyed, she will watch for her when no one else would, and trap her all ripe for the old scums who will pay the price. Oh, she's one of those that are not met with every day. Yet, notwithstanding all her sins, the good woman passes for a very sanctified creature in the neighbourhood. Oh, free constitution! Merry England!" exclaimed Manning, "to thy liberal laws we owe all this freedom."

Manning gave way to this last exclamation in rather too loud a tone to meet the approval of Dashwood.

"Refrain your enthusiasm, my friend," he said, in a conciliatory voice; "why, you spoke loud enough to be heard in the streets!"

Knowing this rebuke to be deserved, Manning remained silent.

"And where is that wonderful head-piece of yours?" Dashwood asked.

"You will see him directly," Manning replied; "I will call him."

And as he spoke, Manning lowered his bull's-eye upon the floor, and taking a chair, jumped upon it, and with a stick which he held in his right hand he knocked at the ceiling.

Shortly afterwards a voice was heard in the apartments above, and the sound of footsteps immediately following were a sufficient guarantee to Manning that his signal had been attended to.

Dashwood then saw an individual, of about fifty years of age, holding a tallow candle in his hand, make his appearance.

At first sight the new comer would not strike one as being anything but an honest engraver, for which he gave himself out.

But if deeply and carefully catechised, it was easy to perceive that he had not always been living from the mysterious sources from which he derived his income, and that there was something intelligent about his features, and a kind of indescribable gait, which would have led one to believe that he had not been born for the *rôle* which he performed.

"This is our master," said Manning, pointing to Dashwood. "Mr. Ferret, sir."

Dashwood looked at Mr. Ferret.

Meanwhile, Manning whispered into the new comer's ears these words,—

"That gentleman, who came with me, is called Dashwood; he has given me four hundred pounds to divide among ourselves, for us to be ready when he may want us."

"And what are we to do for him?"

Manning shook his head in the negative.

"I don't know," he said; "there is a mystery about him which I cannot fathom; he wants us, and as he pays handsomely, I am satisfied—ain't you?"

Ferret nodded his assent.

"Is it anything connected in the woman's line?" Ferret again inquired.

"I know no more than the man in the moon what his object is," replied Manning; "but now, Ferret, our friends will be coming shortly, will you receive them?"

"Yes; and what are you going to do in the meantime?"

"Take our master with me in the adjoining room, and, as the pals come in one after the other, exhibit them to him through the aperture."

"Won't he appear?"

"No; he has his reasons for wishing to keep incognito."

"Is he a swell?"

"I fancy so."

"Has he got any coin?"

"Look here!"

"They are perhaps bad ones," Mr. Ferret now said, the same idea occurring to his mind as that which had struck Manning, as he glanced upon the well-filled portfolio which Manning placed before him.

"No, it is all right."

Mr. Ferret's eyes glistened.

"'Tis enough," he said, "I will attend to your friends."

At that instant a gentle knock was heard at the door below.

"They are coming, captain."

"Who?"

"My five recruits."

"I thought they were within this house."

"Not likely."

"Do they live outside?"

"Of course they do."

"Where?"

"Some at the west and some at the east end of London."

"And how did you pick them up?"

"That is my secret, captain; ask no more."

The entrance door now ran upon its hinges, and it was as much as Dashwood and Manning could do, in the short period which elapsed, to gain the room, from which they could see without their presence being heeded.

CHAPTER XLI.

A FEW LONDON CHARACTERS DESCRIBED WITHOUT EXAGGERATION — AND A CLUE TO THE STORY GIVEN.

MR. FERRET had, according to his promise to Manning, descended to receive the new comers, leaving Dashwood and Manning together in the room adjoining the one where the three personages had just met.

Once Mr. Ferret gone, Manning blew out the light of his bull's-eye.

Two minutes afterwards the sham engraver returned into the room.

This time he was accompanied by a young man of about twenty-five years of age.

Fancy, reader, a skin as white as snow, taper fingers covered with diamonds of the purest water, silken wavy hair, curling naturally, blue eyes like those of a woman, melancholy and loving; a small moustachios of a somewhat darker hue than the hair; a small mouth, and beautifully set teeth.

A small foot admirably well shod.

Light trousers, falling upon a calf of faultless shape.

A dark frock coat, encircling a slim and well made waist, and a tie loosely thrown around a turn-down collar, coming down so low as to enable the beauty of a feminine neck to be perceived.

Fancy all that, and an effeminate gait, like that of those young noblemen who, because they are born to old titles, and bound to come into a princely fortune, think that to be particular about their toilet, and to gloat in their conceit, is the only aim which they should study.

"By Heavens! who is that?" Dashwood asked, his eye rivetted upon the new comer. "That is a woman, I will take my oath, dressed as a man."

"Many people have made that bet already," Manning exclaimed.

"And won it, I suppose?" Dashwood asked in an under whisper.

"No—lost it!"

"Tell me who he is, will you?"

"That young gentleman has a sister called Mrs. Leicester, once a prostitute, now a kept mistress—which is a shade higher, not better. That is one of the young swell mobsmen; he will pick a pocket, ease you of your watch; live upon gay women for months until they are satiated with him; pass himself off for what he is not. He was sentenced to three years' imprisonment for obtaining two hundred pounds under false pretences, and he has only been out of gaol two months. He looks right well over it, does he not? He has no feelings, no religion—nothing. He would cut your throat just as soon as he would look at you. He is a wonderful young fellow! He rides a thoroughbred in the season in Rotten Row; never wears anything but lavender and varnished boots in the summer, and will do anything for money. If you find him useful he is your man."

"But what is his name?" Dashwood inquired, "I would like to hear it."

"He has only one by which he is known by us—Blue Eyed Charlie, as we call him; what title he takes abroad he keeps dark," exclaimed Manning.

"Well, old stick in the mud," Blue Eyed Charlie was saying to Ferret, "what is all this meeeting and parliament for? I understand that all the boys are about to be invited here to-night. How is mother Ferret?"

The manner in which the youth pronounced these last words could only have placed you in mind of one person, namely, of that pretty, clever, and amusing little dancer, Miss Lydia Thomson, when performing the "magic toys."

Old Ferret did not like the intimate manner of his young friend.

"Sir, if you please, when you speak of my wife—my legitimate wife, sir—use a little more respect, or you and I will fall out."

Blue Eyed Charlie smiled disdainfully.

"Why, you old fellah!—ha! ha!—you ought to feel proud at my condescending to inquire in so kind a manner after your better half. However, for the future she may go—o—o—she may go to—"

It is very likely that the handsome youth would have concluded the song, which perhaps a few of our readers know, and sent worthy Mrs. Ferret to a place where he was most likely to find his way himself some day, had not another knock followed.

"Who might that be?" Dashwood inquired.

"Two ticket-of-leave men, I believe."

Instinctively Dashwood placed his hand in his coat pocket.

He felt safer now the poniard which he ever carried was in its place.

The idea that all these people whom he had wished to see together could turn round against him, and illustrate the incident which he had read somewhere, of the spectator who, in his eager wish to contemplate two bears, fell into the yard where they were, and was devoured instantly, had entered his mind.

He was thus musing when the two men entered.

The first of the two was a tall, gaunt man, of about five feet nine inches, endowed with muscular powers that few indeed could have possessed.

He had red moustachios, and a long beard that nearly reached his chest.

The other was a smaller man, thick, but well set, of which the sunken, hollow, black eye showed the determination which he could display when bent upon carrying whatever he had a mind.

They were both dressed in sailor's garbs.

"Where's Manning?" the taller of the two asked of Ferret. "I received his note and I came, not wishing to break my appointment. Is there anything on hand?"

"He is out for a few minutes, but he will soon be back."

"Confoundedly annoying that!" Blue Eyed Charlie said. "People's time ought to be considered. Damn it all! I won a lot the other day—and, by George! I am quite spoony upon a ballet girl, and I would rather be with her now than in this deuced ugly crib!"

Meanwhile Manning was whispering a few words into Dashwood's ears.

"What think you of my men?" he asked. "These two ticket-of-leave men are up to any game—robbery, murder—anything will suit their book. The bigger one was convicted for burglary fifteen years ago, and the other, who is an old man you may perceive, did a bit in the body snatching way."

Dashwood began to think that he had seen enough.

Are there any more coming to-night?" he asked, impatiently.

"Only two, and then I will go and speak to them; but remain here quietly."

It need not be said that Polly's lover required no such advice.

The step of another individual was soon distinct.

He was about thirty years of age, and upon his features were stamped two signs, which one cannot mistake, namely—that of vice and of intelligence.

"What is to be done now, eh?" he inquired, "I've got my tools with me."

"That is our blacksmith," Manning whispered again to Dashwood. "That chap will take the impression of any lock in the kingdom. He is a knowing customer, and the best of the joke is this, he has never been caught yet—but his turn will come all in due time, never fear."

"Who is the last one of all? By Jove! that is a gentleman!" Dashwood muttered, seeing a man of about forty years of age appear, whose manners proclaimed him to have once belonged to a better world.

Manning smiled complacently.

"This is a mixture, is it not?" he asked from Dashwood.

"A strange one," muttered Polly's lover.

"The Honourable Tom Merton that was, this covey is. He will rob, swindle; make a book on horse flesh without ever intending to pay; seduce girls, victimise tradesmen; has threatened twice to kill his father; has forged two bills; married a prostitute, and will die in the workhouse; yet he is a useful man. He goes now by the name of Tomkins, and out of him a good deal can be done—but he will not have anything to do with murder. He is a gentleman born, and a man of the world; and, like one of his friends Hogan, he will be a 'leg' and shake the law only."

"And now, captain, what must I tell them?" he asked.

"Are you going to see them?" Dashwood inquired.

"Yes," replied Manning. "Come with me, and show yourself forth, it will be better than to remain in the back ground."

"No," Dashwood replied.

"Wherefore such reluctance?" Manning asked; "are you not satisfied?"

"Yes—and no; but at all events, I wish only to act with them through you."

"Not much harm in that. Shall I acquaint them with your strange whim?"

"If you think necessary you may."

"Look at me, then."

"Well, what about it?"

"I will quit you now."

"Will you come back?"

"As a matter of course."

"Farewell for the present, then."

Manning made no reply, but left Dashwood and entered the room where the company which we have described were all together.

Blue Eyed Charlie reached towards Manning, and shook hands with him.

The "honourable" did not move a step.

Sullenly did the two convicts look at the new comer.

The blacksmith was examining one of his keys.

"Hallo! my friends, you are all here, I am glad to see."

Not a reply emanated from the lips of those present.

"What is all this about?" Manning inquired.

"It means this," the blacksmith began, "that it is no use to get us all together at a certain hour if you are not more punctual yourself."

Manning looked around him.

"How much money have you got between all of you?"

The convicts felt their pockets.

The "honourable" gazed upon his greasy, shabby coat.

The blacksmith gave way to a sigh.

Blue Eyed Charlie looked at his rings and smiled.

"Well, my boys, to cut a long story short, we have now to deal with a gentleman; he has paid us in advance. Not one of you will leave this place to-night without money in your pockets, and as much, I will be bound, as the most sanguine anticipated."

A yell, such as is heard at Newgate when the drop is allowed to fall by Calcraft, and the culprit condemned to death loses his footing, answered Manning's words.

A moment of silence followed.

"And what are we to do for the money?" they asked.

"Nothing as yet."

"That beats me hollow!" Blue Eyed Charlie exclaimed.

"But you are to promise me that you will come here every Monday morning at twelve o'clock to hear whether you are wanted."

"Need not come on foot, I suppose—may drive up in a hansom?" inquired the former "honourable," who, at the thought of getting any money, was feeling aristocratic once more, and who was not above, when out of such, purchasing his coffee and sugar at a small shop in his neighbourhood.

"You will please yourself about that," Manning replied, rather vexed.

"Do you all bind yourselves to this compact?" he asked.

"We do," was the unanimous reply.

"Upon your honour?"

"Upon our honour, we do," the voices replied.

"That is to say if you have got anything left," Charlie ejaculated.

"But who is our master?" the tall ticket-of-leave man inquired.

"Never mind about that," Manning replied.

"One would like to know."

"Well, he must wait for another day."

"And now for the money!"

"How much?" asked Blue Eyed Charlie, inquiringly.

"Do not be too anxious, will you, sir," Ferret now exclaimed.

"You must give a receipt," Manning now put in.

"We will do that."

"Who shall I begin with?" Manning now inquired of the audience.

Not one sound dissented, and the whole of the company pointed their hands towards the late "honourable," who was really too much astonished by what he had seen and heard to realize the reality of his position.

"You are chosen, sir," Manning said. "Will you step here?"

The "honourable" stepped forward as bid.

"This binds me, I understand?"

"Yes; are you willing?"

"Perfectly."

And he gave his receipt for fifty pounds, which was the part allotted to him, the division being made among the five people impartially, and without any regard to youth or rank, and as the others signed, they muttered,—

"We will be at our post when the day comes."

When it was concluded the entrance door was heard to be opened and closed five times, and then silence reigned once more.

Meanwhile Dashwood remained motionless, awaiting Manning's return.

"Captain," he said, "we are once more alone.

You may rely upon your men—they will act for you in their respective capacities; but what do you want them to do?"

"I may not require their services, but if I do, it is only one man."

"To get rid of one man?" Manning inquired.

"That's all."

"Easy task," replied Ferret.

"A great deal depends upon it."

"How much?"

"A fortune of ten thousand a year, which I now enjoy; but for the present, good bye, ere long I will see you again."

And thus speaking, Dashwood took his departure from Manning, and in the dark groped his way towards the entrance door.

And as his footsteps were heard dying away upon the pavement, the two men sat around the fire which burned in the grate, and smoked silently.

"Ten thousand a year!" Ferret mused.

"Ere five days is over I will have another four hundred pounds, and not a word will I say to the pals about it. That's the way to become rich!" Manning soliloquised.

"Not if I know it," a voice muttered.

And Blue Eyed Charlie, who had been eavesdropping, having returned to the room unnoticed, glided swiftly down the stairs, and banged the door after him, caring very little to disturb the musings of the two inmates above stairs.

———

CHAPTER XLII.

WHERE A NEW PERSONAGE APPEARS—AND WHICH TELLS WHO HE IS—AND WHAT HE DOES.

THE evening which followed the strange interview, which had been held between Martin Dashwood and the band—interviews which we have described in a previous chapter—a four wheeled cab stopped before a large house, situated in one of the most fashionably inhabited parts of a locality which is known in London by the name of South Belgravia.

From the numerous trunks and boxes, which were on the upper part of the vehicle, it could easily be inferred that the inmate within it was returning from some far off journey.

Had any passer by come to this conclusion, he would not have been mistaken—it was the true one.

As soon as the rattle of the cab had ceased, a light had appeared in the ground floor of the house, before which it had halted, and the hall door had immediately afterwards been opened.

Not condescending to wait until the driver had jumped off his seat, the person, who was evidently the traveller, alighted from the four wheeler, and walked quietly towards the house.

As he descended the steps he was recognised by an old man.

He was an old man at first sight, if one could judge by the hair, white whiskers, and the wrinkles which covered his forehead, but his gait was so straight, his eyes were so bright, that it was evident that if he appeared old, there was still freshness and vigour about him.

He might have been sixty years of age, doubtless, but he was as strong as a man of fifty.

He bowed respectfully to the traveller, and with a voice which trembled with emotion, he ejaculated, "Oh, I am so glad to see you back, Major, I have been expecting you home for the last six days; and I thought that perhaps you had altered your mind."

The person who had been denominated by the name of Major, was a man of about thirty-eight or forty years of age, and extremely handsome.

In answer to the speaker's remarks, he replied,—

"Why, faithful John, you are always the same—always happy to see your master return to you. But when one wishes to carry out successfully the plan which he contemplates, it must be said that his time is not his own, he must be entirely guided by circumstances; but had I been away so many years, instead of months, I would not regret it. See that my luggage is safe carried in the hall, and give the man a crown, he drove so well," with these words the young speaker entered the house.

John, who was the new comers confidential servant and butler, was not long ere he saw his masters instructions accomplished, and when he had attended to his part, he joined his master in his study.

Let none of our readers fancy that the new comer was of a studious disposition, or filled any profession where hard work is necessary to attain the pinnacle of it.

No, not so, indeed, his name was Major Blake, and he happened to be an officer in her Majesty's service, and the brother of that Mr. Blake, who from Mr. Haltering's account had been murdered by our acqhaintance Dashwood, in the singular manner alluded too.

Upon his open countenance could be traced the noble and generous feeling which a great many Englishmen possess—and from the ease of his manners, and the kind and friendly tone of voice, it could be seen that he could recognise, even in a servant, a genuine affection, and by his way of behaving, show him he was not above returning it.

"I suppose, sir," John said, "that you are tired, and wish to retire?"

"Not yet—not yet, John," the young man replied, "I have a long manuscript to read ere I go to bed."

Thus speaking, Major Blake sat before his desk.

"If you would allow me, master, to make a suggestion?" the old servant inquired, in an affectionate tone of voice, which he attempted to render as respectful as he could.

"A suggestion? yes, John, by all means, what is it?"

"You have been toiling for many days past, and you must be rather tired after so much exertion—you will kill yourself in this manner, sir!"

"Thank you for the good will which you bear me, John," the master replied, "do not fret about me—God is good, they say, and I have a duty to perform. I must do it; and I feel confident that He will give me the necessary strength to discharge it."

John bowed once more to his master.

He was one of those faithful servants of which the type seem every day to disappear. He had been born and bred in his master's house in the country, and from generation to

generation his forefathers had filled the place which he occupied in the Blake family.

He loved and respected his master, and as he had no ties to bind him to this earth, the regard which he entertained for Major Blake could indeed be compared to that of a father.

"Will you want any supper, sir?" he asked, "before I bid you good night."

The young man mused for a while ere he made a reply.

After a few moments consideration, however, he pursued slowly,—

"Do you remember my sister, John?"

The old man looked at his master.

He could not make out why a question that had so little to do with the point at issue should have been brought forward.

"Who would not remember poor Miss Maggy?" the servant replied, slowly. "She was so kind to us all—she was always so lively, and her voice sounded so pleasant through the house when she sang, that the blank was great when she left home to run away with ——. That was bad enough, sir; but she died so young, too! Remember Miss Maggy!" the old man continued, "who would not, sir, I ask. I cannot forget the day when you heard that she was no more. I thought that my eyes could not shed a tear, but when I followed the body to the grave in that lonely churchyard I could not help myself."

The old man's voice grew weaker, and he remained silent.

"And what would you say, John," Major Blake pursued, "if you were under the impression that she had met her death by foul means, and that the man who had murdered her was capable of anything."

"What, Mr. Dashwood, sir!"

"Yes, John," Major Blake replied. "I suspect that Mr. Dashwood—but never mind yet; one must not speak till he is perfectly certain—and—so good night, John. Do not disturb me any more, as I have to read rather a lengthy manuscript before I go to bed."

The steward replied in the affirmative, and withdrew.

When Major Blake found himself alone, he walked towards a small portmanteau, which he always carried in his hand, and which he had brought in with him—he opened it.

Out of it he drew a packet of paper.

It was rather a voluminous parcel.

It looked like a manuscript.

Slowly he unfolded it, and he read to the line the life of Martin Dashwood!

Martin Dashwood is the son of an Australian merchant, who, having failed for a very large sum of money, was compelled to suspend payments, and who, not wishing to keep his son in a colony where he had been unsuccessful in his commercial pursuits, sent him over to England to be educated.

Not many months had elapsed after young Dashwood had landed in England that he was acquainted with the death of his father.

He was then sixteen years of age.

On the receipt of this news he appeared to be so broken down by his only relative's death—he to all outward appearance became so religious and so good that he enlisted the sympathy of the clergyman under whose care he had been placed on his arrival in England.

On being asked for what branch of life he would follow, he said that he had gained a little knowledge of business in his father's counting-house, and he would like to follow it up in this country.

He was then introduced as a confidential companion in the house of a merchant of the name of Williams, who received him kindly, and made him a member of his family from that moment.

That merchant had one son—much younger than Dashwood—and a daughter, who was just entering into her fourteenth year.

Bessy Williams mingled freely in the company of Dashwood, and, as her charms developed themselves in womanhood, a more lovely creature never was seen; and Dashwood fell in love with her.

It was only a feeling between two that were young. Unfortunately the girl could not bear the sight of her brother's companion.

Dashwood felt and knew that by the girl's manner—although, like many other persons, he was born with strong passions, he so far controlled himself that he never allowed them to be perceived.

Mr. Williams, the merchant, now thought of sending his son to be educated. Young Dashwood went with him to the public school.

Although the boys' dispositions were different indeed, they still retained in appearance the affection of relations.

Dashwood, although young, had yet imbibed the principles of that glorious illumination which demonstrates that virtue and vice are mere convertible terms, and that there is no standard of right and wrong, but such as the cupidity of interested legislators and priests have invented, in order to keep the spoil to themselves; and he formed a plan, which was so vile, and wrought with such daring machiavelism, and impelled by such disgusting ingratitude, that success could not, it would seem, attend it.

If virtue in this world was ever sure to get its reward, and vice certain to be punished, such a design as that which emanated from the brain of Dashwood would have been dashed to nought ere completion by the hands of the God above.

What was his project? What was his aim?

After having been received in the house of a merchant, who, out of kindness of heart only, was willing to give him a collegiate education, subsequently, doubtless, to give him an interest in his business, it would strike us that to love him were but the natural consequence to be expected.

Well, it was the contrary.

He hated the hand that gave him bread, and bent his whole thoughts upon getting Horace Williams, the merchant's son, disinherited—to marry Bessy—and to occupy the station of his son in law and heir.

Such was the scheme!

Whether it was successful or not will be ere long shown.

Upon its success Dashwood relied implicitly; although he did not flatter himself upon its being carried out in a day—or a year.

He knew that to attain such a longed-for object he should have to abide his time—not to hurry his acts—and to watch his opportunities.

There is a certain boldness which in many instances accompanies the deeds of the lowest scoundrel that ever breathed, if he sees the path that lays before him somewhat clear, and if he knows that if he has trouble to remove the impediments in his way, once he has done so, new ones will not spring up to destroy the work which he has hitherto gone through.

Being young, and gifted by Satan with an hypocrisy which would defy description—the victim could not foresee a trap laid by one so insignificant.

The merit, then, was little indeed, the pit was at his feet, and he plunged into it, like the traveller, who, having strayed amidst the endless woods of Siberia, is surprised by the snow storm, and buried within its icy shroud.

Dashwood and Williams junior returned from school.

The former was seventeen, the latter only fifteen.

Before his death, Dashwood's father had left a small sum of money, which was to defray his son's expenses at College.

The merchant disliked a University education.

He had a prejudice against letters, and with a sound wisdom, which is not to be blamed, he concluded that it was not incumbent to make one who was destined to fill his post in a country house in the city, acquainted with classics, and that superficial knowledge, which only ornaments the mind, and is often of no avail to a commercial man.

The young man knew how difficult it would be to induce the old merchant to send his son and heir to the University.

Williams junior was of a frank, lively, impudent, thoughtless disposition; Dashwood, on contrary, was cool, calculating, and reserved—and did all he could to attain in the eyes of the merchant a character for virtue, steadiness, and rectitude.

Everything goes by outside show in this world, unless the actor be a very bad one, indeed. Dashwood's gravity passed for both the virtues in question.

At this part of the manuscript, Major Blake rose from the seat which he had taken, and walked up and down the room, like one who is unable to trust his eyesight.

"That was the man who married my sister," he muttered. "Could such a man ever commit murder? Could poor Maggie have been poisoned by him? How could that be? The physician at the time said nothing about it. I will have her body exhumed! I will see whether she died by foul means! Oh, heavens! Oh, heavens!"

And the military man grasped the manuscript with a feverish hand and read on.

Dashwood went to church twice every Sunday, sometimes three times, and never failed, when catechised by the old merchant, to repeat not only the best, but a considerable portion of the sermon.

He would then expatiate upon the sublime beauty of the words contained in the Gospel, saying that he really believed that he would feel so happy could he be admitted into the church.

Little would he care about a living with a good stipend, a small curacy in a country district would suit him best.

How delighted he would feel could he give comfort to the widow and the orphan—help them with his scanty means, and look forward to the day when he would obtain the everlasting reward promised by that great Omnipotent God to those who have turned their stewardship in this world to the best account.

Dashwood would speak in such glowing terms, his eye would kindle with such brightness and hopeful delight, his voice would be so mellow, and his delivery so genuine, that it would never have entered the mind of a less suspecting man than the old merchant to doubt him.

In rapture he would listen, and bless providence that he had been so fortunate as to meet for his son so good a companion.

Young Williams, on the other hand, was giddy and volatile, and often made an excuse of going to church to visit a friend; would talk of the preacher as being a stupid old parson, who sent him to sleep, and that it was really a bore to be compelled to put up with his constant absurdities, and with his dry text, which he read because he was paid for it.

Dashwood always contrived, under the mask of friendly regret, to pity the young man's foolish ways, and would endeavour to persuade the father that, although he would turn very bad if not carefully looked into, he was young still, and that, with a good deal of persuasion, he would mend ere long.

Now there was a very pretty girl, who acted as servant maid to Bessy Williams.

She was one of those Kentish maidens, with hair so wavy, eyes so clear, skin so white, and there was about her such a wicked longing for the pleasures of Cupid, that she could not but attract the notice of youths, whose warm hearts and budding passions kindled within their breasts desires hitherto unknown.

As boys generally do, they both fancied themselves in love with this pretty abigail,

Young Williams and Dashwood both tried their utmost endeavours to breathe into the girl's ears sweet words of love.

At first she would not listen to either, but being constantly wooed by two youths, who possessed no slight attainments in the shape of good looks, and who boldly and fearlessly renewed their task every day, the poor girl, unable any longer to withstand her own feelings, at length set her heart to sin.

Dashwood had been rejected by her.

Young Williams she preferred, and acted in such a manner as to show to Dashwood who was her favourite, and that it would only be wasting his time to endeavour to revert her affections from him.

The chambermaid was not above seventeen.

She belonged to that period of life when guilty sin ought to be palliated in the eyes of men, because then it is a struggle between the mind and nature, because from the very first the issue cannot be questioned—because it is too old a theme to be expatiated upon, and because nature always carries off the prize.

Dashwood perceived his young companion's superiority wtih growing rancour, and it increased his determination to destroy the companion who had snatched from him, the lips of she—such a picture was ever before his exuberant imagination—for whose possession he longed like the lioness in the desert must long for the embrace of her savage lord and master.

Dashwood knew the steps which he should take under the circumstances.

He made light of the matter; said to Horace that he never cared for the maid; that he was a deuced lucky fellow to have beaten him hollow, and urged him to a criminal connection with the girl, who, on her side, was but too anxious and too willing to listen to the protestations of the merchant's heir.

There was to be an appointment one evening in the abigail's chamber.

Dashwood learned from the unsuspecting youth the evening, when, with all the longing of a girl of seventeen, the maid was to await Horace in her room.

Once in possession of this valuable secret, Dashwood caused some of his companions to come and seek young Williams, to sally forth on a little expedition, which was only to last an hour or two.

Without thinking of the possibility of his being detained out for the best part of the evening, the merchant's son accepted the offer, and, forgetful of his appointment with the maid, who he knew would wait all night for him, he left his father's house.

While away Dashwood took his friend's place.

Noiselessly and swiftly he creeped to the girl's room.

Everything was plunged in the deepest darkness.

Old Williams, after having read the Bible to his daughter, a very suitable step which he took every night, retired to his virtuous couch until the morning.

The chambermaid was eagerly waiting the moment when the merchant's heir would seal by his caresses the love which she knew he entertained for her.

Not a sound was heard beyond Dashwood's cautious step as he entered the chambermaid's room.

Once more he triumphed.

The maid, finding herself deceived, was about to scream and to call for help, but it being, alas! too late to remedy that which, in her ignorance, she had allowed to be performed, she listened to her seducer.

Dashwood then revealed to the unfortunate girl the reasons which had induced him to act as he had done, and, with oaths, threatened exposure and expulsion from the family if she would still remain dumb to her own interests; whereas, if she would side with him, he promised to keep the secret within his breast; spoke to her about the gold which he would lavish upon her, the affluence which he would place in her way, and dazzled her imagination, provided she would join him in his scheme to blast the character of the youth in his father's opinion.

Such an offer was too atrocious to be met at first by the maiden.

But the time flew.

She felt that the old merchant would cast her into the street were he to be apprised of the truth, and she wavered.

Anna—for this was the girl's name—thought that she loved the merchant's heir, but it was only a rising passion, and one which was satiated by accomplishment; and strange, nevertheless true, she began to feel a certain interest in Dashwood, who had been the first to take her maiden kiss, and whoever that man is a woman never forgets it.

THE FASHIONABLE BALL.

At length, overcome by Dashwood's burning caresses, and by his youthful enthusiasm, she yielded, and became a tool in his hand.

CHAPTER XLIII.

WHERE MAJOR BLAKE KEEPS ON READING A MANUSCRIPT, WHICH APPEARS TO INTEREST HIM.

WITH that disgust and that reluctancy which any individual endowed with a manly heart and generous feelings would experience in reading the manuscript, of which we have given the first part, Major Blake threw the paper aside, and was about to convey it to the burning flames which sparkled in the grate.

There are some stories which one can read without feeling one's heart beating with a loathsome and dizzy sensation, but that which purported to give a faithful account of Dashwood's life was so revolting in its conception, that it was as much as the military man could do to allow his glance to run over the characters, which were written in a bold, firm, and manly hand, and which had evidently been trusted to the paper by a person who possessed no slight knowledge of Dashwood's real character.

Perhaps, if Dashwood had not been connected by marriage with him, he would not have been so anxious to become acquainted with the contents of the manuscript, but it should be remembered that Dashwood had been the husband of a Miss Blake, who was his sister.

Within it he had been told that some light

would be thrown upon many circumstances connected with Miss Blake's elopement, and hence he was very anxious to come to the end of the copy in his hand.

He went to the cupboard, and having lighted a cigar, and poured a glass of brandy in the tumbler which stood by his side, he resumed his perusal.

Here the manuscript was divided into longer paragraphs, and it was written much closer, and was headed—

PART SECOND.

Then it ran as follows :—

There was nothing to which old Williams had so great an aversion as licentious amours.

Dashwood knew this, and his one and sole aim was to make him an eye-witness of his son's sensual propensities.

Anna had not consented to act as she had said she would without being handsomely paid by Dashwood.

Besides, we have read what a mysterious ascendancy he held on women, and it is very probable that the girl was sold body and soul to him by the time he resolved upon lifting up the curtain, ere he would allow the old merchant to assist to a play, of which the filthy disclosure would never have been written by us were we not faithful recorders, and as the comprehension of the story depends upon it, we are bound to unravel all things as they occur.

By connivance with Anna, Dashwood left the old father to be a witness of the girl's interviews with his son.

And at length, when everything was ripe, the miserable chambermaid, who was now a slave in her seducer's power, struck the old man and his peaceable family with horror.

She threatened to bring a charge of rape against the unfortunate young man.

This is only but a faithful record of the events of the past, and it would not enter into the view of the writer to dwell upon a parent's anxiety, and the mingled remorse and indignation of the poor youth, who could not fancy that he had fairly brought himself into a dilemma, from which he could not emerge without a most disgusting and shameful exposure.

Matters were hushed up.

Such common occurrences generally are.

A sum over three hundred pounds was given to Anna to leave the country, and to bear to other climes Dashwood's own offspring.

The family of the seduced girl, who could not realise the "mishap" (worldly expression) which had occurred to their daughter, had also to be very largely bribed to abstain them from prosecuting.

Meanwhile, Dashwood, like the spirit of evil, gloated over the success of his satanial scheme, and by his honied talk, played his part as a Jesuit so well, that he induced old Williams to send his son to Oxford, away from London, where he might perhaps swim deeper in the slum of villany.

Dashwood suggested to the father that, it being evident that his son and heir was then totally unfit for business, it would be better to remove him to the country.

Dashwood and Horace Williams went to college.

The former to study for the Church, the latter to improve a mind, which must be corrupted indeed, since he had in cold blood, and yet so young, plotted the ruin of an innocent, artless, and unfortunate servant.

It would be useless to keep up the attention of the readers of this manuscript with all the artifices which were employed by Dashwood to destroy his young friend and college companion, by the intelligence which the old father had desired his adopted son to send him relating to his son's proceedings.

This he did with an artful appearance of sorrow and reluctance, which would have deceived a much more wary man than a city merchant, whose experiences of the world, like all men of his class, were confined to a very narrow circle, though vivid enough as far as that circle extended.

Dashwood at that time, and when his vile ideas were gradually realising themselves so far beyond his most sanguine anticipations, happened to make the acquaintance, at college, of a young man of the name of Brinsley, who was a distant relation of young Williams.

This Brinsley had been left an orphan, with a very fair fortune of three thousand pounds, and although he was gifted with much talents, he managed to destroy his brains by an uncontrollable love for pot-house propensities.

To inform the reader how money is got, how young men are besought to run into debt at Oxford, if they belong to the "fast set," how they can mortgage, under age, every farthing to which they are bound to come into on reaching their majority, is not the purpose here.

Let it, however, be said, that Brinsley had ran through every sixpence which he possessed; the day of reckoning having not yet come, he could still "fly kites" in the market, and manage to run on until he should find that there is an end to all things in this enlightened and delightful century.

The chief propensities of this young Brinsley were selfishness, gluttony, pride, and a carnal indulgence in all the cynical pleasures of low public houses, dog and cock fighting on the sly, and a longing craving for the society of the coarsest and most dissipated, foul-mouthed harlots in Oxford.

Alike to Dashwood he was meant for the Church.

Horace Williams, the unfortunate merchant's son, could not tolerate his relation's company.

He was extremely vulgar in his habits and conversation, a fact which need not be dwelt upon, considering the previous insight we have given into his character, and his conceit leading him to employ a low kind of quizzing when he thought his company were less knowing than himself.

The merchant's son, it must be borne in mind, had but one fault, namely, being too plain, too honest in his way of thinking, and had he been told the conspiracy which was carried on against him, it is really to be believed that he would not have placed any belief in the report.

Dashwood had detected in Brinsley a good deal of ability, the remains of a very high intelligence, and superior attainments, which would have obtained for any one else a very high place in the noble profession for which he had thought himself inclined to follow.

Nought, however, remained to Brinsley beyond a low, instructive cunning, which leads a man to trample on his neighbour, rather than to be borne down by the crowd, and a corrupted nature which would rejoice in the fall of any one besides himself.

A tacit understanding took place between Dashwood and this most promising English Churchman, on the condition that Dashwood should employ his influence with old Williams to get Brinsley a living, while on the other hand he could rely upon him to afford him every assistance in his power to get Williams junior disinherited.

It was a bargain—which the two youths should respectively do their utmost to carry out, because their mutual interests were at stake.

The one wanted the merchant's fortune.

The other wanted his living.

With such a youth as Horace a good deal of persuasion went a long way.

Gradually Brinsley cringed to his cousin, helped him in the many ways which one can help another, and when he was beginning to believe that he had formed, perhaps, too rash and too unguarded, nay, even an unwarranted opinion of his cousin, young Williams was led into all kinds of excesses.

Brinsley had already been two years at college, and he knew the ins and outs so well, that he soon initiated the young recruit to every description of gay resorts which are found at the University.

Livery stablemen, jewellers', perfumers', and tailors' bills, were easily incurred by young Williams.

Dashwood and Brinsley used to introduce him, whisper behind his back the immense expectations which he had, puff up the extraordinary wealth of the old merchant, and the consequence was that, without asking it, he was launched into the vortex of expensive and ruinous extravagance before he knew where he was.

Brinsley knew a very pretty St. John's Wood nymph, who used occasionally to come down to see the fellows.

Between her and Brinsley the young man's ruin was plotted.

This girl, whose name we need not quote, was one of those pretty women who, having graduated through the most hideous stages of ten consecutive seasons in London, was cankered in the body as well as she was in the heart.

She was a woman of marble.

Poor Williams fell in love with her!

Oh, by all that's true and noble! oh, by all the heavenly powers that are supposed to exist! could youths like Horace (and there are many like him) be saved from falling in love with those miserable creatures who, for a few years only, shine like a meteor, and melt gold as fast as the lead thrown in a large burning furnace, of which the capacities are immense.

Whose feelings have fled, whose hearts are rotten, who look upon humanity as a well from which the water is ever and unceasingly to be drawn.

Who considers love a song, who revel in all the blasphemy of polluted lewdness, and by whom a story of incest is listened to with burning eyes and with dilated nostrils.

Who think that to cause suicide to an infatuated drunken lover is a page in their history, which must increase their ephemeral popularity.

Who will not be prudent, and save for their old age.

Who heed not the future, fully aware, yet fearing not to breathe their last sigh on a dunghill of demoralisation, if not of poverty.

Poor Williams saw the girl.

She was one of those who always look well, who are never borne down by ill-luck when it overtakes them.

A daughter of night, who lives amidst gay lights, and subsists upon champagne!

She had velvety eyes, splendid golden hair, and her features were such as to induce you to believe her to be an angel of candour and modesty.

But when, like the serpent in the wilds of America, who, after having slept for months, awakes once more to gratify her burning desires, she, too, sprang from a few days' lethargy to cast the irresistible ascendancy of her devouring passion upon her spotted victim, she was adorable.

This was, then, the girl who had been chosen by Brinsley to entrap Williams.

He was led by her into the most wayward and reckless debauchery.

And, once she had fairly drawn out of him as much as she could fairly expect, she returned to the modern Babylon.

Dashwood meanwhile contrived that the old father should receive an account of them in the most exaggerated colours.

At length, to crown such a very disgusting drama, Brinsley circulated some reports, which Williams had thoughtlessly uttered, upon his courage having been called into question. A duel was fought between the two students, amidst the clashing of wine glasses, and the guttural, hollow, and filthy songs of the reigning harlots.

Williams's antagonist was wounded.

The heads of the college took cognizance of the affair.

Dashwood and Brinsley, who were known to be his companions, made it as black as possible, and as expulsion was threatened, Dashwood then wrote and informed old Williams about it.

His indignation against his son was at first beyond all bounds, but he contrived to avoid the public disgrace of the dismissal from college by removing him at once.

The youth was then sent for to his father's country seat, and Brinsley and Dashwood were included in the invitation.

Their conjoint scheme had succeeded as well as Dashwood's former conceived plan.

The haughty spirit of the young man would not acknowledge a colour of criminalty which did not exist, which had been put on the affair by his designing companions; and he would not yield to anything like reproof.

The result of all this was that father and son quarrelled.

The latter, exasperated by the false accusation brought against him, and in which his father would not coincide, in a fit of very natural despair, struck his own father in the chest with his clenched fist, which laid him prostrate on the ground.

To describe the heartrending scene which followed would be beyond my power.

The whole household heard of the occurrence.

Horace became mad, frantic, and in the most endearing terms asked his father to forgive him.

But he had acted too much in accordance with the wishes of Dashwood and Brinsley for them not to pour oil upon the burning rage which had seized hold of the merchant's frame.

Young Williams was dismissed out of the house on the spot, provided, however, with a certain sum of money, and turned out upon the town, to act as he thought proper.

But the father's heart was not yet entirely closed to all paternal feelings.

He still retained for his prodigal son a lingering affection, which Dashwood and Brinsley soon perceived, and to check the good tendency of which they immediately resolved.

CHAPTER XLIV.

WHERE THE FEELINGS OF A GOOD MAN INDUCES HIM TO PERUSE A GREAT MANY INCIDENTS CONNECTED WITH A NOBLE TASK WHICH HE HAS ON HAND.

At this part of the manuscript the eyelids of Major Blake closed, and the paper fell from his hand.

There are some natures which can sustain an immensity of hard toil and of hard work, who can undergo the most extraordinary succession of fatigues without feeling for the time being any effect from them.

Major Blake was one of these.

But nature at times must resume her sway, as the body of man cannot be kept too many hours and days without any rest, for it is it that will give way first, as in the present instance.

We have seen ere now that the officer was returning from some voyage, and when the reader is told that he had not slept for three nights, his days and nights having been so taken up by matters of importance, that it will not be wondered at when we see him unable to pursue the reading of that wonderful life of a man who has already been introduced to us as a murderer, as the lover of a vicious horse-breaker, and as the chief of a secret band, which he must have evidently paid for some purpose.

Fairly exhausted by his fatigues and what he had read, Major Blake wound his steps towards one of the comfortable sofas which ornamented the study where he was.

And having himself placed some coals upon the fire, he indulged in a wholesome sleep.

It is a well known fact, that when we have something on our minds which greatly pre-occupies us, we will, it is true, be able to sleep for an hour or two, but being restless, we cannot find in slumber the same relief which we do at other times.

And thus it was with the personage whom we saw arriving in a cab but a short time ago.

For a couple of hours he, however, slept comfortably enough, but this short amount of rest having satisfied him, he rose up.

Once more the brandy bottle was called into requisition, and he read on again.

Here the manuscript was somewhat covered with ink blots; a few corrections had been made and subsequently erased, and the matter which he was about to glance over had a heading in large letters, entitled,—

PART THIRD.

To Dashwood and Brinsley the deceived father still committed the task of watching at a distance the steps of a son who had proved ungrateful after so many years of devoted kindness, and to prevent him if possible from indulging in more dangerous excesses than he had hitherto done.

The father had not been acquainted yet with the exact amount of his son's liabilities, which he had contracted during his stay at college, and the two youths knew how very sore the old man would feel, in being compelled, to save the honour of his name, to honour the various acceptances given by Horace as the debts which he had incurred, which were fabulously exorbitant, considering the short time he had remained at Oxford.

Scarcely had Williams junior left his father's roof than they gradually followed each other.

As Brinsley had received a handsome percentage on all the usurious monetary transactions in which he had involved the merchant's son, through his channel they learnt when a fit opportunity was offered to them to send in their respective claims.

It need not be told that old Williams's anger was intense when he had to pay the debts of his son.

But it soon cooled down, owing to Brinsley, who hinted to him in a joke one morning that his son might mend, that *il faut que jeunesse se passe*; that if he did, why, the debts incurred would be comparatively trifling if his spiritual welfare could be insured by it.

It was at this moment that Dashwood seized the opportunity of winning the old man's heart.

He appeared to renounce the benefits of his college education, and occupy the post in his counting-house intended for the son.

The merchant, still deceived, with tears in his eyes—not fathoming yet the low and interested nature of his *protégé*—embraced him, and accepted his proposal.

His ears being then opened to anything he might be asked, he instantly, at his young friend's request, conferred a living in his gift on Dashwood's colleague in selfish knavery in his infamous career.

So far Dashwood's plot was carried out successfully—but he was not by any means yet satisfied.

More, in his opinion, was to be done to consummate his security, and ingratiate himself deeper and deeper still in the old man's good graces.

He needed something else.

He needed Bessy Williams as his wife.

Now, although she had felt shocked at her brother's imaginary excesses, she felt for him with all the tenderness of a sister, hoped for a new result, and was ready to counsel forgiveness to her infatuated parent.

She was then seventeen.

Beautiful, tender, soft age for a maiden who combined all the excellencies of female beauty with a mind which was highly cultivated.

To possess her was the impulse of Dashwood's passion.

To marry her was the suggestion of his craft.

In wishing the first contingency to occur, he only longed for the realisation of a whim which would enter the mind of any admirer of womanly superiority, while such admiration was rendered still greater by the knowledge that Bessy had a loving disposition, which could not but make the man of her choice happy.

On the other hand, Dashwood would have looked forward to the future without any fear of pecuniary want.

Were he united to the merchant's daughter he knew perfectly well that he should then be the heir to all the immense possessions of old Williams, to the irrevocable exclusion of the youth who was fairly entitled to them.

Somehow or another, however, where women were concerned, they had at first an unconquerable antipathy against Dashwood, which his will of iron, and a certain gift of mesmerising them which he possessed, finally always conquered.

Bessy's disdain exasperated her new suitor, while it inflamed his passion, and he knew not what steps he should adopt to enlist at once her favours, since his silver words and plausible pretences were lost upon her.

His hypocrisy appeared as if struck through by her bright black eyes, and as if his affectation of morality only rendered the adulation of his flattery absurd and contemptible.

Dashwood, however, was resolved not to be baulked.

He knew that in the end it would succeed, as he had on his side old Williams, who, although he wished the match, would not force his daughter's inclinations.

There is a proverb which goes to say that "murder will out," and Dashwood felt that he might perhaps go too far, and by too much hastiness ruin, in a few days, the splendid position which his slow course of systematic villany was on the eve of insuring for him.

He turned over in his mind how he should get over the rising difficulty.

He then applied to the Rev. Mr. Brinsley to assist him in his dilemma.

He suggested a forced marriage, and on the plea of what he had done for him, solicited his assistance as a right and not as a favour.

The selfish knave, however, was no longer willing to remain Dashwood's slave.

He had obtained his purpose in the shape of a "fat," good living, and he coolly informed him that a clergyman should be a moral man before all else, and should not be mixed in transactions of so disgusting a nature.

That a priest had obligations and duties to fulfil, which he could not fairly discharge were he to have on his conscience the remembrance of having abetted the consummation of such an infamous plan.

That it was very well to be foolish once, and that he knew he had sinned deeply; but God was merciful.

And, as a conclusion, he did not intend any more to follow the same road, which must lead some day to an awkward exposure and unenviable notoriety.

This gave rise to some correspondence between the two old friends, and the winding up of several letters taught Dashwood that, although the rule is honour among thieves and rogues, still, occasionally, exceptions are to be met with—as the case in point.

The Rev. Mr. Brinsley had replied that he did not care a straw for all the Williams' and all the Dashwoods' in the world — and in a coarse, drawling way, made the weaknesses of the man —who, to be candid, put bread into his mouth —a subject of vulgar buffoonery.

Meanwhile, Dashwood had to rest upon his oars in what concerned his scheme of marriage, and, in the interim, resolved to employ his leisure in achieving the total destruction of the young Williams.

This was not very difficult.

The stricken deer is deserted by the whole herd—and a man undone is sure to receive the kind offices of every fool and knave that can contribute to tread him deeper into the earth.

The sum which Williams junior had received from the old merchant would have been considered a large one by many; but, in the hands of a youth who had run through fifteen hundred pounds in a six months' stay at Oxford, it appeared so small that he never attempted to turn it to any account, and, with that facility which some people have of squandering a fortune, he managed, in a very short period, to exhaust every penny of it.

Young Williams, not suspecting Dashwood, applied to him for some relief; and if the truth, too, is told, it must be confessed that, in the present instance, he really exerted himself to obtain him funds from the father.

This new instalment dwindled off with the same rapidity as the previous amounts; and Dashwood introduced him to one or two casual acquaintances of his, who led him into expensive amusements, and who sponged upon the poor fellow with such renewed tokens of the friendship they professed for him, that he remained blind to the horrid machinations systematically carried against him.

Always preserving his intimacy with the young merchant, Dashwood continually presented objects of compassion to his generosity, which the kindly foolish weakness of his heart could not resist.

At the same time Dashwood was playing a double-game as usual, and representing to the old merchant the life of his son as one undeviating career of debauch and dissipation.

Dashwood had a share in a betting book, which was made by a swell out of luck who he had known at Oxford.

One of those University men who had fallen low, aye, so low as to have become bookmakers on horse flesh, which is indeed the most demeaning position that a man can fill in the scale of social life.

He induced him to stake the best portion of his fathers' remittances upon some "crack," which was a dead certainty for some great handicap, and which turned out like ninety-nine out of one hundred favourites turn out to be, namely, a grand swindle.

When the old merchant would inquire from Dashwood relating to his son, he would inform him that in addition to his other propensities, he had taken to gambling, and had lost rather a heavy sum, by staking it upon a good mare, who, indeed, had a fair chance of " landing" the money —but which had failed to come off fully to the public's expectations.

Nothing on earth could have been more irksome to the unfortunate merchant than to become acquainted with such sad tidings.

He believed his son to be a drunkard, a gambler, and who only delighted in those amusements, which men of business condemn, as they must ultimately bring those who indulge in them to certain ruin; and in his old age, when the merchant contemplated the moment when he should look out towards his son for comfort and for filial love, he found his dream broken, his expectation of seeing his boy reforming, dashed to the ground.

But young Williams, meanwhile, was too proud to return to his father's home.

Another rashness achieved his ruin.

He married the daughter of the landlady where he lived; and as neither had any money, blasted for ever his future prospect.

" Love in a cottage" lasted as long as the father kept on sending money; but Dashwood advised him to stop parting with funds which were only squandered in vice and dissipation.

A family and distress followed.

The father-in-law was incapable of assisting, as he had many children to provide for; besides, a daughter, who took it into her head to marry a gentleman, and to make her position more agreeable, he would have allowed her like a Christian to starve, had not Horace resolved to face the world—by addicting himself to the uncertain profits of literature for subsistence.

The months elapsed—the year followed.

The merchant's son's (now a literary character) family increased, and grew expensive.

When he entered into his matrimonial state, he had furnished a small house at Brompton.

He borrowed some money upon the furniture, by giving a bill of sale upon it.

When the day of payment came, he applied to Dashwood to represent to his father the frightful plight in which he found himself placed.

It was not Dashwood's object to do so any longer; the state of infatuation to which he had reduced the old merchant was so great that he feared to destroy it, by agreeing to his victim's request.

An execution took place in young William's house; the bed from under his wife's body, then lying-in, was the only thing which was left after the sheriff's warrant had been enforced.

Poor Williams, unable to bear so much calamity, cursed God—cursed the world which had treated him so bitterly.

A fire raged in the empty house, and his wife and his children were snatched away from him, and he remained alone—alone in the world.

One morning he strayed into a coffee-house, where he had a cup of tea and a crust of bread and butter; while satiating his hunger, he glanced in the " Times," and saw his father's name figuring among a list of charitable good men, like him! for having subscribed a thousand pounds to a public charity of which he scarcely knew the nature.

Will you believe in the tale of providence after that?

A French soldier once said that " God Almighty always was on the side of the largest artillery."

Would not such a statement appear true in the face of the above heartrending facts?

The heart of Williams was fairly broken.

He was, literally and positively speaking, driven to despair.

There is but one thing in this world which can keep up the heart of man—give him strength to face, with a bold and hopeless mind, the severest blows that the wayward hand of Fate hurls against him.

And what is that?

Religion.

But Dashwood had endeavoured, and successfully, too, to shake young Williams' religious opinions by books of scepticism, and by introducing him into the society of Atheists, who are pleased to call themselves philosophers.

Thus, when he found himself deserted by all, what did he do?

He thought of suicide, and mentioned his intention of doing away with himself to Dashwood.

No information could have been more welcome to that heartless villain, and he conveyed the intelligence of such a rash determination to the old merchant.

Conceive, then, the craft of Dashwood's web, and the infatuation of the father, who, notwithstanding that sad news, never endeavoured to recal his prodigal son to the arms that had so cruelly forsaken him.

The father, on the contrary, wrote a most unfeeling letter to his son, who suddenly disappeared from a city which had been the witness of so many sad incidents linked with his unfortunate and lonely destiny.

Weak persons would have had what is called a tender conscience, and none but a creature of Dashwood's stamp would have been so tenacious as to carry out, to the end, so infernal a scheme.

Meanwhile, everything prospered under his hands, and he required but one thing—to marry the merchant's daughter—and by such a union become the avowed heir of old Williams.

The antipathy which the girl experienced against him was still as strong as ever; and, vexed in the extreme to be thus baffled, he now began in earnest to endeavour to fathom the causes which could lead to such dislike on her part.

Was she acquainted with his low and demonical conduct?

If so, why had she not spoken before?

Did she love some other person?

This was most likely.

What was to be done under the circumstances?

To find out, of course, who the object of her love could have been.

Dashwood was not long in finding a clue to the mystery.

Miss Williams had formed an acquaintance with a penniless clerk in her father's counting-house.

Letters had passed between them.

Dashwood gleaned the information from the girl's confused manner when he happened to mention the clerk's name in her presence—

making, at the same time, allusions which could not but bring a blush on a girl's features.

Her bedroom was ransacked, and a lady's maid bribed.

Dashwood placed him in possession of all those documents which he required to establish her guilt in her father's eyes.

Old Williams was not able at first to realise the truth of such a statement, but proofs being forthcoming, he yielded to Dashwood, who advised that the clerk should be instantaneously dismissed from the office.

Dashwood was entrusted with the task of doing so, and it need not be told that he accomplished it without delay.

Dashwood found now that he had but one thing more to do—namely, to keep on tyrannising the girl so as to force her in the end to submit to his desires.

Had she had a brother to protect her, friends to defend her, maybe she would have resisted; but her father, who was the only person to whom she could rely to wipe the tears which damped her eyes, had been so alarmed at the acquaintance his daughter had contracted without his knowledge, that he openly countenanced Dashwood's proposal.

For a few weeks the poor girl attempted to struggle against her suitor; but submit she did at last, and unwillingly consented to become his wife.

This step, however, was her death blow. She fell into a consumption, and gradually pined away.

Dashwood, it may be scarcely believed, detested his wife for the resistance which she had offered him, and it was with a fiendish joy that he noticed the decline of her health—gloating inwardly over a death that would leave him his own master once more, with the fortune of the wealthy merchant, who had been so infatuated as to listen to him.

When love does not exist on either side, scenes will occur; and a frightful quarrel took place between husband and wife; strong words followed, and she was carried in hysterics to a bed, from which she was doomed never to rise again.

On the following day the physician gave her up, and a clergyman inquired whether she had anything upon her mind, and what was her last wish.

She replied that she desired to be left alone with her husband.

Dashwood went like a culprit to the seat of judgment.

Before no one had he trembled before.

But when he saw the angelic expression of the woman's face—when that countenance became lighted up with anger, and when upon her deathbed she opened her lips to tell him that she knew his vile character, and that if she had not spoken before it was because she did not wish to break her father's heart—he was fairly cowed.

Dashwood, however, soon recovered his confidence, and laughed her to scorn.

Her passion supplied her with strength. She attempted to ring the bell to call her father, and to reveal all to him.

Her violence was frightful to witness, and she seemed to be so roused that her listener knew not what to do, lest in a moment all his villany might be exposed.

At that instant a fainting fit slowly and gradually came upon her.

Dashwood watched the effect of it.

Sitting by her bed side, he looked like the angel of death awaiting his victim.

Suddenly the girl opened her eyes wider and wider.

Her faint glance met that of her husband.

What if she were to come to life?

What if the physician had made a mistake?

What if she were to recover?

A few words spoken by her would have the effect of undoing what had cost him so much time to place together.

"Dashwood," she muttered, "I want to see my father."

A smile of heartless ingratitude overspread the husband's countenance.

He remained motionless and silent.

And then he heard sounds of footsteps.

It seemed to him that it was the old man's tread.

What was to be done?

It was come to the issue of life for life!

He rushed towards the woman—grappled her throat with his nervous and feverish hand, and pressed it till life was extinct.

She uttered a weak groan, her teeth rattled, her eyes sank deeper and deeper in her head, her lower jaw dropped, and she became a warm corpse, which was the only sight which awaited the father as he entered the bedroom.

Dashwood's features were as pale as death.

"The time has come, he said," whispering softly and mournfully into the merchant's ears, "she is no more I fear, but her soul is now in heaven, for she died like a true christian."

When the old man saw his daughter's pale features his heart gave way.

He clung to Dashwood's arm, and he was led by him to a chair, upon which he fell exhausted.

The merchant did not survive his daughter very long, and when he died, he left behind a will, leaving Dashwood the heir of his business and of all his possessions.

Major Blake was about to pursue the reading of the manuscript which he had been perusing, when he heard a gentle tap outside the door of his apartment.

"Come in," he said, quickly.

No sooner had he spoken, that his old butler entered.

"What brings you hither, John?" the military man inquired, gazing fiercely upon his butler's countenance,

"A message has come for you, sir," the servant replied quickly. "A man on his death bed wishes to see you."

"A man dying!" he exclaimed, "what can it mean."

"I know not, your honour," the servant replied; "what shall I say?"

"That I will go, of course, as soon as I have placed some order in my toilet."

"The messenger is downstairs waiting for you, sir."

"Tell him to wait. I will not be long."

Thus speaking, Major Blake prepared to take his departure.

And it was only now, that he perceived that he had been up all night, and that so busy had he been in the perusal of the manuscript, that he had not noticed the first streaks of morning peeping through the curtains of the room where he had been sitting.

Major Blake opened his desk, and carefully placed the manuscript within it, and having seen that it was safely locked, he walked along the steps which led downstairs, to see what the messenger wished to say to him.

CHAPTER XLV.

WHICH DESCRIBES AN INTERVIEW WHICH TOOK PLACE BETWEEN MAJOR BLAKE AND ONE OF THE PARTIES OF WHICH HE READ OF IN THE MANUSCRIPT.

A MAN, whose face Major Blake had never seen before, awaited him in the hall.

"What do you want, my friend?" the military man asked, with that polite tone of voice which gentlemen always assume before strangers, whoever and whatever they may be.

"It is Major Blake I want to see, sir."

"I am Major Blake. What is it?"

The messenger bowed, and held out to the major a letter, of which he at once broke the seal.

He looked at the writing.

It was unknown to him.

He afterwards glanced upon the signature, and he read a name which was familiar to him.

"Williams!"

"What can this be?" he muttered.

Then, musing, he read on—

"SIR,—

"Although I have not the honour of your acquaintance, knowing the generous and noble feelings which you are endowed with, I take the liberty of asking you to come to my bedside. The doctor says I have not six hours' life in me, and if you will abide by my request, I will acquaint you with a secret, which I must divulge."

Major Blake gazed upon the messenger.

"What is your name?" he asked.

"Manning, sir," he replied; "I live with Mr. Williams, and he begged me to give you this letter."

And Manning assumed the appearance of a man who was innocent in the extreme, and it would have been difficult indeed to recognise in the servant before us Dashwood's lieutenant.

"Where does Mr. Williams live?" Major Blake asked.

"St. John's Wood Road, sir."

"Very well, call a conveyance and I will go with you."

In less than twenty minutes afterwards Major Blake reached the residence in question.

It was a detached villa, which seemed to be rather tastefully ornamented outside.

As soon as the cab stopped, the Major was led into a small lobby, which extended to a flight of steps.

"Will Major Blake follow me?" asked a man of about forty years of age.

Having replied in the affirmative, the military man was conducted into a bedroom, which was furnished with sumptuous elegance.

Upon a large bed he perceived an individual, who would have been between thirty-five and forty years of age.

He bowed to Major Blake with the hand, and beckoned him to sit down.

Then he made a sign to the servant who had brought Major Blake within to retire.

The military man was gazing upon the individual who had sent for him, and was wondering whether the unknown person who had written to him in the manner he had was really about to die, or whether there was not some snare laid to entrap him.

"Major," said the sick man, who apparently guessed the reflections which were crowding his visitor's mind; "I do not appear, you think, like a man so near his last hour as perhaps I am."

The Major was about to speak, when he was prevented from so doing by the sick man, who said,—

"But this is not the point at issue, sir. I have not sent for you without very serious reasons. I have just returned from India, where I have made a very large fortune, and I wish to dispose of it ere I die. I have no near relation in this country beyond a brother-in-law, whom I would on no consideration see."

"What might be his name?" Major Blake inquired in a softened tone of voice.

"Martin Dashwood," the sick man replied, faintly. "He married my sister, who died very shortly after her marriage. I can't say that she was made away by foul means, but the man who was united to her could be guilty of any deed. The other day I received a manuscript, giving an account of his life, which was written by one who knew him well, and who, upon his deathbed, acquainted me with the whole truth."

It may easily be fancied that Major Blake's attention was rather kindled by the revelation he heard.

"Who could that be?" the soldier asked.

"A clergyman, of the name of Brinsley, who died repenting of his sins."

Within the last few days Major Blake had seen and heard too much to be able to realise to himself the truth of the many statements which had reached him.

"Where is that manuscript of yours?" he asked, in a quick tone of voice.

"I sent it to you when I heard that, actuated by the same motive as myself, you were endeavouring to investigate the character of a man, who must be too great a rogue to be allowed to live at large."

Notwithstanding what he had heard, Major Blake could not understand why he should have been the party with whom the late merchant's son should communicate.

Thus, when he had allowed him to remain silent for a few minutes, and thereby giving him an opportunity to recruit his strength, he asked him why he did so.

"Why, Major Blake," he said, "I was told that your sister married this Martin Dashwood, and, as she died rather early after marriage, we were both interested in sifting this matter through."

"I have sworn," replied the soldier, "to hunt this man out, and, with the help of Providence, I will; but, with the exception of the manuscript which reached me, I cannot say that I have yet found out anything which could warrant me in

THE UNEXPECTED MEETING.

bringing this charge against him; what I could substantiate is out of justice."

The sick man shook his head.

"In a few years, Major Blake," the patient continued, "I have made a fortune which brings me in ten thousand a year, and if I die intestate it would go to my family, and my brother-in-law is the only one which remains of all my relations. Think, then, how hurtful it would be to my feelings to leave such a fortune to a man whom I cannot but loathe after the reports which I have heard."

"What you state is perfectly true," the Major replied, "but all rests entirely with one man—with that clergyman. His statements were made before witnesses, no doubt, but his word is only one which can be contradicted by the party accused. The murder of your sister would ap-

pear to me a worthy conclusion of his previous deeds, but so many years have elapsed since she was no more, to prove such a crime now would not only be a difficult task, but an impossible one."

The sick man was listening to these words with increasing interest and anxiety.

"Oh! I wish I could live," he said; "but I feel that my last hour is drawing nigh."

Thus speaking, the merchant's son placed his hand upon his heart.

"Have you made a will yet?" Major Blake asked.

"I wish I had," he muttered, "I never thought of it yet. I will do so now if you will bring me a sheet of paper, a pen, and some ink."

The voice of the speaker was so firm, his eye was so bright, that Major Blake could not be lieve that he could die in the short period in which he said he feared he should.

"I will go and fetch a lawyer and a couple of witnesses," he muttered; "what will you do then?"

"I will make you my executor, and in the event of your proving Dashwood innocent of the crimes which he is charged with, the fortune is to go to him; whereas, if my anticipations prove correct, the whole of my property will become yours."

Major Blake rose.

"I will not be five minutes away," he said; "rely upon me to be back very shortly."

Thus speaking, he rang for the servant to show him down stairs.

Anxious to carry out his promise, Major Blake hurried out, and having called a cab, drove away to the nearest lawyer's in the neighbourhood.

But scarcely had the Major disappeared from the room of the sick man, than a closet opened suddenly, and Dashwood, with a fierce eye bespeaking vengeance, rushed upon the son of the man whom he had so cruelly deceived.

"Dashwood!" shrieked the sick man, as soon as he saw the appearance of his old college friend.

"Yes, it is Dashwood!—it is me!" he hissed. "Yes, it is Dashwood. You want to make a murderer of me; well, you may do so—but your will is not made yet, and it will never be!"

Williams tried to rise out of bed, and to reach the mantlepiece, to lay hold of a loaded pistol which he ever had by him.

But he could not, his strength failed him.

"What! do you think you could struggle with me?" Dashwood exclaimed, in a frightful passion. "I wish I could torture you and make you suffer all night, or until the moment when you will die—but, alas! there is no time to be lost."

As he uttered these words, he took the patient by the shoulders and held him on his bed.

A dozen times he shook him as strongly as he possibly could.

But the man would not die.

Life was yet in him.

"I must do away with you," he muttered: "my fortune depends upon it."

"Oh, mercy!" exclaimed the sick man; "if you are guilty of one murder, do not soil your hands with another."

"Who told you that I was?" he asked.

The dying man wished to cling to life, to revenge himself against one about whose guilt he could now have no doubt.

"You are too emaciated to live long," Dashwood exclaimed; "no one will ever dream that I have done away with your life, because you just told Major Blake that you would not live long; so suspicion in this case will not await me."

"Oh, spare me!" the sick man replied, "and my fortune is yours."

Dashwood replied by a hollow, satanical laugh.

"Yes, yes; I heard you just now talking about me. Die, die, die, you accursed scoundrel!"

With these words, Dashwood gave a blow to the temple of the sick man, with a strength which rendered him powerless.

Then he placed a mask, which he carried about him, upon his features, thereby preventing him from breathing, until he felt that his heart had fairly ceased to beat.

Williams, the merchant's son, was now dead.

With the swiftness of the doe, Dashwood resumed his hiding-place, having withdrawn the mask from the corpse's features.

Scarcely had he done so than Major Blake returned.

Manning received him at the door.

The military man was accompanied by a doctor and a solicitor.

As the fortune of Williams was immense, he wished to see that everything should be carried out with the minutest accuracy, and with due deference to the most intricate rules of the law.

He entered into the bedroom.

The two men followed him.

A death-like silence reigned within.

What could have happened.

The patient did not rise as he had done before.

Had his forbodings come to pass?

Had life fled from him already?

Was he no more?

Could he have died without making his will?

Such were the quick thoughts which crowded themselves in the mind of the military man during the time which elapsed between his entering the bedroom and reaching the bedside of the patient.

He gazed upon the body.

He retreated three steps backwards.

There is something so repelling and so ghastly in the appearance of a corpse—especially when the corpse is that of one whom we knew but a few minutes previously—that we cannot prevent ourselves from shuddering with feelings of undefinable awe.

The physician, in his turn, took the place which had been vacated at the bedside of the patient by Major Blake, and began to examine minutely the chest of his late patient.

Never dreaming that murder could have been committed in the very short space which he was away—namely, twenty minutes at the utmost—Major Blake did not think of speaking about the last thing which would have entered into his head.

The lawyer was disappointed at his having lost his fee, and he did not hint at the deceased's having met his death by the violence of some person or persons unknown, because he saw no way to substantiate his opinion.

And the doctor proclaimed the merchant's son to be fairly dead, because he expected it for many days past; and the quick way in which he went off, the more reliance would then be placed in his word for the future.

Thus Dashwood came in for the handsome fortune of one more of his victims, and thus Major Blake was baffled.

But he was not going to stop there.

Though he had failed in his first attempt, he still trusted in the Power above, and, with renewed strength and vigour, he decided that he would make further researches.

Half-an-hour elapsed, and the three professional men now left the death-room, and shaped their course to their various destinations.

When the room was once more lonely and deserted, Dashwood again stepped into the midst of it.

Soon he was joined there by Manning.

"Poor fool! stupid hound!" muttered Manning, speaking to the corpse, which was gradually assuming that dark shade which is to be noticed among those who have diseased liver. "You thought yourself very clever, eh, didn't you? You took me into your service, knowing not who I was; you gave me food, bread, and liberal wages, never suspecting that I came into your house, sent by your bitterest enemy, who knew what could be got out of a bachelor with ten thousand pounds a year, and without any direct heir to bequeath it to."

"Poor fellow!" Dashwood pursued; "you have been the most ill-used man that I ever knew; but shake hands, I can fairly do so now, since I come into a fine fortune by you."

And the ruffian, not fearing to carry out such an atrocious joke, took the hand of the corpse, and shook it vehemently.

At that instant the corpse opened its eyes, and Dashwood thought he heard it muttering something audible, and he ran out of the house as if he was pursued by some apparition.

"What is the matter with the governor?" Manning muttered, as he finished the toilet of the corpse; "does he think the chap is a-going to come back to life? No, it ain't likely, not in these days of enlightenment and civilisation."

Thus soliloquizing, Manning placed the blanket over the features of the body, and went out of the room singing a pot-house song, which was a blasphemy to the scene which he was just leaving.

CHAPTER XLVI.

WHERE HOGAN GOES AHEAD, AND WHAT HE DOES.

OUR readers doubtless remember the opening of the International Exhibition, about which we have already spoken ere now.

That day had formed an epoch in Langdon's life.

Through the endeavours of Mrs. Haltering, he had been thrown into the society of the dashing heiress—of Laura Wylde, with all her thousands.

More than once had Langdon thought over the pleasant walk which he took with the girl in Hyde Park.

He believed in his own mind that he had created an impression by no means unfavourable.

At least he thought so.

Nay, we can go a little farther.

We can state, without the fear of our being contradicted, that he had seen Mrs. Haltering since, and she had led him to hope.

"Laura Wylde likes you," the worthy lady had said. "When you see her again, mind that you behave yourself. I do not doubt but that she may ultimately be brought to ——"

"I know," Langdon replied. "But, Agnes, one thing must be done."

"What's that?"

"We must not rely too much upon what a girl may say."

"Why so?"

"Have you read Shakespeare?"

"'Frailty, thy name is woman,' my dear Langdon; I knew that was what you were going to say, but spare me the bore of listening to it once more. This is too old, too universal, and too hackneyed a saying to be worth repeating."

A good deal of "balderdash" of a similar nature had been indulged in by the two "outsiders," and Langdon felt that he would perhaps be so fortunate as to secure the coveted prize at some day not far distant.

But if we direct the attention of our readers to that memorable day, it is to revert to other matters of which we are called upon to treat, as we have already devoted a few lines to them.

We allude to the exclamation which Langdon had given way to when he had seen his acquaintance Hogan driving away with the Duke of Ellingtown.

He had hinted that he would not be astonished to see or to hear of his friend Hogan turning the illustrious patrician to some profitable account.

Now, how could that be?

How could a man like Hogan obtain such a hold on a patrician's friendship as to cause him to do that which Langdon had hinted at, namely, to get a proud nobleman to lend his name to an accommodation bill for a few hundred pounds—a thing they are very shy to do towards helping their own equals?

For to commit one's name to paper is not by any means a very agreeable step to take, as it generally lets many people know what we wish to keep from them, namely, that we are in want of that despicable, and yet so useful an accessory to man's life, and which in the English dictionary is termed by the name of money.

It would be imagined that a man like Hogan, who was previously unknown to the Duke of Ellingtown, and whom he only met at such a doubtful place as that of Mrs. Haltering, would have a great difficulty in becoming intimate enough with the patrician to ask him to help him in the manner above alluded to.

That he could have asked him is no criterion, because in this world we meet people who would ask us for the coat off our backs, were there a million chances to one against them getting it, but that he should have carried his point seemed so preposterous to sensible and thinking men, so fraught with difficulties, that to enter fully into the subject may be found interesting.

And again—is this country not one of the most exclusive ones on the continental map of Europe, in the shape of acquaintance-making, as a rule.

And now for the solution of the riddle.

The acquaintance of Hogan with the Duke began at Mrs. Haltering's.

Who was she?

We have already told our readers that she was an officer's wife, who had been separated from her husband to prevent the filthy revelations of a national disgrace in our British legislature, namely, the Divorce Court.

Mrs. Haltering's husband had impressed her with the necessity of doing that which a great emperor, an illustrious general, and a wonderful statesmen, advised his subjects to do—*de laver son linge sale en famille*—which in English can be translated thus—to wash one's dirty linen in one's own family.

In driving from the Exhibition to some west end hotel, Hogan had taken very good care to do everything in his power to win the good opinion of his companion, and when the Duke had reverted to Hogan's name as that of a person who had been familiar to him, the crafty black-leg had quietly hinted that he was indeed the son of a general, who in years gone by had known his lordship.

Some patricians are very particular, others are far from being so; and we remember having seen one of the bearers of one of the oldest names in "Burke's Peerage," paying a visit, in the broad daylight of noon, to some unfortunate creature who could be bought for the trifling consideration of a five pound note, or, perhaps, less.

That the nobleman alluded to was made the dupe of a designing "outsider" there can be no doubt, but, considering the place where he met him, he could not have expected any other treatment than that which he received.

When the Duke, then, reached his destination, he wished farewell to our gallant acquaintance, Hogan, who pondered on the good occasion which came in his way.

By some of the extraordinary oddities of London society, or London outside society, whichever the reader prefers, Hogan was acquainted with Dashwood, and he knew that in his house he happened to have, prisoners, two girls, meant for some of the disgraceful spendthrifts who care not what amount of money they have to pay to gratify, by some astringent, or by some strong tonic, the weakened organs of their ill-used and impaired constitutions.

It then struck Hogan that if he could obtain for his lordship a lady by birth and by education, still uncontaminated by man's embrace, like Lord Vineyard, the old Duke of Elling-town's pride would be flattered, and he would not afterwards refuse Hogan any favour which he might ask from him.

Thus Hogan reasoned with himself.

He had, besides, a plan of his own.

He never did things by halves.

When he wished for success he began in earnest.

Now he did so.

He looked upon the Duke as a windfall to him —as at the time he met him he was frightfully hard pushed for cash.

Days passed, till one afternoon, Hogan happened to meet the Duke.

"Fine weather this," the Duke said, and taking Hogan's arm, they walked on to Mrs. Haltering's.

With that Jesuitical pleasant smile which ever sat upon her countenance, she received the two gentlemen.

On a sofa in a corner of the room sat a young girl, of sixteen years of age at the utmost.

She was of an exquisitely fair complexion.

Her eyes were blue, large, and bright, and the silken fringes which softened their intense radiance, enlivened the melancholy of an interesting languid physiognomy.

When she saw the two gentlemen entering she blushed.

The Duke noticed that.

Girls of sixteen must be very innocent and very bashful, now-a-days, to blush before the appearance of two members of the male species.

She was duly introduced to the two gentlemen.

The Duke entered into conversation with her, while Hogan and Mrs. Haltering were discussing matters of everyday life, seeming not to heed

how very smitten the nobleman had become in a very short space of time.

This girl, whom we now introduce to our readers, was one of those whom Polly had seen at Dashwood's house.

Unable to bear any longer the girl's entreaties to send her into the open air, he had placed her under the tuition of his worthy friend Mrs. Haltering.

He knew that she could not be in better hands.

Nay, he felt that she should play her part well.

When the Duke spoke to the girl—whose name was Ady—he could not help admiring the brilliant enamel of her white teeth, the quick expression of her blue eyes, and the loving and intellectual look of her whole countenance.

Thus it occurred to him that he longed for the possession of this beautiful bird who had been kept so long in the cage.

But how can love at first sight be explained?

It seems strange, yet it is true.

But can one judge of a woman's qualities and attractions sufficiently well to be enamoured of one in less than half-an-hour?

We cannot tell about that; but that which we know is, that such loves, kindled so abruptly, last much longer, in many cases, than those which have been preceeded by a long courtship.

There was a mutual understanding at the conclusion of the interview, that Ady should become the Duke's own.

"A devilish fine girl that," the Duke said, on leaving the house.

"None but the brave deserve the fair," Hogan replied; "and, my lord, she will be yours."

The two men shook hands, and made an appointment, which we will describe in due course.

CHAPTER XLVII.

WHERE MAJOR BLAKE STILL READS THE MANU-
SCRIPT OF DASHWOOD'S LIFE.

It would be difficult for our readers to form an adequate opinion of the disappointment which Major Blake felt on reaching his home.

He had made up his mind to carry out a design which, considering the motives which prompted it, was praiseworthy in the extreme; and yet he now discovered that he was as far from his destination as on the day which he first conceived it.

He did not want help from any one—he believed that with God's assistance, he would be able to accomplish successfully a task which was fraught with immense difficulties.

But it was provoking, indeed, to find that he should have met with an unexpected incident, which had dashed to the ground his design, and had rather forcibly shown him the small space of ground on which he had walked, and the long distance which remained before him ere he could reach the end of the journey upon which he had set out.

The Major had been rather astonished when, by post, he had received the manuscript which we have seen him reading, but he had been still more puzzled when the strange message, which the dying man had sent, reached him.

He thought then that the finger of God could be traced in the singular coincidence, upon which he pondered at the time, and for many years afterwards; and with an eagerness which can easily be imagined, he sallied forth in search of further information.

To him it was most welcome news to hear, and any one who might speak the truth, for he doubted not that, with the manuscript which he possessed, and a *viva voce* statement, he would have no difficulty in establishing Martin Dashwood's guilt, and in revenging the death of a beloved sister.

But the death, the sudden death of Williams shortly after the interview which the Major had had with him, was one of those extraordinary and unaccountable whims of fate, which awkwardly interfered with the plans before him.

For although we may believe people, whom we meet daily in the intercourse of life, to be guilty of the most horrid foul play, we cannot lay any accusation against them, unless we have the clearest of evidence on our side to substantiate most palpably what we assert.

Major Blake thought of all these things, and scarcely had he entered his studio than he rushed to his desk to withdraw from it the manuscript.

It was there safe enough.

He opened it and read on.

Dashwood was now the heir of Williams the merchant, and in looking over the returns of the business which was yearly transacted by the house, of which he was now the proprietor, owner, principal, &c., &c., he discovered to his satisfaction that it was yielding an income of four thousand pounds a year.

He knew that from the style of living of the old gentleman, Williams senior must have had at least that income, and he was also agreeably surprised to find on reading the will that he was set down in a very handsome round sum of hard cash invested in the three per cent. Bank of England stock.

It might be thought, perhaps, by many that, after having worked for so many years with unremitting steadiness towards obtaining old Williams's wealth, Dashwood would have taken a great interest in the fine business which had been left him; and endeavoured to improve it by applying his brains to that purpose.

A great many merchants in the city, who had admired Dashwood's steadiness, and learnt the fate of Williams junior, who could not let the other get rid of his "wild oats" in a year or two, and who was launching into a career of recklessness and debauchery, at least (so the *on dits* informed them), fully expected to see the lucky youth now a man, double the business which he came into, and out of a large capital build one of those immense fortunes known only in the city of London.

For the eight or nine months which followed old Williams's death, Dashwood remained remarkably reserved, and it was noticed by one and all that he grieved deeply for the loss of one who had proved a protector and a kind father to him.

Dressed in the most simple mourning attire, his hat surrounded with a dark crape, he would never smile, and when he would be induced to speak to some of his late governor's friends, he would appear so serious and so genuine, that these would willingly excuse old Williams, and respect his memory all the more, for his having disinherited a spendthrift son, to bequeath his wealth to so steady and so good a person as Dashwood.

Dashwood was imbued with one idea, before which he ever bowed like the Hindoo before his idol, and he beleived that, if properly handled, hypocrisy was a tool in a man or woman's hand which had the power of levelling any obstacle, and of clearing for the clever actor the many impediments which obstruct the road of the casual wayfarer.

When the success which had attended his endeavours is taken into consideration, it will be admitted that no one can wonder at such an idea being still more strengthened in Dashwood's mind, and on his turning it to other purposes.

In every man's mind there is one certain feeling, which goes by the name of ambition.

Ambition is always laudable, provided it is directed in the proper channel, and, but for it, we would never have read in history of such men as Alexander, Cæsar, Napoleon, Wellington, and, later still, in our days, of that extraordinary, talented genius, namely, the reigning Emperor of the French, who can, indeed, be looked upon as the wonder of the nineteenth century, so chequered was his career, so great was his triumph.

Dashwood was ambitious.

In the city counting-house where he had spent a few years of his youth—from nine in the morning till five thirty in the evening—after his return from the University, he had obtained an insight into the old merchant's accounts, which was deemed by Dashwood a very good stepping-stone towards something better.

Being young, handsome, and possessing an education far beyond the average of those he met, Dashwood longed to be admitted into the society of the aristocracy and gentry, and which he hoped to be introduced by some of the heads of some of the leading firms.

To effect this object he naturally went to work very slyly, and as he knew that he could not attend to two things, to pleasure and to business, he acted upon an old saying which old Williams was very fond of quoting, namely, between two stools you must fall to the ground; he sold his interest in the business and started off in the world.

This ambition of Dashwood, to which we have alluded, was not so easily realised as many may be induced to believe, and it required an extra amount of hypocrisy, for he had to tax his brain on more than one occasion to devise upon certain plans which would place him into possession of the prize which he so ardently longed for

We English people are a very exclusive nation.

At home we admit within our intimacy none but those who belong to us by family ties, or who, holding the same position and standing in life as ourselves, are welcomed by us as freely as we are welcomed by them, at home we do not like to demean ourselves (there are exceptions of course) by keeping company with people below ourselves, or, by asking beneath our roofs characters whose antecedents, family, and wealth, are matters of doubt; but abroad, we alter like the silk-worm, whose skin changes of colour; we know and wish to know everybody; we become patronising; we do not care about our family; we men become enraptured with the ways of coarse and vulgar foreigners, and our daughters fall in love with the first "commis" whom they meet, and who, besides the particle "de" before his name, happens to have sixty pounds a year salary.

Dashwood had to struggle against the many difficulties which he had before him, and which we have briefly alluded to, and it was not until he had displayed as much policy as would be required for a Yankee citizen to obtain the presidential laurels of the White House, that, he at length obtained entrance into two of the weathiest English families, belonging to the county of L— where Dashwood had bought a large-sized house, which he called a hall, where he kept a stud of hunters, and where he took a great delight in entertaining the jolly married men, and the bachelors, living around and about for miles and miles.

Although the sum which Dashwood had received from the person who had bought the business of old Williams had been a considerable one (the exact amount we never heard), it could not long stand the never-ceasing taxation which the extravagance of its owner placed upon it, and he found himself, after a few years of fashionable life, on the brink of ruin—tolerated only by the aristocratic portion of humanity, and despised by the commercial community upon which he had looked down in his days of splendour and giddiness.

A wife—a rich wife; nothing but a wife would do for Dashwood now.

Although he was what a nobleman might call "hard up," Dashwood had a few thousand pounds left, with which he could weather the storm, hunt up the heiresses at all the fashionable watering places, and after having watched his opportunity and abided his time, hook within his net one morning some fine fish of the female species, with golden hair, golden looks, and, better still, a golden purse, to spend the golden hours of life in never-ceasing happiness.

Another shade of hypocrisy there again was needed.

It was incumbent upon him to ingratiate himself in the good opinion of such of those old ladies who, having young and pretty wards to look after, are sometimes exceedingly particular in allowing them to make acquaintances.

Even if they permit them, as a special favour, to make them, they do not allow them to cultivate them when they are made.

But this, for Dashwood, was only child's play.

He had, in a trip which he made to France, copied some of the manners and customs of that nation, and although many in the attempt bring themselves to the level of an educated dancing-master—he had not; and he had about him a smack of politeness and of courtesy, which were greatly relished by the wrinkled old dowagers for whom this premeditated pantomime had been purposely got up.

The exchequer of Dashwood was steadily but gradually getting low, as he never grudged any expense which he thought should be incurred, to meet the emergencies of the times.

The "hall" in the country was at length going to be sold, to meet certain liabilities which Dashwood had incurred while staying at Torquay, when an old lady with her niece came there.

The niece, it was whispered, was immensely wealthy.

But there were several rumours afloat anything but creditable respecting the origin of the lady's fortune.

The people spoke of a fish stall, and all those nasty remarks, which as much as implied that Mrs. Tomkins and Miss Snooks belonged to a fishmonger's race, and that the latter's father had accumulated a very handsome competency by selling lobsters, bloaters, natives, and sundry other fishes, which, however, enabled young Miss Snooks to live in great style.

It was a great blow for Dashwood, when he found himself, through "sheer necessity," compelled to set aside his dream of entering a fashionable family, and obliged to eat "humble pie" by associating with such people as the aunt and niece about whose respective characters we have already spoken.

He occasionally fancied, when he drove with worthy Mrs. Tomkins and Miss Snooks, that they spoke a little too much about shell-fish, and so on, which however did not prevent Dashwood to propose, and become Miss Snook's husband.

Dashwood then returned to the hall, hoping that, with his new acquired wealth, which was always supposed to be his own, as he had the sense of keeping his own council, and never to allow his affairs to get known, he would be visited by the neighbouring nobility.

This was Dashwood's dream.

This was his ambition.

He was disappointed.

Refined people, who had tolerated a pleasant, handsome, wealthy bachelor, who had intruded himself in the county, were not likely to hold the same indulgence towards the married couple.

Shortly afterwards Mrs. Dashwood died suddenly.

There the manuscript concluded rather hastily.

At the bottom of the page there was several remarks, which Major Blake endeavoured uselessly to decipher.

The characters were written very small, and in various places they were blotted out with heavy spots of ink.

Major Blake turned the manuscript over and over again, hoping that he would find some light thrown upon his sister's fate.

But, beyond what we have read, there was not another line.

As abruptly as we have written it, the paper concluded.

There were no remarks, or no signature, to indicate from whom the manuscript had been taken, and by whom it had been penned.

But it was evident that it had been written by some one who did not intend to stop so very quickly, and so very awkwardly, as there were a least twelve sheets of paper, and of which the folios were carefully numbered, devoid of any writing.

Major Blake folded up the manuscript, and replaced it, where he had taken it from, namely, the desk.

What was to be done under the circumstances?

How was he to find out the truth?

The merchant's son was no more.

Could he have some other manuscript among his papers?

How could that be?

If it had been so, would he not have forwarded it to him?

He would set his mind at rest soon.

He would not remain in the state of anxiety in which he was.

Over and over again he thought of visiting Martin Dashwood, and of accusing him of those things which he suspected.

To plead the wrong to find out the right, and thus by his behaviour, and by these means and proceedings set his mind fully at rest.

For he could not believe that one who had acted like Dashwood had done, if reliance could be placed upon what he had read, would have the boldness to face an honest man's accusations, or to deny his guilt.

In this instance Major Blake was sadly mistaken.

One who could have behaved like Dashwood had, must naturally possess a strong mind and a fearless nature, which would defy any attacks from a stranger.

The only loophole which remained to Major Blake, who had determined that he would sift matters through were he to spend his life and his fortune, which was considerable, to do so, was to obtain against Dashwood such information as would warrant him in taking immediate steps against him.

But the military man knew that this was a difficult object to accomplish.

Then, as now, in London, where one man is as good as another, and Dashwood happened to have so well managed his affairs, that he had obtained an entrance in several fashionable families, was, besides, a member of one or two west-end clubs, which admitted as their members none but men of the highest respectability.

Major Blake, though, felt that his was a design, which, although praiseworthy in its conception, could not be carried out without the most paramount difficulties, and without creating a scandal, and obtaining for himself an unenviable notoriety were he to fail in his object.

For his suspicions, after all, were perhaps groundless, for, although he had once thought that Dashwood was a murderer, this idea would not have haunted him so strangly and so powerful, as it did had not the perusal of the manuscript, which our reaeers have read, fortified them in his mind, and stengthened whatever doubt he might previously have had.

Besides, the strange interview which he had had with the dying man, in St. John's Wood, had produced upon his imagination, one of those sad and gloomy impressions which cannot easily be forgotten, and he thought, that by some unknown links, Dashwood had something to do with that man's death, and the sudden disappearance of the manuscript which he so much prized.

But he never dreamt of the possibility of Williams having been murdered.

He never dreamt that there could have been any underhand machinations set in motion to get rid of that man, who had sent to him to acquaint him with a secret which he had to divulge.

Major Blake, however, knew that by the death of Williams, Dashwood would derive considerable benefit, inasmuch as his being the nearest of kin of the dead man, he would step into his fortune.

Ten thousand a-year was, indeed, a princely income.

Major Blake was aware of that, and he could not remain blind to the fact, that, if wealth can in many instances be used for very worthy purposes, in others, a very different use can also be made with it.

He knew that if it is used to help those in distress, to further the welfare of needy but deserving people, and to do a great deal of good, it is sometimes disposed of to buy the mercenary services of the most degraded beings that can be found; and to destroy the virtuous minds of many who are unable to bear against the unceasing pangs of hunger and despair.

God knows what Dashwood might not do with gold and time on his hands.

It therefore devolved upon Major Blake, now more than ever, to try to take away from Dashwood's features the mask that he kept over them, which for so long a time concealed his wicked behaviour.

But the great point at issue was this, how could Major Blake see Dashwood.

Why to go and pay him a friendly visit, and during a few hours interview endeavour to ascertain from him that which he wished to know.

But Major Blake was alone!

He had no one to help him

The only one, who had evidently bent his mind to unite his efforts to his own, was now no more.

Had he only sent for him a few days previous, matters would have been arranged much better.

Major Blake thus thinking, was apparently forgetting that any message which might have been sent him previously, would not have reached him, as he had only returned to town but two days ago.

Now Major Blake, needing fresh air, walked towards the window.

He opened it and looked out.

"Oh, London," he muttered, as his gaze wandered afar, " sublime panorama of the Queen of the Universe, you are indeed, the enigmatic emblem of the world.

"Smiles and tears mingle together within the large dimensions of thy vast radius.

"In one place, pleasure to night will be at its height. In another, the artizan will slumber heavily, after his day's hard toil.

"Here, the melodious sounds of the ball-room band will warble forth their soft strains in the open air.

"There, the tread of the workman, wending his steps towards his morning's task, will be heard.

"On the right, the song of those who know not what care is, the radiant smiles of those who love each other, and the prayers of those whom hope has not forsaken.

"On the left, the tears of those who suffer, the sobs of a parent, who mourns the loss of a beloved son, the despairing cries of the orphan, and the heartrending shrieks of the bridegroom, whose feverish hand clutches his betrothed's cold body, who is suddenly snatched away by some terrible disease."

And then, when night came, Major Blake muttered, "What a picture of life, of death, of opulence, and of misery.

"Near me, I hear the rattle of the brougham,

carrying away in its swift course the wealthy citizen; a few yards further off the shrill whistle and the ominous sound of the crowbar of the housebreaker.

"Oh, London! what is there in thee?

"Thou might'st indeed be compared to a wide stage, upon which we perform dark and terrible dramas, where infamous deeds are wrought, and where daily are perpetrated crimes which the law is powerless to punish.

"London, where crime elbows virtue, where the guttural laugh of the rake drowns the genuine sob of the needy and destitute widow, and where the burglar treads the same road as the honest man.

"What is there in thee?

"And yet, who is there among us who, having not visited the English metropolis, does not, at some period or another of his life, long to do so?

"Who does not know the story of Dick Whittington, thrice Lord Mayor of London, who, finding his home dreary and unbearable, with a sickened heart, yet hopeful mind, ran away from his ancestral demesne, in Gloucestershire, to set off on his weary journey to London, wherein he hoped, and with some reason too, to carve his own fortunes."

And we ourselves, my dear reader, will exclaim with Major Blake—"What is there in London?"

Yet the labourer in the field working at the plough raises his head in astonishment to gaze upon the train as it hurries on towards the capital of the civilized world; and the youthful maiden and the rosy-faced boy stand outside the door of their humble cottage, as the smack of the whip, and the sound of the trumpet proclaims the departure of the coach for the city of London.

All professions and all trades look forward to the day when they will visit the great centre of attraction, towards which the eyes of the whole civilized world are turned.

The apprentice in the studio, as his pencil runs over the canvass, the reporter on the provincial newspaper, and the clerk who bends his head over the voluminous ledger in the counting-house, occasionally dream of the Big Town where such wonders are said to be wrought.

But why should such sentiment be felt by one and all, by those who have not to work for their living, namely, the upper ten thousand, and by those who, being less fortunate, have to rely upon their own energies and their own exertions?

Is it because London is a town, dazzling, lovely, and gay during a few months of the year, where royalty, in all its gorgeous pageantry and gilded display, holds its sumptuous drawing-rooms and its aristocratic lévées.

Is it because Parliament, in its long sittings, frames the laws of the land and watches the British Constitution while assembled in the halls of Westminster, where can be seen all that is noble and enlightened.

Truly, indeed, from the above description, the metropolis would be a veritable Eden, where misfortune is unknown, where tears are never shed, and where the days, months, and years glide on with a swiftness that, our happiness being so great, does not permit us to notice.

But it is not so.

Notwithstanding all these dazzling attractions,

London is not to be sought by those who long for happy hours.

It might, indeed, be compared to the Well of the Danaides, within which, slowly but gradually, many a stout heart leaves the dreams of his youth—the hopes of his manhood—the bitter remembrances of his old age.

With an avaricious thirst, it takes all and returns nothing.

Oh, you that circumstances have not brought to London, come not within its polluted, burning, and vitiated atmosphere!

If your imaginations, still innocent and true, need days of faith and calm, seek them not here.

Cast away from you dreams of celestial worship; and if you think that it is a noble thing to bind your heart and soul to one lovely being—to follow and worship her—ah! do not come to London to seek her.

For it is *par excellence* the town of wealth and patronage: where the poor man will struggle many a long year ere he attains that independence which he so anxiously hopes to obtain; where the poor girl will have to struggle hard indeed, if she wishes to emerge successfully and without stain from the many temptations which beset her path at every step she takes.

Seek not happiness in London, for the woman whom you will love, will lead you from the pinnacle of sublimity to the positiveness of every day life.

You will see her among beings, who will speak to her with indifference, when you would be ready to worship her on your bended knees, who will have a derisive smile upon their lips when addressing one, before whom you tremble, and, then you will believe her to be true and pure, you will believe her to be an angel among demons; and alas, you will find that mercenary interest and selfishness swayed all her motives, that she sought not you, but wealth and consideration, which you cannot give her.

No! Come not to London, if the harmonious sounds of an angel voice, of one faithful and kind, whom you may have left behind you, vibrates in your heart, for you will soon forget her among a thoughtless crowd, who have no sympathy, and who cannot understand how sad the mind can be, when assailed by the bitter regrets, which causes the soul to weep for the loss of the joys, and of the bliss that it had once dreamt of.

No; in conclusion we will say, if the ambition of a praiseworthy glory devours you, dismiss it at once, for you will not obtain it now-a-days by singing of things pure and sacred.

We have given way to the above reflections as they were those which entered Major Blake's disappointed mind.

We cannot wonder at them, for it was really the kind of musings which would assail the imagination of one situated as he was, who suspected a man of murder, and who had no means of convicting him, owing entirely to his want of evidence, and who had moreover, the dissatisfaction of seeing the individual stepping into one of the handsomest incomes ever heard of, when his downfall would have gratified everybody much better.

————

CHAPTER XLVIII.

**WHICH SAYS A FEW WORDS WHICH ARE NECESSARY
FOR THE COMPREHENSION OF THE TALE.**

WE have not been in this work, of which we find
that the dimensions must be much more limited
than we expected at first, so very particular as
to localities as we should have been had we had
occasion to refer oftner to the place described.

But it is necessary at times to do so.

Our readers donbtless remember that we have
said ere now that Dashwood stood in the middle
of a field which was totally uncultivated.

It was one of those high white houses which
we cannot but notice as we walk along, and as it
stood by itself in the outskirts of London, over
and over again the neighbours had asked who
lived within its walls.

The servants in the house were all dumb, with
the exception of a very pretty housemaid
whom Dashwood kept in the house, doubtless to
throw a little gaiety over the gloom of the whole
place.

As Dashwood got all his provisions from west
end tradesmen, and as they were regularly
brought to him twice a week, the neighbours had
no means of ascertaining the rank and position
of the inhabitant of the White House.

Besides, people in London are not as inquisitive as they are in the country; and a man may
live for twenty years in London, and die without
your neighbour knowing anything about it, or,
what's more, caring very little about your being
dead or alive.

The deaf and dumb servants which composed
Dashwood's household had no opportunity to
speak, were they even inclined to do so, and the
housemaid knew that it was as much as her
place was worth to breathe a word abroad, and

hence she had remained hitherto as silent as the grave.

The life of Polly the horsebreaker, whose early career we have watched, and whom we have followed step by step, was indeed a dreary one, and she would have been delighted at any incident which might occur and give her back her freedom.

Occasionally she would ride out with Dashwood in the surrounding neighbourhood, drive to town with him, but his company was not so agreeable as to render her stay with him at all lively.

Besides, Polly happened to know that Dashwood had been the means of destroying the life of Lady Florence, and we can easily believe that, although she might have had a certain amount of fear for one who had behaved like he did, such a thing as affection had never caused her heart to beat for him.

Polly and the housemaid, in the absence of their master, had often conversed together, and although the latter was not aware of the master's corrupted nature, still she knew that there was some cloud hanging over his forehead which he would not have wished any one to become acquainted with.

Repeatedly had Polly asked her lover whether he intended to remain for ever in the lonely house which he inhabited, and in answer to her questions he had answered her so roughly and so sharply that she had not ventured to broach the subject again.

Polly, besides, could easily see that the love which Dashwood had at first experienced for her, was gradually dwindling down to indifference, and she dreaded the moment when the feeling which he might once have entertained for her, might perhaps turn into hatred.

We may fairly ask why Polly should look upon such a conclusion as likely to pass, but when it is told that Dashwood's character exhibited such strange whims, that to describe them would be impossible, it was not difficult to understand her fears.

Such a change as love turning into hatred is not an uncommon occurrence, and she sadly feared that if she did anything to offend Dashwood he would be terrible in his revenge.

She was, besides, in possession of a secret with which she could compromise Dashwood's freedom, nay, jeopardise his life, and she thought that if her lover reflected upon the knowledge which she had, and to what ends she might turn it, he might feel inclined to do away with the existence of another woman.

Had Dashwood for instance resolved upon such a step, he could easily have carried it out, for there were none in the house who would have in any way hindered him in the accomplishment of such a nefarious deed.

We believe that Dashwood had received from Captain Morgan the price of Lady Florence's death, and, further, we are in a position to state that he did not know by what means she had been made away with.

Doubtless, had Captain Morgan been acquainted with the bloody drama which had been enacted at Dashwood's house, he would have grieved sadly at having required the services of one who could so faithfully and so mercilessly carry out his instructions.

One may, when grave considerations are at stake, suggest the idea of such a murder as that which had been perpetrated, but when it comes to the execution of it, few, indeed, can be found to be the instruments to work out the terrible object in view.

We have shown ere now Dashwood's character, and related his story.

We have described how he had acted towards the invalid in the house in St. John's Wood, and how those who had been called in by Major Blake, in compliance with the sick man's request, had not discovered any marks of violence upon his body.

Dashwood, up to the present period, had found all his deeds crowned with a success which far surpassed his most sanguine anticipations, and he was thinking of reforming his ways.

To carry out successfully so praiseworthy a design, he would have no difficulty to contend with, as he would soon be master of Williams's fortune, which no one could withdraw from him.

With the wealth of the merchant's son he would dazzle continental society, and return to London to end his days.

Those were his plans, if he could fulfil them.

He had not yet made up his mind as to what he should do with Polly, as she had never asked him any questions relating to the state of his affairs.

Although she was as intimate with him as a woman can be with the man she lives with, yet she dreaded to ruffle his temper by too much inquisitiveness.

She remembered the night she first accompanied him to his home, and the strange feeling which crept over her.

Since then she feared him.

She knew that Dashwood was her master.

She knew she was the mistress of a murderer.

This thought was one which hung heavy upon her mind.

What could she do to escape from him?

Left alone for nights and nights, she fretted deeply.

Besides, Polly was of a superstitious nature.

All those who have no religion are generally so.

She fancied that at nights she heard groans and murmurs of pain.

She fancied that she heard Lady Florence's voice shrieking for help.

But those were only the wanderings of imagination.

Dashwood had broken his word to Polly.

He had promised to furnish a house for her in the fashionable part of the town.

Had he done so?

Had he not kept her closeted within his lonely residence?

What was to become of Polly?

And where did Dashwood spend all his evenings?

This she resolved she would find out.

But, perhaps, ere long she would become acquainted, without seeking it, with the knowledge which she longed to obtain.

In the meantime we will leave her to attend to other matters, and begin a fresh chapter.

CHAPTER XLIX.

WHERE WE SEE THAT A CONVERSATION WHICH WE
HEARD SOME TIME AGO IS PRODUCTIVE OF
SOME SATISFACTORY RESULT—AND WHERE WE
MEET TWO OLD ACQUAINTANCES TOGETHER.

ABOUT half a mile from Dashwood's residence
there stood, and we have reason to believe that
there stands now, an old, broken-down, sus-
picious-looking public house, which was called by
the aristocratic name of "George the Third."

It was situated at the extremity of a lane,
badly paved and ill-lighted, with slimy damp
walls on each side, and as one strolled towards
it, he ran a very good chance of missing his footing in treading upon the slippery stones which,
unevenly laid down as they were, served as a
foot-path.

It was not a place where one would be tempted
to go.

It was only "business" that brought you
there.

We mean that "particular business" which is
carried on between twelve and three o'clock in
the morning, by men who, having no calling, and
not wishing to work, think that to rob and murder
is an occupation which, if fraught with danger,
is not without its many redeeming points.

The "George" was supposed to be closed between twelve and six o'clock in the morning.

But this was a rule which was seldom if ever
adhered to.

Little indeed would the landlady have studied
her book, had she been green enough to conform
with one of the many injunctions which are
framed by an intellectual chief of the police at
White Hall, and the trade of the house was at its
culminating point at the witching hour.

The police knew that it was rather a suspicious
"crib."

That it was a place which should not remain
open, but some how or another the "George the
Third" had kept its licence.

Nothing wrong had ever occurred in the
house.

Aristocrats did not patronise the "George," as
the landlady would say, but still, they were hard
working people in their way.

No one could deny that.

They worked hard sometimes.

We will soon show how.

An old gaslight hung over "The George the
Third," and it shed its flickering glare upon the
low roofed entrance; it presented truly the appearance of what it was, a low pot-house.

Besides, the stench and the miasma which arose
from the pavement of the lane was really stifling,
and it was indeed a query how people could live
in such a spot.

At the entrance of the lane there was the road
which led to London town.

At the moment that our attention was drawn towards it, there were two men sojourning along
the road.

One was a tall, rough-looking fellow.

The other was smaller than his companion.

His waist was slim, and as the moon shone
upon his features, it was not difficult to recognise one of the individuals whom we have seen
before.

Who were they?

For it was past midnight.

What was their errand?

Were they going to "The George the Third?"

We should say so, for as we follow their steps
we see them wending their way towards the
lane.

"Let us stop here for awhile," one of the
men said, "and see that we are all right."

The speaker was Brassy Bill.

His companion was Charlie Wood.

"What do you want to stay here for?" Charlie
Wood asked. "We will be much better away
from this open space, we might be seen."

"What then?"

"The peelers might ask us what we are doing
out here so late."

"Well, I would soon settle them."

"What would you say?"

"I'd tell them to mind their own business, as
we mind ours, and not to be interfering with honest
people, who work hard for their living."

And as a sequel to these words, there came a
sigh.

Yes, Brassy Bill breathed with a sigh!

Had he been performing at some west end
theatre, he could not but have provoked roars of
laughter.

He was so genuine apparently.

"We we will go down and see Mother Redmond, and have a swig there, and prepare ourselves for the 'job.'"

What did Brassy Bill mean by the words he
uttered?

Did Charlie Wood understand him?

Doubtless he did.

His lips quivered, and his eye beamed bright
and fierce.

"It will soon be one o'clock," he said.

"In an hour's time it will," Brassy Bill replied; "twelve o'clock has just gone."

"Yes—I forgot," Charlie Wood replied. "I
reckoned the strokes as we passed the church."

"It will come quick enough," his elderly
companion replied; "what is an hour after
all?"

To Charlie Wood the hour which was about to
elapse seemed a century.

The evening we saw him he was about to be a
tool in Brassy Bill's hands.

He was to assist him in some daring burglary.

He was to shed blood if necessary.

To commit murder!

To become Brassy Bill's accomplice.

Why had he done so?

Had his trade become so bad as to compel him
to become a thief, a burglar, a murderer?

No.

He had given his word to Brassy Bill.

He had pledged himself to act as he should
bid him.

He had sworn not to retrograde, not to fear,
now that he had gone so far.

What was he to receive to compensate for the
loss of his liberty, and the forfeiture of his life,
were he to fail in the scheme which had been
plotted by Brassy Bill?

Any monetary consideration?

Of course he would get that.

But was that enough?

Was that sufficient for the loss of his good
name.

For the heart-rending remorse which would
haunt his brain were he to soil his hands with
blood.

For he knew not what was to take place.

He was led like a sheep to the slaughter house.

And yet he walked on.

Why?

Because he felt confident that, once his part should be carried out, Brassy Bill would keep his promise.

Would tell him the whereabouts of Polly, of that girl whom he wished, nay, longed to see, like the traveller in the wilds of the desert prays for the discovery of the oasis, where he will find a drop of water to quench the excruciating pain of an unbearable thirst.

_____

CHAPTER L.

THE BURGLAR AND HIS COMPANION—THEY PAY A VISIT TO THE HOUSE-OF-CALL — THE PLOT DEEPENS.

ALONG the dirty, slimy, narrow lane, the two men walked on.

The light of the "George the Third" was the beacon which served them as a guide.

Over and over again as Brassy Bill proceeded towards the tavern, he turned his head around.

He wished to ascertain whether he and his companions were followed.

He thought that he had heard the monotonous sound of the constable's step in the distance.

That was to Brassy Bill an ominous sound which he by no means liked.

Although in a joke he might have said to Charlie Wood the answer which he would have given to any person who had authority to question him, still he was not so bold and so courageous as he wished his friend to believe him to be.

Besides, with a very few exceptions, such men as Brassy Bill are cowards.

Were they to know that a tough resistance would be offered to them, they would never venture upon their expeditions of plunder and of sin.

As it was, Brassy Bill thought that he had settled everything to his heart's content.

"My boy," he said, tapping Charlie Wood on the shoulder in a friendly way, "we have a pot on to-night, and the place where I will take you will indeed be worth visiting."

"I hope," Charlie Wood replied, "that violence will not be necessary."

The burglar gave a shrug of contempt.

"What if there is," he groaned, "ain't you strong and healthy, muscular and powerful, and with regard to myself, I can do a bit of 'cracking' at times, and I never looks to what may be in the way."

A voice, a subdued voice was now heard.

"Hush, hush!" the coster had whispered.

"What are you at, hush! hush! hushing for?" the burglar whispered in a sharp tone of voice, "why, my friend, it is only the old landlady of the 'George the Third' who is closing her window."

Charlie Wood listened again.

To do so, he had however to stay his course.

A few seconds attention, convinced him of the truth of Brassy Bill's words, then he resumed his march.

An instant brought him outside the low-roofed entrance.

The door was closed.

Brassy Bill had a pair of pistols hidden beneath his attire; with the handle of one of them, he knocked at the door.

No answer.

Brassy Bill knocked again.

Still no answer.

Charlie Wood was beginning to get literally disgusted.

"If such success attends us everywhere, why, it is no use to go on," he thought.

"She will not let us in, that is plain," he then said aloud; "why stop here?"

"Won't she though! That is all you know about it."

Still no answer.

And the burglar knocked again.

Still the silence remained unbroken.

"By God! that's too bad," Brassy Bill said. "Let us see."

And he whispered a few words through the key-hole.

Apparently the woman inside did not hear them.

This time Brassy Bill pronounced them in a louder tone.

"I say, Mother Redmonds, don't you recognise old friends?"

This is what he ejaculated.

This phrase might have been heard twenty yards off.

It had the necessary effect.

It brought an answer.

"I will be with you in an instant; why do you get so impatient?"

It was a woman who had spoken.

What was she like?

Who was she?

Was she young or old?

Such were the thoughts which entered Charlie Wood's brain.

He was thus musing when an old hag appeared.

Brassy Bill went and gave her a kiss.

Her appearance was repulsive.

A low forehead, grey sunken eyes, a long, hooked nose, and a protruding jaw without any teeth, were the features of old Mrs. Redmonds, whose countenance was furrowed with deep wrinkles, and whose browned skin was covered with long black hair, which made her look more like a female gorilla than like a human being.

Instinctively the coster started back.

At first he thought that within that low pot-house he would have met Polly.

Now, his was a feeling of bitter disappointment.

"Give us a glass a-piece, m'am," Brassy Bill said, "and we will be off."

"Anything on hand?" the old hag asked, mysteriously.

The burglar nodded his head in reply.

"Where?" asked the landlady.

Close by.

"Ah, ah!" she muttered, taking no heed of Charlie Wood, who she took of course to be one of Brassy Bill's pals, although she had never seen him before. "Ah, ah!" she continued, "I did not think that there was fish for their net about here."

"You know that lordly house in the fields, mother?" the burglar pursued.

"Yes, I have heard Charlie (our friend blue-eyed Charlie) speaking about it. He said that occasionally he had seen a very pretty girl, a fair haired girl, something meant for his betters!" and the old hag smacked her lips wishing more forcibly to convey to the burglar what she wished to imply.

The coster youth's attention had been kindled.

Who was that pretty girl?

Could it be Polly?

Could it be she whom he so much wished to see?

How very odd if he should meet her thus unexpectedly!

He resolved to find out.

"What about the girl, marm?" Charlie Wood asked.

"What about her?" the old hag replied, "why nothing particular, only my Charlie, he has a look out for beauty, and he says he has seen a very pretty girl occasionally come out of the lonely house in a very handsome conveyance more I know not, and now you must be satisfied with what I tell you, my boy."

The coster knew that silence was now the order of the day.

Polly!

Polly!

Polly! he muttered to himself three consecutive times.

"What are you at, soliloquising in that kind of mysterious fashion," the burglar asked, "the girl can't know you, man."

"I know that," he replied, roughly.

At that moment Brassy Bill looked up.

The dial of an old clock struck his gaze.

The hands showed him that it was fifty minutes past twelve.

"We must be thinking of moving, Charlie," he said, "come on."

And the two men drank off their draught, and shortly afterwards the bang of the door of the "George the Third," told that Mrs. Redmond, had definitely closed for the night.

CHAPTER LI.

STILL MORE MYSTERY—CHARLIE WOOD'S IMPATIENCE INCREASES—THE TWO MEN ENTER THE LONELY HOUSE IN THE FIELDS.

ABOUT ten minutes had elapsed since the departure of Brassy Bill and of Charlie Wood from the "George the Third."

With the swiftness of men who have something to carry out, they cleared the distance in no time, and it was just one o'clock in the morning when they reached the outskirts of Dashwood's house; that lonely residence which we have visited before.

The night had become pitch dark, and in the moonless heavens could be seen inky clouds, which threatened to burst out every moment in a thick heavy rain.

The darkness was welcome to Brassy Bill.

Followed by Charlie Wood, he soon came to the side of the entrance door.

Not a light was to be seen in that large house, situated amidst uncultivated fields,

All the better for Brassy Bill, for the inmates were all asleep.

"Where are you, Charlie?" the burglar now asked.

The dark form of Charlie Wood glided by his side.

The warm breath of the youth, in the cold morning air, acquainted the speaker with his companion's presence.

The youth's features, could indeed, be said to be as white as those of a clammy corpse.

He was about to commit a daring burglary.

And who was that for? we may ask.

To see Polly once more.

"Stay by my side, Charlie," the burglar said, "we must arrange our plans."

The coster replied in so faint a voice that it was scarcely audible.

"You ain't a going to funk at the eleventh hour," he hissed between his teeth.

"What makes you think so?" the youth replied eagerly, "don't bully, if you please."

Vexed and annoyed at the remark which had been made by his companion, and, moreover, being unable to deny the truth of it, Charlie Wood became bold and courageous.

The answer which he had given had been pronounced in a firm tone of voice.

Brassy Bill noticed the change in the youth.

"That's better," he muttered, "cheer up, Charlie. Faint heart never won fair lady, and, by the son of God, to-night we will be rich."

"Who lives in this house?" Charlie inquired.

"A man that is wicked and wealthy."

"Do you know the ins and outs of the place," Charlie pursued.

"Trust Brassy Bill for getting reliable information, why, my boy, I have been in this ere crib ere now; the apartments from top to bottom is as familiar to me as this little toy."

Thus speaking the burglar drew forth a shining crowbar from underneath his garments.

Although the night was dark, the steel shone somewhat brightly in his hand.

"I must lay that down by my side," he said, "in case I want it."

And he placed the instrument upon the ground.

"I say, boy," Brassy Bill began, in a friendly tone, "have you got the skeleton key?"

"Here it is."

"Where?"

"Here."

"Give it into my hand, man; I cannot see you, and I don't want yet to light my bull's-eye; time enough when we are inside."

Charlie Wood approached nearer to his companion.

He held the key in his right hand.

"I have got it all right," the burglar said, eagerly seizing it with a feverish clutch. "Excuse me, lad, if I take the job away from you, but I am more accustomed than you to these things."

And as he spoke, Bill was feeling the hall door for the lock.

He soon came upon the key-hole.

Charlie Wood trembled like an aspen leaf.

It was not fear, reader.

But he wondered whether he would meet Polly that night, or at least in the course of that eventful morning.

Perhaps she was in the house.

Perhaps she was not twenty yards away from him!

How would she greet him?

What would be the nature of his interview?

But, after all, perhaps she was not an inmate of that house.

Thus he was musing when his companion spoke.

"By Jove! the door gives way," Brassy Bill whispered. "How is that? I thought they were wont to bolt it within!"

It was indeed the case.

The door was gradually and slowly receding before Brassy Bill.

As it ran upon its hinges it made a slight creaking noise.

The door was now ajar.

"Ere we proceed, Charlie, look after your barkers," Brassy Bill muttered, "and see that your poniard is all right."

This was wholesome advice.

The coster had perceived in an instant the wisdom of the remark.

He took one pistol out of his pocket, he cocked it, saw that the cap was fastened safely upon it, and having ascertained that the trigger was in a good condition, he re-placed it back from whence he had withdrawn it.

Then he satisfied himself that the fellow-one was also fit for use, and when he had ascertained beyond doubt that he was armed with a good pair of pistols, he replied to Brassy Bill, in a voice which trembled somewhat with emotion,—

"I am perfectly ready now, what is the next thing?"

He got no direct answer to this last query; but he heard Brassy Bill thus soliloquising.

"Cursed fool that I am, I should have lighted up my lamp, ere I came here; how the deuce am I to do now, I've got no matches."

Brassy Bill found that he had no means to light up his lamp.

Thus the expedition must naturally be broken off.

"You're a nice old bloke to be sure!" Charlie Wood whispered, "and what's to be done then?"

"Proceed in the dark, that's all. It will render our errand more dangerous but we can only die once, and we may just as well go off to-day as to-morrow."

"Very nice sentiment indeed! but I do not quite see it."

"How are you to help yourself?"

"By producing a box of lucifers that I bought this morning.

"Come inside then, we will soon see what will be our first step to take."

And Brassy Bill gently pushed the door before him.

The two men were now in the hall,

"In a minute I will strike a light," Brassy Bill said. "In the mean time go and close the door."

Charlie Wood did as he was bid.

It did not take him long to walk backwards and forwards.

And once more he was by the side of his companion.

CHAPTER LII.

CONCLUSION

In the foregoing chapter, we have left Brassy Bill and his youthful companion in crime within the hall of Dashwood's house.

But they were doomed to be disappointed in their nefarious purpose, for three days after the events which we have related, a paragraph appeared in the *Times* newspaper, informing the public, that a daring attempt at burglary had been defeated by the vigilant hands of the police, who had obtained, no one knew how, information of the dark plot which had found conception in Brassy Bill's brain.

Brassy Bill was transported, and he is now in a penal settlement abroad.

The other characters of the tale are still in the land of the living, and but the other evening we heard that Lydia was going on rather fast, and so fast, indeed, that she was threatened with a galloping consumption, were she not to repair her ways.

May be at a future period, we may return to Dashwood and Polly, and inform our readers with their fate.

Laura Wylde is not married yet.

And now, readers, " au revoir."

THE END.

www.ingramcontent.com/pod-product-compliance
Lightning Source LLC
Chambersburg PA
CBHW080829250626
47160CB00008B/2887